POWERS
James A. Burton

POWERS
James A. Burton

PRIME BOOKS

POWERS
Copyright © 2012 by James A. Hetley

Cover art by Matthew Hughes.
Cover design by Telegraphy Harness.

Prime Books
www.prime-books.com

For more information, contact Prime Books:
prime@prime-books.com

ISBN: 978-1-60701-336-5

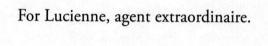

For Lucienne, agent extraordinaire.

I

The air hummed, oily golden liquid condensed out of sparkling haze, and a demon took human shape across the kitchen table from Albert Johansson. The thing stood at an angle to the world until it put one glowing hand on the scarred Formica tabletop and twisted to vertical without apparent movement, as if concepts of up and down were optional and it had to locate itself in space. It smiled. The smile showed too many teeth for comfort. Large needle-pointed carnivore teeth, suitable for ripping flesh—living or dead, human or other, it didn't matter.

Albert froze. He sniffed. Nothing. No brimstone, no incense, no arctic chill or furnace heat or moldy damp earth-smell of the unquiet grave. Nothing. And he trusted his sense of smell, closer to hound than human. His nose told him that the form, those teeth, weren't even there.

Then, as if he'd asked for it out loud and the demon thought to add another sense and more reality to the scene, an ozone tang of nearby lightning spread through the room and stung his eyes.

Albert tore his gaze away from those teeth and stared at the hand instead, wondering if now the plastic would begin to smoke and bubble and char. Or maybe freeze and shatter with bitter cold. You never knew with demons.

Nothing happened. The hand continued to be a golden hand with the dull luster of true pure metal. The table continued to be a table, no more worn and scratched and battered than it had been before, pale green plastic-laminate top with a pattern of faded almost-daisies to disguise spills and stains, zinc edging with the dings and dents of fifty years of abuse.

More nothing happened.

Albert blinked three times and took a deep breath, feeling ice settle into the pit of his stomach and spread chills out to his fingers and toes. He'd been minding his own business, building a sandwich at his kitchen counter and listening to Bach's solo cello suites, intellectual and sensuous at the same time. Home-baked dark chewy rye—baking bread cost time rather than money, and he had a lot more of the former than the latter. Besides, he enjoyed baking bread—the smooth warm resilient touch of kneading the loaf, the earthy living smell of first the damp flour and then the rising yeast followed by the baking. It never got boring, even after a few hundred years.

He was passionate about good food and good music. Damned little else, and his apartment reflected that—peeling wallpaper, cracked plaster, stove and refrigerator and furniture that had seen better decades or centuries rather than just years. But he couldn't quibble with the rent. His family owned the place.

He *should* have been safe and private, savoring first the thought and then the deed—fresh-baked rye bread just cool enough to slice, parchment-thin salty dry Westphalian ham layered with nutty Emmenthaler cheese, fragrant and full of holes, brown stone-ground Raye's ginger mustard from a century-old mill powered by the giant tides in the Bay of Fundy . . .

The room had hummed around him and he glanced up and this golden ectoplasm materialized next to his kitchen table and took the shape of a man. Demons, angels, spirits, djinn, whatever you called them—they didn't usually waste time with doorbells. They didn't have to. At least this one hadn't felt the need to manifest with a clap of thunder and cloud of brimstone smoke. Or blast the apartment door into cinders and flinders for the dramatic entry of a desert whirlwind.

He'd seen that sort of thing in his long, long life. It stuck in his memory. He had forgotten a lot of things, important things, over the centuries, but *that* sort of thing he remembered. Demons had that effect on people.

It didn't seem to care whether Albert knew its true nature. It didn't bother with clothes. Neither male nor female, no visible genitals, no nipples on a chest shaped halfway between pectoral muscles and breasts. No bellybutton. "Man" as "human." Sort of. Or at least that was what it showed to *him*. Other eyes might have seen other forms. A burning bush, maybe, or wheels within wheels within wheels.

Or maybe they wouldn't have noticed anything at all. Sometimes Albert saw things that others thought weren't there, heard words that other ears ignored. It was part of being what he was.

Whatever that might be.

He took a couple of deep breaths. He blinked and felt cold sweat breaking out along his spine. The demon was still there. He cut the sandwich in half and put it on a plate and offered it. The demon grunted its thanks, pulled out a chair and sat on it without even singeing the wood, and Albert started to build another sandwich.

Thoughts spun through his head. *What the hell am I supposed to do now? Fall on my knees and genuflect and pray? I'm not sure there* is *a fixed etiquette for such meetings. If they want you to take off your sandals because you stand on holy ground, they'll tell you. If they want to rip your head off and crunch it for an appetizer, they'll go ahead and do it.*

One did just that to Johannes. Brother or not—from what Mother told me, the damn fool asked for it. Elaborate suicide. I'm not that bored with life. Yet.

He'd lived long enough to see plenty of weird shit. He'd seen friends die in agony or wish they could, had plenty of enemies try to kill him and fail. He'd had a few centuries of practice in keeping calm under pressure. Sometimes it helped. But his hands shook enough that he had to concentrate on spreading more mustard, layering more ham and cheese. Angel or devil, it didn't matter. Long history said that visitations from either tend to be rough on the neighborhood.

He stopped working on the sandwich and studied the knife in his hand. He loved good food, good music, *and* good iron. Iron and steel and him, they understood each other. They talked to each other.

Most people would look down at him and sneer at the idea that he was a master smith—him standing maybe five foot three on a day when he was feeling tall, and no more muscle than most people his size. But good smithing, that wasn't a thing of forcing metal to do what you wanted. It was more a discussion and persuasion, not domination but partnership. He did blades and fine-work and didn't need a lot of bulk to heave cart-horses around for shoeing. He just had to set his anvil a little lower than some others in the craft.

His kitchen knives had been an experiment—nickel-iron born from a meteor's corpse, to give each blade the flaming magic of steel pulled from heaven to earth by the implacable drag of gravity, steel worked and folded and folded again at the forge, carbon infiltrating the grain of the metal from a reducing fire, thoughts and words of making until the steel took meaning from his hammer, a shape and meaning that maybe could skin and gut a god and chop him into cubes for stew meat. The blades could slice a tomato paper-thin as well, or bone a slaughtered cow, and he only needed to sharpen them once a decade. He wondered what would happen if he leaned across the table and stabbed this knife, this *living* knife, into the body of the demon.

But he wasn't about to try.

He finished building the second sandwich, sliced it in half, and put it on another plate. He grabbed a bottle from the refrigerator—

dark Shipyard ale, strong-hearted enough to keep company with the sandwiches—waved it in the direction of the demon and got a smile and nod of acceptance. At least its mommy had taught it not to talk with its mouth full. If demons *had* mommies . . . .

So he opened the bottle, poured straight down the middle of a glass to let the bubbles breathe into a good head, and opened and poured another for himself. Before his knees collapsed under him, he sat down. Sat down on a worn scarred wobbly-legged blue-painted wooden kitchen chair, about as mundane as it gets, across his battered 1950s yard-sale kitchen table from a demon. With a ham sandwich and a beer. Surreal. It had rattled him enough that he'd forgotten the pickles, had to get up and open the refrigerator again and look a question at the demon. Again, it nodded that it would like one. Strong sharp Kosher dills.

Kosher. Like ham and cheese sandwiches maybe slipped past Leviticus? But that's why he kept thinking of it as a demon. Legend said that angels kept Kosher, demons didn't. Albert wouldn't know. He'd only met two, maybe three for sure, never had offered one a sandwich, and the last was more than a hundred years ago. He knew the theory, but half-remembered legends didn't compare with smelling ozone in his kitchen and then sitting down across the table from the Other.

He couldn't even tell if there was a real difference between angels and demons, or if that was just a label we put on a mirror that reflected what we found inside ourselves. Taxonomy of the spirit world got awkward. It was too . . . *other.*

Anyway, it ate the sandwich and the pickle in alternate bites, drank the beer, belched. Albert wondered if he should ask some priest or rabbi or mullah whether it had to shit afterward. As far as he knew, spirits didn't *need* food, but this one seemed to enjoy the snack. It belched again. Maybe it wasn't used to beer.

Or maybe it hung out in a society where belching after a meal offered compliments to the chef. Albert knew such places, such people, from centuries of travel.

"Simon Lahti, I thank you for bread and salt. A blessing be upon this house."

Albert twitched at the name. He'd used dozens, maybe hundreds, moving from place to place down the years. It got to the point where he had to concentrate, remembering just who he was supposed to be *this* year and city. That name went way back. And then there was the angel/demon thing again. Demons were supposed to go in more for curses than blessings. Maybe it was trying to keep him off balance. If so, it was doing a damned good job.

Its voice sounded . . . peculiar, again neither male nor female, but with a hollow resonance that didn't seem to fit that pseudo-chest, more like the echo of an oracle's cave. It stopped there and looked at Albert as if expecting some kind of ritual response. The man nodded and looked a question. His tongue didn't seem to be working right just then.

"Simon Lahti, we wish you to act for us."

A heap of coins formed out of nothing and clinked together on the table. They *looked* like gold. The ones Albert could see *looked* like old U.S. "eagles" and "double eagles"—ten- and twenty-dollar gold pieces, last minted in the 1930s. He picked up a palm-full. Heavy, heavy, heavy in his hand, the way metal money used to mean something serious, and it took him back a ways. Some fives and even tiny ones mixed in. Different dates—1880s to 1920s—different designs, different scratches and dings and level of wear, as if they'd come from a real hoard rather than minted fresh by magical imagination.

A *large* heap—somewhere between five hundred and a thousand dollars in face value, he guessed, more money in one place than he'd seen in years. Hell, in *decades*. Sold piecemeal to collectors, he could eat well for years off that pile.

Living in fuzzy shadows of the modern world, using borrowed names and forged papers, he'd never make that kind of money in a daylight job. That's why he lived on the fourth floor of a slum that wanted to collapse into its cellar, eating beans more days than not.

Cassoulet with lamb sausage, chili in a hundred variations, home-baked beans, no reason they had to rank as fodder. His brain chased after that tangent to avoid thinking about the demon. *Yellow-eye beans soaked overnight, add chopped-up onions and garlic, a good chunk of salt pork, molasses, ginger or mustard, sometimes sliced Greening apple. Slow-baked, all day in the oven blending those flavors and perfuming the air, and the pizza joint downstairs paid for the gas. Served them right—lousy pizza, skimped on the sauce and cheese . . .*

He dragged himself back to present danger. What he did next probably wasn't smart. He did things like that now and then, things that gave him the total shakes when hindsight kicked in. Then he'd start thinking about his brothers, the ones he knew about, and his sister, and how their stories all ended with them seeking death. And finding it.

He stood up, walked over to the old gas stove, and dropped three coins into a cast-iron skillet he'd left out to dry over the pilot light after washing up from breakfast. Clinkety-clinkety-clink, the proper sound of gold hitting iron, they bounced and rattled and settled and stayed put. They didn't vanish with a sizzle and puff and a stink of rotten eggs when they touched cold iron. Not fairy gold.

He picked them up and turned back to the table. The demon's "face" looked vaguely amused. Or maybe not—Albert didn't have that much experience in reading demon expressions.

That's the point where second thoughts kicked in and he realized the chance he'd taken. He could have ended up as a smeared layer a molecule or two thick, adding fresh stains to the peeling wallpaper, for insulting his visitor. He wished his brain worked faster, but he'd never claimed to be a genius. Just slow and steady and persistent to the point of pig-headed. Mind or body, he wasn't built for speed.

He bulled ahead, his usual move when he stepped in that kind of shit. "Who wants to hire me? What do you mean by *act?*"

"Our name is Legion. One of your kind has been abusing our companions. We wish you to stop this abuse."

Companions. Albert sorted through memories of Mother by gaslight, or did that flickering yellow gleam in her eyes come from a candle, an oil lamp? *A fire at the mouth of a cave to keep the dire wolf and saber-tooth at bay? Tales in the drowsy fog before sleep, anyway, tales of the land where she was born across the sea or under the mountain or in flying castles above the clouds.*

Too many tales, too many words, with no proof that any single word was true. Mother could weave a tale that made you smell the spilled guts of fresh-dead corpses on a battlefield and hear the rustle of raven wings over the groans of the dying, then the next day tell another story with the same heroes very much alive ten years or ten centuries later.

Companions. Companions to spirits, demons, angels—not *pets,* as such, not something owned. Not something equal, either.

Elementals.

Sprites of earth, wind, water, fire, not things of thought and speech and reason. The heart or soul of the grove, the spring, the stone, the mountain cave, the deep and darksome tarn. Blue flame dancing free of the coals of a dying cook-fire.

And someone had been . . . *abusing* . . . them. This could get messy.

"Why don't you deal with the problem yourselves?" Hey, King David or Elijah or some other Bible guy got away with arguing with *God.* This was just a demon.

Mother had warned Albert to never trust a demon. Legends again, most cultures—demons didn't care what happened to mortals, and they seemed to enjoy playing tricks. Plus, they twisted language for their own amusement, seeming to promise one thing and then delivering something quite different. *Nasty* different.

The demon squinted at Albert, as if it read his mind. Maybe it could. "Your kind created the problem. Your kind must deal with it, or face the consequences."

Talk about guilt by association. "Consequences"—Albert didn't like the sound of that. Brought up images of Sodom and Gomorrah, it did. Another example of why he didn't really care whether he was talking to an angel or a demon. Either could be just as rough on innocent bystanders.

Not really. His brain ran off on another tangent, still trying to dodge. *Angels generally get the worst of any comparison. Demons tempt or torture individuals. Angels visit the Wrath of God on whole cities or tribes or nations and they don't bother to file an environmental impact statement first.*

"Why me?"

As soon as he said it, he realized how silly that sounded. He'd meant it as an actual question rather than the classic whine of Job goosed by God's fickle finger. *Why do they want to hire me, rather than a detective or some wizard or perhaps a priest? I'm just a maybe-man who has managed to live a long, long time, and forgotten most of it.*

Detective, wizard, priest. In all the various and nefarious ways I've earned or stolen a living, I've never been a detective. Outside of a special bond with iron and steel, I don't have enough magic in my whole body to light a match without striking it on the box. I've never been able to sort out the true Word of God from the lies men spin as easily as they breathe. Like I said, why me?

At that point he decided he needed another beer. Maybe the demon wanted another, too. He had no idea what effect alcohol had on the spirit world. If he'd stopped to think about it, the vision of a drunken demon probably would have pushed him over the edge to run screaming down Main Street. But the demon nodded when he waved another Shipyard in its direction. Albert pulled a fresh six-pack out and set it on the table between them, no reason to stint. Hell, he might not live to finish another.

The demon smiled. Albert *thought* it was a smile. It still showed too many pointed teeth and a hunter's eyes, like a leopard or wolf shape-shifted into human form. "You see things that others do not see. You hear things that others do not hear. You do not seek dominion over men. We know that you respect our companions."

It gestured toward the living room on the far side of the kitchen doorway, at the old fireplace that used to be the sole heat of the room, back when Albert's family first bought the pile of crumbling brick and dry rot fronting on South Union. Four fireplaces on each floor, originally, one drafty pitiful heat-waster for each of the front and rear rooms of this deep narrow row-house apartment, with a long cold tunnel of space in between. Say what you want about the sad decline of civilization and the golden Elder Days, Albert thought central heating and flush toilets were grand ideas.

He'd had a mason reopen and line one fireplace and flue when he had the whole apartment torn apart for renovations about fifty years ago. He didn't like to let strangers past his door, but roof leaks had gone far beyond the drip-bucket stage and he didn't mess with gas lines and electricity. They bit.

Yeah, I don't like strangers in my lair. More to the point, skilled work costs money. That pile of gold—I pinch every penny that comes my way. I have to. I can earn a dollar here and there by day labor, but a steady job, paying good money? With every piece of official paper forged? Not likely. My driver's license, the other documents, they're good enough by themselves. But I can't afford the kind of paper that stands up to a serious check.

Sell my blades? Custom knives and swords bring real money, but you need to be a public person to make the sale, fair to middling famous in the collector's world. I don't dare walk that path.

He couldn't even wave a birth certificate under some official nose. As far as Immigration was concerned, he was another illegal just arrived from Canada or Mexico. Sure, he'd lived in the U.S.

for over a century and a half. Fat chance on proving *that* to a judge. Only reason he didn't get hassled more, his blond hair and blue eyes made him *look* like he belonged. Except for being short, and even *that* made the cops ignore him. Short people, especially short people walking with a cane and limp, aren't seen as a threat.

So, most repairs, he did himself or did without. Besides the money problem, too many awkward questions could come up, like the almost-human skeleton in tarnished silver chains bricked up inside an offset in one wall. He could remove that one and dump it, bone by bone out on the river or in the woods, but he couldn't guarantee that the bones would stay separate and dead . . .

He shivered at the memory. There were other memories of this place that could give him the shivers too, but now he let salamanders come and go and play in the fireplace, kept dry wood laid on the hearth for them. He'd come back to the place in the morning or late evening and find cold ashes where he'd left wood, sometimes felt and smelled a difference when he started a fire himself to give life to the space. Elementals of air and fire helped clear out the ghosts, the must and dust of old wood and plaster, made the air smell fresh and clean and friendly, and they respected the limits he'd set for them.

His eyes stung. He took a deep swig of beer, probably drinking too much too fast, or not—considering he had a demon sitting just across the table.

Yes, a lot of bad memories tied to this place. Still, bad memories or not, every time he'd given his feet to Mother's wanderlust, turned nomad and gone on walkabout for twenty or fifty years, somehow he ended up back in this same room. He'd come back to find everyone he knew and cared about had vanished, or been replaced by grave markers.

Even Mother. I don't know if she's alive or dead. Or something else.

"Simon Lahti, we know that you respect our companions, and you do not trust powers that are beyond mortal control. We know of this."

That . . . name . . . repeated a third time as a charm. Icy fingers ran down his spine. "Simon Lahti" was *not* his name, neither the name on his current driver's license nor the name he was known by many years ago, but it said things about him he'd prefer that no one knew. Not even demons.

Sure, in theory, he knew that Others lived all around him, not seen but seeing. He *knew* this, but he was just as capable as any man of forgetting it for years at a time. Now Legion kept rubbing his nose in it.

But that had nothing to do with finding out who abused elementals. The past was gone, and often had little connection with any particular future. And he couldn't change it. The future, now, sometimes he could change *that*. What he *could* do . . .

Dangerous. Likely fatal. He refused to think about it. He got up from the table, surprised that his knees seemed willing to hold his weight. Crossed the kitchen to the front parlor, to the old oak roll-top desk that held those papers connected to his current name and station in the world. Found the nerve to pull out the bottom drawer on the left and took from *that* a linen bag, lurking alone in the solitary space *it* wanted, hand-loomed fabric brown with the grease of generations of fingers, smelling of time and graves.

II

A stream of yellow-brown dice spilled into his palm, small bone cubes hand-cut and less than perfect, the scratches and chips and grime of centuries not masking the runes slashed across the faces of each die. They'd belonged to Mother, and she'd left them when she vanished. Where *she* got them, God alone knew. But *which* God?

Sometimes they'd speak to him. He didn't know how. Their magic lived inside them, came from the songs and smokes and potions and whispered spell-chants of whatever forest-witch or desert shaman had formed and smoothed them centuries ago. *If* they spoke, they spoke true.

Generally, they didn't speak. No use at all for the stock market or picking horses. He didn't know why. His small powers didn't run that way.

He rolled them clicking in his cupped hands, looking off through plastered brick walls into the distance rather than at them. He thought about their number, twenty-seven, three-cubed of cubes, probably important and if he lost or cracked one they'd never speak again, or would speak gibberish. He thought about the demon, behind him and making the skin crawl up and down his spine. It had manifested small, no larger than Albert and he was practically a dwarf by modern standards. He knew that it could grow to the size of a mountain in an eye-blink if it wished, or shrink to a gnat and fly up his nose to eat his brains out from the inside.

He cast the bones on the floor, against the baseboard so they bounced and muttered and rattled on the broad pine boards. Out of that rattle, he heard a word, syllables and sounds in some language he'd never heard on any human tongue. But he knew what it meant.

<Refuse.>

Nothing vague and Delphic about *that*. He shuddered. Saying "no" to a demon . . .

He thought about the heap of gold on his kitchen table, wealth enough for lots of good food and good music, even a stereo or refrigerator newer than the last ice age. He got by, just barely, by not owning a car, not paying rent, staying away from medical care. His palms *itched* for that gold.

He found it hard to think straight with gold in the room. It wasn't *just* money, that heavy soft rare metal. It seemed almost like a drug to him, sensuous in the way it called, the way it blocked sense and self-preservation—lust and envy and covetousness and the rest of that list rolled into one. Sort of like sex to humans.

But when the cubes spoke at all, they spoke true.

He gathered the cubes into a pile in his hands and cast them again, this time staring at them, at the spin and bounce and tumble of the runes, hoping against hope that the bound spirits or whatever would change their minds. Six letters formed among the runes, Roman characters, and then vanished again as soon as he'd noticed them.

REFUSE.

All capitals. The magic thought it needed to shout.

He decided he didn't want to try again. After all, the bones just told him what he already knew.

Never trust a demon.

As he thought that, the letters flashed again before fading back into dark runes cut into yellow bone and shaded with what looked like ancient blood. Runes he couldn't read, runes he'd never seen in any book or museum in all his years and wandering. Maybe the magic itself had made them, for just this one set and purpose.

He shivered again. He gathered the cubes, dumped them rattling into their bag, and tucked the bag into its drawer, to wait in darkness for the next time someone called them, whether that someone would be him or Mother or some stranger that the magic first called to itself. He had a general idea of what would come next. Not specifics, no, but he *had* been getting bored with life.

His brothers and his sister finally hunted for their deaths. His kind couldn't count on age or disease to find them and give them rest.

But evidence said they weren't immortal. Which might be just as well.

He stood up. He faced the demon.

"No."

The demon lifted its right eyebrow, just the ridge of "skin" over "bone," no hair—Albert noticed for the first time that it didn't have any hair at all. That oversight told volumes about how his brain was working. Or wasn't.

Fire spread from Legion's fingers, coating walls, floor, ceiling, wood and plaster and brick alike, scorching and curling the faded wallpaper and boiling centuries of varnish and paint off wood. Black smoke filled the air, biting deep in Albert's lungs and throat, and when he lifted his hand to cover his mouth he saw his skin blister and char. The pain hadn't hit him yet, but heat drove deep into his flesh and bone, the demon raising the fires of hell to torment him.

"Breaker of guest-law!" He coughed the words out and tried to hold what little breath remained behind them. It had been easy to be philosophical about death, until he looked it straight in the face.

The burning froze. The demon walked through the flames to stand in front of him, frowning, a curl of smoke hooked in one nostril.

"Yes, your kind would use those words. And we accepted bread and salt from you, even if you did not bind us with peace-words in the giving."

It gestured, and the flames vanished. The *damage* vanished. No smoke, no heat, no charred flesh on the hand in front of Albert's face, no sense that anything at all had happened in his rooms. No pain.

Demons.

"We obey 'guest-law.' This house and hearth are sacred. But we will find you in another place."

Which could mean the instant Albert stepped out of his door, or ten years or a hundred years from now, on the far side of the world. Who knew what time and space meant to a demon? Nothing, most likely . . .

The demon had made him an offer he couldn't refuse. He decided that maybe he wasn't ready to die yet.

"Where and when has this abuse happened? What can I do to stop it? Can I call on your kind and your companions for help?"

Time grows short. A week, two weeks, as mortals measure time. The demon had said that. *Already, we feel change. Your kind broke the balance, opened the path. Repair it, or this world shatters.*

The demon wasn't telling him everything. Albert knew that. He headed down the stairs anyway. Down through the dark abandoned third floor of drifted musty dust and peeling wallpaper and chunks of age-broken horsehair plaster gritty on the wide-plank flooring, avoiding the first and fifth and eighth treads of the stairs—he didn't invite people home, and anyone who fell through those worn old cracked boards should never have been there in the first place.

Shatters, and becomes what? "World" as universe, or planet, or laws of physics, or society? Repair what? This isn't just about "companions." This was a demon speaking, maybe lying, maybe twisting double-meaning words into something hidden, very different. *Armageddon? Ragnarok? Or some demonic joke?*

He stepped into the second floor, fancier with varnished hardwood flooring and plaster moldings around the ceiling but just as abandoned and stale with last year's air, the old gaslight fixtures still in place, dust-furred gray sheets shrouding mahogany Victorian furniture: monstrosities bought new at the height of fashion back when Mother invited strange men home and lightened their pockets of excess gold. They'd owned this building for something like a century and a half, through a corporate fiction that didn't draw official notice if it lived forever. The pizza joint's rent paid the taxes these days, successor to a dozen similar greasy spoons or beer halls in the past.

He paused at the fireplace in the front parlor where a marble mantel and columns framed a blackened brick hollow that hadn't felt heat in decades. Stooping, he left a pint of vodka, a brick of dark chocolate, a wedge of Emmenthaler, and half the remaining loaf of rye on the hearth. They wouldn't be there when he came back. He didn't know what happened to the empty bottles, or *want* to know.

Most people ignored the hearth-spirits of their homes. Mother had taught him the price of that. They'd take their due without the gift, and you'd never know why you lived under an unlucky roof. He'd give a pint of cheap vodka any day to keep those little . . . friends . . . out of his hair and cupboards. If they held drunken midnight parties with punk-rock music cranked up to "ten," they did it in some pocket universe where he couldn't hear.

On his way out, he picked up his cane where he'd left it next to the parlor door. He kept almost-innocent things like that scattered around his home, always in the same places where he could find them in the dark, a habit of long survival in dangerous places. Most people wouldn't see a cane as a weapon, especially an orthopedic cane—rubber grip and rubber tip and what looked like a shaft of brushed aluminum. Sign of a cripple, not dangerous . . .

That's why he carried it. He hefted the cane, stainless steel, much heavier than your eye would suspect, just in case. Enough weight to break a wrist, a knee, a skull—he'd done all three. Like many small people, he was much stronger than he looked.

He let his hands and the steel remember each other and loosed a twist he thought only his peculiar brain could work. The cane separated below the grip, unsheathing a foot-long blade of laminated steel, a fighting blade much more complex than his kitchen knives. The sight of it woke memories of smelting the raw ore, furnace panting like a live animal, carbon blending with iron under the blue-flamed red bank of charcoal. Then time outside of time at his forge fold-welding yellow-hot sparking metal again and again and yet again to judge the grain of the metal by its bending, wrapping keen brittle steel around the tough heart that made it strong, forming, grinding, heating, quenching, polishing to bring out the grain of watered silk—as keen and deadly a blade as his centuries of skill could conjure out of iron.

His city wasn't a nice place. He didn't live in a nice part of it. He didn't think he'd *ever* lived in a nice place.

If the cops got nosy about why he always carried a cane, even if he walked like he was perfectly healthy, he could point to the sole of his right shoe, built up more than an inch—that leg was shorter than the left and not quite straight. Result of a tangle with a freight wagon, so Mother said, when he was two or three and playing where he shouldn't. Medical care being what it was, or *wasn't*, back then, he was lucky to have two legs. Another bit of his past he'd have to take her word for. He'd always limped from it, as far back as he could remember.

He headed down another set of dark dusty stairs, another set of treads that creaked their warning if he put a foot wrong. No, he hadn't booby-trapped the place. He'd just learned to guard himself with what was available. Obvious traps were harder to explain to curious policemen than "accidents" and the wear of age.

The demon wasn't telling him everything. He wondered, though, whether the things it *did* tell him were truth or lies. Why would a demon need his help? If it could flick its fingers and turn his apartment into hell's inferno, it could do the same to whatever mortal was "abusing" its companions.

Or were those flames illusion? They'd looked real, felt real, smelled real, even to him. The demon wasn't using metaphor when it said Albert could see things that others did not see. His senses weren't human. He could see beyond the human range, into infrared and some into the ultraviolet. Likewise, he could hear above and below the human normal range. His nose twitched at scents that eluded most people.

Those were not blessings without price. They helped in working metal—judging fuels and fluxes and ores and the metals they become, judging heat, listening to the metamorphosis of iron becoming steel under his hammer—but he couldn't stand crowds. People *stank,* and the modern world screamed noise at him from near and far.

Why would a demon need human help? Or mortal *help, anyway, given that best guess says I'm not human? Maybe it has a bet down with its buddies? Betting on me, for or against?*

He froze, one foot up in the air, and then put it back down on a safe stair tread. Another possibility had flitted through his head. He needed to examine it before he stuck his head into the noose.

If there was more than one demon involved . . . not bets, maybe, but either pranks or deadly warfare. Mother had told him that demons—angels, spirits, whatever—they didn't get along any better than mortals. Just study Loki and his chummy relations with the other Æsir.

One demon was enough, more than enough. Getting involved in demon politics could be suicide. But did he have a choice?

He didn't. He chased that idea down at least five dead-end alleys. Legion would kill him if he didn't play its game, whatever its game turned out to be. Probably kill him in a way that took five days. The demon had made that plain. If Legion said "Shit!"—the only questions it allowed were "How much?" and "What color?"

Those thoughts got Albert nowhere, as well as to his front door. He checked the sidewalk through his peephole, unlocked, unbarred, and stepped through. With another twist of thought he reset it all from outside—that door was a lot stronger than it looked, a burglar would find it easier to break in through the brick wall to either side, and that was two feet thick.

He didn't want visitors.

A gesture to convention and any watchers, he touched the crosses that marked and guarded both jambs of the doorframe, invoking God on this journey. He looked right and left, checking for threats again and then freezing like a suspicious rabbit. Dusk had crept in, somewhere during his encounter with the demon.

He didn't know why or how, but they screwed up time as well as space. He'd been making lunch at noon. A few minutes later, he stepped out into late spring twilight heavy with the scents of threat and promise—a whiff of sweetish smoke from the opium den across the street mixed with the tomato and oregano and baking crust of the pizza joint, roasting coffee from the warehouse district, traces of coal tar from the gasworks and the paving.

Albert shook his head. Demons.

He walked across town as the town grew dark around him. Yes, walked. He knew it wasn't normal, marked him as *different*, but he didn't own a car. Beyond the budget problem, he didn't *trust* cars. He should, he supposed, they were just clever metal-working on a larger scale, but he kept looking for the horse or team that wasn't there. Besides, most machines felt . . . empty to him. Worked metal should have a heart, a soul, the trace and memory of the smith who'd forged it and woke life in it. Machines made by machines lacked that.

Irrational, maybe, but that's what you got when you brought an old mind into the modern world.

He still twitched when one of those new electrics or hybrids whispered up behind him, not just horseless but without the rumble and whine of an engine to warn you it was coming. He didn't have a phone, either, or a computer or a lot of other modern magic. Airplanes? He still remembered the first one that droned over his head, a kite of sticks and wire and cloth and an engine reeking of burned castor oil. You couldn't make him fly in one for his weight in gold.

He walked in and out of the pools of light, through the reek of humans and their lives, past whores and street-side drug peddlers offering strange deaths. As always, he saw the city as the outsider he was, wondering why laws forced a man or woman into the risk of buying and selling on the street, the traders of flesh or chemicals working corners and alleys rather than a licensed house. He shuddered, remembering some of the published lab tests on street drugs, some of the rates of blood-borne and venereal disease in street whores of either sex. Make prostitution legal, allow it in designated areas, and neighborhoods wouldn't be plagued with the crime. The sex workers would be safer, healthier, and so would their clients. Make drugs legal, they would cost maybe one percent of the black market price and wouldn't kill the users anywhere near as fast. No *legal* house would risk its reputation on the psychos currently running the business.

Sanction and license the drug house across the street from his apartment, you'd pay a lot less and get exactly what you paid for. Content and dosage certified by independent lab. If you wanted to fry your brain, at least that way you fried it the way you wanted and sank into oblivion or hallucinations with a sober guard covering your ass.

But then the criminals *and* the cops *and* the politicians wouldn't get rich off the transactions. Albert had grown cynical with age.

Flesh and drugs didn't tempt him. Maybe that was part of not being human. Temptation *did* reach out and try to grab him by the ears, a whiskey-rough blues voice wafting down a side street from a bar he sometimes visited. Two blocks further on, a snatch of saxophone reached out to him, first clear and then fading back to a whisper even to *his* ears as a door opened and closed, split-note and trill followed by a smoky sultry glissando, and he froze in his tracks. He *knew* that sax, a tone and style unique to one blind jazz genius escaped from the slums of São Paulo, but the short phrase wasn't on any recording or broadcast he'd ever heard . . .

He'd never seen Lula perform live, hadn't known he was in town. The jazzman never booked gigs. He just showed up sometimes at a bottle-club door for a one-night stand, no publicity, take it or leave it, and word spread like wildfire among the fans. Live music was so much better than any recording, almost a different species. It was, well, it was *live*.

By whatever God you recognize, he was tempted. Another night he would have followed that sound, his own peculiar vice. He stopped and listened for a few minutes, there in the electric darkness, even turned. The demon's chore could wait. Then he thought about what he knew of demons. Odds were, Legion wouldn't just kill him, it would burn down the whole block with Lula and the audience and a hundred random strangers added to the toll. Sodom. Gomorrah. Pillars of salt optional.

Or maybe not. Never trust a demon.

Albert winced, remembering his apartment and the flames of hell, remembering the sudden searing heat and his flesh turning black in front of his eyes. He walked on.

That same hell kept his appointment book, and he had already decided he didn't want to die just yet. Add that missed jam-session to the "bad" side of Legion's karma account.

Did demons have karma? Damned if he knew. Maybe literally.

First a whiff, then stronger—cold char rode the evening air, not smoke but the memory of a fire not long dead. Not the resin smell of wood in a fireplace or stove, not sulfurous coal or greasy sooty oil, not the burned-rope of hemp smoke—a dead building. Most humans couldn't tell the difference, but Albert could. A stench of death hung over and after a building fire, a mix of smoldering wood and cloth and plastic and tar and hot metal, all quenched by the fire-company's cold hoses. He could have followed his nose to find it, rather than searching for the address Legion had given him.

This neighborhood was *bad*. Albert stopped and scanned the shadows, weighing dangers. He lived in a slum, yes, but borderline in the many grades of slum. Now he'd walked through three, maybe four levels straight down in the economic strata. Gaps opened out along the street, places that had burned out or just lost their battle with gravity and weren't worth repair. He passed under dead streetlights, saw candles flickering behind broken windows patched with cardboard or plastic sheets, smelled drifts of trash and burned-out cars and moldy mattresses in the weeds of vacant lots.

He hadn't walked this neighborhood in maybe twenty years. Too dangerous. But Legion said to go there, so he went.

And then Albert stood in front of it, a burned-out shell with blackened ragged holes for windows and door, an old ill-kept frame building surrounded by fresh yellow plastic "Fire Line" tape. He searched his memory. Paired six-pointed stars flanked the gaping doors. He remembered plain-dressed gray-haired men with beards and black hats or yarmulkes, Orthodox Jews long ago. A synagogue.

He smelled something faint within the char—a whiff of sandalwood, almost a trace of incense. His nose pulled him along those drifting traces, past the yellow tape and inside.

Salamander? That made no sense, no sense at all. The Star of David, Solomon's Seal on the doors, should have kept it out.

He thought about the decaying, no, *decayed* neighborhood. He thought about the peeling paint and cracked clapboards even where the fire hadn't touched. Had they abandoned the building when they couldn't raise a *minyan?* Without the living faith, the stars would not have guarded. He smelled something else, something of worked iron there, old and beyond old, heated and broken by the fire or by something else. It had a touch of Other about it . . .

White light blazed in his face, sudden pain behind his eyes. He struck at it without thinking. His cane rang on metal and sent the light spinning, sparking, into darkness. Another swing, shaft thudding on flesh-padded bone, crook of cane grabbing, pulling, a thrust into body and grunt of breath; upward jab and switched grip and clunk of shaft on skull; rustle of falling cloth, silence.

He spun away, staggering toward the faint light of the door, heard movement and muttered oaths behind him. Light flared again, searching, stabbing, light that missed him as he dodged. Light that found him, followed him.

"Halt! Police!"

A snarling voice, female but no way feminine.

He ducked and turned a corner. Bullets whined off brick and stone, followed by echoing booming gunshots.

Running now, panting, he grabbed at another corner, winding deeper into the labyrinth of alleys and courtyards, hoping against dead ends. Each turn blocked sightlines, trajectories from that gun . . .

He'd just attacked a policeman, maybe killed him. At least one cop still lived back there, a cop who had seen Albert's face. Up close and well-lit. Defy a demon and follow up with *that?*

Albert had had better days.

III

The way the rest of the night worked out, maybe he should have just trotted straight back to that bottle club where he'd heard Lula's sax. Sure, Legion might have killed him. He'd have died a happy man. Instead, he stumbled into night-hidden alley potholes and around stinking garbage bins, past lunging snarling shadowy dogs maybe chained or behind fences, maybe not. He stopped, listened, waited, darted through pools of light, sorting through memories twenty years, fifty years old for the alleys and mews and stairs up hillsides too steep for streets and other back ways of a person on foot and hunted.

All this while twitching at the echo of every footstep within three blocks, every whiff of fresh human sweat. All this while his shoulder blades cringed away from that bullet without warning—"hot pursuit" and legal. He couldn't shake the fear, even though he didn't hear or see anyone following him through all the twists and turns and doubling back. That included crossing the river twice, long open stretches of bridge where he had clear views ahead and behind under the streetlights.

Some people have always been the sort who cops call "sir," but those people never have been hunted. Albert had been down a lot more than he'd been up and knew cops from the underside. Most cops were okay, no worse than the average human. But attack, maybe kill, one of their own, and they turned *mean*. Suspects had a way of getting killed while resisting arrest or attempting to escape.

And he was carrying a cane with *stuff* smeared on it, blood and hair and skin cells for sure, maybe a dab of brain tissue, maybe not. He almost threw it in the river, both times crossing, except he couldn't count on it staying there. A simple magnetic drag would probably catch it—a finding spell certainly would. Wiping it down wouldn't help—even a bleach bath. Physical evidence might be erased, but the cane's aura would still match the dent he'd left in that shadow's skull. They also *knew* each other—easy enough to detect.

He didn't want to throw away that blade, either. It carried part of his soul, from the forging.

He made it home un-challenged and un-shot. After a long twitchy wait in the shadows, watching for trackers while sweat chilled on his back, he unlocked a cellar door off the back alley and made damn sure he locked it behind him, setting a bar across it before climbing down through gloom into dark stone-smell and into darker shadows, placing another bar across the second door at the bottom of the cellar stairs.

He kept his forge in the cellar. Less noise to disturb the neighbors that way, no windows for snoops to look in on his work, and besides, he'd like to watch some random stranger drag a two-hundredweight anvil up three long straight flights of stairs. Follow that with about five more trips each for the fire-pit and the bellows. This way, the anvil block sat firm on an honest sandstone ledge rather than perching on some floor joists of questionable virtue spaced too far apart thirty feet above street level.

Underground seemed more fit for his kind of working, anyway. Even if he wasn't a dwarf. He'd hung a light over the anvil and a few other spots where he needed to see fine detail. Most of the rest lay in shadow where he could best judge the fire's heat and the glow of metal.

With doors locked and barred behind him, he felt tension leaking out of his shoulders and back. If someone or some*thing* tried to come down those stairs, he had ways out that his family set up long ago. Not that those would help with Legion or any of *that* kind. But he had entered his heart, the place of his power. If he had any.

He switched on the lights. Forging. He needed to reset his brain from flight to forging. He took three deep breaths and closed his eyes, letting his thoughts settle into the steel of his cane, thinking air and fire and iron and anvil and wakening new life. How to change that cane so that even a wizard wouldn't feel its past in his hands? Couldn't trace it and find it from the wounds it'd left in the shadowed ruins of the synagogue? Trace it, and through it find the hands that carried it?

Things once connected always stay connected. The shaft and grip were the heart of tracing, the parts that had struck his enemy. Not the blade lurking inside—that hadn't tasted flesh and blood, he wouldn't need to change *it* . . .

He laid a charcoal fire in his forge—he'd never been comfortable using coal or coke to heat and work his iron. He felt a touch of memory of the wood in charcoal, of the tree and soil, rain and sunlight, *something* alive that made the fire listen to his needs. Coal and coke might have been alive once, but that was far too long ago for them to remember. They felt like stone now to him, not something he could talk to, listen to.

This working wanted a long fire, to heat the whole shaft at once, change the whole shaft at once, not doing things by pieces. He kindled shavings and splints at one end until the charcoal caught, pumped the leather bellows with foot-lever and spring-pole—blowing fire through the length of the bed of coals, waking sparks, waking blue jets and miniature orange demons in the glowing heart of heat, again the old ways of working metal as he'd learned them in a past turned to mist and dust and vague shadows.

Letting the fire-bed grow and settle, he prepared for working. He had his rituals, setting out tools and stock and plans just like a normal smith. He chose a light hammer for more control than force—*talk* to the steel, discuss rather than argue with it—and a two-faced swage for grooving. Then it was time to loose the blade from its sheath inside the cane's heart, unpin blade from the grip. Lay the cane shaft and grip in the fire. Check slack-tub, brine quench, oil quench. Free the vise and set it again just as he wanted it and waiting, with brass jaw-faces that wouldn't bite his iron.

Feel the iron, smell the iron, hot in the coals. Read the temperature by eye. No welding here, no blazing white sparks flying from each strike of hammer on hot metal. Uniform red heat, a human would just see it as a glow, he saw something more—he saw iron willing to change in certain ways. Tongs came to his hand as if he'd called them, griping, setting the glowing cane shaft between the jaws of the swage, tapping rather than pounding, matching rounded grooves along both sides of the shaft, up the length and then back down again, to taper out a couple of inches from each end, up and back, widening, deepening, then back into the fire, judge the glow, up and down the shaft again, smoothing, fire again, swage again. Turn a quarter in his tongs, a second set of grooves, four total as he saw the finished work in his head.

His world focused on the steel. Nothing else existed. Talk to the steel, talk to the fire, listen to the steel, listen to the fire. Smell them, taste them, *feel* them, discuss, agree. Heat to red again, one *particular* shade of red, clench the tip in vise jaws, twist free end turning grooves into matched spirals, two full turns in the cane's length. Judge by eye, close to the glowing steel, heat baking tears to steam and singing eyebrows. Back to anvil and tap here, tap there, smoothing the flow of iron. Heat again. Mandrel for the sheath, the blade. Drive mandrel into red glowing heart of cane. Judge shaft again, swage again, mandrel again.

Quench the steel's heat. Polish, first grit and then rouge-wheel, foot-treadle power for the *feel*, banish scale and scars of forging. Reheat gently to draw the temper, anneal, judge colors flowing and swirling across the shiny cooked steel, working by eye and ear and nose. Let cool just enough and quench again, from the lesser heat. Tough, strong, not brittle.

Again for the handle, change the shape, change the grip from molded rubber—now purged to untraceable ash and smoke sent up the flue—replace with diamond-checkering in the steel itself, change the *soul* so none could read it.

Metal hot to the touch, still expanded, set and pin blade before grip cools and shrinks, slide into now-cold sheath with a sliding rasp and snick, test the fit and release. Set blade aside. Heat a brass ferule instead of rubber for the shaft's tip, slip over cold end, quench to shrink and clench around the steel. Same for knurled brass ring to hide the joining between grip and shaft for hidden blade.

Done. Breathe deep, step back from forge, step back from anvil. A new thing lay on the anvil face, shaft of blue and purple swirls, black grip, old blade in new setting. No connection to the shadows and soot, the blood, the crime. He wiped gritty sweat from his face and looked upon his work and called it good.

"Now *what* in the name of Allah's eight million afreets are *you?*"

The voice came out of the shadows on the far side of his forge. He jerked and blinked and tried to shake himself out of the trance of working iron. He got *involved* in metal. When he was at the anvil, the world could end with trumpets and earthquakes and the unfurling of the last scroll and he wouldn't notice. Not until he finished his forging.

She had a welt across her left temple, and blood-matted black hair above her left ear—injuries that looked too much like the work of his cane. She kept her left hand tucked into a pocket in her coveralls, some kind of working uniform with lettering and patches he couldn't read in the gloom. She had a gun in her right hand, pointed at him.

He wasn't an expert on guns—some large blued-steel automatic that meant business. The muzzle on the thing looked big enough to shove his thumb down it. He didn't feel like arguing. He lifted his hands.

"I'm Albert Johansson." His current name, matched the license and all. Johansson went with the eyes and hair, and, well, nobody *ever* took an Albert seriously.

The apparition shook her head. "I didn't ask *who,* I asked *what.*"

She shouldn't have been there. Yeah, he got involved, wouldn't notice things. But he'd locked and barred those doors, and his cellar forge didn't have any windows. She must have climbed down a chimney flue. With a broken wrist, it looked like.

"I'm a man, just like any other."

"Pig farts. I'm the seventh daughter of a seventh daughter, heir to the Woman of Shamlegh. I've *Seen* the Hidden People, but I've never seen your kind before. Neither man nor gnome; not troll, not djinn, not dwarf under the mountain. I've watched dwarves at the forge. They're good, but they can't talk to steel that way."

He knew he talked when he worked. He'd never recorded what he said, couldn't remember afterwards, couldn't even tell you for sure what language he spoke when he and iron got together for a little chat. For damn sure, he never let anyone watch and listen. All he knew was, it worked. He and iron understood each other.

She waved the gun, moving him away from his anvil and fire and bellows, away from the finished cane shaft and the blade still showing bare steel. She limped forward into more light, and he could see her jaw muscles clenched. He'd hurt more than just her head and wrist, in that scuffle in the dark.

Even taking away the soot and bruises and the blood, you wouldn't call her pretty. Nose like a beak, broken years ago, dark hooded eyes, hollow cheeks, chin with rather too much character. He'd seen brown hawk-faces like that before, the dry dusty tribal hill-fort villages of Pushtu and Paktia, where he watched and learned from smiths who could forge automatic weapons out of tin cans and scrap cast-iron pots. The women of those tribes wore veils or full burkas when they went out at all. She didn't. He wasn't sure the change improved the landscape.

She studied the cane. She started to pull her left hand out of her pocket, winced, and sagged against his anvil. Maybe he could get to that gun . . .

Her glare said, *Don't even think about it.* She straightened up, it looked like sheer will, and followed the glare with a shake of her head. "In your dreams, runt." Yeah, she was taller than him, maybe half a foot. No trace of a Hill accent there, more like Bronx. He guessed second or third generation away from the tribes. Not that he could see any sign the move had softened her.

She poked at the blade with her pistol, keeping her eyes on him. "Where did you get *that?*"

He was proud of that blade. Watered-silk folded steel, rival to the best pre-Meiji *tanto* or *katana*, keen enough to cut a thought, cut the wind, yet springy as a fencing foil, he'd sweated blood on that one short blade. He didn't know that he'd ever done better work. Equal, yes. Not better.

"I forged it."

Her eyes widened, and he didn't think it was pain. She stepped back from the anvil and raised her pistol to her forehead in salute.

"I know men who would give several thousand dollars U.S. for that blade, alone. Two, three times that for the whole cane. What the hell were you doing, poking around my crime scene?"

Tell her a demon twisted his arm? Not likely. "You had a salamander there. I smelled it."

She cocked her head to one side and then winced. "You *smelled* it? And my Sight shows at least three hundred years behind you. I repeat, what *are* you?"

He shrugged, as well as you can shrug with hands in the air. "If you find that out, please tell me. I don't know. I just am."

Taking another of those risky moves that he was making habit, he lowered his hands without asking. She let him. Maybe that Sight she claimed didn't call him a threat. Not that it had warned her in the burned-out synagogue. He never asked how another person's gift worked or didn't—he had enough trouble with his own.

Now that she stood closer to the light, he could read the patches on her coveralls. City police, indeed, and a name tag that said "el Hajj." From what he knew of Muslim names, that meant someone in her ancestry had made the pilgrimage to Mecca, from a time and place where that was notable.

"I thought I'd checked for anyone following me . . . "

She managed a wry smile. "I'm very good at following people and finding things. That's one reason why the Chief puts up with me."

She waved her pistol toward the door and the cellar steps. "Now, if you'd just let us out. Don't move fast enough to make me twitch. I had a gunsmith spend a few hours on the trigger sear."

"How'd you get in here?"

Another wry smile. "None of your business. I'm here. That's what matters."

He didn't agree with that. But she held the gun—a Colt .45 automatic, now that he could see it well. Nothing he wanted to argue with.

He'd never needed to know much about police procedures. He hadn't been arrested in something like fifty years. Still, he thought she was being awfully casual about this. He went ahead, unbarring and unlocking, up the cellar stairs, unlocking and unbarring again, her staying well back with that cannon in her hand. He could have dodged out and around the corner at that point, he didn't think she could move fast enough to catch him or even get a clear shot, not with her limp and all it implied. But she was good at finding things and following people . . .

No gain there. Like with the demon, running wouldn't do him any good. She already knew where to find him.

Outside, in the alley that stank of wet dust and the pizza joint's garbage and a winter's worth of dogshit now thawed with the spring, she waved him back and tucked the pistol somewhere under her coverall. At that point, things clicked together like the blade locking into his cane.

He blinked. "You aren't arresting me?"

She started to shake her head and then didn't. "What for? I'm pretty sure you didn't start that fire. As for the rest, if Allah so wills, I'll drink your blood. When the demon lets me. I don't need some soft-hearted law of the infidel dogs for vengeance."

She turned and limped off along the dawn alley, went around the corner and was gone. Yes, dawn. He'd lost the night in his forging. Vanished time again. Until he saw a newspaper, he couldn't even tell if it was one night, or two, or three. Working iron, he got *involved*.

But she'd left some puzzles behind. The demon? She didn't give a Name, so he couldn't tell if she meant Legion or some other. The vengeance that she named so calmly you could almost miss it? No puzzle there. Hill people were like that. Blood must be washed out with blood. But the way she invoked the will of Allah? That had sounded like mouth music. No meaning behind it. He didn't think she cared whether Allah willed or not. She'd do it either way.

The way she'd said "the Woman of Shamlegh"—a title, a title of power, *her* power. Matriarchy, not patriarchy. With some of those hill tribes, he'd learned that Islam was little more than a surface gloss. True beliefs lie hidden deep beneath, far older.

Then he started to shake and felt his bones turn into rubber. He'd been coasting on the high his forge always gave him, one reason that the drug houses didn't tempt him and he could take good beer and wine or leave them—he had better ways of stepping outside his brain. But, just as with alcohol or opium or hemp, he paid a stiff price after.

Anyway, high from forging, he probably wouldn't have cared if Legion had shown up with all his buddies, Allah's eight million afreets, much less a single woman from the cops. Not even with a gun pointed at him. The whole scene had lasted maybe five minutes, his stepping back from the anvil to her limping away down the alley.

Now he cared. Now the drug of his magic washed out of his blood and left him exhausted. A pounding hangover and a rush of fear broke sweat down his spine again.

He stumbled back to the cellar door, down to his forge, and cleaned up from the night's work. Killed the fire in cold water. Married cane, shaft, and blade. Climbed up again. Locked up.

He limped his way out of the alley and around the corner to his front door—no connecting stairs from the cellar up. Yes, he had ways from attic to cellar, hidden, abandoned chimneys and the shaft of an old dumb-waiter, that sort of thing. But he couldn't trust his legs to a ladder just then, or to the scattering of brick nubs and rusty brackets that made a climbing path up the alley wall.

Brown paper caught his eye: a long envelope sticking out of his mailbox. It hadn't been there last night or whenever it was that he went walking. He pulled it out.

No address. No stamps or franking. Sealed. He felt too washed-out to care about modern trivia like evidence or letter bombs or even privacy. He ripped one end open, in the dawn light on the street.

A feather. One solitary tail-feather from a hen pheasant. He blinked and tried to shake some sense past the fog filling his brain.

Mother had taught them a dozen codes and signals, objects you could leave anywhere and people wouldn't notice them, or, if noticed, make into any sense. Pheasant feathers, well, they meant danger—like his family, they weren't native to this land. People introduced them as tasty self-propelled targets for the hunt.

And the tail feather of a hen pheasant meant Mother.

His stomach didn't just growl, it snarled at him. He hadn't eaten anything since that ham sandwich with Legion, yesterday's lunch or whatever, and his body *needed* food after the forging. He couldn't make sense of the feather there, on the street, with fog for brains.

Through the door, lock up and bar again—little good *that* seemed to do against not just Legion and its ilk but the Afghan harpy on his trail. He stumbled upstairs, one step at a time, glanced into the parlor and yes, the food and vodka had vanished from the hearth.

On to his apartment perched on the fourth floor, up stairs long and steep to the gold coins still gleaming in the sunrise on his kitchen table. At least Legion hadn't decided to lay another jest on the stupid mortal chump. Him.

Yet.

He grabbed some food, random calories in quick form, gulped a beer, and collapsed on his bed. Didn't bother to shuck off the sweaty gritty sooty clothes first.

Laundry and personal hygiene didn't make it onto his list just then. Or the end of the world, whichever came first.

IV

nd the evening and the morning were of the third day. Or
whatever day it was, anyway. He woke to sky glowing pale
yellow in the east, just about what he'd seen before crashing into
bed, and had to assume he'd slept the clock around. At least
once. Maybe twice. He really needed to start keeping a diary,
if Legion was going to add even more gaps to already sketchy
memories . . .

He lay in bed feeling like three kinds of shit, still down
after the high that working serious iron gave him, a kind of
whole-body hangover that wasn't exactly bone-ache fever or sore
muscles or exhaustion. He woke alone, of course. He'd slept
alone, lived alone for fifty years, a hundred years. Sometimes,
dark times awake in the middle of the night, he understood
why his brothers sought death, why his sister sought death. He'd
come close to following them. Their long lives weren't *lives* as
such, just existence.

Living required getting close to other people, and they didn't
dare. Besides the dance of moving and changing names, dodging
questions, pretending they were human, they always faced the
pain of watching someone they loved grow old and change into
a dry shriveled husk that once was vibrant. After the third, the
fourth, he'd decided it was safer to never love again. He didn't
keep cats or other pets, either. They become part of your life and
then vanish into smoke at the blink of an eye.

A shower helped some, clean clothes, and coffee. Mozart helped more. Like all mortals, he had died, yes, died young, but he left lasting joy behind him. Albert threw some ingredients together and turned them into buttermilk pancakes with orange-blossom honey instead of maple syrup, and added rounds of bulk sausage heavy on the sage and pepper. Eat, drink, and be merry, for tomorrow we die. Or today, if Allah so willed.

Besides, he was rich. At least temporarily. He kept staring at the demon's pile of gold and the pheasant feather while he cooked and ate.

Talk about ambiguous. That feather—the problem with codes and signals lay in interpretation. Mother always liked to be a mystery, even to her own children. She liked to keep things vague. He'd jumped to conclusions when he saw it, his brain dull and dizzy and too full of that day's things. The infamous cold light of morning gave him other answers. Or, more accurately, other questions.

He didn't know if the feather was Mother warning him that he was in danger—in which case she was a little late—or saying *she* was in danger and needed help. Or maybe the end of the world loomed, just like Legion said, and she wanted him to do something about it. In any case, a few details had gone missing. He hadn't seen her in twenty years or so. He hadn't known if she was still alive, much less in town.

He didn't even know for sure that the feather came from her. She could have taught the same code to someone else. He had those brothers and a sister, all dead years ago. At least, he *thought* they were dead, although all he had was second-hand reports. Never saw the bodies.

He had some cousins, an uncle and aunt, a niece and two nephews that he knew about. He hadn't seen any of *them* for over a hundred years. For all he knew, he had family he'd never met. Like maybe a father.

Hell, he'd been away from Mother long enough at times for her to bear a child and raise it and send it out into the world without her bothering to tell him. His family, well, it was a little strange. Private. They all kept their lives in little boxes and were damned careful about what they let out past the walls. *Nobody* got straight answers out of Mother. She'd find some way to evade and muddle anything, even if she was standing next to a window and you asked her if it was raining. What he knew about her, she'd let slip in passing, or as part of a tale that could be nine parts lies or even the whole cloth.

The feather might tell tales, itself. It would remember who had touched it, where it came from. Like with his cane, things once connected stayed connected. You just needed to ask the right questions in the right way.

The dice wouldn't work for that. Besides, he wasn't happy with those bone cubes at the moment. They'd tried to get him killed. He only had the one small magic—he couldn't see the future or the past. He didn't trace things, find people, walk through walls like that Afghan harpy, read tea leaves or palms or entrails or stars or hear voices from the cave. He just could talk to iron.

A thought chilled him, and he ignored it by brewing another cup of coffee. The image waited and still lurked there in one corner of his brain when he came back to it with the mug warm in his hands. He made it wait some more, sipping hot bitter caffeine. It didn't go away.

That woman, el Hajj. She claimed to be very good at finding things and following people. She also wanted to cut out his heart and eat it. You need a definition of "vendetta," go to the Pamirs and the Karakoram country and the tribes. They held grudges and blood feuds that reached back to Tamerlane.

He'd once lived ten years in those unforgiving hills, learning the ways they talked to iron. They knew him as a member of the tribe of smiths, a different kin-tie but one they recognized. They'd accepted him for that. If he'd set a foot or hand wrong, though, they would have killed him without a second thought.

They didn't have laws. They had guns and knives and what they called honor instead, some of which he understood and some he didn't.

As far as he was concerned, *she'd* attacked *him*. Shining a high-powered flashlight in dark-adapted eyes from four feet away, that's assault. She hadn't identified herself as police, hadn't said a word or even made a noise before that. Her blood was on her own hands.

He didn't think he could make *her* believe that. Besides the tribal honor thing, he'd noticed that cops never made mistakes. That was another tribal culture.

The second cup of coffee didn't help. He'd never heard of anyone finding visions of the future in the brown liquid. A third would just crank up his twitching nerves another notch.

He gathered the demon's gold into a paper bag and stowed it in a plumbing chase behind the bathtub where he'd chipped out three bricks years ago. No reason to leave temptation lying around—Mother still had keys, if she really was in town, and she'd see that pile of coins as hers. All wealth and property belonged to the Queen, you understand. Anything she left you was just a gracious gift.

He needed more information. To him, that meant "library." As far as he was concerned, public libraries ranked up there with flush toilets and central heating as great advances of civilization. He remembered life before those good things, and had no wish to return.

So he grabbed his cane and headed down three long flights of creaking dark stairs through the dust and out, no mysterious brown envelopes sticking out of his mailbox this time, but enough advertising and financial offers and other junk that he suspected he'd lost more than one day to the demon and the forging and the crash that followed. He dumped everything unopened in a trash bin down the street, no keepers—if someone wanted to steal those credit-card offers to a name he hadn't used in a generation, fat lot of good they'd find in the theft—and walked across town to the pile of yellow brick and stone and arched windows under a green copper roof that served as the local temple of knowledge. The place even *smelled* of learning: centuries-old paper and dark waxed wood and radiator dust in the long close-spaced shelves of books.

Also smelled of homeless people—stale cigarette smoke and layers of unwashed clothing and sour cheap-wine breath—but that was decreasing with the spring warmth and less need to get out of the arctic wind before you froze to death. He didn't know why homeless people always smelled of cigarettes. There was *true* addiction for you, scraping up the bucks for a pack of smokes when you couldn't keep a roof over your head.

Anyway, he got there just after the library opened, giving him first shot at the morning newspaper and a quiet chair in a corner. Early enough that he had to ask for the paper from the gray-haired librarian in the periodical room, and he gritted his teeth a bit before walking up to her with a smile he didn't feel.

She recognized him, of course. "Good morning, Mr. Johansson." She stared at his face for a moment like she always did, before pulling the newspaper out of a pile waiting for her to shelve. She shook her head, again like she always did.

The librarian thought he was his own son, or maybe grandson. He looked a lot like a man who used to come in thirty, forty years ago when she'd just started working. Charming little guy, they'd talked a lot, she'd had dreams, embarrassing dreams. Of course, that man had a beard . . .

Couldn't be the same man, obviously.

She'd commented on this several times when he checked out books. He'd told her the truth—he never knew his father, and his mother didn't talk about him. That hint of personal scandal meant the librarian wouldn't ask again. Much.

This was one of the reasons he didn't stay around any one place longer than twenty years and allowed long intervals before he returned. Good thing most people don't or won't believe their eyes.

A quick look at the date and yes, he'd lost two days. Lucky it wasn't three, or he'd have wasted his walk and found the library closed for Sunday. Legion said the world would change, was changing, doom rushing toward the world like an express train on a single track, and Simon Lahti had two weeks at the most . . .

And Simon Lahti didn't exist. Never had.

He found his story, page one but below the fold, a follow-up on the synagogue fire. The sixth in a year, the article said, complete with map on page five showing how the sites clustered in an area of a few blocks. All were of "suspicious origin," quoting a police detective named Melissa el Hajj. There appeared to be a "human element" in most of the fires, besides the obvious pattern of the crime locations.

She hadn't mentioned the inhuman element. Her business, not Albert's. But *Melissa?* He'd expected something exotic like Fatima or Mumtaz. He revised his estimate of how long ago her family had left those Afghan hills.

Know your enemy—sage advice from a hundred sages. He couldn't find a listing for her in the telephone directory, not even another el Hajj. Several el-Haj names, Hajji, al-Hajj, but the paper and his memory agreed on her chosen spelling. Nothing in the city directory, either. Well, he couldn't blame her for an unlisted phone, not in her position.

He thought about calling up the central police station and asking to speak to her or leave a message, but that didn't seem like a good idea. Maybe it had something to do with how she wanted to kill him.

That done, he made a quick check of an old city map, one with an "aerial" view faked with sketched-in buildings as they'd been in the 1880s, points of interest named. The synagogue was there, of course, it had been there since Methuselah was a puppy. He tried to match up the other fires with buildings in the picture, and no connections jumped out at him. At the time of the map, they'd been stores, hotels, a livery stable, a warehouse. The neighborhood had been upscale then, a couple of private clubs made the roster and a couple of banks long gone. He couldn't see any pattern except proximity, and that they'd all been abandoned for years, "current owner unknown."

He shrugged and headed back out, passing the gray-haired librarian now at the circulation desk, who nodded to him with a repeat of that quizzical smile.

The research had gained him little. At least he had a fine spring morning, blue sky, trees bright green in first leaf, birds singing, and a warm breeze from the south to bring a touch of brine-smell upriver from the bay. He walked, as always.

The synagogue's neighborhood didn't look any prettier by daylight: empty weed-grown lots where buildings once stood, now turning into dumps. The survivors looked like smallpox cases, pocked with boarded up or broken windows and a couple of places where he could see daylight through openings where no daylight should shine—evidence of collapsing roofs or walls. He walked past several of the previous crime scenes on the way, all empty lots, whatever burned-out shells the fires left had been leveled and the cellar holes filled in. No clues, no lingering smell of elementals beyond the slight residue of charred building on adjacent walls. He couldn't see why anyone would *care* if the whole neighborhood vanished in smoke. Save the cost of demolition.

People lived there, though. People who didn't look him in the eye but who studied his back or glanced sideways as he passed or who watched from windows until they made sure he wasn't stopping at their doors. He didn't know if they filed him under "Predator" or "Prey" or "Cop"—some label that made them keep their distance, anyway. Which, given the general atmosphere, suited him just fine.

The synagogue sat where he'd left it, a lot more detail visible in sunlight. It had been a smallish low plain building—there had never been a lot of Jews in town and most synagogues he'd seen tended to plain architecture. Traces of yellow paint still clung to the clapboards. He didn't know if that was whim or a good price on bulk paint or a reference to the pale yellow stone of Jerusalem and the Temple.

Except for a small dome over the entry, now a blackened skeleton, the roof had gone—walls reached up to end in blackened ragged stubs, empty fire-gnawed windows down both sides with less wall at each until the last ones in the rear barely had sills. Even *he* could see that the fire had started at the rear, around the pulpit or whatever Jews called that space. That screamed "suspicious origin"—not that many fire sources for a pulpit, outside of God's lightning striking down the preacher.

The place had been *old*. He saw timber posts and charred beams lying in the sodden ash on the floor, axe-hewn timbers and boards with the irregular faces of pit-sawing, clapboards split rather than sawn, the materials and methods he remembered from centuries ago and lands across the ocean.

He'd seen the peeling paint even in the night. Now, in daylight, he could see warped clapboards hanging askew with rust streaks telling him the damage came long before the fire. He saw rot in one unburned windowsill, then another, gray weathered breaks on the sash, piles of gray droppings and white streaks on the remaining eave trim where pigeons had gotten into under-roof spaces and nested.

Yellow tape still guarded the ruin, warning people away from a crime scene. Somehow that added to the mournful sense of a building abandoned, a building that had outlived its people and use. He could still smell the salamander and sandalwood again but much fainter, fading, he might not have caught it if he hadn't been searching. No wonder Legion had wanted him to get there while the smells hung fresh.

He picked up a nail lying close to the wall and inside the tape, pulled from interior trim the firemen had ripped loose and thrown out through a smashed window in their haste. Wrought iron, not steel, it hadn't caught enough heat to destroy its memory. He rolled it across his palm. Square shank, hand-wrought, rose-headed by five hammer blows on a nail plate, pointed by four taps on the anvil, he remembered making them by the hundreds, by the days, the weeks as an apprentice. He'd learned to *hate* nails. He touched it to his tongue.

"What can you taste from rusty iron?"

He jerked and looked up, finding his nemesis. She'd done it again, materialized like a ghost out of the shadows, moving without sound, now standing inside a burned-out window of the hulk. That woman was trying to give him a heart attack. At least this time she didn't have a gun in her hand. She *did* have a shaved patch and bandage on the side of her head where he'd hit her, didn't make her look any prettier, and some kind of cast on her left wrist and hand that left her fingers free.

Both cast and bandage were stained with soot. So were her blue coveralls, especially the knees and elbows—she'd been poking around her crime scene. He got the impression that she'd be pure hell as a patient. Doctor had probably told her to stay in bed.

"Age," he answered.

She cocked her head to one side. "Age? Talked to a guy at Historic Preservation this morning. Near as he can tell, this was the oldest synagogue in the western hemisphere. No record of construction, but it turns up in town records from 1700. What does your magic tongue say?"

He tasted the iron again—cold, rusty, bitter, tired. "About three hundred winters, I guess. It's a simple working, not enough soul for a good memory."

She blinked at that, and looked skeptical. Hey, he didn't know *how* he knew that sort of thing. He'd just spent so much time and sweat and blood and skin on working iron, they recognized each other. He could tell the man who forged the nail hadn't been a Jew, hadn't liked or trusted Jews, hadn't thought they should be allowed to build in town. They denied the Son of God. Unhappy smith, unhappy nail, endless years sunk into the wood of a building it despised. He tasted that in the iron.

He remembered a scene from long ago and another city, a burning building with dark-coated men dashing through the flames and smoke and falling embers, coming out with their clothes and hair smoldering and red shining burns on hands and faces but joy glowing through those burns, bodies protecting long rolls cased in rich cloth with knobs of silver on the ends . . .

"Did they save the scrolls?"

Lifted eyebrows—she didn't understand what he was asking.

"The, what do they call them, the Torah? The Word of God? I've heard that a Jew should protect it with his life."

The cop shook her head. "Nobody's used this building in something over forty years. Anything that important, they'd have taken away long ago."

He could still feel *something* under that ash and char, just as strong as it had been a night ago, two nights, whatever. A piece of iron called to him. *Old* iron, old beyond anything he'd felt before, and that included Roman iron.

And it was hurt.

Iron didn't usually cry out like that, even to him. He could walk past steel-framed buildings every day and barely feel all those tons. Even touching the metal or tasting it, like the nail, he needed to really pay attention to get something out of it. He had to heat iron, hammer it, forge it, want to make it into something, to get a good conversation going.

"Are you going to shoot me if I come inside?"

She lifted an eyebrow. "Probably not."

He ducked under the yellow tape and followed his nose through a side door splintered ajar by fire axes, into the sodden lye-smell of ash and char. The floor thumped solid under his cane, stone or tile—he'd been in burned-out buildings before and knew they sometimes hid nasty surprises, shells of a floor or wall that looked whole and sound but just wanted a touch to collapse into black empty hollows behind. He didn't *know* that Ms. Detective el Hajj would let him walk into a death-trap, but he wouldn't put it past her. Most likely, though, she needed to spill his blood with her own hands. An "accident" wouldn't satisfy her honor.

The iron cry for help pulled him toward the rear, where pulpit and choir would sit in a Christian church, the focus of the sanctuary, the worst damage of the fire. He thumped along, step by step, testing each bit of floor before he trusted it. Even natural fires could skip and concentrate within a matter of a few feet.

He found the remains of a cabinet of some kind, quality woodwork, even a smith could tell a skilled craftsman had put a lot of work and pride into that. Further proof of something unnatural about *this* fire. It shouldn't have survived at all, that close to the heart of the fire, even damaged as it was.

In the still-damp ash, under charred boards, he found a hexagram—the six-pointed star known as the Star of David or the Seal of Solomon—forged thick and the width and height of his joined palms. He found two of them, as if they had ornamented matching cabinet doors. One felt normal to him, just wrought iron, maybe the same age as the nail. The other . . .

The other one was *old*. One point of it had cracked. Had *been* cracked, judging by the feel, by some outside force, and it wasn't heat, wasn't the building burning down around it. This was wrought iron, not cast iron, tough instead of brittle. It could take heat and the quenching cold of the fire hoses.

It knew him, knew his skills. It wanted him to fix it. It *needed* him to fix it, it was *important,* something dark and dire would happen that he couldn't see, couldn't understand, if he didn't take this seal back to his forge and make it whole—

"Drop it!"

She had her cannon out and pointed at his heart. Gripped in one hand, rested on the cast around her other, steady, the huge bore swallowing light. She stood between him and the door.

She didn't understand. "I have to repair this. It holds the worlds apart. It seals the way."

The words came from the iron, not from him. He couldn't say how or why. He didn't know what they meant.

"Drop it. Nobody takes evidence from my crime scene."

V

Possessive young lady, calling it her *crime scene.*

He studied her face, harsh and concentrated over the gunsights. No, not young. Crow's feet at her eyes as she scowled. More, indefinable, a sense of weight, of having seen more than a few years. Forties, he guessed, maybe as old as fifty, from all the humans he'd seen grow and fade. So fast.

He didn't drop the star. That would have been rude, after it had spoken to him.

He bent over and laid it back in the mold it had formed for itself by settling into the bed of damp gray ash, careful to fit the edges and points exactly as he'd found them. He covered it with the charred boards that had been a cabinet face, again matching the pieces to the marks they'd made, leaving her crime scene as undisturbed as possible. Then he stood up. She still had that gun pointed at him.

"Why don't you just shoot me and get it over with?"

"Can't. The demon won't let me."

There it was again. He shook his head. "Look, I wouldn't *be* here if a demon hadn't started to burn me alive for refusing. I don't have much choice. How about you put that cannon away so we can talk like civilized people?"

"Drop the cane and I'll think about it."

So much for people not seeing that his cane was a weapon. But she still wore the bandages and bruises from it, and had seen the blade inside. She was a cop—he was surprised she hadn't asked to see his concealed weapons permit. Which, of course, he didn't have.

She didn't seem to care much for standard police procedure. Breaking into his forge without a warrant, however she'd done it—that could count as "hot pursuit" under the meaning of the act. Leaving without arresting him, standing by in the shadows watching while he destroyed evidence? Not really. Likewise for letting a civilian poke around in a crime scene.

"Look, I need to get out of here. That seal is making my teeth ache. It's whining at me. Either let me get some distance from it, or let me take it back to my forge and heal it. Or shoot me."

At that point, he wasn't sure he cared which way it went. That thing's whine *was* making his teeth ache, throbbing from his wisdom teeth up inside his temples and pressing on his brain until his eyes watered. Yes, he still had his "wisdom" teeth, small wisdom they conferred on him. Dentists hadn't been invented when his teeth grew in, and he was just lucky they grew in straight.

Or maybe his species didn't have the same problems with teeth that humans did. He wasn't sure which.

He moved across to the broken side door, still testing the surface with his cane as he went. Solid. Solid like rock, not even the echo you'd get from a concrete slab or stone paving over empty space. Which didn't fit . . .

"Does this place have a cellar?"

She kept her distance, kept the gun braced on her left wrist and cast and pointed at his chest, kept the remains of benches or pews between them, as if he was maybe a kung fu master in the movies and could drop her with a flying side kick from twenty feet away. She just shook her head at his question.

Outside, in a narrow alley next to crumbling brick walls that still showed scorch marks from the synagogue fire next door, the star's whine faded back to a thin plaintive buzz like a fly trapped on the other side of a window. He ducked under the yellow tape, took a deep breath, and dropped the cane to rattle on cracked potholed asphalt. After all, he'd already decided that he wanted to live a while longer.

"Cellar?"

She'd followed him through the door but still kept her distance, trash and bits of burned building between them, still kept her pistol ready. She shook her head again. "Not that I know of. Why?"

"When I held the star, it wasn't just talking to me. I could see something. A black space that felt hollow, like a cave, with moving lights in some kind of haze or smoke. They scared me. I don't know what they were, but I didn't want to meet them."

"Salamanders? That's how they got in to cause the fire?"

He closed his eyes for a moment and shuddered, remembering that dark vision. "Not salamanders. Those things were *mean*. Salamanders are just big friendly puppies that happen to start fires. Give them a safe place to play and they make the whole room happy. What I saw and felt, those things fed off pain and hate and sorrow, not wood. And they were *hungry*. A long time since their last meal."

"Nothing I've ever heard of." She paused and clicked something on the side of her gun. He *hoped* she was setting the safety on. Then she moved the muzzle so that it pointed just a bit away from him, letting him breathe a little easier. That muzzle looked like the tunnel of the New York subway.

Her eyes looked almost as dangerous, memorizing him from hair to boots. "Little man, what's your real name? 'Albert Johansson' wouldn't stand up to a record search, would it? Not if you go deep enough? That guy at Historic Preservation had a photo of your block, 1883. Put a suit and bowler hat and mustache on you and you'd be twin brother to the man standing in front of the storefront bakery. I doubt if that's coincidence."

Oh, *hell*. Photographs. He tried to avoid them, but sometimes he got caught by accident. He wondered what he'd been doing that made him stand still long enough to be frozen in one of those old wet-plate photos. Probably drooling over a pie or pastry in the window display—if he remembered right, that place baked the most amazing cherry strudel, sour and sweet at the same time, flaky layered crust. It would melt in your mouth . . .

She gestured her left hand and the cast at the side of her head. "I wasn't feeling too good the other night. Head hurt. But I still can't See the beginning of your lifeline behind you. Who are you, *what* are you, why are you tied up in this shit?"

He shrugged. She had the gun, she knew too much already, she'd proven that she was very good at finding things and following people. Whatever trouble he could get into, he was already hip deep. Maybe neck deep, but he was short.

"I've used dozens of names. Can't remember all of them. The demon called me 'Simon Lahti.' I guess that makes it as permanent as any. I've already told you I don't know *what* I am. As for why, the demon says I have to stop someone from abusing their companions. Or mortals will suffer the consequences. My demon claimed to be called 'Legion.' Is that the same as yours?"

She frowned and narrowed her eyes. "Police ask questions. We don't answer them. Keep talking."

And here he'd been thinking she wasn't a typical cop. Still, putting two and two together and adding them up to five, somebody wasn't telling the whole truth. Somebody with golden skin, no sex, and no hair.

"I don't trust demons. They lie, they play tricks, their goals aren't my goals. I *think* Legion wanted me here because I'm a smith. I can heal that star. Nothing to do with stopping the fires. You're the detective—that's *your* job. My job is working iron. Let me take the star back to my forge and make it whole. It's *important.*"

Her frown turned into full-blown scowl. "Little man, I don't know about you, but I've lived long enough that I don't believe everything I hear. I've come across old broken magic that damn well should *stay* broken. I want to find out what that star really does before I'm going to let you fix it."

Her "little man" phrase was starting to annoy him. Which was probably why she used it—he was getting a sense of why she said the police "put up" with her for her special skills. The woman *liked* to piss off people.

"Look, that thing feels about as old as Solomon."

"You expect me to believe that Suleiman bin Dauod was a *blacksmith?*"

"I didn't say Solomon made it himself. Just that it was too old for me to tell. I've heard plenty of stories about Solomon as a powerful wizard, not just a king—commanding the winds and the djinni and knowing the language of the animals. Aren't some of those straight from the Qur'an itself, the words of the Prophet?"

She blinked at that. "Peace be upon him . . . Four or five, yes."

She broke off and shivered. Not the cold, not with the warm spring day, blue sky and sun. "I'll get a police magician out here to look at it."

He'd been ignoring the buzz while they talked. It spiked for a moment, another twinge from his teeth up to his temples and pressing on his eyeballs from the inside even at that distance, a sense of urgency.

"Don't take too long. Something bad happens soon." He paused, following branches and possibilities that had sprouted in his head while they talked. "Who owns this place? Maybe we can find someone who knows the history of that thing, where it came from, what it does. Get your answers that way. Faster."

She cocked her head to one side. "Funny you should ask. We don't *know* who owns this wreck. We've been trying to track it down, but Jews don't have a bishop or a diocese or anything like that, no national organization that runs things or owns things.

The congregation owned the building, and the congregation seems to all have died or moved away. Like I told you, this place hasn't been used in decades."

"Doesn't the city have an address for the tax bills?"

"Tax exempt. Religious building. Not even utility bills—water, electric, gas. All cut off years ago. That's one reason why I went to Historic in the first place. If nothing else, we need to figure out who pays to tear it down."

He looked around. Roof gone, except for that bit of dome in the front, walls damaged or half gone, no windows left, wood posts and beams charred to the point where half of them collapsed—a hot fire that had plenty of time to work before the fire company got here. Historic as hell, maybe one of the oldest synagogues in North America? Maybe, but she was right. It wouldn't be a repair job, and rebuilding to historic standards would cost a ton. No congregation, he had to assume no insurance.

She could see him working his way through that. A faint smile twitched her mouth. "Now get lost. I'm supposed to be on sick leave, and you're keeping me from a cold beer."

He thought she was joking. "Doesn't your Prophet forbid alcohol?"

She stilled and that muzzle came back to his chest, unwavering, with a click that meant the safety was off again. Her face settled into a slit-eyed glare that could have frozen the bay.

"Little man, I once killed a Badakhi because he thought he should beat me for going unveiled. He was much larger than you. I killed him with my knife, slowly, starting with his manhood. Then his brothers came for his blood, and we killed them. Then their cousins came, and *their* cousins. We had better rifles, from the *farangi,* but this grew tiresome, and the ammunition cost much. So we left our mountains, and came here. Do you wish to start such a thing?"

She'd slipped into the sing-song cadence he remembered from the Bengali delta to the Pamirs, English as a second language. The

New York accent had vanished, leaving him with more questions than answers. He gulped and backed away.

That might be *another* reason why the police *put up with* her. None of her bosses dared to chew her out or fire her.

She let him live. She let him go. He picked up his cane and backed all the way to the end of the alley, turned, and hiked up the street with a crawling sensation between his shoulder blades, wondering if she'd shoot. All the way, Kipling's words kept chasing their tails through his head:

When you're wounded and left on Afghanistan's plains,
And the women come out to cut up what remains,
Jest roll to your rifle and blow out your brains
An' go to your Gawd like a soldier.

He wondered where Kipling had met her grandmother. Or however many generations back it had been—when he'd lived in that country, both men and women bred young and died young, even for humans. He didn't think it had changed much.

He wouldn't have minded if Legion had materialized out of thin air just then. He had some questions for the damned demon, and felt up to arguing with it. But that Kipling reference kept nagging at him.

Part of being old was remembering things that had long gone out of fashion. Kipling was one of them. People didn't read him much any more, particularly his poetry, didn't memorize it. Nationalistic racist doggerel, they said, "white man's burden" and all that. But it was catchy and stuck in his brain. The tale she'd spun sounded like one of Kipling's, or part of it—a century, century and a half, past his time. Albert would have thought even those hills had moved a bit beyond it. But she'd told the tale as *hers,* not her grandmother's or a memory of her tribe. *Her* knife, carving pieces from that Badakhi as he screamed and writhed and turned the dusty stones black with his blood.

Most parts of this world moved at the same pace, existed in the same time. Some didn't. Some were even farther away from "today" than that. Places where human slavery lived on, just for example, an example a lot of people wouldn't believe.

He'd seen it. He'd had people want to make *him* a slave. Like Legion, they had wanted to own the way he could talk to iron.

He looked behind him, just in case she was following, gun or knife in hand. Bad memories did things like that to him. Not that he'd see her. She was just another demon chasing him, able to walk through locked doors or find him across gaps of space and time.

Demons. Connections. He remembered the feather, a warning that might have come from Mother or might not have. He remembered the things that Legion knew about him, how the demon seemed to be playing around the edge of some kind of demon law in maneuvering him to the fire site and that wrought iron star. Legion hadn't *told* him to fix the star, just made sure he would be where he could feel it. Wheels within wheels within wheels, the surface didn't tell you much about what hid beneath the water. He *had* to be tangled up with more than one demon here, even if Legion was the one persecuting el Hajj as well as him.

Legion knew a name for him that he hadn't used in centuries. The damned demon or another of its kind might know Mother's code, as well. He couldn't trust anything. "What is Truth?" asked Pilate, and washed his hands.

He shook his head at all the religious references, but this whole story boiled down to gods and demons, both the real ones and the ones men made for themselves. He lived with enough demons of his own making. He didn't need outsiders screwing with his life.

He made it home with thoughts still chasing each other through his head. His hip ached with so much walking—orthopedic shoes didn't take away all the stress from his unequal legs.

And his body was still paying for the forging, tired and hungry and headachy with a dull throbbing from toes all the way out to fingertips. Straight smithing didn't cause it—he had to sink into the heart of forging, "become one with the iron" so that he was worked as much as working, before accumulating such a debt of pain. Zen blacksmithing, the arrow loosing itself into the heart of the target.

The el Hajj woman had said she knew people who would hand over thousands of dollars for his cane. He didn't think that was enough.

He collected the day's mail, more junk, no brown envelopes, and clicked his way through all the locks and reset them behind him. Plus the bolts and bars, of course, even though he had more than a hint they wouldn't stop el Hajj or other demons. Or Mother, of course, because she knew the secret ways.

Then up to his apartment, hip and muscles complaining about the steep climb of old stairways, dusty air more of a contrast than usual with the fresh spring breeze outside. He needed to open some windows, even on the second and third floors. He tended to treat his building like a cave.

Into his kitchen, food at the front of his brain, and he found a new pheasant feather on the table. A hen pheasant, of course. Next to it lay a note:

Don't worry about Solomon's Seal.

Balkis

Which was a name Mother sometimes used, as a joke and also as a code. No, she did *not* claim to have been the Queen of Sheba. That would have been extreme hubris even for her. She just wanted people to treat her as if she was.

Well, he thought she was beautiful enough to fit the legends. But then, he knew he was biased.

Solomon's Seal? Capitalized? Yeah, that iron felt as old as Solomon. The legends he knew, though, said Solomon's Seal was a ring. A signet ring, the kind you used to seal letters and royal decrees, maybe with magic bound in it. Twist the ring on his finger, a djinn appeared to do the great king's bidding.

English was a slippery language—seals could be many things. He didn't think the star ate fish, for one . . .

But the star had told him it sealed the way. Another meaning of the word, something that closes, like the seal on a jar or can. Closing out nasty germs from food, closing out those hungry spots of light.

Mother liked to be vague, confuse people with double-meaning words. When she didn't want to lie outright. Sort of like a demon, that way.

The star—the Seal—*called* to him, wanted him to fix it. And Legion had led . . . forced . . . him to find it . . .

Maybe Solomon had made more than one Seal.

He stared at the feather. He still had no way of knowing if it or the message really came from her. He walked around the table, not touching it, and it looked pretty much like a pheasant feather from all sides. He'd sort of hoped it would go away or turn into an asp or something.

Then he walked through the apartment, checking the closets and the little tell-tales he left on various secret ways and false walls. All undisturbed—a clump of lint here, a hair across a crack there, dust that would show the sweep of a door. The place was untouched, with no evidence of entry except the presence of the feather—empty. Shame, that, a little heart-to-heart talk wouldn't have hurt. At least the demon's gold still sat in his hideaway behind the plumbing. He wasn't naïve enough to think she wouldn't have found it if she looked. Mother was always death on secrets—other people's secrets, that is, she kept her own locked tight.

He didn't know whether she'd cared to look. Or if the feather came from someone—some*thing*—else, that didn't know every little twist and quirk about her.

A bit of a love-hate relationship, the way he felt about Mother, and he knew it. Dominant personality, somewhat like those gods he despised, she'd make you pay if you crossed her even in small things. Could be petty and vindictive, with a long memory for real or imagined slights. Living under the same roof didn't appeal to him much. He felt some level of relief along with the frustration when he didn't find her anywhere.

He grabbed a beer and thawed a chunk of venison chili for lunch, not enough energy left for cooking or even building a decent sandwich. Plus, the rye bread had gone stale with his lost days, and he didn't have the energy or patience for baking fresh.

He always kept some good food frozen—the mere thought of canned pasta made him shudder, but sometimes he needed fast and easy calories. Likewise with the music, some Tallis a-cappella choral motets he knew he could trust to soothe his aching brow. He tended to say a lot of rude things about religion here and there, but he couldn't deny that faith had inspired a lot of lovely music. Other great arts, too, but music was his peculiar vice.

Then he collapsed into bed, the past few days claiming their toll. At least this time he had enough energy to undress first.

A sense-memory nagged at him in the gray drift between waking and sleeping. Sandalwood. When he held the Seal, he'd smelled sandalwood, stronger, as if he sensed it through his fingertips rather than his nose. Was the salamander trapped in that iron, somehow? Like so much else in this confusion, it made no sense . . .

He woke in darkness, his head ringing from the wall he felt against his left ear. He seemed to be sitting on the floor, in a corner. He felt hot blood trickle down his cheek. Light blazed in his eyes—the same bluish dazzle he remembered from that night in the burned-out synagogue. He blinked and shook sleep and pain out of his head, shielded his eyes with one hand, caught the glint of steel held a couple of feet away from the glow.

Knife. It waved back at him.

"Little man, what did you do with that star?"

VI

He shook his head again, groggy, trying to clear it. He studied the blade gleaming in the side-splash of that light, all he could really see, all *she* meant for him to see. Yes, he knew who held the knife, the light. That damned Afghan harpy. Again.

But he concentrated on the blade, squinting. Slight double curve to a fine stabbing point. Double-edged blade, to slash as well. Strong central rib. He couldn't see guard or hilt, in the black behind the dazzle . . .

He *was* a bladesmith.

"I would have thought that style of *khanjar* came from well south and west of your people."

"I took it from a Persian who annoyed me."

That made him snort, even facing the knife. He wasn't awake enough to be scared yet. If she'd meant to kill him, he would have woken up in hell. Or wherever. Besides, a demon wouldn't let her. She'd said so.

"This Persian didn't object?"

"He could not object, being dead."

Pretty much what he'd expected.

By that time, he had a start of some wits about him. "I didn't do anything with that star. You claim to be a seer. You claim to be able to find things. Can you see that forging anywhere around here?"

He raised his hand to the side of his head, chancing her nerves. After all, a knife wasn't as twitchy a weapon as a gun. He'd stared at the wrong end of both more than once. He'd survived. A knife was more dangerous at close range, but it wouldn't go off by mistake. If she cut his throat, she'd mean to do it.

His fingers met slippery hair. Yes, blood. Skin tender, throbbing already. Not serious, scrape on his scalp about an inch long, no apparent break or even crack to the bone underneath. Sometimes a thick skull paid off.

Not as bad as what his cane had done to her, and that hadn't slowed her down. He held those wet red fingers out into the light.

"Does this make us even? Blood for blood?"

"In your dreams."

There it was again, the idiomatic speech, just like that "Melissa" thing, the signs of someone who had lived in this society all her life. Contrast that with the dead "Persian" who'd donated her knife—*nobody* called them Persians anymore. *Persian* meant a long-furred and somewhat ugly breed of cat, not a nationality or race.

Chills shot through him as he woke up enough to be scared and shake his brain into action. The woman liked to torture people. With a knife. She'd said so. That wasn't the worst of it.

"The star. What about the *star?*"

"Gone. I took our tame wizard out to the scene and the star was gone. You and I and Allah in His infinite mercy were the only ones who knew about it. So I thought we should have a little talk with Allah, you and I."

That star had touched him somehow, tied itself and its hopes to him. His chest turned hollow and he started to sweat with fear. He had to concentrate on breathing.

"You're *positive* it's gone?"

"Boards tossed to one side, empty print in the ash. The wizard said he could feel where it had been. He also gave me a strong sense that he was frightened, once I told him what you'd found, what you'd said. Wouldn't talk, couldn't make him. *You'll* talk, one way or another." She waved her knife in front of the light, adding emphasis.

The light irritated him—just as she'd intended. The whole damned *game* irritated him, Afghan Harpy and Mother and Legion's tricks and all. Few people could manage to live as long as he had without developing a little control over their tongues, but midnight interrogations were *designed* to strip all that away.

"Screw you, your flashlight, and the goddamned camel you both rode in on. You don't need a knife to make me talk. I don't have your Allah-damned Solomon's Seal, don't know where it is, and haven't been anywhere near that synagogue since you chased me off. No, we're *not* the only ones who knew about it, you and me and Allah. I got back here and found a note about the star on my kitchen table. It's still there, and I never touched it. If you can sense people from objects they've handled, you might be able to follow that."

"Bullshit."

More Western phrasing—from his memory of her ancestral homeland, he would have expected some long and flowery invective that added up to the same thing. Probably including detailed references to his ancestors unto the tenth generation and their kinship with pariah dogs and the undoubted fact that none of the women had kept their noses. And she hadn't reacted to his blasphemy, one way or the other . . .

"You don't believe me, I'll show you. Let me get up." He paused, considering her culture and general attitude. "Now I'd like to get dressed, if you don't mind. I'm feeling a little naked here."

The flashlight gestured up, which he took as permission. He stood and turned toward the chair where he'd dumped shirt, pants, and underwear before collapsing into bed. He heard a swish of movement and froze as a needle-sharp point pricked the skin over his right kidney. The rough surface of the cast on her left wrist sandpapered his throat and chin, pressing just enough to suggest he should move with care if he wanted to keep an uncrushed trachea.

Breath touched his ear, and a whisper. "Skip the clothes. I'm not in any hurry to find out what you hid under your shirt. I've seen naked men before. Some of them even uglier than you."

Okay, maybe she actually *was* a seer. Just like with the cane by the stairs, his little habit of keeping weapons scattered around his home included a few close by his bed. Not a knife or gun—a can of pepper spray that wouldn't be too particular about exactly *where* she hid behind that light.

He felt less touchy about clothes than most people, especially when it came to keeping all his internal organs where God or evolution put them. And he did *not* offer any quotes from the Prophet about modesty and the proper demeanor of women. He was capable of learning, under sufficient duress.

"The note's on my kitchen table, like I said."

She let him turn, keeping the knifepoint just touching his skin. No sudden moves, they walked like slow-dancers through the darkness to his kitchen. Still nothing sudden, nothing to startle that knife hand, he reached across to the wall and switched on a light. Blinding brightness. She spun him away with a kick to the back of his knee that stole his balance. He fell, smacking nose and cheek against the refrigerator. He leaned there blinking, stupid, mixing dazzle and dizziness. Feeling warmth oozing down his upper lip. More blood? He licked it. Salty.

He groped at the counter, bracing himself. His hand bumped something chilly and hard, cylindrical: a can, a full can of sour cherries. He'd thought to make some strudel in the morning, in memory of the bakery window that had betrayed him into a photograph. Maybe make it after he'd slept the clock around again, to have the energy and patience.

His fingers closed on the can and he spun and threw, aiming for the sound of her breath, at the shadow of her head forming in his dazzled eyes. Vertigo took him and he sagged back against the cold door of his refrigerator, blinking. He heard a dull thud, the sound of can against flesh and bone rather than a wall or the floor.

When he could focus again, she was on the far side of the kitchen table, staggering, her gun replacing the knife in her right hand. The hand jerked, the gun jerked, and he saw the orange flash of half-burned gunpowder at the muzzle, *felt* the boom of a large-bore pistol in a small room, saw the dull gray lead and shiny copper jacket of a bullet. His brain traced a straight line from the bore to his chest and knew he was about to die. But she'd said the demon said she couldn't kill him . . . yet.

Somehow the bullet took its damned time as the muzzle jerked up and settled back on target and jerked again with a second shot. A second bullet. Slow in the air. Hanging in the air, a few inches behind the first. Impossible.

A shadow formed and became solid black between him and the bullets. A black hand plucked the first bullet from the air, squeezed it until the molten gleaming lead core popped from its red copper jacket, and then did the same with the second slug, gathering the pieces together, molten lead in one black palm, molten copper in the other. One hand tossed the lead into a mouth that formed as the shadow grew human shape, swallowing. Albert could see the throat muscles pulsing. The moves repeated with the other, the copper.

"You may not harm Simon Lahti. We commanded this."

Another damned demon. Or the same one.

The black fingers plucked glittering brass from mid-air, the ejected cartridge cases also defying physics and refusing to submit to gravity. The brass melted and followed the lead and copper into the demon's mouth.

Albert's eyes adapted and he could see again. Her knife had landed on the floor in the scuffle. He inched toward it, reached for it. Settle this vendetta once and for all . . .

The knife skittered away and levitated, settling on his table at the far end from the feather and the note from Mother. The far end from Albert.

"*You* may not harm *Noshaq*. We command this."

Damned demons. "You told me you could not guard me or help me."

"We may enforce our commands."

Thus proving that the Afghan bitch's demon was the same as his. Legion.

Apparently Legion could *not* command whoever was abusing the salamander, whoever damaged and then stole King Solomon's Seal. Demon laws, or another demon got there first?

The demon reached out toward the woman, the woman in dark coveralls *without* patches or a badge this time, Albert could finally see details, and plucked the pistol from her hand. "Defiance must cost. We do not wish to reduce your value by damaging you."

The pistol disappeared into the demon's mouth, somehow it fit even though it seemed too large, and again Albert could see it lumpy and collapsing in the "throat" of that black shape. The demon belched after swallowing, muffled popping sounds echoed off the plaster as the remaining cartridges exploded in whatever passed for a demon stomach, and a final belch or fart left the smell of brimstone in the room as the demon faded into nothing.

"You bastard, that was a custom Gold Cup! Cost me two weeks pay!" She lifted her hand and touched the side of her head, exploring a patch of short hair where Albert had last seen a bandage and shaved scalp. Either his time-sense was totally gone to hell, a bad metaphor in this case, or she healed damned fast. Her fingers came away stained with fresh blood.

The can. He'd always been good at throwing things. If he'd hit the same spot on her skull, she ought to be dead or at least out cold.

She focused on him. "You owe me a new weapon, little man.

That's worse than blood." Another pistol appeared in her hand, smaller but looking no less deadly, pointed at him.

He shook his head. "You want to lose that one, too?"

Dark eyes blinked. Then she glanced down at her hand as if she was surprised. "Reflex. Always carry a backup." The pistol vanished into her coveralls.

Sirens echoed from the street below, several different directions, converging. He sorted memories and cities and decades in his head. Police cars—this city used different sounds for police and fire and ambulance. When he looked a question at her, she had a handheld police radio next to her ear and lifted her free hand in a "shut up" gesture. But she didn't answer whatever she heard. The radio vanished. He'd never run into anyone who moved that fast, faster than he could see, even staring straight at her and not blinking.

Was she human? *Whatever* she was, she cocked her head to one side and listened. "Anyone live upstairs, either side of this dump?"

"No. North side, for two buildings over, nothing but pigeons above some second-floor offices. South side doesn't even reach this high, one floor lower. The upper floors have been empty for ten or twenty years. Building codes."

She nodded. "Report of gunshots. They won't be able to locate a source. And they won't search too hard in this neighborhood. Afraid they might find the shooter still holding the gun . . . "

That last sentence came with a sneer—didn't look like she thought too much of her fellow officers: not up to Afghan hilltribe standards. Then her eyes narrowed into a glare. "You don't want to talk to them."

No, he didn't. For any number of reasons, most of them nothing to do with her. Hell, he didn't want to talk to *her*. But she wasn't giving him any choice.

"Even if you keep your mouth shut, you still owe me a weapon. And blood."

He sagged back against the cold enamel of his refrigerator, adrenaline gone and with it his muscles. "A demon eats your gun and you blame *me*? You break into my home in the middle of the night, slap me out of bed, threaten me, try to kill me, and it's all *my* fault? Shove it up your ass." He pushed himself upright. "I'm getting dressed. You can leave by whatever way you got in."

He paused, propped up by one hand against the frame of his bedroom door. "I don't make guns. I've never seen or touched a gun that had even a piece of a soul. They're just machines."

She was still there when he came out of his bathroom, dressed, hair damp from a quick swipe from a cold washcloth. His scalp had quit bleeding. He felt a little steadier on his feet, a little clearer in his brain. But she was still there, the too-solid remnant of a bad dream.

She had rummaged through his refrigerator while his back was turned, had a full pan of sausage on the stove and some cinnamon-raisin bread toasting. Damned familiar of her. Also, rather trusting on the ingredients of that lamb sausage, if she made any pretense of devout submission to the will of Allah and the words of the Prophet . . .

"I don't think that lamb is *halal*. Farmer's market, the butcher didn't make any claims, I just buy for the flavor . . . "

"*Halal, haram*—Allah is more compassionate and merciful than the beards want us to believe."

The knife lay on the table next to her flashlight, he didn't recall where that had ended up in the scuffle, and she was staring at the feather and the note. "Who the hell has the nerve to call herself Balkis?"

Short and to the point. "That might be Mother. She's as casual about names as I am."

She gave him a long stare, squinting. "You have a *mother*?"

"Most people do."

She stared at him some more.

"What's with the feather?"

"Family code. Maybe. I haven't touched that, either."

She stepped back from the stove and hovered her left hand over the note and then the feather, not touching—he guessed that a broken wrist and cast didn't dull whatever sense she used.

"Look, can I get past you to the refrigerator and put some ice on my nose? Stuff some tissue in my nostril? I hate cleaning up blood."

A lifted eyebrow. "I'd bet the Prophet's best mare that you'll stop bleeding in another minute or two. Like that scalp wound."

So she'd noticed, or expected, that. She knew some things about him, about his family, that she shouldn't have known. They could be killed, but it wasn't easy. They all healed fast. They didn't get infections. Something like her broken wrist would slow him down for a week, maybe two. Mother had told him that his broken leg had been closer to amputation, a loaded beer wagon rolling right over it with an iron-shod wheel.

He had to take her word for it. Which, with Mother, complicated matters.

He studied the blade without touching it. Gentle double-curve of watered steel, keen and with some wear of use and sharpening—"Persian," yes, and no flat-faced long-furred kitty-cat about it. Isfahan steel with the faint yellow tint peculiar to the composition of iron and alloys of that province. The smith had worked it to display the *Kirk Narduban* pattern, the ladder that the faithful ascend to heaven. Two hundred years old, at least, probably more, a museum piece of Islamic craft. Good steel, good forging, work *he* could have been proud of.

The design, less so. Whether smith or after-finish, someone had narrowed the tang to fit the fancy curved pistol-grip of a Persian *khanjar*, paired flats of lapis and amber and then lapis again to the heel, bound with thick silver spacers between the sections of stone and a small silver guard at the blade, all the metal engraved with what looked like calligraphy, well worn. Much more wear on the grip and guard than on the blade, speaking of decades spent inside its sheath. Whoever had carried it hadn't needed to use it much.

Something dark and curled and pointy, perhaps a tiny scorpion, sat trapped in the amber on the side he could see. Pretty knife, conspicuous wealth, but the abrupt shoulder cut between blade and tang would concentrate stress, and that stone grip would turn greasy with the first hint of sweat or blood . . .

"A fancy-blade," he said, with some contempt. "I hope you never trust your life to it." He looked up. She seemed to have been studying him as he studied the blade.

"That's a strange thing to tell an enemy."

"I never meant to call you my enemy. You scared the shit out of me the other night. What I did was reflex, like you with your second pistol. Nothing more."

"You should not have crossed the crime-scene tape." Then she cocked her head to one side and her eyes narrowed, her face turning cold and harsh again, like her mountains. "Little man, I've thought of a way for you to wash out the blood between us. Forge me a blade to kill a god. Then we're even, for both the blood and that Colt."

The flat tone told him she meant it. All of it. He thought she meant Legion, and agreed with the intent. But he remembered and the ache of old broken bones woke in his wrists and hands.

"You want me to set up my forge between the salt water and the sea sand, while I'm at it?" He didn't expect her to catch the reference, but "Scarborough Fair" had ruled even *his* radio for a brief while . . .

"Gods aren't immortal. Although some of the bastards would like to think they are."

So she *did* understand his meaning about impossible tasks. "I don't think that's a good idea. I forged a blade like that, once. Someone offered me a pile of gold. I needed it. The blade worked." Then came the unpleasant part. "He'd seduced her and left her, so she slit his throat and cut his body into seven pieces and scattered them on the Lake of the Dead for her fish to feast on . . ."

"The blade worked. But the god didn't stay dead. And they hold grudges."

VII

She froze and stared at him across the kitchen table, one eyebrow lifted. But she didn't ask the obvious questions. He replayed what he'd just said, in his memory.

"No. I don't know where that came from. I don't remember his name, I don't remember her name, I don't remember where or when or what tribe's Lake of the Dead that was, whose gods they were. Haven't thought of that for years. Centuries. My brain is falling apart."

He shook himself. "Forget I said that."

She was still staring at him. "Falling apart, or falling together? I've remembered things, the last few days . . . "

And then she added, "I still want that blade."

He shook his head, not saying either yea or nay. The air stayed chilly. Nothing to do with physical temperature—the kitchen felt warm enough with toaster and stove going, the mingling reinforcing aromas of sausage grease and cinnamon toast weaving their perfume and stirring his taste buds in anticipation—but the psychic temperature Legion had left behind . . . nerves jangling, tension and distrust in full force. Albert skirted her personal-space to reach and turn on the radio for its distraction. It offered him Mozart. Flute. Probably Jean-Pierre Rampal playing, by the distinctive tone of the instrument.

He recognized it by the first few bars in the middle of a movement, one of the strange things his memory did. He could remember some things for centuries. Others slipped into fog within a month—like that demon-blade and who had wanted it. Damned annoying.

Mozart was good. Soothing, bright, no thunderstorm drama of Brahms or Beethoven or praise to whatever-Name-of-God-you-chose Wagner there to crank the friction higher. He'd never liked Wagner. Disliked the story lines as much as the music. If Ms. Detective Melissa el Hajj or Noshaq or whatever the hell her name was didn't like Mozart with breakfast, she could walk her Afghan émigré ass out of his life forever any time she wanted.

They ate. He savored the lamb and sage with a touch of coriander, the toast thick with butter. Various thoughts crossed his mind, like how he'd intended to add the sausage to dried beans and onions and tomatoes and basil, long-baked to mingle and take on each other's savor. Stretch the costly meat into dinners for three days or four, rather than squander the whole of it on a single breakfast. But he kept those words behind his teeth. She didn't seem to feel like talking, either.

Lamb sausage and the way she'd seared it brown and then started to move the skillet to the edge of the "fire" to cut back the heat set off memories. Habits die hard. She hadn't learned to cook on a stove . . .

"Oh ye who believe! Eat of the good things that We have provided you with, and give thanks to Allah if Him it is that you serve."

She stared at him, gaze like a knife pinning him to the wall behind. "Sura II, verse 172. Are you of the *umma* or the *ulema?*"

The Islamic faithful or the clergy. Why the hell did those words slip from my memory into the open air? Muslims behave differently towards believers and unbelievers. That difference can be very good or very very bad, either way. I don't even know if she is Sunni or Shia.

Tell the truth. It's simpler. "No. Neither. I lived with a Muslim family for some years. The head of the family would recite that before we ate."

"In *English?*"

"He had served with the English army. He would say the words in Arabic and then translate as a courtesy to a guest."

"Some scholars say that the Holy Qur'an must not be translated."

Again giving no hint of her own beliefs, no mention of imam *or* ayatollah *or Sufi sage . . .*

He quoted her own words back at her: "Allah is more beneficent and merciful than the beards want us to believe."

Let's not discuss how long ago Ali Akhbar Khan served with the British. The gaunt silver-bearded patriarch had carried a Snider rifle, while the Kipling Tommy privates in the next column carried Martinis. Nineteenth-century military metal.

A hint of a smile touched the corner of her mouth. At least she had *some* sense of humor . . .

Then she shoved her empty plate toward him. "I cooked. You clean."

Not something he'd ever expect to hear from a Muslim woman. Yet, she wore a veil of a sort, never showing her true face to him. Or maybe one of those sets of nested Russian dolls, each one a *different* face, smile or fierce scowl. Or sometimes, a derisive grimace with tongue sticking out.

If she wished to shame him by handing him women's work to do, she failed. He'd *prefer* to wash up, particularly that cast-iron skillet with its baked-on "seasoning" from a century or two of use. She'd probably feel the need to scour it with steel wool and ruin the finish.

Or look around for some sand, scouring agent of choice in her water-poor hills. He'd eaten enough sand in those years, it had been coming out his pores.

He started to gather dishes in the sink, then turned to her, with a thought. She was headed for the bathroom, *his* bathroom, without asking. Just move right in, take over. Like Mother—the only boundaries that mattered were *hers*.

Turn about is fair play, sauce for the goose is sauce for the gander. Gender. Whatever. "You asked if I was *umma* or *ulema*. Are you?"

She paused in mid-stride. "I ask questions. I don't answer them." Then, over her shoulder, "Telling you will make life easier for *me*. The answer is the same as yours. No. Neither."

Hence her thirst for a cold beer at the end of a long day's work in the ash-stink of a burned-out hulk.

"Well, you *can* identify two sentences out of thin air by chapter and verse. In translation."

He saw the back of a shrug. "Scripture—Muslim or Christian or Jew, it's useful to throw their own holy words back at them. Even Shaitan can quote scripture for his own purposes. Which *isn't* scripture. I haven't found a holy man yet who obeys every single word. Or a holy woman, either."

Then she vanished behind the bathroom door.

He remembered scripture easily, too. One of the few things he *could* remember with precision, one century to the next. Funny thing, that, with him not believing it. It had to be those three—Jewish, Christian, Muslim. He couldn't remember Hindu or Buddhist or Sikh writings worth a damn.

Belief could be useful, could have kept Legion the hell out of his apartment, if Albert had faith. Crosses, the mezuzim of the Jews, graceful flowing Arabic calligraphy from the Qur'an—they guarded home and hearth for believers. Symbols and belief hold power, great power, even over the hidden world. Every opening into Albert's building showed crosses to the outside, even the plumbing vents through the roof, remembrances of previous owners. They hadn't had much effect on Legion. Just as those six-pointed stars, Solomon's own Seal, hadn't kept a salamander out of that abandoned synagogue.

The salamander had been able to enter the synagogue because believers had abandoned it. The faith had left, decades ago. Legion had gotten into Albert's apartment because Albert wasn't a believer.

Oh, yeah, he *knew* gods and demons and angels haunted the world. That wasn't faith, that was personal witness. What he didn't do was worship them. He'd consign them all to their own particular hells if he could. The best of them acted like spoiled brats if they didn't get every whim satisfied, right down to the brand of toilet paper you used and whether you washed your right hand first or your left, and the worst turned nastier than Caligula with a hangover and bad hemorrhoids.

That wasn't even considering the way humans had warped religion to serve their priests and kings and tribal elders. After a few centuries of perspective, he'd started noticing things like that.

So crosses and the like didn't do him any good. He'd take the trade and call it even.

Those thoughts saw the dishes stacked in the drainer and his skillet back drying over the stove's pilot light. He was swabbing the counter and kitchen table with a rag when she came out. Hair damp, bleeding from her scalp wound stopped. He touched his own head, tested his nose. Same thing. No blood. Maybe they were cousins, improbable though that seemed.

That name Legion had used for her, Noshaq or however you spelled it, that was a mountain in the wilds of Afghanistan if he remembered right. He'd seen it once, far on the horizon, menacing. A *serious* mountain, in serious wilds, one of those kill-you-as-soon-as-look-at-you high places ruled by a bitch storm goddess, the weather and the rocks and the ice as much as the people.

Whereas he was some kind of northern European, as best as he could tell. Simon Lahti, the one name out of hundreds that Legion had chosen to use . . .

"Simon." Yeah, Mother used to call me Simon among other things, pretending we were Christians, but the last name . . . I have no idea what my father's name might have been. I never knew him, don't know if she had more than a few minutes' acquaintance with the man or if I shared his genes with my brothers and my sister.

The "Lahti" part, that just means I was born in a dark smoky room on some back alley of that town of the Troll-King's Finnish realm. Or so Mother told me—I'm not in any position to say. I can't tell you which king or even the dynasty. We weren't Saami. We didn't care. We left there when I was so young the memories merged into dreams. Not true Gypsies, outsiders even to them.

"You. Wake up!"

He shook himself out of those thoughts. She'd vanished her pretty-pretty knife somewhere in her coveralls and was staring at the note and pheasant feather, still lying on his table. Something about her face, her eyes and the squint-wrinkles around them, made the hair on his arms prickle—she seemed to be focused about ten miles beyond the table-top, somewhere deep in the earth below.

"Arm yourself. We're going pheasant-hunting."

"We?"

"We. Legion won't let me kill you, and I'm not going to chance you talking to your so-called mother. I want to know where you are. Safer."

So-called? Not many places where people would raise doubts about your mother. Father maybe, but motherhood is usually not an item of dispute.

Not that he really cared. Legion wouldn't let *him* kill *her*, either, and people usually thought killing was the proper response to that kind of slur. As if knowing his father or his mother changed who *he* was.

People were strange. Albert shrugged. *Arm yourself? That implies some interesting things about her "pheasant hunt."*

Arm yourself. He thought about this and that and the other thing. His cane, of course. Nothing else that people could see—walking out the door into maybe a swarm of cops? He checked the street-side windows, saw two police cars angled into the curb with flashing lights, saw one officer scanning rooftops and sidewalks and windows, talking to a microphone on a long coiled cord reaching back inside the cruiser he leaned against. Leaning rather casually, not crouching to use the car for cover.

That wasn't the body-language of fear and a sniper-hunt, there. Looked like he'd already decided they'd been called out for firecrackers or an engine backfire.

Ms. Detective el Hajj should be able to talk him past that, being a fellow cop and all—as long as he wasn't carrying a rocket launcher over one shoulder or some other obvious threat.

Which eliminated the katana or any other kind of long blade. Well, he wasn't much of a swordsman, anyway. Being short suited him better for close-in fighting. Cut 'em off at the knees, then you can reach the throat.

Short blades he had in plenty. Weapon only, or something shaped for utility use, prying and cutting and splitting as well as stab and slash? He didn't know where they were going, what they would face . . .

The front room closet gave him a choice of cloth-wrapped bundles. One felt comfortable in his hand, balanced, well remembered, even while still hidden. He'd custom-forged many of his blades for others—they'd never felt *right* to him, even though his hammer and anvil knew they were right for the man or woman who would carry and swing that metal.

This one, though, he'd felt growing to his own hand as he formed the glowing steel. He'd started in to make a blade for sale to some stranger, needed the money. Ended up with something that carried more than the usual splinter of his own soul bound within its working.

And it wanted to come along on this hunt.

He unwrapped it while walking back to the kitchen, then laid the sheathed knife and the linen wrapper on the counter and turned away to dig a padded jacket out of the closet. A little warm for the season, but no need to advertise his weapon.

A quiet gasp behind him made him turn back. She was staring at the knife like a mongoose waiting for the perfect moment to pounce on a cobra. He studied the knife like it was a new thing, trying to see what had caused her reaction.

He'd formed the hilt as a traditional *aikuchi tsuka ito*, including the Japanese-style *kumihimo* raw-silk braid wrap, patterned black and red, that would give him a firm grip even soaked with sweat or blood. Not like that stone on *her* knife. Minimal dark bronze guard and pommel: simple, smooth and flush with the sheath, just a single rune cast into the guard on each side of the blade—*Þurisaz* for "Thor" on one side, giant-killer, god of the hammer even if not known as a smith; *Tiwaz* for "Tyr" on the other, god of single combat, victory, and heroic glory. Bits of Nordic, consciously *ironic* whimsy when he was carving the lost-wax forms for casting.

Her hand reached toward the grip and then pulled back, once, twice, doing a shy dance as if outside her control.

"May I?"

First time she'd *asked* for anything. He nodded, reluctant. Knives were personal, weapons were personal, if they had any value at all. Touching his knife was moving inside his personal space, too much like touching *him*.

She grasped the hilt and the matching *kumihimo* of the black-lacquered wooden sheath. Drew the blade—seven inches, eight inches, he'd never measured it, it was what it was, what it had asked to be, fitted to *his* size. Straight, edged partway down the back, heavier and broader than his sword-cane blade, he could clamp the tip in his vise and support his whole weight on the hilt, no spring to it. Closer to *yoroi tōshi*—"armor-piercer"—than the slim blade of a traditional *aikuchi*. The Japanese language used great precision in naming blades and other parts of weapons. Told you things about a culture and its history.

Funny thing, after all his years in a village a day's walk outside of Edo—the words he remembered mostly tied to weapons and steel. Little else had stayed with him. Told you things about *his* culture and history . . .

She stared at the steel as if hypnotized, lost in the matte gray acid-etched surface—the "storm-wave" pattern of his forged laminations. Her left forefinger reached out to test the edge, just her nail.

"Don't—"

Blood beaded on her fingertip, below the split nail. She kept her nails short, just like her hair—made sense if she spent her days poking around the insides of arson crime-scenes. Now she stared at the blood.

"I didn't even *touch* it!"

She looked up, met his stare. "*This* would buy your blood away from me."

He shook his head. "It doesn't fit you. You need a longer knife. A larger grip. A guard for meeting blade with blade. A style for someone who seeks danger, not the last defense of a hermit."

No, he didn't quite know where he'd come up with that horoscope in steel.

She weighed the knife in her hand, fluid grace shifting through different combat grips and tossing it from right hand to left and back, then nodded. Sheathed it and set it back on the counter, her hand lingering as if reluctant.

"We come back to my first question the other night. What *are* you? That blade didn't come from any human forge."

He shrugged, slipped his arms into his jacket, and settled the sheathed knife into a pocket sewn below the collar and angled across his back between his shoulder blades. No guard, the knife would lie flat and concealed by the padding to either side, pommel just out of sight, while the pocket held snug against the *kumihimo* braid on the sheath so he could draw his weapon with one hand. He tested it. Smooth. Attention to detail had saved his ass more times than he could count.

"I am what I am. Nobody has ever put a name to us, not even Mother." He glanced at her hand. "Your finger okay?"

She held it up. No blood. "Enough talk. Legion seems to think we're working with a deadline. Get your ass down those stairs. You first." She picked up the pheasant feather and the note. "Since Allah in His beneficence has given me a star to follow . . . "

"Speaking of stars, why aren't you tracking that Seal from the ashes?" Ali Akhbar Khan spoke again from his memory, on the roof of his mud fort and enjoying the spectacular night sky of his hills, "And He it is Who has made the stars for you that you might follow the right way thereby in the darkness of the land and the sea . . . "

She cocked her head to one side and studied him. "Because that manifestation of Allah's infinite mercy led nowhere. Two steps and gone. That's why I came here. You're the only person I've ever had trouble following. *Quod erat demonstrandum.*"

"You found me . . . "

"I was following my own blood on your cane."

He headed down the stairs, avoiding his little ineffective traps, picking up his cane on his way.

Her voice followed him. "You really should replace some of these steps. A person could get hurt."

"That's the general idea."

VIII

"Turn left down the next alley."

She'd led them back into that beyond-bad section of town, the bombed-out-Berlin landscape near the synagogue. Or what was left of the synagogue. *"Led" isn't accurate, either,* he thought. *It's "No way in hell I'm gonna let you behind my back. Not with* those *blades. You take point."*

Apparently she didn't trust Legion as a mediator. That was okay. Neither did he.

He heard rats in the trash, snowdrifts of trash that oozed out from dingy graffiti-splashed windowless brick canyon walls to nearly block the alley, too narrow for a car, trash that had been picked over with even the dubious-value rusty metal sorted out to sell by the pound to junk dealers to buy junk. The kind you injected or smoked or sucked up your nose. How could you find so damn much trash once you pulled out any scrap metal or burnable wood or even cardboard sheets large enough to block a draft? Plastic jugs. Broken glass. Discarded clothing too far gone even for the homeless. Tattered remnants of plastic sheeting, rattling in the wind. Cotton-stuffed mattresses spilling their piss-reeking guts onto the cracked asphalt and brick pavement. Dogshit. Damned if he knew what the dogs found to eat back here. Maybe the rats.

Some of those rustlings probably *weren't* rats. People sheltered in trash igloos braced against the crumbling bricks. He felt their wondering, paranoid goggle-eyed straggle-haired stare from the shadows, what those two clean strangers were doing in this filthy down-and-out world. Stranger means danger . . .

He wondered what they thought he could take from them, what they thought they could take from him, and resisted the impulse to reach back and touch his knife-hilt to prove he still had it.

Never tell the world where you hide your weapons.

She kept about fifteen, twenty feet behind him, calling out directions now and then, far enough back so one grenade wouldn't get both of them. *Where did that image come from? Was I in some army somewhere?* But he couldn't shake the feeling of being on patrol in hostile jungles, her "point-man" reference, with her as backup rather than enemy. She had at least one gun still, and that silly gaudy Isfahan dagger. Plus whatever else she hid in her coveralls.

From what he'd learned of her so far, that probably included a brigade of heavy dragoons held in reserve. *Another army reference. Damned memory. Was I drafted at bayonet-point, sometime since gunpowder came on the scene?*

Which could have been three or four centuries back, lost in the mists of time . . .

Armies don't have much interest in drafting a midget with a limp. Big strong not-too-smart farm boys, that's what they want, and lots of 'em, the kind of soldier you could expect to march across a mile of open field into the cannon's mouth. March in neat skirmish lines through barbed wire against machine guns.

More likely I heard soldier jargon while I repaired their weapons in the armory. Or made pretty-pretty swords for the officers.

Or I picked the phrases up from Ali Akhbar Khan. Heavy dragoons and grenadiers—those sound British enough.

He kept scanning the alley as he walked. And wrinkling his nose. No indoor plumbing in those trash igloos. "Do the note and the feather lead in the same direction?"

"Turn right at the next alley."

So she wasn't going to say. He turned. The next alley looked vaguely familiar, wider and also somewhat cleaner. You could drive down this one. Someone bothered to keep it clear. Backs of buildings, not the sides, loading docks and rear entries and such. No windows below the second floor, to make breaking-in harder.

Third building down on the right, a blank wood door, fancy inset panels with the varnish weathered off, wood gray and splintering, stone-trimmed gothic arch capped with some kind of shield surmounted by a cross. The shield had eroded far enough by acid rain, he couldn't read what it once carried—words or symbols. Church-type detail but not a church. Chapter house? Rectory? Offices for a church no longer standing? Or maybe the cross just warded against demons?

He'd seen that before, something to do with Mother, something at least forty or fifty years gone in the mists of time. Weeds grew on the threshold, rooted in dust and sand blown into the eddy over years. Door not used.

"This one?" He glanced back at her.

"No. Keep going."

Why did he remember this? Blank brick wall except for the door and its stone trim, no windows. Judging by the change in brick, a narrow building about forty feet wide, maybe four stories high, a story taller than the ones to either side. Looked like old work, not machine-made uniform brick, slightly lumpy and uneven but in better condition than its neighbors. Anonymous. No hardware on the outside of the door—no lock, no knob, no knocker or bell. Not unusual on an exit door . . .

"Move it, little man!"

He moved it.

Two buildings further, on the opposite side of the alley, she focused on a blank steel door with locks and handle. Locks, plural, three of them. Even standing back, he could see dings and gouges along the lock-side jamb where someone had tried to pry it open. Old rust on some of the scratches, others looked newer.

"This one."

He remembered it too, vaguely, again something associated with Mother. But then, they'd been in this town a long, long time, even by his standards. Faded scratched peeling letters on faded scratched gray paint, HAIRSTON'S ANTIQUES and ATLAS SECURITY on a badge-sticker that looked like it had been there forty years. Buzzer-button to summon your genie, if you had a delivery to make.

Antiques? In *this* neighborhood? New lamps for old, pottery jars big enough to hide forty thieves? She had thrown him into metaphors of the *Thousand Nights and a Night*. Always had thought Scheherazade would be a pretty little girl, soft hands and voice, not that harsh hill-tribe face as sharp as her blade or tongue, gnarled strong fingers scarred by the decades and callused to knife and pistol . . .

No keypad to disable the alarm system. Probably inside, have to punch in the code within a minute of opening or it would start screaming for the cops. He tried the knob. Locked.

"Back off." She waved him across the alley, as if she planned to blow the door open with a limpet mine. Military idioms again, probably *her* fault again. Bent over the locks as if she was talking to the pins and tumblers and bolts, her body blocking his view of the door.

"There's an alarm system . . . "

"Dummy sticker. No such company."

She *was* the cops. She'd know.

He couldn't remember what day it was, weekday or weekend, with Legion's habit of screwing up the flow of time, whether they were breaking into a store that was open or closed. Or even, from the outside evidence, whether it was still in business. Again he wondered, antiques, in *this* part of town? But she didn't look like she planned on walking around to the street side of the block and using the front door like a law-abiding citizen.

She turned the knob and the door swung in, unlocked by whatever words and incantations she'd muttered. Or lock-picks, more likely, with incantations like, "Come on, you mangy slit-eared misbegotten son of a yellow pariah dog mated to a pig . . ."

Darkness inside. She pulled her flashlight out, splashing blue-white probes into the shadows, side and floor and ceiling, not trusting. He didn't hear any alarms. No shouts or threats from inside, either. She stepped over the threshold and studied the door's frame behind her, probably checking for wires or switches or a keypad. Then moved on into darkness.

He crossed the alley and followed. A quick sniff told him that they weren't burglarizing a working business—stale air, dust, damp, winter's chill lingering in the unheated darkness. Her stabbing flashlight beam and thin light filtering past boarded-up shop windows told him what kind of business it had been. Junk. The "antiques" label covered old battered tables and dressers, cookware better suited for scrap metal, some console radios that dated back halfway to Marconi without being old enough to start gaining in value once again. Electric heaters with exposed coil elements that could burn down whole city blocks given any chance.

Veneer peeled off dusty sideboards and china cabinets. Stacks of crockery, he could see chips and cracks even in the gloom. This stuff would drag *his* apartment down a notch or five in the *Gracious Homes* décor scale.

Then the stabbing light settled on feathers. A cobwebbed hen pheasant—not even good taxidermy when it was new—sitting in a forest of table lamps with frayed cords and decayed shades.

Minus all its tail.

The flashlight beam poked here and there on the floor. No recent footprints in the dust. Mother, if it had been Mother, had collected those feathers a year or more ago.

He saw the harpy's silhouette against the light, cocking her head to one side, as if listening and . . . sniffing. She pulled the feather out of her coveralls and left it lying on the dusty table next to the stuffed bird. No further value, except as a message if Mother came back?

She turned back and waved him out. "Okay, now we track the paper. Probably same result, but what the hell, won't know if we don't try . . . "

So the two traces didn't lead to the same place. Nice to finally get *that* answer.

Out in the alley again, blinking against the light. She locked up behind him, click and clunk and click again. Generous of her, not leaving Ali Baba's Cave open to the neighborhood looters. He hadn't seen it, but probably they could find *something* in there worth stealing. If you looked hard enough. If you were desperate enough. Or maybe, just break up the furniture for firewood to heat a can of beans and hold frostbite at bay.

She marched him two blocks down the alley, back past that door he recognized—she didn't give it a second glance. Then through another narrow alley, out on a different street with a few stores hanging on, teeth and toenails, and she picked a security-grilled door with a dingy sign that offered news, magazines, and smokes. Once they stepped inside the narrow tiny store he saw it was mostly cigarettes and cheap cigars, some loose tobacco and a variety of wrapping papers for dope, but the place also offered a few racks of newspapers and lurid gossip tabloids. There were a few girly and muscle-boy magazines in plastic sleeves so you couldn't peek at the goodies without paying. He wondered what they sold out of the back room.

El Hajj pulled a tablet of lined paper off one shelf, carried it over to the cashier behind his scarred Plexiglas shield, paid for it, and waved at the door. Albert took the hint.

Outside again, on the cracked sidewalk under the tattered canvas awning, she pulled Mother's note from one of her pockets. She unfolded it and fitted the torn top edge against the matching ragged edge of the tablet. Mother hadn't even bothered to steal or buy the whole thing, just had taken the one sheet.

Ms. Detective Melissa el Hajj held the tablet up to the light and squinted along the surface of the paper, detecting. Shook her head. "She wrote out the note on this, in there, used one of the pens from the rack. Nobody saw her. Went in, wrote and tore it off, and walked out. In a shop where the cashier keeps a nine-millimeter automatic in the register and they have security mirrors covering every sightline in the store."

He shrugged. "We're good at not being noticed."

"Now that's *two* people I can't trace. You and the woman you call Mother."

She tossed the tablet in a nearby trash bin, bonanza for some dumpster-diver, making him wince. Apparently she had more money to waste than he did.

Which doesn't take much. And why does she keep harping on whether or not Mother is my mother? Maybe it's a cop thing. "Just the facts, Ma'am, nothing but the facts."

Then she cocked her head to one side and narrowed her eyes. "Okay, what had you so interested in that wooden door, back there in the alley?"

So she *had* noticed.

"Wooden door. You saw all the scratches on that metal door, the junk shop. Why hasn't anybody tried to break into the wooden one? Hell, even the rats could gnaw through it, the length of time since anyone used it."

"And?"

Damn her. "I remember seeing that door, years ago, decades ago. Going inside, with Mother. Can't remember why."

"Worth a look. Let's get a view of the front side first. Maybe I'd rather go in that way. Not that I think you'd lead me into a trap . . ."

A relationship based on mutual trust.

She pointed down the street. "That way."

Left and right and left again and then straight for a couple of blocks, filthy stinking alleys and streets with no traffic and furtive shadows here and there in darkened windows, she seemed to carry a map of the city in her head. This wasn't the way they came. As if he had an army of minions looking for a place to set up an ambush. They turned and stepped out on the street that should have had the front of the back they'd seen. He remembered the street names.

This one offered him straight storefronts, no sign of the old brickwork or any gothic arches. Not even boarded-up storefronts, so they could see into the spaces—empty, most of them, but still dreaming of tenants. Hadn't given up yet.

Three buildings in from the alley, he counted, a tattoo parlor. Windows painted over for privacy. Peering through the door, he saw a waiting room with tattoo flash designs on the walls: voluptuous girls, grinning biker skulls, Chinese dragons, intricate Celtic knot work—some of it considerably better than average art. Cracked vinyl sofa and a small counter and doors leading back into the working space. No customers. Two-sided sign on the door turned to say: *Closed. Please Come Back Again.* But no hours given.

He stepped back and looked up. Counted floors. Three. Same height as the buildings to either side, continuous parapet at the roofline, even the same brickwork trim—vague memory called them corbelled dentils. Damned stupid memory, why couldn't it offer him useful facts, dates, and names, instead of architectural trivia? Windows aligned straight down the block— all the same size, type, trim—age-browned shades or tattered curtains inside. The whole block looked like it had been built at the same time, maybe a century later than what he remembered from the mystery in the alley.

Sometimes buildings split a parcel of land. Across the street and down a bit, he looked again and couldn't see any higher floor in the back. He *could* see a chimney back there. It wasn't tall enough to clear any hypothetical fourth floor.

He looked at her. She looked at him and shrugged. They walked back down the alley, about eighty feet he guessed, and turned and counted buildings. Third one in, the arched doorway sneered at them, set into a type of brick and style that didn't match the street side. He couldn't see how far forward that fourth floor reached, couldn't get far enough away in the alley, but what he *could* see had blank walls just like the rear.

Blank door. No hardware, not even hinges on this side because it opened inwards, just as he remembered. Did you get into the building from one side or the other, through one of its neighbors? Which one? He was pretty sure he remembered Mother using *this* door. As much as he could trust his memory . . .

The door opens in . . .

He knelt, careful of the dirt, the evidence, and examined the line where door met dust and weeds. A thin dark line separated them, dust not tight and molded against the wood. The door *had* been used sometime since the winter, since the last rain.

She waved him back across the alley, just like she had with the junk-shop door.

"How can you pick a lock that isn't there? You got a battering-ram tucked away in one of those pockets? Dynamite?"

She glared at him, it began to seem that was her permanent expression. "Probably can't hide this any longer. If you tell anyone about it, I'll kill you. But I have a bargain with locks and doors. If they don't try to keep me out, I won't break them. I don't use lock picks."

As if she wasn't planning to kill him anyway.

That explained how she'd followed him down into his forge. Without explaining, really. And how she materialized at his bedside at midnight, in spite of all the layers of locks and traps and straight heavy bolts with no lock cylinder to pick.

Well, Mother had a few little tricks that physics denied were possible. For that matter, so did he. Chemists and metallurgists wouldn't like the things he did to iron and steel.

She laid her hands on the door as if feeling for vibrations. "I can open this."

A chorus of barks answered her. Sounded like a whole pack of dogs in there, six or eight *large* dogs, German shepherd class, growling barks from deep chests. With large teeth and attitudes. She backed off.

"I carry six spare magazines for the .45 auto. Only two for the .380—never figured on getting into a war using the backup. You can go in there alone if you want. I'm hiking back to my apartment and getting another gun."

"So you're not one of those fairy-tale princesses that insists on opening the forbidden door?"

"Not without superior firepower and air cover, that's damn sure. With *you* guarding my back, even the .45 starts to look iffy. Maybe I want a 12-gauge street-sweeper in my hands."

Such trust and confidence. But the "princess" part apparently suited her just fine.

IX

She unlocked the outer door and waved him in. "After you . . . "
"You're inviting me up to your apartment?"

"I told you, I'm not letting you out of my sight. Besides, some people in this neighborhood aren't smart enough to leave you alone. I don't want their blood on my hands."

He blinked at what that last bit implied and went through the door. It handed him an industry standard cheap-apartment-foyer—dirty scuffed brown tile floor with a threadbare mat to wipe your feet, damp-stained nondescript sheetrock walls with mailboxes set into the wall to his right, steel door marked STAIRWAY on his left. Her neighborhood didn't look much better than his. Some better, but not much. About the same age, since damn near half the town had burned down from a stable fire spread by wind back in the late eighteen-hundreds. A lot of people had rebuilt in brick, with heavy walls between buildings, in a move to prevent another firestorm.

Three mailboxes, four floors, that added up to one narrow deep apartment for each floor. This place had a Chinese take-out on the ground floor rather than a pizza joint, but the main difference *that* made was the soaked-in smell of stir-fry pork and scorched garlic rather than tomato paste and burned mozzarella.

No elevator, either. If you wanted handicap access in this town, you paid a lot more, lived in a newer century's floor plan. She unlocked the stairwell door, different key and second layer of defense, and waved him through. She still didn't want him behind her. Trusting woman.

"I thought you enjoyed a good blood feud. 'Then his brothers came for his blood, and we killed them.' Old tradition, back in the hills."

Stars exploded in his head. His cane rattled away across the floor as she spun him around and slammed his back against the wall, the cast on her wrist against his throat. He couldn't reach behind him for the knife, the way she had him pinned. Her breath growled warm on his cheek.

"Little man, do you think I *enjoyed* that? I had to speak the words of the Prophet in language they understood. Some things that Allah forbids, the knife and the bullet follow. The *customs* of their graybeards are not Islam. Their *tribe* is not Islam. I taught them this, and then I left, growing tired of blood."

She thumped his back against the wall again for emphasis and then released her grip on his jacket. Backed away. Tucked her .380 back into her coveralls. He felt an ache where she must have jammed its muzzle up under his ribs with her right hand. Hadn't noticed it at the time.

"You left, so they can return to their *customs*." There was his idiot tongue again, careless.

"We go back now and then, little man, me and some of my people. We walk their hill paths. Stand on their ridges against the sky, looking down on them. They remember us. To this day, you ask about a certain village and men will deny that it exists. That it ever *has* existed. Ask them to guide you through a pass that goes by a certain name and they will guide you through another. They remember, and obey the will of Allah. *Their* women go unveiled and speak with whoever they wish, still showing proper modesty but fearing none but Allah. Say the name of our village to their *women* and see the answer in their eyes."

She backed further, to where his cane had fallen, keeping her eyes on him. Squatted and picked up his cane. Tossed it to him. "Upstairs. Fourth floor. I don't like people above me."

He glanced over at the mailboxes. There it was, *Apt. 4* and *el Hajj* written out for the world to see. She hadn't bothered to check it for any credit card offers or sale fliers. The other boxes said *Abdullah* for *Apt. 2* and *Meshud* for the third floor. Probably some of her "people" and if he made the mistake of kicking up a fuss, he would have hostile company in a hurry.

For that matter, he didn't know if he would face a suspicious husband upstairs, and seven little el Hajj children, lined up in order of height. Each with a face like a hatchet and a knife tucked into the belt.

But somehow she didn't seem like the husband sort. The mother sort. But then, neither did Mother.

He led the way up wooden stairs that popped and creaked and sang like a Japanese nightingale floor. Nobody was going to sneak up unnoticed, but none of the treads seemed to be traps. Second floor, single door off the landing, double locks, third floor the same. Fourth floor, he didn't see any locks, just a knob like an interior door. He tried the knob and the door didn't budge. Big surprise.

This time, she didn't bother to hide what she did behind her body. She just laid her left hand on the door and turned the knob with her right. The door opened. She waved him in, to a dark room of shadows with light bleeding in from either end, doors into front and rear rooms, rooms that had windows.

His nose told him he could quit worrying about any Mr. el Hajj, any little el Hajj children. She had a distinct, a *unique*, smell—she'd just given him a fresh in-your-face sample—and that was the only human odor lingering in the air. There hadn't been another body in this space in months. Perhaps years. He couldn't decide if that was a good thing or a bad thing.

Then she flipped a light switch and he froze. Light flooded an austere room nearly bare and obsessively clean, no furniture, off-white walls and ceiling, dark gleaming hardwood floor, a brick fireplace on the wall toward the street side. But that wasn't what caught him. A small Kazakh rug covered part of the floor, with a meditation pad in the center, clearly aimed at the far wall from the door. Which held . . .

The Great Wheel, the Wheel of Life, he couldn't tell if it was Tibetan or Nepalese, but the ones he had seen were small ink drawings or paintings, a couple of feet on a side at most. She had a tapestry or rug, must be eight feet square, with vibrant colors that told him the threads had to be silk and never exposed to sunlight, incredibly detailed. He'd never seen such a thing, never even heard of one.

Afghanistan had been a Buddhist land once. He remembered the statues, the caves. A lot of the old art, Buddhist or Animist, had been destroyed by religious fanatics who said that all images were abominations to Allah. Somehow, she'd kept this and smuggled it out. But that weaving belonged in a museum under glass, or some billionaire's mansion . . .

It drew him. Each step closer revealed more detail—knife-edged fang-red mountains, evergreens that glowed against a clear lapis sky and brilliant snow, the scarlet Yama gleaming with ivory skulls in his golden fiery hair, the pig and snake and cock in the center so lifelike he expected them to start moving in their eternal dance and battle of sin. Ignorance, anger, and lust incarnate.

Probably if he stared at them long enough they would. Start moving, that is. A mandala for meditation was meant to suck in your mind and consciousness. He shook himself loose.

A statue stood on the floor just below the Wheel, about two feet tall. Nude Kali in her dancer's grace standing on the ball of one foot, garland of skulls hung between her breasts, left hands holding a knife and severed head, right hands in gestures of fearlessness and blessing. It glowed with the peculiar luster of old gold, and he could feel its weight without touching.

It also would be worth hundreds of thousands of dollars at

an art auction, particularly tempting for the new billionaires of India. He wondered how she dared let him see this.

She'd vanished into the front room, probably her bedroom, leaving him alone with the treasures. Maybe she knew the door wouldn't let him out? He turned and checked it. Three deadbolt locks on this side, no turn-knobs for unlocking. They couldn't be tighter shut if they'd been welded.

He crossed to the fireplace mantel. Simple white-painted wood about six feet long over a square shallow fireplace with recent ashes, it held four jade carvings each about six inches high and varying widths. The first, white jade, a plain bowl that made your fingers ache to touch it, caress it, thin enough to glow translucent in the down-light from the ceiling. The second, a Chinese dragon wrapped around a brass incense burner, pale green. The third, a Buddha in deep green jade, the ascetic Buddha with his ribs like a picket fence and eyes sunken in his skull, not a common image in the Western world. The fourth . . .

The fourth was a naturalistic portrait bust, he'd never seen that done in jade before. It was old. It was exquisite, both detail and proportion. Pink jade.

It was her.

"Gifts to my family, long ago."

"Including your portrait?"

She'd reappeared next to him while he was sunk in the jades. Or maybe while the mandala had hypnotized him, and he hadn't noticed her, under the spell. She'd stripped out of the coverall, leaving her in a deep green bodysuit hung with holsters and pockets—and a padded yellow vest that he assumed was bulletproof. Or whatever technical term they used, ballistic nylon maybe. She looked a lot thinner without the bulky shapeless clothing, wiry. Somewhat like the Kali, this one a tough stringy warrior-woman rather than the voluptuous earth-mother depiction often used.

"Actually, my grandmother times seven. Or maybe six or

eight—oral history confuses generations, sometimes. All our women look a lot alike. Strong genes."

"Including the broken nose?"

She fingered hers. "That's genetic, too. Not broken, just bent to the left. We've never bothered with that 'symmetry equals beauty' thing. We're Picasso-women, one eye higher than the other. In case you hadn't noticed."

He hadn't. But there it was, both her and the sculpture, subtle. It seemed to fit her face. The eyes balanced the nose.

She held her left wrist between their faces, glaring at the rough cast, pale green almost like the jade but with the pattern of the reinforcing mesh, from her forearm down to the back of her hand and circling the thumb. "I want this thing off. Can't seem to get the proper angle at it one-handed. Make yourself useful."

A pair of heavy kitchen shears thumped from her right hand to his, the sort of cutlery you'd use to dissect a raw chicken or goose.

"I'm no doctor. Don't they use saws for that? You might make the injury worse, taking a cast off too soon."

"Thy mother never knew thy father . . . "

She broke off whatever followed, sounded like a particularly vile spitting dialect of Pashto too fast for him to grab specifics. The sense, though, was clear.

"I can't reload with this thing on my wrist. Can't get the magazines out of my pockets. Trust me, the bone is healed. It was just a hairline fracture. Cut the damned thing off!"

He'd been right about quick healing.

"And thy *father ran on three legs, and howled in Baluchi!"* he said, and the words that followed. He tried to give his bastard Pashto exactly the inflection he'd learned from Ali Akhbar Khan, one of the old man's favorite curses.

Her eyes widened. "We can discuss each other's families at another time. For now, just help me out of the damned cast. Please?"

He tried. The tip of the shears barely fit under the cast edge. Each time he tried to cut, the blades just wedged back out from the hard fiberglass surface. If he angled exactly *so*, he could nibble away, maybe a molecule at a time.

"This will take all week. The doctor wrapped heavy gauze around your wrist before putting on the cast, yes? Padding? I can cut down to that with my knife a lot faster." He paused. "Of course, that would require you to trust me . . . "

He could see what she thought of *that*, written clear on her face. Her jaw worked for about a minute as she chewed on his offer. Then she nodded and led him into the back room of her apartment, the kitchen, just as austere as the other room— plain off-white walls and plain white refrigerator and stove and cabinets. One table, white Formica top; two chairs, white wood. She sat down and laid her left arm on the table, palm down, as much of a fist as she could make with the cast hindering. Her knuckles paled against her dark skin.

"You cut me, I'll kill you."

He stared at her for a moment. "I'll be sure to cut deep, then."

"The man who taught you those curses, he served with the Old Khybers. Havildar or higher. Only *they* stretched 'Baluchi' into tomorrow in quite that way. They did not like Baluchis."

Ali Akhbar Khan rose to Havildar-major. What she calls the "Old Khybers" were disbanded after the Great War. Colonial rebellion. But how does she know how their sergeants cursed?

He pulled out his knife and touched the point to the forearm end of her cast. Drew it along the surface, no weight at all, testing the hardness of the resin and mesh. The tip left a scratch. Back to the beginning of the scratch, a feather more weight, and the tip bit partway into the mesh, hissing against the resin. Again. Again. Through the first layer. The second. The third.

She brought her other fist up to the table, white knuckles, tendons standing out. He pulled the knife back and looked up. Sweat beaded on her lip and forehead. No, she *didn't* trust him.

She'd tested the edge of that knife. She knew what a slip could do.

Again. He felt some of the last layer part, different drag at some points of the cut as the blade slid into cotton instead of fiberglass, he hadn't kept the pressure even or the doctor hadn't wrapped it exactly the same or the faint shake of her arm affected the cut. He used even more care, as if he was finishing on the anvil with the barest tap of his hammer and thought.

The two sides of the cut sprang apart a hair's-width, tension in the cast and compression on the cotton. He pulled the knife back, she pulled her wrist back. They both dared to breathe. She flexed the fingers of both hands. Red lines marked where her nails had bitten into her right palm.

She grabbed the shears from where he had laid them on the table and ran them up the hairline break, cutting the gauze underneath and spreading the cut. Pulled the two edges apart with a crackling rip, breaking the back of the cast. Slid the corpse off her wrist over her fingers and thumb. Threw the wreck across her kitchen into a corner.

"Fuck *that!*" Cursing in English rather than Pashto.

She ran her fingers, both hands, through her hair and panted for more oxygen. "Thank. You."

She stood up, twisting her freed wrist, bending it, testing it, and smiling at what she found. Apparently all present and correct. Then she walked over, picked up the cast, and opened a cabinet under the sink to a trashcan with neat plastic bag liner. Dumped the cast. Closed the cabinet. Everything proper again.

He glanced around, itemizing—nothing on the counters except a microwave and toaster oven. Nothing on the refrigerator top, no refrigerator magnets holding notes, top and front of the stove far cleaner than his. He bet that if he got into her bedroom, small chance of that, he'd find the bed made to military precision and the top of her dresser bare. This woman was a neat freak. He didn't want to know what she thought of *his* place.

Over by the door again, she spun and stared at him with a gun in her hand. Reflex pulled his knife up until he realized the gun was pointed off to one side. It looked like it was aimed at the center of the clock on the stove. She turned her head without moving her hand, checked the sight picture, holstered the pistol, turned away, and spun back again, repeating the whole sequence.

She stared back at the knife, still in his hand. Blinked, as if she just ran through how her moves must look to him. She was used to being alone here.

Shook her head.

"Damned things are supposed to be identical, consecutive serial numbers and all. They aren't. This one always feels a hair muzzle-heavy compared to the one that fucking demon ate. Machinist tolerances. Doesn't matter when I use the sights, but I need to reset the instinct shooting. Sorry."

Again, cursing in English. Did she run multiple personalities under that black hair? He sheathed his knife after checking the point for any wear from cutting the cast. If she was going to go to the extreme of actually apologizing for something . . .

"Let me see that."

Again, the considering stare. She dropped the magazine into her other hand, worked the slide to eject a live round, and caught the cartridge out of mid-air. Fast hands, very fast, as he had noticed before. She handed the pistol to him with its slide locked open.

He checked the chamber anyway. Empty. Then let the slide snap forward and hefted the pistol with one hand, then the other, then a two-handed stance menacing the same clock on the stove. She wanted a gram, maybe more, off the muzzle weight . . .

She'd been playing those games of hers with a round in the chamber. Well, loaded weight *would* make a difference. She *had* kept her finger out of the trigger guard, and the safety on.

Still . . .

"You know how to handle a pistol. I thought you didn't like them?"

He ignored her, sinking his thoughts into the Colt in his hands. Old design, 1911 model, he'd held them before, stripped them down, repaired them. But couldn't remember where and when.

Have to stay away from the barrel bushing, don't screw up fit on the firing-pin and chamber end, but there's free space between slide and barrel in between . . .

Fingers bracketing the slide, he thought about the slow flow of metal like a glacier under his fingertips, dragging molecules toward the grip, humming a few words over and over, talking to the metal. *Sliding down the slide. Sliding down the slide. Sliding. Sliding. Do not pinch, do not distort the metal. A few molecules . . .*

He shook himself loose, worked the slide a couple of times to verify it was just as silky-smooth as before, and locked it open. Handed it to her.

"I've used guns. Even own a couple. But I don't make them. As I said, no soul."

She took the gun, staring at him. Reloaded it, including a round in the chamber. Dammit, sure the weight of all that brass and lead would change the balance but it would change again every time she fired. This model had an inertial firing pin and no safety block—if you dropped the weapon it could go off. Military protocol said to carry it with an empty chamber . . .

He couldn't remember where he'd learned that.

The detective, or whatever she was, went through her instinct-shooting drills again, then nodded. "We get a free morning sometime, I have some other guns I want you to sing over. And you still owe me a knife."

That appeared to be as close to another "thank you" as he was going to get.

Over her shoulder as she headed back toward the front of the apartment, "Get yourself a beer and a sandwich. I have to sort out the gear I need to pull a raid on a place that doesn't exist."

"Huh?" Brilliant comment, but . . .

"You wondered why the local boyos haven't tried to break into that wooden door. They can't see it. It isn't really there. You can see it. I can see it. But we aren't human."

So she *had* noticed.

X

"Let me get this straight. You've been on the city police force for twenty years, and nobody notices that you don't get any older?"

They walked through the streets and alleys, dirty streets and filthy or worse alleys, Albert with a backpack full of whatever Melissa el Hajj thought they needed for "a raid on a place that doesn't exist"—damned heavy, whatever the whatever was; he suspected ammunition sufficient to start a small revolution. She was wearing uniform coveralls—badge, patches, name-tag, gun belt, and all—and carrying a pump shotgun slung over her shoulder. This time, she was willing to walk in front of him. Some kind of barometer for a change in their personal weather, he guessed. She seemed like the kind of woman who turned her back on damn few people.

The weather spoke of probable change, too. Gray clouds rolled in from the northwest, a suggestion that long walks weren't a good idea, and gusts of cold wind stirred the winter residue of dirt and trash. He sniffed. Threat of rain on the air as well as other things—garbage lost and buried in a snow bank and recently surfaced and thawing. Not air you'd breathe in a better class of neighborhood.

People weren't noticing them. As she'd said, "Mostly, people in places like this don't *want* to notice cops. Subconscious theory is, if they can't see me, I can't see them. Plus, like you said back at that smoke shop, people like us can be very hard to see. That clerk didn't see you and wouldn't have noticed me if I hadn't slapped the pad down on the counter in front of him. They don't *want* to see us, whatever we are."

"Us" meaning something other than cops, in this case. But that brought him back to thinking of cops and her blue uniform coveralls and the lieutenant bars on her collar. That rank implied her captain or chief or whatever did something more than "put up" with her. Which was how they got on the subject of her twenty years on the force, and nobody noticing that she hadn't changed much from "thirty-ish" to age "fifty" and standing on the edge of retirement: "twenty and out."

"I overhear comments about how silly it is for someone who looks like *her* dyeing her hair—like it would make *her* look young and sexy. Overheard a sergeant in the break room, couple of months past an ugly divorce, say he'd rather try to fuck an axe."

Ouch.

But she looked more amused than hurt or offended.

He relaxed a bit, quitting the dance of evasion that had started when she mentioned that old photo of him from the 1800s.

Probably she still planned to kill him, once Legion was through with them.

"How do you handle ID? I mean, cops are big on background checks . . . "

She turned into the alley that led to the alley they wanted. "Pretty easy, if you plan ahead, and don't let locks argue with you. Plant a birth certificate, city clerk usually has the forms right there in the office and you're already using the right typewriter, wait twenty years, then ask for a certified copy for Social Security, driver's license, you name it. Let that ride for another ten years, racking up points. Just don't get impatient. People like us have the time. I never claim to be younger than thirty."

Two men had been picking through the trash. He thought they were men but in the dirty shapeless jackets and baggy pants, hair tucked up under ragged knit caps, they could be women. Ms. Detective *Lieutenant* el Hajj unslung her shotgun and carried it braced on one hip aimed at the sky, and they vanished. Sort of like a Western movie he'd seen once, citizens going *poof!* off the dusty main street when the bad guy and the sheriff appeared at opposite ends of the block. No bad guy for *High Noon,* here, not that he could see.

"Is that part of the police procedure manual? Scaring citizens off the street?"

She glanced over at him and then turned back to scanning the roof-parapets overhead. Probably watching for snipers. "You planning to file a complaint? You think *they* are planning to file a complaint?"

"No and no."

"Then it's proper procedure."

Maybe she got promoted because they didn't dare do anything else with her.

"Do you have a real name?"

They walked on, dodging trash and dogshit on the rough pavement, scanning the blank brick walls for threats. They passed the place where the men/women had been. Damned if Albert could see where they went. Magic trick. He'd just about decided she wasn't going to answer his question . . .

"No. Not that I can remember. You?"

He *also* wanted to think a bit on that, before bringing things out into open air. Then, "No. That name Legion used, 'Lahti' is a place in Finland. 'Simon' is religious camouflage that Mother used, nothing more."

Since she apparently felt like talking, he asked, "How do your 'people' handle it, the ones from your village, this business of living forever? Or are they all like you? Us?"

"They help. They provide references, fake job experience for me, that sort of thing. They're humans. They grow old and die, but they do what I ask them to do. Humans are like that, facing their goddess." She looked bleak. "They help me remember who I am."

Oh, hell. "That Kali in your apartment, that's another portrait, yes?"

"Not my choice."

"I never noticed the second set of arms."

"I keep them hidden." Then she shrugged, with a grimace. "That's how they explain my speed. I can't remember the last time someone managed to hit me, much less hurt me. That's part of why I had to follow you."

"I'm not fast. I just caught you by surprise."

"And *that* was the surprising part."

They turned into the wider alley. No people. The door was still there, the door that didn't exist into a four-story old brick building that also didn't exist and didn't even bother to offer an illusion on the street side of the block.

"Why so talkative, all of a sudden? You told me that you ask questions, not answer them."

"Little man, you're the first new thing to cross my path in over a *century*. I'd decided to open up before I invited you into my apartment, let you react to it. Then, hearing you curse with a tongue long dead, that was a breath of mountain air here in the lowlands. No one has dared curse me since that dying Badakhi. I hope you understand what you said."

"I think so. Ali Akhbar Khan explained each word and the cultural meanings each carried."

"Good. Never give offense without intending it."

With that, they faced the door.

One of the dead weeds was broken, still hanging on its stem and drawing arcs back and forth in the gathered dust with each gust of wind. It hadn't been broken when he looked before, a few hours ago. The slit between wood and dust looked different.

"Someone's been through this since we were here."

She nodded and waved him back. Nerves made him reach back and touch his knife hilt under the backpack, make sure it waited free. The dogs inside broke into frenzied barking and growling, he could hear claws scratching at the wood that blocked them from their lawful prey.

"It isn't locked. Not even latched. Anyone could push this open. If they could see it."

He remembered a pack of wild dogs, years ago under hot dry dusty sun in another land. Not a good memory. *Don't let them get behind you.* He drew his knife and backed up until he bumped against the wall across the alley. Solid and reassuring.

She braced the shotgun against her side, finger inside the trigger guard, and nudged the door with one boot. It opened about eight inches, about one dog wide. She knew what she was doing, that was obvious. Albert flinched. Nothing happened. A splat of rain hit him at the same time he realized the dogs had fallen silent. She nudged the door again, half open now, and still no dogs. She kept the muzzle of the shotgun low, dog height. For a large dog, that is, not ankle-biting Chihuahuas.

Nothing but another gust of wind, another short burst of rain. Cold rain, with a hint of ice to sting his cheek.

He saw worn flagstone paving inside, a narrow view of a courtyard with galleries around, a marble fountain with a weathered green bronze maiden pouring water from an amphora in the middle. In sunshine.

No guard dogs.

She kicked the door wide. No dogs, no people, no rain. Four floors of galleries, white marble columns and Moorish-style marble pierced screen-work carved in floral patterns serving as rails between the columns, he'd seen something like this in a courtyard in Spain. Doors off the galleries were solid-looking dark wooden rail-and-stile doors with faded flaking varnish like the one into the alley.

He inched forward, seeing more of the same, following her through the door as she swept the corners with the muzzle of her shotgun, then scanned the galleries. Three doors per side on each level of the galleries. Red tile roof over the top level, courtyard open to blue sky and a hot sun. Open stairway with more pierced stonework for a rail, switch-backing up the rear corner to his right. He stopped in the doorway, staring back and forth between the dry courtyard and the spitting sleet of the alley. He moved one hand back and forth through the plane of the wall and could feel a line between the weathers, cold and wet to hot and dry in a razor's edge.

He stepped all the way inside, and studied the place. Three doors times four floors equals twelve. Mirror image on the other side, twenty-four. No doors on the narrower front, one old casement-style double window, small leaded-glass diamond panes, on each floor instead, including the ground floor where the tattoo shop stood on the other side of this block. He moved out into the courtyard and checked the back wall. One door into the alley, one door on each of the three floors above. Where the hell did those go, through a blank brick wall?

One door in, twenty-seven doors out. Mystical numbers?

"Should I close the door?"

She kept sweeping the four sides with her shotgun, nervous. He couldn't blame her. Hairs prickled on the back of his own neck.

A quick glance at him, one eyebrow up. Then a shrug and back to the sweep. "Go ahead and cut off our retreat. If we can't get back out, well, that backpack you're toting is my jump bag—food, water, basic camping gear."

Jump bag. Emergency supplies for evacuation, recommended kit for hurricane or flood or brushfire country where you might have to cut and run on a few minutes' notice, live on your own resources for a week or more until you could go home again. It figured that *she* would keep one, here in a city that fit none of those categories.

Of course, he had one too. In case he needed to leave town in a hurry, for a non-natural cause.

He closed the door, after checking that it had a handle on

the inside. He opened it again. Alley still there. Still filled with gusts of rain, streaking the brick and turning the dust to cratered mud. The wind didn't pass through the opening. But his hand could. He closed the door again. No reason to invite alley rats in, two-legged or four.

She'd been watching him. Nodded. Went back to threat assessment. Put her foot on the bottom step of the stairway. "I'll go up and scout. You keep lookout down here."

Words echoed down, a clear alto voice. "I'd rather you stayed down there, too, O Goddess of the Mountain Winds. I prefer to hold the high ground."

He knew that voice.

Albert's eyes searched the upper galleries but couldn't see her. Pierced stone-work had been invented to serve as a privacy screen as well as decoration, and it was doing its job. There might be a shadow darkening it in the far front corner of the fourth floor . . .

Metal clicked behind him, and he glanced back. A shotgun barrel pointed at the same corner. A hint of police baseball cap and eye peeked over the railing of the stairway. Boots in the shadow underneath. Ms. Detective Lieutenant el Hajj, in full combat mode.

At least she hadn't fired. Yet.

"Don't shoot. That's Mother."

"Move away," she whispered. "Split the target."

Laughter above. "Simon, dear boy. Please introduce me to your girlfriend. I know *what* she is, but I don't know *who*."

He still couldn't see her, and the voice seemed to jump from one corner to the other. Mother had tricks like that.

He stepped out into the courtyard, completely contrary to Official Orders. "Mother, this is Detective Lieutenant Melissa el Hajj of the city police's arson division. She's here to arrest you for abuse of a salamander."

More laughter. "You always *did* have a sense of humor. How about if I promise to never do it again?"

He turned toward the shotgun barrel, still pointed comfortably upward. The blast would hurt, add to his long-term hearing loss from the forge and all, but nothing more damaging than that . . .

"Well, that gets Legion off our asses. We've solved your crime. We know who did it, and she says she'll stop."

Then he remembered the other thing and twitched, the thing Legion *hadn't* ordered them to do. That Legion had dodged even mentioning, but had set up with great care. Demoniacal care, even. For whatever reason.

"Mother, you have to give that star back. I have to fix it."

The laughter held an edge now, bordering on sarcasm and . . . insanity? "Fix it? *Fix* it? I spent a thousand years learning that the thing existed, fading a little with every minute of every day and never knowing why. Another thousand years finding it. A third thousand following its travels and waiting until the faith that guarded it died. Seven times seven years since they took the Torah out of that cabinet and left, leaving forgotten the last remaining relic from Solomon the Great. That long for the guard to fade, so I could enter. It still took all my power and the life-heat of a salamander to even crack the foul thing. And you want to *fix* it?"

So she had killed the salamander. No wonder Legion was pissed.

"No, little Simon Lahti, you do *not* want to fix it. That Seal was killing you as well as me. Killing your Mountain Goddess girlfriend. Even cracked and leaking its own power, it still holds your names, sucks power from you. Old Solly was a bastard, yes he was. 'Thou shalt have no other Gods before me.' That's all his God asked, admitting that other Gods existed for other tribes. But Solly had to be a hero, make his little tribal God supreme. He forged that thing in the fires of his own soul, subtle but strong, to drain us over centuries. And the sneaky little shit said that he loved me . . . "

She broke off.

Albert felt movement beside him, glanced over, saw the . . . Mountain Goddess? . . . still holding her shotgun aimed at the corner of the gallery but out from behind the stair. He couldn't read her face—no expression at all, except concentration.

"Who the hell are *you?*"

He looked back up. Mother had moved forward, stood just behind the screen-work railing. She wore something classic in gold cloth, a sari perhaps, but wrapped and draped across her dark skin so that right shoulder and right breast remained bare. Typical of her, style and casual body-sense that never paid much attention to whatever culture they were visiting. She made the rules. Everyone else obeyed them. Even in past centuries, when dark skin meant slavery in this land, no one had ever questioned her. She was what she was.

Like a goddess. A fertility goddess out of prehistory, short with big breasts and big hips and dark and beautiful. He'd forgotten how beautiful.

"Who am I? Balkis, goddess of Sa'aba am I. I heard of a human dabbling in our powers, and went to see. He acted nice. We exchanged gifts and knowledge and . . . other things. I left and returned to my own land and worshipers. I never knew how he took my secrets and betrayed me, until the Seal worked its evil through the years. By the time I knew that I should kill him, he was already dust."

A snort of derision echoed in his right ear. "Forgive me for questioning your tale, O Goddess, but how do you know *your* name if the great Seal of Suleiman bin Dauod is sucking *mine* away? If we are all gods and goddesses together . . . ?"

Again the laughter, even wilder. "Solly was a bastard, like I said. He worked my name into the Seal, to hide what he had done from the only goddess who could have hunted him down and stopped him while there was still time. He left me enough of my powers that I wouldn't suspect him. Like I told you, it took me a millennium to know what he'd done."

Then her voice sobered. "Don't bother trying to follow me. I don't have the Seal. I hid it. When it leaks enough of its own power through that crack, I'll destroy it and we'll all be free once more. The gods *will* come again."

She vanished. Albert heard a door open. Then her voice came again, hollow and echoing as if she spoke from a cave.

"Beware these doors, Simon Lahti! Your mother warns you! Half of them lead to places that will kill you if you don't know where you're going. Plus, they sometimes change. Will it be the Lady or the Tiger?"

A door closed.

He stood staring up. Mother? That "Balkis" thing wasn't a joke? Gods and goddesses? The Seal had cried out to him, begging him to forge it once again, guard the way between the worlds.

Gods and goddesses loose in the world once more. That would fit Legion's warning about the world changing. He didn't *like* the bastards, even if he was supposed to *be* one.

Another metallic click echoed beside him. Probably the *other* goddess, setting the safety on her shotgun.

"Well, that raised as many questions as it answered. Should have tried to shoot her."

Albert turned, shaking his head. "But that's *Mother*."

"Whoever or *what*ever that was, that woman isn't your mother. Skin can lie, but no lifeline connects you to her. The winds tell me this."

Goddess of the Mountain Winds.

XI

Goddess of the Mountain Winds—cold, thin, deadly, remote. You can't keep secrets from the winds. You can't hide from them. Even the strongest door can't keep them out. They'll find some way to sneak inside and chill you to the marrow.

And the killing will be just as cold and remote. Not passionate death, she's not *an avatar of Kali. The mountain winds just don't care. Make one mistake and die.*

They can touch you, but you can't touch them.

Well, *that* explained a number of things. *If* he could believe Mother, which required a leap of faith at the best of times. The world-myth held a multitude of forge-gods, some even with a bum leg and "vertically challenged." Smithing was the kind of work that people everywhere knew *needed* gods, and somehow involved dwarves. And spitting in the east corner before firing the forge.

Too bad he didn't know his own name. If Mother could be trusted, he might yet remember it. Soon. As soon as enough power drained from the Seal.

"I don't *like* gods."

The Wind Goddess was staring at him, furrows of intensity above her nose. She shook her head. He couldn't tell if that meant she agreed with his statement, or disagreed. Communications breakdown.

If all else fails, ask. "Do you believe Mother? That we're gods?"

"She's *not* your mother. Whatever else she is, she's not that. But her life *does* stretch back out of sight. Which takes some doing. Yours disappears in fog. Hers goes over the horizon off *that* way." She bobbed her head generally east.

An answer that wasn't an answer. Mother could be thousands of years old *without* being Balkis, either Queen of Sheba or Goddess of Sa'aba. Without him and . . . Ms. Detective Lieutenant Melissa el Hajj . . . being gods.

"So what do I call you? What do I call *her*?"

She wrinkled her nose. "Call her Mother, if that's what flows easiest off your tongue. Or 'that bitch' will do just fine. From what little I've seen of her. Me?" Another shrug. "The few people who don't call me 'Lieutenant' or 'Goddess' call me Mel. 'Noshaq' is a mountain." She thought for another moment. "I don't think anyone alive today dares to call me 'Mel.' You may."

He blinked at that. All of it. Including the regal graciousness of the last bit. It meant something important, but he had no idea what.

Or should he concentrate on the bit that no one left alive called her that? "Dare to call me Mel, you die!"

English was a slippery language. But "Melissa" wasn't an English name—his chancy memory said it was Greek for "honey bee," and he wondered where she'd picked *that* up. Alexander's wandering army? Where and when had *he* learned Greek?

Anyway, she'd chosen a venomous insect for her name.

Her eyes had gone back to scanning the . . . building? The galleries, anyway. Over her shotgun sights, of course, although she held the gun against her hip rather than her shoulder.

"I want to talk to those doors. Not open them yet, just ask them what they hide. I think your Bilqis was telling the truth when she said some of them would kill you. Doesn't have to open straight to *Jahannam* or a *djinni* lair—Antarctica will do. The center of Rub Al-Khali also comes to mind, before they mucked it up with oil wells. Or even underwater, if the sea level has changed since Allah created this place for His amusement."

She was back to studying *him*, those disconcerting dark eyes narrowed and weighing him over the balance-point of her sharp nose. "Guard *this* door." She cocked her head at the one leading to the alley. "I don't want any distractions wandering in and interfering with my winds."

Another stare, followed by a nod to herself. She laid the shotgun down and started to unbuckle her gun belt. "You said you knew how to handle a pistol. Looked like you meant it. Have you practiced recently?"

Valid question. Pistols are tricky tools, not like a rifle or a shotgun. You can't lay off pistol practice for a year or so and still count yourself a gunman.

"Two hundred rounds on a practical pistol range, little over a month ago. I scored eighty percent lethal hits, including clean on the shoot/don't-shoot section."

Two hundred rounds plus range-time was damned expensive, on his limited budget. But, he couldn't see any point in keeping the guns if he wasn't able to hit a barn from inside it.

She handed him the gun belt. Heavy—holstered pistol and four spare high-capacity magazines. Plus handcuffs and pepper spray and portable cop radio, the whole *meghilla*. He wondered just how many laws and department regulations she broke by handing it to him.

"I'm thin. That should fit you okay. Rather have someone at my back with a gun than with that knife and sword-cane, impressive as they are."

"That leaves you with just the shotgun."

She grinned, a hard smile with a touch of nasty in it. "Not on your ass, little man. I still have my Colts, the .45 and .380. What you have is just the duty gun. Chief says every cop has to carry the same hardware, interchangeable magazines and such, we're a *force*, a *unit*, not a goddamn mob of individuals." Her snarl told him exactly what she thought of *that*. "I've practiced with it, but a few thousand rounds downrange can't make me like it. Different balance, bad grip, and it jammed a couple of times. My Colts never have."

Great. Maybe she *was* an avatar of Kali.

He drew the gun from its holster, cleared it—round in the chamber, dammit—and examined it. Smith and Wesson 9 millimeter semi-automatic, double action, polymer frame and metal slide, he'd never handled one like it before. That double-stack magazine made the grip seem fat to him. He'd really need to use both hands for good control—he could understand why it felt odd to her as well. But he could live with it.

Or die with it, more likely, if it jammed in a situation where a knife just *wouldn't* do.

Maybe he could talk to it about smooth feed and ejection, if they got a few minutes free. Safety came ready to his thumb, anyway, and it pointed where he meant it to point. Ambidextrous safety as well, he swapped from hand to hand, trying the feel. Mel watched his antics for a moment before issuing a curt nod of approval. Or, that's how he chose to read it.

She grabbed the shotgun, stood up, and walked over to the nearest door, the first one on the ground floor on the right, and placed her left hand on one of the recessed wooden panels. He loaded the pistol, including the round in the chamber again— that was the way *she* carried it, and she was probably going to ask for it back. Besides, as a modern weapon, he assumed it had a firing-pin block and wouldn't go bang if he dropped it on those pavers with the safety on.

Gun belt was wide, heavy stiff patent leather and shiny— he'd prefer matte nylon webbing, lighter and more flexible—but probably police force standard again, not her choice. He took off the backpack and buckled the belt on. Needed to use one notch over from the faint crease where she usually wore it, he was wider around than her for all she stood at least half a foot taller.

Slim. Like that gold Kali, all lean muscle, marathon-runner build. Being a goddess, she probably didn't have to exercise to look like that. Part of the god-package . . . like he'd never been able to change the way *he* looked.

She'd moved on to the second door and stood leaning her forehead against it. Asking deeper questions? She shook herself, stepped back, shook herself again, and walked over to the third.

Not his problem. If she wanted him to know, she'd tell him. Meanwhile, that left him with an unfamiliar gun and holster. This one had a pretty serious top strap, probably designed to keep an alleged perpetrator from grabbing an officer's weapon in a scuffle, so Albert needed to practice actually getting *to* the gun if he ever needed it.

He didn't need a cowboy movie quick-draw, nothing like that, just reliable transfer from holster to hand. Without dropping the damned fat-gripped gun in the process. Same with grabbing a replacement magazine from its belt pouch in the middle of scare-the-shit-out-of-you violence. The snaps on the pouch cover-flaps wanted to stick. Metal, he talked them into a smooth release. Probably should have been Velcro in the first place, but you couldn't polish that.

She'd moved on to staring out the front window, shaking her head, and then starting on the other bank of ground-floor doors. Just out of curiosity, he opened the back door again, disturbing her winds. Hard rain swept the alley outside, sleet mixed in, he could feel the sting of it when he reached his hand through that boundary. Cold, raw, not a place you'd want to be. Particularly if you happened to be homeless and living in a cardboard hut.

He closed the door and crossed the courtyard to the front window. It looked out on a streetscape, just as he remembered from their earlier check except raining now. Broken window on the second floor across the way and three rust-rimmed bullet-holes in the "No Parking" sign. He remembered those too.

He went back to unsnapping the holster strap and drawing the pistol and flipping off the safety and getting a sight picture, slow motion, just engraving muscle memory with unfamiliar hardware. Then he sat on the marble curb of the fountain, in hot sun next to gentle splashing water, and let the rays soak up some of the tension this place woke in his shoulders. Illusion, all of it. A damned convincing illusion, he could smell the water.

I don't like *gods.*

The building wasn't the only cause of tension.

She had worked her way up to the fourth floor galleries, he couldn't see her but followed her footsteps as they echoed along spending only a moment or so with each door. Rather longer with the window to the front. And rather longer with the one he thought Mother had used. *Balkis* had used.

Gonna take a bit of time to digest that news, that Mother isn't my mother. Not really bad *news, considering who She is, but it shakes up my world a bit. Probably says that my brothers and sisters and aunts and uncles . . . aren't. And that the reports of deaths in the family may be greatly exaggerated. Mother never let facts interfere with a good story.*

The weird thing was, he believed it. Mother not being . . . Mother . . . fit in with too many things through the years. She was the kind of person who would tell a lie when the truth would serve as well. Or better. *She* was the center of the universe, and truth could twist itself as necessary to fit.

Mel clumped down the stairs again, boots heavy on stone treads, and walked over to sag down a few feet away from him on the fountain lip. She stared off into space. Little as he knew her, her body-language said she wasn't happy.

"Doors won't talk to you?"

"Oh, they talk, all right. Ones on the first two floors lead to places in this world. Except for the rear on the second floor. None of those three rear doors will open, for me or anyone. Not until *Yawm al-Qiyāmah*, maybe. If such a thing will ever come."

"Well, nothing on the brick wall outside . . . "

She shook her head. "They lead somewhere. They just won't open. Maybe direct routes to *Jannah* and *Jahannam*. Outside means nothing. Illusions."

Yawm al-Qiyāmah—"The Day of Resurrection." And the Muslim paradise and hell.

Maybe.

"The third rear door?"

"The Blessed Qu'ran does *not* contain all knowledge. The Prophet, may his name ever be praised, never had enough paper for that. All I know is all three doors go somewhere."

"What about the upper two floors?"

She glanced up. "Those doors go to . . . other places. The winds are odd behind them, but they still speak to me. The one Bilqis took, that goes to an oasis of strange powers and smells. I think we would be unwise to take that door."

"Where do the doors to this world go?"

"Some of them I know. The middle door on this side," she nodded to the second one she'd tried, "goes to my mountains. Not to my home, but close. What you call Tibet, maybe, or Nepal. I know those winds. I could walk to my home from there. I wish that I had found this place many years ago."

Something in her voice . . . he saw a glint on her cheek, and the breath caught in his throat. Tears. The Goddess of the Mountain Winds was crying. *Kali* was crying. Homesick. He looked away, quick before he shamed her.

This would be a good time for him to go sniffing at doors. He did so. He couldn't feel or smell anything unusual about that middle one on the righthand side. Or any of the others on the first floor, for that matter. The second floor, he caught a whiff of northern forest out of the front-most on the left side, the particular mix of fir and pine and spruce and birch and autumn ferns around a lake in Finland. A lake that he could not put a name to, nor remember visiting.

Third floor, he glanced out the front window and then stopped. Not raining. Sun shining. The store and building across the street looked neat and clean, prosperous but not new. The streetlights were gas units. Gaslights, but he saw cars parked on the street. Cars that looked modern.

Alternate world? What did that say about the doors that the winds had told her were normal? Did that door open into *her* hills?

Fourth floor, the window looked down on a meadow surrounded by forest, stream running out from under his feet and down the middle to a beaver pond and mounded brown lodge and sharp-gnawed aspen stumps. Did that version of the world even have humans in it? Or maybe lacked grabby Europeans, to come and build cities and bury trout streams deep in sewers? Or had the buildings fallen down from age or earthquake and weathered away to nothing, and the trees returned? Man had been here and left?

The door Mother . . . *Balkis* . . . had used—Mel had accepted and used that name, pronounced in the Arabic fashion—didn't tell him or his nose anything. He continued widdershins around the fourth floor. The last door on that side . . .

No, don't open it.

He glanced over the railing. The Goddess of the Mountain Winds still stared out into her memories. Not a good time for him to clatter down the stairs, bubbling over with news.

Just for kicks and killing time, he tried the rear door, the one that *should* open out over a clear drop to the alley and broken bones at best. That might actually open into Muslim paradise, or the fires of hell. The door handle wouldn't budge. He felt his way into the metal. Knob on a square shaft, passing through a square hole in a cam inside an old mortise lockset that moved the latch against a spring. Exactly like dozens of locks in his apartment building. Not truly a lock at all, just a latch.

He asked the parts to move. They said, "No."

Iron had never said "no" to him before. This wasn't a loud "NO!" with the exclamation-mark of defiance, just a quiet and almost apologetic "no."

It couldn't. He could break it, he could feel that in his hand, no problem. A lot of the parts were cast iron, brittle and old beyond old. But he couldn't move it. Breaking the lock wouldn't open that door. Something beside the latch held it closed. Mel's winds had told her true.

The moral of this story is, even gods have limits. Even Kali gets homesick.

He finished off the top gallery of doors, no further news either good or bad, and looked down into the courtyard and . . . Mel . . . was up and prowling like a caged tiger, shotgun held at the ready. No, not a tiger—a leopard, smaller and quicker and sleeker.

He was free to notice her again.

He thumped down the flights of stairs, white marble treads with green-gray veins, treads without a trace of wear in spite of the feeling they had been there since the rocks first cooled. How many feet had pounded them, without leaving a mark?

Illusions, too?

He waved around at the galleries. "Your winds give you any idea who made this?"

Head-shake. "I don't think 'made' is the right word. It just is. What we see is what we want to see. The only part that's *real* is the doorways. You probably saw what Bilqis thought she saw when she first brought you here, and now I see that, through you. Other eyes that could see it at all would see something else. Something with one way in and twenty-seven ways out, that's the only constant. If there's a Beaver God to go with the view out the top window, it probably sees a giant beaver lodge with many tunnels. Who knows?"

He stopped about halfway down the last flight of stairs and looked around, full circle, before turning back to her. "How do you find it in the first place? If you're the kind of person who can see it at all, how can you tell one doorway from another, one cave mouth from another, and know you ought to walk inside?"

Another shrug. She did that a lot. "We both were drawn here, just like we both felt the Seal and were drawn to it. That's probably why we're in this damned backwater city in the first place. The Seal is a god-magnet, pulling us closer to better suck us dry. If Bilqis isn't lying, she would have felt it more than we do. She still has more power. She still knows who and what she is."

So Mel was buying at least part of that story. With reservations and questioning the source. Wise move.

"What did your winds tell you about *that* door, the last door on the fourth gallery?" He pointed.

She cocked her head to one side, looking up. "They didn't like it. Nothing poisonous, that one shouldn't kill us unless we do something stupid, just that it's a closed space, tunnel or cave or cellar. No place for winds to play." Then she turned back to him. "Why?"

"The Seal went through there. I felt it."

He'd felt the painful and pained whine he'd left at the burned-out synagogue, faint and distant. Since he didn't know how much the Seal had weakened, he couldn't tell how far away, whether it sat behind still another gate into still another world. Or two, or five. But it had gone that way, and left its . . . scent, was the closest word he could find on such short notice. And, he'd smelled, no, *felt*, that touch of sandalwood, as well. That impossible touch, that might be the soul-trace of a dead salamander.

Did Balkis know he had touched the star and formed some kind of bond with it? And, if she knew, did she care? After all, no *sane* god would pass up the powers she offered. The name she offered. Let the damned Seal die.

He had as much power as he wanted. *More* than he wanted.

But he *would* like to remember his own name.

XII

The doorway framed . . . *nothing*.

Albert's stomach churned when he stared at it. Or *into* it. He *saw* blank gray without depth or texture, but something wired into his brain knew it wasn't a flat surface like a painted wall. It made the building spin around him. It offended his sense of where he stood in the universe. He tore his glance away and his feet settled back onto solid marble. Except he knew *that* also was illusion. He turned back to the Goddess of the Mountain Winds. Kali. Mel. *Whoever* she was.

"Why do the windows give us a view, but the doors don't?"

She sat in front of the doorway, full lotus position on the cold stone floor of the gallery, about as far back from the open door as she could get without pushing through the illusionary railing and falling the illusionary height of several illusionary floors to the illusionary courtyard, and his butt ached in sympathy. She didn't carry much padding around with her.

It made the very picture of a serene *yogini* except for the shotgun pointing into the void, balanced on her right knee with her finger inside the trigger guard. He'd heard the click when she flipped the safety off before he'd pulled the door open. Not a particularly trusting woman. But he already knew that.

"Not exactly windows," she answered. "You'll have noticed, they don't open. No hinges or latches or other hardware. And I think you would find the second floor view isn't *quite* the same as the first, if you look and compare them for long enough. I've changed my mind. I think only the first floor doors open into *our* world."

"I wonder what would happen if I tried to break the glass . . . ?"

That pulled her "meditation" away from the doorway. "I'd really rather you didn't try. What happens to the contents of an illusion when it breaks? Makes a good Zen *koan*, but I'd rather not find that *satori* through personal experience."

She focused back on the doorway. "Now, bug off. I'm trying to meditate here."

So far, her public face added up to a maze of contradictions, some more dangerous than others—a Buddhist Kali who practiced yoga with a shotgun on her lap, identified quotes from the Qur'an from memory, and tossed off slang Americanisms like "bug off" at any random moment. "Bugging off" looked like a reasonable choice. He headed down the stairs to the second floor.

That door to Finland gave him the same gray nothing. Now they'd tried one on every floor, with the same result. Apparently one of the rules of this place was, you couldn't see what waited for you beyond the gate. The homesick smell of northern forest didn't get any stronger, just like the pained and painful whine of the damaged Seal hadn't strengthened when he opened *that* door. She'd said her winds hadn't changed, either. They still felt trapped, unable to use or even sense the open door.

Just for kicks, he poked the tip of his cane into the gray and watched it vanish, inch by inch up to just short of the grip and his hand. He tapped down with it and felt ground, soft lumpy ground, underneath. Then he pulled the cane back. Got it back, all of it, with a tuft of dead pine needles stuck to the end. He hadn't been sure things could go through and then come back. He could replace the cane, but replacing a hand or foot got a little . . . complicated.

Water beaded on the surface of the steel. He sniffed. Rainwater, with the resins and aromatics of drips from pine boughs. It smelled good. He didn't ache for the place, not as if he was bonded to it, didn't think he was any kind of Finnish "god," but the memories he didn't have of it were pleasant ones. Maybe as a god of smiths, he didn't tie as tightly to any one place as she did. His realm was the forge, no matter where it sat and who pumped the bellows.

He could step through that door. He could leave this whole stupid "quest" and re-forging the damned Seal, let it die, gain his memories and the powers of a god. If Legion wanted to argue, they'd met the letter of its contract. They'd found out who'd abused the salamander, who'd *killed* the salamander, and stopped her. Albert didn't remember anything in the agreement about repairing magical artifacts. Or getting paid for that repair. And he objected to working for free . . .

But I don't like *gods.*

Mel hadn't tried the door into her hill country. She wouldn't even go back to that gallery of doors on the first floor. The ground-level door they'd tried had been across the court from hers. He could understand.

He wandered over to study the second floor window, the one that *might* look into a different version of the street he'd walked.

Details. Two rust-rimmed bullet holes punctured the "No Parking" sign beyond this one. He climbed down to the first floor and verified his memory. Three. He climbed back up the stairs again. Everything else looked the same, on a quick scan. He doubted that it held down to molecular-level detail.

The glass felt cold to his finger-tips, as glass on a rainy day should. Tapping with a knuckle gave a hollow thump, about as resonant as his ear expected from a pane of glass that size. Nothing . . . disturbing . . . like that formless gray. His cane would shatter it, no problem.

A half turn and he glanced up. She stared down at him from that upper gallery. She didn't speak, didn't nod or shake her head. Just watched.

He had a sudden flash-image of a popped balloon, a stroboscopic photo with shattered stretched rubber blasting out from the pin-point that had caused the catastrophe. What would breaking an illusion look like, if he could break it—something like that, with both of them thrown into the gray as "reality" pushed out into nothing? Or would they appear in the center of the tattoo parlor, suddenly contesting with a chair or cabinet or bit of structure for that particular volume of space-time?

Maybe not a good idea. He lowered the cane. He walked around the gallery, out of her gaze, and climbed back to the fourth floor. When he looked down again, the door to Finland, whatever alternate Finland, was closed. He hadn't closed it.

Back up the stairs, her dark eyes studied him. "I sometimes get bored with living, too. Do you know if we *can* die?"

He shook his head. "Mother told me that my brothers and sister died. I never saw them killed. Never saw a body. She's not the most reliable source."

Her eyes shifted to staring across the courtyard, but their focus seemed far beyond any wall, any illusion. "I asked you for a blade to kill a god. Not for Legion, or for any blood feud cherished and kept warm through the centuries."

She paused for a moment that ran on to a minute. Then, in a flat cold voice, "For me."

Her stare came back to him. "I don't know if I would use it. I don't know if I have the balls. But *having* a blade like that, having a *chance* of dying after all these years, that would be a comfort in the night. I don't sleep well."

Neither did he. Except when he'd worked himself to exhaustion, one of the attractions of his forge. Then he could sleep. Working metal was a drug.

Gods sleep fitfully, if at all. It's part of the job description.

She shook herself loose from the black mood. "You want to poke your cane through *this* door? I'd like to know if we'll need parachutes when we step through. A fifty-foot drop might not kill us, I've tried it once or twice, but broken bones still hurt."

So she'd been watching him for a while, over that gallery rail. Watching him, and making no move to stop him if he'd stepped through the door, if he'd tried to break the window.

He poked his cane through the . . . nothing. Wiggled it around, up and down and sideways.

"We've got a floor, feels like natural rock, rough and uneven, pretty much on a level with the gallery. Nothing within reach to either side or up or straight in. Nothing has tried to bite or grab my cane."

He tapped and tapped, could feel the hardness beneath the opening, but heard nothing. Again, he got the full cane back when he pulled on it. It felt cool when he ran his fingertips down to the brass ferule, like it would in "room-temperature" air. And dry this time.

"Your winds are sure we can breathe in there?"

"If we can't, we'll die. What's the downside in that?"

Great. Encouraging attitude there. We'd better make sure our depressive cycles stay out of sync.

Which supposes that we're stuck with each other for long enough that it matters.

She took a deep breath and scowled. "Something you'd better know. I said that my winds weren't happy in there. Trapped." Pause. "That means *I* won't be happy in there. I don't like closed spaces. Claustrophobia. Probably comes with the territory, *if* Bilqis has my territory right." Another pause. "That's why I spent so much time staring at the gate. Not meditating—*scared.* I don't *want* to go in there. To put it in crude American terms, it scares the shit out of me." She held up her left hand, keeping a white-knuckled grip on the shotgun with her right. Her fingers trembled. "You can laugh now. Kali *scared.* Go ahead."

As if he dared.

Closed spaces didn't bother him. Underground didn't bother

him. He actually felt more comfortable, protected, there, as if he had been raised in a cave. Maybe he *was* a Nibelung, after all. He thought for a moment.

"You have any rope in that pack?" He nodded toward where he'd left it propped against the gallery rail when he went back downstairs. Light rope is good for lots of things in emergencies, he kept some in *his* kit . . .

"Two hundred feet of nylon parachute cord, about an eighth of an inch, woven sheath around a core. Holds a quarter-ton, more or less. Why?"

"I'll tie one end around my waist, you hold the other, I go through the door and scout. I can hold my breath for a couple of minutes. If I haven't come back by then, pull on the rope."

She stared at him. She stared some more. A minute passed. Then, "You . . . are trusting . . . me."

With my so-called life? No. Yes. Maybe. Probably better not discuss it.

He didn't want to plunder her pack—God, whichever God, only knew what he'd find in there and whether it would bite. "Where's the rope?"

"Upper left side pocket. Under the bug net and bug repellant and toilet paper and soap bar and towelettes."

He leaned his cane against the marble railing and started to unzip the pocket cover.

"No. *Other* left. I was mapping it for reaching back over my shoulder, not for facing it."

Pack had at least five outside pockets, two on each side and one on the back face, plus a puffy top flap that probably contained another pocket. He switched side pockets and dug down through the precise inventory she'd listed. Rope. Tightly-wound hank of heavy green cord in a plastic bag to keep it from tangling with anything. The other equipment had been tied off in separate bags, as well. He remembered her kitchen, everything stowed with fanatical neatness. The spare openness of her whole apartment, just three large rooms and a bathroom, which probably tied into her fear of closed-in spaces.

If she could reach into that pocket while the pack stayed on her back, she was incredibly flexible. Probably a version of a yoga *asana*. Anyway, he stowed everything as close to exactly how he found it as possible. Same reason he'd reloaded her pistol exactly the way she carried it.

Never give offense without intending it.

He wrapped several loops of the cord around his waist, tied them off with a standing bowline, not that he could remember where he had learned the knot or its name, and handed the loose end to her. "Surely those who say, Our Lord is Allah, then they continue on the right way, they shall have no fear nor shall they grieve."

She accepted the rope with a small nod. "Not that the Surah offers any hope to either of us unbelievers . . . Surah 46, The Sandhills, verse 13. Although others are similar."

Just to muddy the theological waters further, he offered her a *namaste*, which she returned. He then drew his knife, going with the weapon he knew best, faced the gray blank entry, hoped he *was* continuing on the right way, and stepped through, leading with his blade.

He felt tingling dislocation move up his leg and arm, as if his hand and foot knew they weren't in the same world as his head. Then blackness. Warmth. Why the *hell* hadn't he asked her if she had a flashlight in her kit? An enclosed space like a cave or cellar, whatever her winds had told her, even a half-wit might anticipate it would be dark in there, even blind *drunk* he should have had more sense.

Dots sparkled before his eyes. Hazy pinpricks of orange light, like charcoal sparking in the air-blast of his forge. Only these danced up and down and sideways, rather than rising in the heat. And they didn't die away. He tried sniffing. Not smoke— fog in cave-damp air. Air, yes, seemed to be safe to breathe.

He'd had a dream or vision of this place . . .

The sparks flowed toward him, he felt their focus, angry or hungry or both, growing brighter and larger. One brushed the back of his left hand and pain flashed and he cut at it and it exploded in sparks, branching firework sparks like his hammer threw from forge-welding, and then another and another, seemed like dozens of them, looming out of the fog, clouds of mosquitoes drawn to him from the bogs and ponds of the Finnish woods, frantic for blood, and he backed away and slashed at them as they closed with him and cut more into sparking death.

And then he was back in the gallery, had stepped backwards through the door or gate or whatever without thinking, and had proved that it worked both ways. He blinked at the sudden light.

His left hand throbbed. He held it up, saw a bloody welt there. That floating glowing something had bitten out a chunk of meat. The bleeding stopped and healing started, even as he watched. It still hurt.

Like with her broken bones, being a god didn't mean you were immune to pain. He shook his hand in the air, trying to throw off the blazing hornet's-sting of it. At least he'd killed the bastard. Whatever it was.

He remembered a smell of wet ash and charred wood. He remembered where he'd seen that cave, those hungry angry sparks. The synagogue. The Seal had given him that vision when he'd held it. Connections clicked in his head.

"The Seal doesn't just suck our memories and powers. It keeps other things from coming through that gate. It stops leaks between the worlds. I wonder if Mother didn't know that, or just didn't care."

She was staring at him. Not Mother—Mel, he'd forgotten about her waiting in the gallery, her holding the other end of the rope tied around his waist in her left hand, shotgun in her right still pointed at the "door." Being scared, being focused on surviving did that sort of thing to him. One-track mind.

"They can't come through. Yet. Not until the Seal weakens more, or dies. Otherwise they would have followed me. I felt like the first meal they'd seen in centuries."

He saw her relax a shade. Not more than a shade, a hair, a pinch. He took a couple of slow deep breaths to calm himself, and sorted through the confusion in his head.

She needed a report on his scouting expedition. "We can breathe in there. It's dark. Floating sparks that bite, you saw the wound, it wasn't a burn." He held his left hand up again. "I could kill them with my knife." He paused. "I *think* I could kill them. They broke apart and vanished, anyway. Mean things. A lot of them."

Another bit sorted late out of the confusion although he'd noticed it as soon as he'd stepped into the doorway: "I felt the Seal out beyond the darkness. It's a little stronger there. That *is* the right path to reach it. I don't know how far, but that's the way to go."

He held his knife up close in front of his eyes, checking the edge after battle. Soot smeared the blade in several places. He touched it and it came off on his fingers, fine-grained and slippery, like lampblack or powdered graphite. So the sparks had something organic to them. They weren't *just* energy. But the steel told him they hadn't damaged it, whatever they were, edge still keen and temper good.

"You willing to go in there? Closed space and all?"

She thought about it. "Willing. Not happy." Her face echoed the last bit.

He pulled the knife's sheath out of its sleeve behind his back, sheathed the blade, and offered it to her, hilt first in a formal gesture, one hand over the other wrist. She started to reach for it and then stopped.

"I'd rather use the shotgun. Really."

Albert grimaced. This wasn't going to be easy.

"I'd rather you used this. It *will* work against those things. It doesn't run out of ammunition. I'm scared of you blasting away at things in the darkness with the shotgun or your pistols. Tight space. Felt like stone around me."

"Shotgun pellets, bullets, most of them will just mush against rough stone and drop," she said. "I use hollow-points in the pistols, they're more likely to blow apart in fragments than ricochet."

He shook his head. "Most and more likely aren't the kind of odds I want. And I don't want to have to stand still in a fight. I've never seen anyone check *beyond* their target in a melee . . . "

"So-called friendly fire." She took a deep breath, slung the shotgun over her shoulder, and then accepted the knife. With obvious reluctance. "What are *you* going to use?"

He untied the rope and rewound it into a tight hank, stowed it exactly as he had found it, shouldered the pack, and picked up his cane in both hands. Applied that little mental twist to unlock the blade. Drew it.

"This. I'm used to it. You'd have to learn the balance. That knife—don't try to tell me that a hill-woman doesn't know how to handle a knife."

She balanced it, palm, fingers, different grips again, tossing it from hand to hand and back. She nodded.

He remembered. *This* time. "Flashlights. But I think we should go in with them off. Makes the targets easier, bright against darkness."

Drive off those hungry sparks and *then* worry about what hid in the shadows.

XIII

Again his hand and foot knew they had moved into a different world than his head and body, and telegraphed an SOS to the rest of the nerves. Particularly those up and down his spine. He told the prickles and the instant cold sweat to go to hell, and followed his hand and blade through the gray portal and stepped to the left in the darkness, clearing the way for her to step to the right. A quick poke and ping from the barrel of his cane told him that stone lurked in the darkness over there, about another three feet. Stone over there made him happy. A reliable guard. Stone rarely stabbed you in the back.

Assuming the *things* couldn't get at him through stone, that is. He didn't know their rules. Didn't know *anything* about them except that they were dangerous, and that added to the cold sweat.

Again, the *things* floated in the darkness, unblinking dull orange fireflies. They noticed him. They flowed toward him, again, and he cut one in half with a slash from the sword-cane blade. Sparks scattered and faded into darkness. More scattered off to his right, a shadow fighting her own fight. One of the flies tried to sneak by on his left, away from the blade, a move that implied too much knowledge of tactics. He blocked it with the barrel of his cane, and *that* one exploded and faded, leaving an afterimage of rough stone and a low arched ceiling overhead.

Apparently they didn't like iron or steel. A blade wasn't necessary. Or maybe he'd twisted and folded some bane into the metal without knowing it, that part of his own soul that he donated to all his work. He'd forged the cane as a weapon, after all. Intent matters.

One came at him high, as if aiming for his throat, and he stabbed it with the point. Two more firework-flashes sputtered off to his right, also about throat-level. And then the other sparks retreated, at least a dozen, he couldn't count with them dancing around like that. He'd only killed three. Maybe another three for her.

He'd thought they'd have to kill them all. The things knew fear. They knew how to fight, where to find a weakness. That meant they had some kind of thought, some kind of sense of self. Kill a hundred mosquitoes, the others kept on coming. Kill a wolf or two, the rest of the pack would back off and think things over. They might decide to follow you through wind and snow and ice for the next week, looking for a better chance. Late in a hard winter, losing two pack members to bring down a few hundred pounds of reindeer meat started to become a decent price. The pack would survive. Wolves were smart enough to weigh that balance. Get in a bite or two on the hindquarters here, wait for the wounds to stiffen up . . .

That wasn't a good thought.

Three of them dodged forward, faster than before, flying in a staggered formation so he couldn't slash two of them at once, and still aimed at his throat. Then they jinked up, down, sideways, just out of reach of his blade. They *knew* that reach. Fencers. Feints, trying to draw him into a move they could exploit. Three others tested *her* in the darkness, not any closer, shorter blade but longer arms, equal reach. She nicked one with the point in a quick stretching slash and it trailed sparks as it fell to the floor of the cave like a wounded fighter aircraft going down in flames. A final burst of sparks and it died.

The survivors retreated again.

He heard a dull scrape to his right, her boots sliding over the rough stone, testing the footing as she moved. The sounds edged closer. Tighten up *their* position, protecting her unarmed left side, the hand that held the flashlight.

"Close one eye. I'm going to try the light, just get an idea of what we've jumped into."

Her voice sounded . . . tight. He wondered if one of the things had gotten through to bite her. They'd worked this out ahead of time, just like deciding which way each would step once through the door. As soon as they had time to breathe and quit dancing around just staying alive, she'd turn on the flashlight for a count of five, pan it from right to left, and then turn it off again, keeping one eye closed to protect night vision.

He closed his right eye, the dominant eye, the one that told him where to stab and slash. Light blazed and washed over stone, a broad beam fuzzy in the dank fog. Her police flashlight could focus tight or spread to cover a wide area, and she'd set it as broad as possible back in the gallery. Dark stone, gray, fairly smooth, rippled, a squashed tube about ten feet across that meandered away down-slope into blank gray that told him nothing. Fog. Floor and ceiling curved gently to meet walls with a tighter arc. It looked natural, no tool marks. Looked like hot stone had sagged before it froze, maybe.

Darkness. He opened his other eye, closed the dazzled one, picked out the fireflies again. They seemed to have retreated, vaguer in the fog. *Don't like light? Nocturnal or underground species?* He hadn't counted, but there seemed to be more of them. They kept an even spacing, grouped by threes, the whole mass moving like a school of fish. The threes were grouped again in threes that moved as one, and he got a sense of a still-larger grouping of nines. They moved too much for him to sort it out.

This coordination bit bothered him. It looked too much like intelligence.

Three groups of three broke from the mass and darted forward, toward her side of the tunnel, throat-high and belly-level and low. Attacking the light? Checking to see if the two of *them* could coordinate? He inched forward and stabbed across with his sword-cane, out beyond her reach, breaking two of the sparks into fragments with one thrust. They hadn't staggered in depth as well as height and width. The others froze in mid-air, she caught one and then another, lightning cuts and firework bursts, and the five survivors retreated. Fast.

He retreated, too, keeping their defense tight. The backpack bumped against the grit of the wall, cutting into his sense of where he stood. He'd never liked fighting, but liked it a lot less when he felt awkward, didn't know his balance. That pack was *heavy*. It threw him off when he tried to move fast. They'd better damn well *need* every ounce of it.

They act like they don't like light. "Turn on the flashlight again. Leave it on. They retreated when it was on."

"Yeah." Her voice growled like she forced the word past her teeth. "Light . . . *now!*"

He scrunched his right eye shut just in time. Blazing brightness, not as dazzling, his left eye hadn't recovered night-vision. But he couldn't see the things. "Aim the light toward the floor."

"Got . . . it."

Definitely gritted teeth over there. But he could pick out the orange specks against the darker tunnel now. Cave. Abandoned sewer. Whatever. The things had floated further back. No, they didn't like the flashlight beam.

"What's wrong? One of those fireflies get through to bite you?"

Another growl off toward her side, like a caged leopard. Then, harsh voice, "We've got a mile of fucking *rock* on top of us, wanting to squash down, and you . . . ask . . . what's . . . wrong."

Oh. The claustrophobia.

Only way he knew to treat *that,* was get her out of here. He checked the buzzing ache in his teeth, found the Seal's whine in front of them. Beyond the fireflies.

"We can back out, if you have to." He glanced behind them,

over his right shoulder, shadowy gray doorway in the gray stone. "The gate's still there."

Idiot thought, he wondered if she had pulled the door closed behind her as she came through. If they'd have to reach through *that* to turn the knob. The Finland door had closed itself . . .

"Where's . . . the . . . Seal?"

"Ahead. I can feel it. Not close. Closer than it was."

"Then . . . we . . . go . . . ahead."

He glanced over at her, letting the fireflies go hang for a moment. Sweat glistened on her forehead. The flashlight, now, that was steady. Just like she'd held her arm steady while he cut the cast off her wrist. Even though she hadn't trusted him.

"MOVE IT!"

He jumped, then snapped his gaze back to the fireflies, still glowing out there away from the light. "You have another flashlight in this pack?"

"WHY?" Stress apparently made her shout.

"I think we can herd those things ahead of us. Two lights, more force. Plus, I like backups. One burned-out bulb, we have a *real* problem."

"Main . . . pack . . . left . . . side."

He shed the pack, opened the flap, found another police-style metal flashlight, long and heavy, club as much as light, just like the one she held. That made sense—be able to swap parts between them if she had to. This one looked unused—the one in her hand had the black finish worn off to bare silvery metal in places, years or decades of use, a couple of fresh scrapes probably from his knocking it to the ground, back however many nights ago at the synagogue in a world beyond the gate. He pulled the spare out and closed and re-slung the pack.

"Help any if you close your eyes?"

"NOT A DAMN BIT!" Then he saw her swallow. Take a deep breath. "Sorry. I can still feel all that rock squeezing in on me, eyes closed or open."

Another thought. "You have anything in the pack we could use to mark this gate? I wouldn't be surprised if we find more of them. Or need to mark corners to find the right path back."

"Fat crayon, upper right pocket. Lumber crayon, we use them when checking ruins in disaster areas. Flood, tornado, earthquake, whatever. You leave a mark—this building has been checked, three bodies, no survivors. That sort of thing. Marks on damn near any surface, won't run in the rain."

Apparently having problems to solve helped take her mind off the space squeezing in on her. It freed up her tongue, anyway. He dumped the pack again, found the orange crayon just where she'd said, marked the door with three quick strokes for an arrow, slung the pack again and tightened the waist-belt, sticking the crayon in his right jacket pocket.

Maybe he'd just marked an illusion, and the arrow would vanish as soon as they moved out of sight. He shrugged at the thought. If so, so. You do what you can, and move on.

"So. Forward the Light Brigade?"

He could feel her glaring at him. "I don't much care for your choice of literary allusions. Go back to the Blessed Qur'an."

"What? Just because the Noble Six Hundred got slaughtered?" Hey, if it got her mad, that helped. "How about, 'Cowards die many times before their deaths. The valiant never taste of death but once.' Shakespeare work any better for you?"

He sheathed his sword in the cane, freeing his left hand for the flashlight—the cane itself was a weapon and he'd just proven that it killed "fireflies"—then switched the flashlight on, aiming it low so he could still see the fireflies. They started forward at a slow walk. The bugs matched their pace, backward. So far, so good.

"I think Hamlet's suicidal 'To be or not to be' depression fits us better. If I thought those things could actually kill me, rather than playing Prometheus on my liver . . ."

Great. The whole reason I got involved in this was that I didn't want to die just yet. Now I have to trust her *to guard my back.*

Then, a tangent thought, *Could Legion actually* kill *a god? Was that all bluff? More illusions? I've just seen how real they can be.*
Never trust a demon.

Meanwhile, literary criticism had moved them a few hundred feet down the tunnel. Lava tube. Whatever. It definitely felt like down, anyway. They walked a slow slope that varied less or greater, but always the one trend. Gravity had helped make this, whether with water or molten rock. More important, that meant they headed for some kind of exit. Water or rock, it had to flow somewhere to leave this empty space behind.

The fireflies continued their retreat from the light. They didn't make any sound. Or, none that he could hear—he had no idea what *she* got from them. Or what her winds could hear. They didn't find any branches in the tunnel, any other doors to confuse the route. No echoes from their boots thumping on the clean stone.

Just a tube burrowing through dark gray rock, wider and narrower and taller and shallower, with smooth ripples on the rough-smooth surface. The fog stayed constant, too, moist stagnant air. Now he smelled a taint of death in it, carrion, not heavy but enough to make him wish for another choice of route. He could understand why her winds weren't happy.

"This fog has to come from somewhere."

Apparently she was fighting her internal demons back. She was right—seamless stone, no cracks, no water on the "ground" under their feet. The chill air and stone wouldn't create fog without a source of vapor.

He sniffed. Just water vapor and old meat and cold damp stone tickling his nose. No sulfur, no touch of swamp or even earth. The fireflies didn't leave a trace behind them, either. He'd caught some char and bitter musty squashed-bug-smell from the ones they'd killed, but nothing since.

They weren't retreating anymore. They'd stopped and spread out in a cloud across the roof of the cave, denser, as if they'd run up against a wall. But the flashlight beams just continued on—the light picked up bones on the cave floor beneath the glowing bugs. Lots of bones.

Ivory-white bones picked clean and then gnawed, until the bottom layer looked like dust and gravel. That explained the smell of death hanging in the dead air. Horned skulls topped the freshest layer, looked like goats or sheep. Some skulls that didn't have horns.

They stopped moving down the tunnel. So did the fireflies. The orange dots packed closer together and milled about faster. They still kept the group-by-three going.

"Your winds say anything about that?"

"Which?"

"The fireflies. They won't go farther. They crowd up against the ceiling, getting away from the light, but we're at least ten feet closer than they used to let us get. Something stopped them."

Her flashlight beam panned across the floor. "Something dumped a bunch of bones. I get the feeling those weren't just bones when they arrived. Now we know what the fireflies live on when they can't eat wandering gods."

"Your winds?"

She cocked her head to one side, as if listening to voices only she could hear. Which was probably true.

"Moving air." A sigh, audible tension flowing out of her. "Something slows it down, doesn't stop it completely. Like a filter. Wouldn't be surprised if that's why we can breathe here. Slow air exchange."

Albert stared at the floating glows. "Can *we* get past it?"

"Don't know. Depends on which way those bones came, before they were bones."

He glanced behind them, sweeping his flashlight beam over the cave floor. Bare stone, not even dust. "You'd think, if they came down our way, we'd have found bits and pieces before this." Then another, closer, look at the pile of bones. "I can't see goats working their way through the doors. No thumbs."

"Maybe those goat skulls were avatars of the Great God Pan. Or goat-headed demons. With hands."

Pan didn't have a goat skull, just horns. But thanks so much for the image. "If the . . . something . . . stopped bones completely, they'd pile up against an invisible wall. They don't. They taper off, and the ones further down haven't been chewed. As if the fireflies can't go there, but anything falling off the pile can. I think I can see wool and dried meat, even."

Which could explain why some body parts lasted long enough to rot before the floating piranhas ate it to dust . . . and he was shading the truth on wool. It looked more like hair, human hair. Hanging off a half-stripped human skull.

The fireflies had oozed forward a bit while his flashlight beam scanned their back-trail. They'd kept to the far wall of the cave, though, the part where he'd been aiming before. Maybe . . .

"Can we force them to one side and slip past them? They *really* don't seem to like light."

She played her beam down and up along one side of the cave and focused it tighter with a twist of her wrist into a sharp almost-laser-beam through the fog. The fireflies flowed away from each move, hugging the shadows.

"Don't think we have much choice. Except for going back. The Seal still out in front of us?"

He checked the buzzing in his wisdom teeth. "Yes. As far as I can tell. Not any closer, yet."

She answered him by pressing her back against the right side wall of the cave, her coveralls scraping along the rough stone as she inched forward. He pointed his flashlight at her feet and followed, the backpack forcing him further out from the . . . basalt? Granite? He wasn't a geologist.

The fireflies packed tighter against the opposite side. They milled around faster. They flowed back toward the entry gate, away from their hoard of bones. And then they swarmed . . .

Fiery needles lit on his skin, his hand and face and side of his neck, any place they could reach flesh. He pushed along, slashing at them with his cane, bursting the glows into sparks, but more and more rushed at him, always in threes, replacing each kill with another trio, another trio squared, and the sparks from her slashes had just as little effect. She turned and backed over the pile of bones, inching out from the wall to leave space for him, and he felt like he was pushing into a feather bed, a wind, and the fireflies weren't at his right side anymore, and he also turned his back to the pressure of whatever blocked them and shoved stumbling backwards until he thumped down hard on his ass and the things hovered beyond his face and he sat there staring at what was left of a human hand, gnawed down to sinew and bone and still clutching the pitted remnants of a femur in a death-grip.

Literally.

The wrist bones tapered to nothing. That probably marked the farthest limit the fireflies could push into whatever was stopping them.

He looked at his own hand. Blazing pain, five bites he could see, blood flowing and then ebbing and then stopping as his god-powers started to heal him. He touched the left side of his face and then his neck and his fingers came away with fresh blood there.

They didn't seem to have gotten to his carotid.

When he ran the battle through his memory, they'd been concentrating there. They knew where humans and gods were weakest. He'd been guarding his neck and eyes and throat by instinct. To hell with low attacks, those wouldn't kill him as fast.

He looked over at her. Blood on her forehead and cheek, her throat, but it wasn't flowing. She was panting, shaking her head, staring back the way they'd come at the milling swarm of thwarted fireflies. She leaned against a door set in the center of the tunnel, steel in a steel wall.

The fireflies didn't like steel.

He looked back the way they'd come, at the cloud of frustrated fireflies pushing at . . . whatever held them away from their next meal. The hand still lay there on his side of the barrier, what was *left* of the hand, bones held together by sinew and dried flesh, on the edge of the pile of bones and bone dust. He stared at it. That person had been alive in there, fighting, screaming, bleeding, dying, grabbing the only weapon he could find. A leg bone from a previous victim. He gagged at the visions.

He poked it with the tip of his steel cane, back through the barrier, back into range of the fireflies. They swarmed, covering it, glowing brighter as they fed, chewing it into fragments of bone as he watched.

He didn't bother with the skulls—the human skull still with a hank of dark hair and dried flesh in the rictus grin of death, the goat skull with one horn gnawed down to the bony roots and the other still curling. Again, lines defining where the fireflies could reach.

XIV

He could smell animal, *goat*, in the air now, faint, not fresh, and a trace of dirt and rain and growing things—outside air. *I hope that calms her claustrophobia a bit. Either that, or she included horse-tranquilizers and a dart gun in her emergency kit. I'm not much good for dealing with heavily-armed psychos.*

She'd been hanging on the edge back there, he'd felt it. He glanced over, about to ask what her winds told her *now*, and she hushed him with a palm. She cocked her head to the door, listening. The *blank* door, no hardware on this side, just a slab of gray steel with a few streaks and patches of rust—he *hoped* it was rust—and a couple of suspicious scratches at one jamb where he'd expect to find a latch on a normal door. He glanced around. No light, except for their flashlights. No doorbell, no security peephole, no mailbox. They, whoever *they* were, didn't expect the neighbors to come calling.

Looks like the fireflies are their guard dogs. Which have to be fed now and then, to keep them in fighting trim. That explained the goats. Not fed enough, *though, have to keep the dogs hungry.*

She nodded to herself, laid her flashlight on the stone, stood, and waved him to his feet and over to the right of the door. Taking command, officer and squad, which he preferred to her either freezing up or going all bear-shirt and chomping on the edge of her shield.

Then, just like at her apartment, she laid the palm of her left hand on the door. He heard clicks and clanks beyond the steel, and the door shifted a fraction of an inch, swinging away from them. She pushed, slow, gentle, eyeing the edge, knife at the ready. Light oozed through the widening crack. No alarms, no screams of rage or terror. She pushed the door further, flooding light into the tunnel. Still no reaction from the other side.

She nodded again, picked up the flashlight, turned it off, and stowed it somewhere inside her coveralls. Produced his sheath from the same place, sheathed the knife, and handed it to him. Reached back for her shotgun, shook her head, and pulled out her .45 automatic. Eased the door wide enough for her body, and slipped through.

He tucked his knife back into his jacket—it felt more comfortable there than in her hand. Wondered whether he should switch the cane for her police pistol, wondered whether he should stow his flashlight back in the pack, ran out of hands. Just kept on with cane and flashlight. Nobody was shooting yet, and he could drop either, damned fast.

Then he followed her through the door. Bright, after the tunnel, but not eye-squinty dazzling. They'd entered a hallway, what looked like poured concrete walls and ceiling, rough and unpainted. Doors marched down one side, tan-painted steel, with small barred grills and what looked like prison hardware on the corridor side. He'd seen the inside of jails now and then.

The other side of the hallway looked more like a couple of barn stalls with plain latches on grilled doors rather than locks. That's where the smell of goat came from. His nose sorted out aromatic hay and feed and clean straw bedding, as well, and fresh water, and outside air from screened vents. Steel screens, in case the fireflies got loose. The jail-cell side didn't give any good smells, hole-in-the-floor toilets and unwashed human bodies, days or weeks old, nobody in there now.

I've never met them *and already I don't think I want to. I can understand not wanting random strangers wandering in from another world, but it sure as hell looks like they* trained *the fireflies to attack humans. Using live bait.*

He revised his opinion of the people who ran this place. Downward. His nose said the cells didn't have windows or running water or any food. Whoever ended up there—political prisoners, heretics, torture-murderers, rapists—got treated worse than sacrificial goats.

She had moved, faster than he had gotten through the door, about twenty feet down the hall, and stood like a statue next to another door, listening. Twenty feet. Two ten-foot stalls for the goats, four five-foot cells for the humans, barely enough room for cell doors. Ugly.

She waved him forward, still with a hushing finger in front of her lips. He stopped and dropped the pack with as little noise as possible and stowed the flashlight. She nodded. Pack on his back again, waist belt unbuckled in case he needed to dump it in a hurry.

He shifted the cane to his left hand and drew her pistol. She held up one finger, not her middle one so it wasn't social commentary, hooked a thumb past the next door, and shook her head. He holstered the pistol again. Apparently her winds only found one heartbeat on the other side of the door, and she didn't want any chance of him touching off a round through clumsy fumbling. Still not a lot of trust there.

We probably ought to work on signals, if we're gonna spend much time hunting as a team.

She pointed to the wall beside her, then gestured that he should go to the right immediately when she opened the door. And, left hand on the door . . .

The locks clicked and she banged the door open, no stealth this time, through the door and he followed. She had moved *fast*, fast as the wind.

A little stupid there, not adding two and two and ending up with four. Wind *goddess, moves* fast . . .

A shocked guard with a bleary wide-eyed stare sat behind a scratched metal desk, leaning back in his steel swivel chair because the muzzle of her pistol pressed into his forehead. Albert had time to take in the scene. Plain painted concrete walls with high barred windows, steel screens again, and file cabinets and a couple-three blank doors to one side and one out the front, all steel, couple of chairs, a coat rack. Magazine lying open on the desk, not dropped or flung, only visible thing inside the room beside him that might serve as food for the fireflies, looked like maybe he'd been sleeping on the job.

No TV monitors. Albert had been expecting monitors, some kind of surveillance system. Not seeing one bothered him. He glanced back at the doors they'd come through. Both had four deadbolts, keyed this side, one at top and bottom and two on the latch side. Three heavy hinges, pins welded in place so you'd need a torch to remove them. They'd designed this place so you couldn't just wander around, that was certain.

He looked back at the sole guard and saw his hand creeping down his side toward a . . .

"GUN!"

Again she blurred and he heard a muffled crunching snap and the guard's head ended up leaning to one side at an angle, her hands on chin and back of skull. Somehow, she still had the pistol in her right hand, she'd done that with the heel of her palm. The guard jerked a couple of times and settled lower in the chair. His pistol clattered to the floor.

Dead. Just like that. And he was a fellow cop, uniform, badge, patches, clean-cut cropped-blond-hair look. She let go, stepped back, and surveyed the room. She gestured Albert toward the side doors. Still silent.

He drew her pistol and this time she didn't shake her head. First door—a storage room, animal feed and bedding, his nose told him that before his eyes confirmed it. Also held steel shovels and rakes and a bin of what looked like coarse bone dust. Recycling. He bet *they* made the prisoners clean that out, sort of like digging their own graves. Second room—toilet, just flush and sink and mirror.

Third room—small office, unoccupied, metal desk and filing cabinets and a couple of the hard, uncomfortable chairs you give subordinates when you want to . . . discuss . . . their job performance.

A nameplate sat on the desk, lettered in lines and ovals and squiggles in no language he'd ever seen before. He walked back to the guard's desk and studied the magazine. More lines and ovals and squiggles. He *could* read the pictures. Porn. Bondage and torture porn, and it didn't look consensual . . . he glanced a question at her.

She nodded. "I can understand six or ten languages. Recognize about a dozen others. That isn't any of them."

Writing is an arbitrary thing. Those squiggles could still represent English or Arabic or Russian. A small battery radio sat silent on one corner of the desk. He turned it on. The knob turned counter-clockwise rather than clockwise. Knobs also represent arbitrary conventions.

"Gahn ab yhgen, rehnf ab yesten." Sounded like the tail end of a poem or chant. Then music with voices. He looked at her. She shook her head. He turned it off. Not English or Arabic or Russian or Finnish. Languages evolve and diverge on their own pace.

He caught himself staring at the corpse-guard's badge and patches, then compared them with hers. Lettering he couldn't read, but shapes the same. Colors the same. He looked up at her.

"Don't expect me to mourn. You saw what kind of place this is. He wasn't a cop, he was a death-camp guard. Some people are just too stupid to live. Going for a gun like that, he *asked* to die. Not even worth a cartridge."

Albert checked the room again, still looking for surveillance cameras. He couldn't believe they'd lock this place up as tight as they had, without monitoring it. They had radio—they had transistor technology by the size of *that* radio—they had fluorescent lights. One man on guard, alone, the scene made him twitchy.

"Can we get moving?"

"First things first. I've got an experiment to run and a body to ditch. Good thing they go together. Grab an arm."

She stowed the man's pistol back in his holster and grabbed the corpse under one armpit. Albert grabbed the other. He already knew she wasn't big on explanations. They hauled the dead guard through the cellblock, back into the tunnel. He weighed a lot, deadweight, floppy. Albert had moved bodies before. They *always* weighed more dead than alive. Always seemed to catch on the floor or doorsill or ground or whatever, as if they fought you.

Then she hauled him upright and pushed his feet against the barrier, the cushion that stopped fireflies but let persistent humans or gods shove through. You had to keep pushing, a certain amount of continuous force . . .

"Any idea what this is?"

She shook her head. "Magic. Or maybe a quantum entanglement field. In other words, damn if I know. It works."

The corpse set its feet into the bone-heap and then fell through, face first, boots and calves at the edge of the cushion but knees and everything above flopping across the bone-chip pile that the fireflies *could* reach. And they did. They swarmed. They coated the body. Flesh and hair melted away. More fireflies appeared, streaming down the tunnel, he didn't have a *clue* where they came from. The first ones crawled away, sated, too heavy to fly and their orange glow muted. They all settled. The air cleared. No new ones came.

"Thought so. Give them a big feed, you can walk right past them. That's why the goats. Don't have anybody you want dead, you can still use the gate."

So the people who ran this place, *Them*, kept their options open. At a price.

"Any idea how Mother got through?"

Mel cocked her head to one side and studied him. "Way I see it, any number of possibilities. At least two of them you won't like. First, Bilqis is Big Boss of the crew running this. Their goddess. She calls ahead and they make smooth her path. Second, she didn't come this way at all, just set up things so you'd hear and follow the Seal through that door. Brought it to this end of the tunnel and then hid it elsewhere, maybe. Anyway, a deliberate trap. She isn't a very nice woman, you know."

Albert felt gut-punched. Mel was right. He didn't like either suggestion. Problem was, either one fit the Mother he knew. Nobody else mattered quite as much as she did . . .

Or at all.

Humans called that a psychopath. Or sociopath, he guessed they had renamed the trait. The description fit a lot of gods. Part of the definition of god-ness, even.

I am God. Do what I say, or suffer. And even if you do *obey, you'll still suffer. Because you don't count. Humans are less than dust to Me.*

I don't like gods.

"Can we get out of here, now? I keep expecting the whole place to blow up on us, or the army to break through that front door with machine guns."

"Patience please, the night is long. You'll have noticed the front door is also locked on the other side. Our late host was locked in here alone to deal with anything that could get through the tunnel. Not even a coffee pot. Punishment detail. He didn't hit his alarm button. I got to him first."

Albert hadn't seen any alarm button, but she'd been on the other side of that desk. "These shall be rewarded with high places because they were patient, and shall be met therein with greetings and salutations."

"Surah 25, verse 75. Which talks about rewards after death and judgment day. Go back to Shakespeare. Or Tennyson, if you have to." She paused and stared him in the eye. "Seriously.

Stop quoting the Holy Qur'an at me. Given what you know of me and my background, it comes across as mocking." Pause. "Little man, that's mocking *me*, not Muhammad or Allah."

"Yeah, and mocking the *Goddess* gets your city melted into radioactive glass. You're a lot like Mother, that way."

Her palm exploded over his ear, he hadn't seen her move, and he fell into stars and darkness but managed to sweep her legs from under her as he fell and rolled to pin her gun hand, her right hand, and smacked her left wrist when *that* hand came up with the *other* gun, and he twisted and reached and had his knife at her throat. They froze, him half on top of her and feeling hard lumps poking him from inside her coveralls and also soft lumps and the hard curves of hipbones, she *was* a woman.

Not that it mattered.

He could push the knife down on her carotid. An eighth of an inch, more or less, and they'd both find out if gods could really die. The knives he made, a good slash and he'd cut her head right off. The knife didn't move. It had a will of its own, and he didn't force it.

She took a shallow breath, her chest moving under him. A deeper one. Her stare left his hand—what she could see of it—and the hilt of his knife and met his eyes.

"I guess Legion didn't follow us here. Either that, or that damned demon is afraid to get between us now."

Then she grunted and moved her left hand slowly, slowly, making sure he saw everything she did, and pushed his hand and the knife away from her throat. "Three times now, you'd think I'd learn. You don't *look* fast, you don't *look* dangerous . . ."

Then another pause, "I may not have a conscience or what humans use for one. No sense of right or wrong. I just am. I *do* have a code of honor, of what *I* want to be, things I don't want to have to remember, and I try to stick to it. It feeds my own ego. Part of it is, I don't burn cities. I *could*, I allow myself to *think* about it, but I don't. I only kill people who *need* killing. Because of what *they* have done, to other people."

"*Three* times?"

She squirmed a little under him, probably some of her hardware caught between soft feminine bits, difficult as he found it to think of anything about her as soft, and the concrete floor, pinching. "The synagogue, that can of cherries in your apartment, here. Three times you've got past my guard and hurt me. And every one of them my own damned fault." She squirmed again. "Now, if you aren't actually going to kill me, would you let me up? I've got the grip of a twelve-gauge pump shotgun trying to drill into my right kidney."

Trust. It all comes down to trust. She hasn't had much practice at it. I'm not too big on that, myself.

He rolled off her and sat up, still trying to shake the daze out of his head. His left ear hurt, and he wouldn't hear too good out that side for a while. Other bits ached and throbbed and burned, suggesting he'd be carrying bruises in the morning. Yeah, he'd proven yet again that concrete was hard.

Another slow learner.

If *she* wanted to kill *him*, now would be a good time. She had both guns out and handy.

She didn't do it.

They both staggered to their feet and shrugged kinks out of backs and shoulders and shook some kind of linear thought back into heads. They each checked and stowed weapons. Truce.

He didn't want to talk about what just happened. Apparently she didn't either.

He glanced at the outer door, still locked. "*Now* can we get out of here?"

"We still getting closer to that Seal?"

He checked with the ache between his ears, the one that had nothing to do with her right palm, and then consulted the buzzing whine that set his teeth on edge. "Closer, yes. But I don't like the feel of it. I think that crack has gotten longer."

She massaged her left wrist and bent that hand back and forth a few times. Wrinkled her nose.

"Did I break it again?"

"No. Just bruised, this time. It'll do."

They walked back through the cellblock and the outer office, leaving those doors open and to hell with the fireflies. She laid her palm on the outer door and listened. Shook her head. She unslung her shotgun and checked it yet again.

"Something out there, something my winds don't know. Also a couple of guards. You might want that Smith."

He drew the pistol and checked *it*, round in the chamber and safety off. She waved him to one side of the door, up against the concrete wall: looked to be a foot thick at least, would stand up to light artillery. Then she moved to the other side, tucked herself up against *that* wall with the shotgun in her right hand and braced against one hip, and reached around to do her wind-magic on the locks.

He heard the locks click. He saw her shove on the door, hard, heard it swing open and bang against a doorstop. Another click.

Black smoke and orange flame blasted through the doorway, an explosion that knocked him flat. A second followed, felt rather than heard, his ears had quit and gone on holiday, and then a third.

Black.

XV

Bitter reek of explosives, dust, burning, tortured metal—Albert's nose sorted through the smoke. *If I can smell things, that means that I'm probably still alive. Against the odds.*

He opened his eyes. That didn't help. Except . . . a faint light defined the billowing black, low against the floor, white rather than orange. Not fire. If he wanted to *stay* alive . . .

He tried breathing, nose scraping the floor. Oxygen content low, dust content high. He coughed and scuttled toward the light on hands and knees. The air got better.

He broke into light and cut left, on the general principle that he didn't want to stay in the doorway. That doorway wasn't a healthy place to be. Now he could see green. Trees, grass, shrubs. A green metal post with three scorched green metal plates welded to it, angled low-middle-high, he guessed they had held booby-trap mines triggered by the door. Unfriendly greeting.

A man in blue uniform stood beside a tripod-mounted green tube. The tube belched and farted orange fire, soundless, a stream of fire that disappeared through the hole that had been a door. White light burst back out of the smoke, trailing white smoke. Albert centered the sights of the automatic on the man and fired twice. Fired without sound, even though the gun jerked in his hand. The man clutched at his belly and fell writhing to the grass. Bad shooting, Albert had been aiming at the chest.

No bang. Okay, I'm deaf. We'll see whether that's permanent. Just keep moving. If you're moving, you're still alive.

He had the gun, damned if he knew how. Convulsive grip, probably. For that matter, he still had the cane in his other hand and Mel's pack on his back screwing up his balance. *Her* pack. Where the fuck was *she*?

Did *she* get out of that hell? She'd been shielded by the concrete, like him . . .

Two uniforms struggled, off on the other side of the belching smoke of the door. Fifteen, twenty yards, maybe. Damn near same uniforms, blue coveralls with patches, and no snowball's chance he could read patches at this distance. One had black hair, one didn't. One had a shotgun, one didn't. He aimed, but didn't dare fire.

One of the uniforms staggered and fell. The dirty one, the ragged one, the black-haired one. You couldn't have been inside that shit-storm and come out clean. He fired twice at the standing clean uniform, saw it twist away and fall. Then he ran, weaving, ducking. She'd only waved two fingers at him before the blast but he expected more damn soon. She'd rolled to her hands and knees by the time he got to her. He pulled her up by the collar of her coverall. Blood and soot and tattered cloth. She started to yell at him, he could see her lips moving, her throat moving. He pointed at his ear.

She grabbed the shotgun from the ground, spun around for a quick check, and staggered off toward the nearest clump of trees. As good a guess as any. He glanced back at the door, the belch of thick black smoke climbing into a cloudless sky. They'd come out of a concrete bunker on a hillside that led up to a wild mountain, looked volcanic and tall, with trees halfway up and then gray jumbled stone above tree-line. The door hung askew on one hinge. Side window slits also smoking. That rocket must have blown them out. Or the first series of blasts.

Shit-storm. He was repeating himself.

People could see that smoke for miles. Time to leave, but not up the hill. That had "trap" written all over it.

She had headed downslope. He wondered if she could still talk to her winds, hear her winds. Her ears must be just as shot as his. *His* just gave him a dull ringing.

Should be a perimeter fence, to keep people out as well as in. So far, everything seems focused on stopping anyone or anything coming through that tunnel without an engraved invitation. The Big Men here know where it goes, what it hides. Don't want any strangers coming out.

Anyone going in, is their own problem.

Wetness trickled warm down his nose. He swiped at it with the back of his fist, found blood. His right knee hurt. Other parts didn't report at all—no feeling in his left arm, but it still seemed to work. Still gripped the cane, anyway.

She'd reached the first trees, leaning against one with both hands, panting. He caught up with her. She looked as bad as he felt. Uniform torn and black with soot, other spots red with blood, blood on her forehead and trickling from her nose, left eye swelling shut underneath a raw red scrape. At least that wasn't her shooting eye, judging by the way he'd seen her handling guns.

She was talking again, he could see her lips move. He held his fist and the pistol up by his ear and shook his head. She nodded. Cocked her head to one side, wincing. Swiped one finger through the blood running from her nose, drew a pair of triangles interlocked on the back of her other hand. Star of David. Solomon's Seal. Looked a question at him: *Which way to the Seal?*

He shrugged. Shook his head again. He couldn't feel that bit of annoyance through the rest of the noise. Maybe later. He needed sign language.

She seemed to get the meaning, anyway. Waved downhill again, toward thicker forest. Pushed herself off the tree, swayed, and started off at a ragged trot. They needed distance.

Albert glanced back at the wrecked bunker, the sooty smoke still rising. Still no signs of other troops. Still no sign of an outside fence or wall. Maybe the Big Men—maybe Mother, he had to admit—didn't care about people on this side. But best guess was, he wouldn't be able to use this gate to get back home again.

If he could count his apartment as home. But his forge sat there, too . . .

He glanced around at the trees, trying to get some sense of place. They looked like maples and beeches and scattered hemlocks—northern hardwood forest and well grown, not cut in at least a generation. Season looked like late spring or early summer, fresh leaves but not just budding out. Downhill would be water, would probably be people. People they didn't want to meet, wouldn't be able to talk to if they *did* meet.

The bridge, by whatever metaphor, burning happily behind them.

Albert stumbled and caught himself, stumbled and fell. He couldn't keep this pace. Back upright, he saw Mel leaning against another tree, panting, now both hands and forehead holding her up. She had to slow down, too. Even if all the Hounds of Hell were after them. Which might well be true. Tracking hounds, and handlers with guns.

She forced herself upright, licked the forefinger on her left hand, the hand that wasn't gripping the shotgun, and held it up into the air. Testing wind? Or listening to winds she couldn't hear with her ears? Anyway, proving she didn't have any tribal prejudices about the left hand being unclean. Then she pointed across slope, and staggered on.

That took them into thick woods with little undergrowth where the trees interlocked against the sky, not much to hide them except the tree trunks. A heavy bed of last-year's leaves blanketed the ground. They probably shuffled and crackled enough to scare any wildlife for a mile around. His ears gave a ringing roaring in his head instead of sound. They walked a hundred yards, two hundred, more, dodging, scanning the forest around, his shoulder blades well aware that they could be the star attraction of some hunter's sights at any moment.

The ground sloped down a bit, different trees—cedars, more hemlocks, thinner scraggly maples—wetter land. Then squishy under foot, and they skirted a marsh, cattails and reeds and dead gray rotting tree snags and a few acres of open water. She stopped, dug a broken pencil and small bent notepad out of one chest pocket, a tiny hole straight through the pad. He remembered the bullet-proof vest she'd been wearing, back at her apartment. Looked like maybe it had earned its keep.

She scribbled. PACK.

He unbuckled the waist belt and shrugged out of it. Couldn't remember when he had buckled it. She rummaged around inside and came up with two fist-sized lumps wrapped in plastic and a heavy knife. He recognized *that* at least, Marine Corps "utility knife"—common name KaBar for the manufacturer. Honest steel, even if machine-made, honest grip of grooved leather rounds that wouldn't slip. You could trust that knife, much more than her stupid Isfahan show-dagger.

At least she wasn't carrying *that* on her body. He'd been expecting her to pull a kitchen sink out of an inner pocket some time.

She stabbed a narrow hole in the ground with the blade, shoved one of the plastic packages in it, squeezed the edges together. Looked around, ten feet off and slightly up the slope and to one side of their track, second hole, second package. She waved him to take the pack and head on around the marsh, bent over each surprise left for any followers, then joined him and led on.

That little bit gave his shoulder blades another reason to itch. *He* didn't keep explosives in *his* emergency bag. Just exactly how sensitive was that stuff? Well, it hadn't blown up *yet*.

The pack felt about two pounds lighter. Dense, compared to the size, probably included a fair amount of metal.

She led him around to a fair-sized stream that fed out of the marsh over an old rotting beaver dam, then moved upslope again. And stopped. She waved PACK under his nose again. He obliged. She pulled a pair of compact binoculars out this time and focused back across the open water. Steadied herself against a tree. Then settled into a squat, as if her knees gave out under her. Good idea. He settled his back against another tree and concentrated on knitting his raveled body back together. Even gods have limits.

The ground bumped under him, he looked up, and a puff of black smoke billowed up from the far side of the marsh. More black smoke, shot with orange flame, and another dull bump followed. He didn't hear anything. She focused binoculars on the scene and started cursing. At least, her body-language and jerking head said cursing. He couldn't see her lips to read a guess at what language.

She handed him the binoculars and then headed off into the woods, expecting him to stow the gear, grab the pack, sling it over his shoulders, and follow at a slow trot. Which he could muster, after that brief rest. Various parts of his body complained about the jolting, but none of them threatened to go on outright strike.

Yet.

She kept glancing around, not just looking for threats but judging terrain. At least, that's the only way he could explain the things she slowed for and studied. Then she nodded her head to herself, stopped, and waved PACK again.

Another package from the depths, a second, smaller one, and she took her police radio from his belt. Her belt. Whatever. This gear-swapping got confusing, with his head still addled from the blasts. Maybe "traumatic brain injury" applied. How many brain cells had he lost, was he losing, with blood oozing into the spaces twixt damaged synapses and axons . . .

He shook his head to snap out of it, not a good idea, as the instant stabbing headache told him.

She'd planted the third bomb by then, at the base of a rock shrouded in tree roots, gnarled roots of a gnarled father pine rising into the canopy. Attached the second package to it. Covered it all with leaves laid with precision, blending into the winter's leftover cloak. She waved him on and followed, scuffing her feet as if to make their trail even more obvious than before. No sense.

One hundred yards, two hundred yards through the forest and then she swung off to the right and curled back the same distance and he understood. He settled behind a tree trunk in a hollow where she pointed him, then watched her jog to another spot with a crossing field of fire over the boulder and tree and surprise hidden there. He couldn't see the booby-trap beyond its backing rock. He hoped *it* couldn't see *him*. That the rock wouldn't spray as much shrapnel as the bomb.

She vanished. He waited.

This was the part of her he'd guessed at before, the cold dispassionate killer like her mountain winds. Double-back ambush. He waited some more, contemplating another set of military terms that he remembered but couldn't remember remembering.

He couldn't hear them coming. Something moved on their back-trail. It resolved into a man in green camouflage fatigues, green military helmet and face shield, advancing step by step behind a dog. The dog, brown and black and heavy and low, nose to the ground, wanted to go faster than the man, tugged at the leash. Tracking was *fun*. Man was having none of it. He looked over every step before he took it. A survivor.

Then, maybe fifteen-twenty yards back, where one grenade or mortar round would *not* get all of them, two more men scuttled in a darting crouch, eyes over weapons searching front and to each side and a fourth, still a bit further back, searching behind. They all looked scared.

Albert expected that she'd wait to get the second group and maybe the trailing man with her spiffy little command-detonated mine. They could then pick off the point man themselves. He sweated a little more, wondering if she had another receiver/detonator tucked away in her backpack, maybe switched on by a random jolt in the rough life it had been living . . .

The blast bounced him from the ground, sweeping dog and man with shrapnel and raising a cloud of leaves and dust to match the black smoke. He switched his aim to the second man, aiming low—probably chest armor by this time, he'd gotten lucky back at the bunker. Go for the legs and arteries, neck or face if the helmets gave him a chance. The man dropped before he could fire. Two shots at the rear guard, who tipped sideways and fell sprawling, leg hit. Everyone down by then, but he didn't know if they'd been hit or not. Assume not.

Answer—leaves and dust flying from a stuttering burst of automatic rifle fire low on the ground, wood-chips spraying from the tree beside him, dirt thrown in his eyes. He burrowed behind the little ridge of his hollow and rolled to his left. Faint blasts thumped over his ridge, he actually *heard* them—not full-auto or even burst mode—one shotgun boom and then another and another, aimed shots. He reached a further tree, poked his head out next to the roots on the far side, ducked back and let the images form.

She was out there. In the middle of them. Shotgun aimed at something on the ground. Another boom and another, heard through thick cotton stuffed in his ears.

She moved fast. Fast as the wind. He kept stumbling over that.

He looked again. She just stood there, shotgun braced on one hip, reloading with red shells pulled from inside her carryall coverall. That told him they were all down, all dead. He stood up and checked the function of all his moving parts. No worse. Not much better, either, but no new holes. He pulled a fresh magazine out of a belt pouch and swapped it for whatever was left in the old one.

Then forward, through the reek of the plastic explosive she had used and the sweeter gunpowder smoke and the earth mould-smell of disturbed leaf litter. The trackers lay dead, both man and dog. Helmet dislodged from the man, and a shotgun blast close-range to the face added to the carnage of the mine's shrapnel. Overkill. Second man, third man, both extra shots. Fourth man, large pool of blood, Albert *had* hit the femoral, but a close-range shotgun blast had shattered the skull there, too.

Not like her, what he *imagined* of her, to waste ammo. Played hell with that cold dispassionate killer bit. He looked up at her. She pulled out the spiral notebook and scribbled in it. Shoved the page under his nose.

THEY FORCED ME TO KILL A DOG. PISSES ME OFF. Another page. 2 HITS, 40 YDS, IN COMBAT WITH A STRANGER'S PISTOL. DECENT SHOOTING.

From *her*, "decent shooting" probably rated as an Olympic gold medal.

Then she flipped the page back to PACK. He pulled it off and she stirred around inside until she came up with boxes of ammo, shotgun shells for her and 9mm for the pistol he'd used. She stowed fresh shells wherever they lived inside her coveralls while he refilled his magazine. It turned out he'd used eight rounds at one point or another, although he could only answer for six. Ammo boxes back in the pack, pack back on his back. She didn't seem to be in any hurry now.

He signed that he wanted the pad and pencil.

HOW MANY BOMBS DO YOU HAVE LEFT?

A shrug, followed by a wince. Gestures still hurt. She reached for the paper.

NONE. BUT THAT SHOULD BE THEIR LAST TRACKING TEAM. MY WINDS DON'T FIND ANY MORE.

So she could still talk to her spies. Maybe they spoke inside her head, rather than using actual sound.

He gestured at the guns lying on the forest floor, looking like guns should in order to be guns but no precise match to any he knew. Drew a question-mark in the air—should they pick up some free hardware? At least a rifle for long range?

She scribbled away, then shoved the new page at him. No. NEED TO MOVE LIGHT AND FAST. WE'VE NEVER PRACTICED WITH THEM—LIKE, WHERE'S THE SAFETY?

Yeah. He could just see fiddling around with a gun that wouldn't shoot when he wanted it, safety in the wrong place or magazine catch he couldn't find in a hurry . . .

Like that radio knob that turned in the "wrong" direction. Stick with familiar weapons and stay out of fights. If you don't get into firefights, you don't run out of ammunition.

He puzzled a bit over her rage at having to kill a dog. Afghan society, Indian subcontinent society in general, didn't value dogs that highly. They tended more toward pariahs than pets.

As far as the "last tracking team" went, he had his doubts. He kept trying to catch glimpses of the sky through the forest canopy. Didn't these people have airplanes?

Then he took a last look at the faces of the men they'd killed. She'd pretty much shattered them with the shotgun. But, brown skin. Black hair. Not European. What was left of the faces said "Indian" to him, Native American, First People, whatever.

Did the army use "Indian scouts" here, like they had in the Old West of Real America? The guards back at the bunker had been brown, too. He hadn't thought anything of it, too damn busy getting out of there, but two points define a line.

XVI

Albert wormed his way low around a rock outcrop at the forest edge, focusing Mel's binoculars on a cluster of buildings about half a mile away, down in a valley in the middle of a large clearing that looked suspiciously like a field of fire—no brush, no boulders, flat land and mowed hay without hollows and ditches that could hide a man. His first glance had bothered him—bad memories. He needed more detail. That meant a belly-crawl to a clear view.

He'd made sure that the cut-over forest brush behind him didn't contrast too much with the mud smeared on his face, that any movement wouldn't stand out against the skyline, that he was in shadow with the sun over his left shoulder so the binocular lenses wouldn't flash a heliograph to the world. He didn't swat at the mosquito whining in his ear. Just in case anyone in those guard towers happened to be looking in this precise direction at this precise time. With binoculars as good as these.

Mel lived in a different world, for sure. Her Leica binoculars exuded wealth—solid and balanced in his hands, silky-smooth focus, sharp, bright image. She might live in a monastic walkup three-room apartment in a slum rather like his, but she didn't have to scrimp pennies when it counted.

Yes, those were guard towers. With some large searchlights mounted on the catwalks outside. Four towers, steel boxes sitting atop open steel frames marking the corners of a square compact camp—two firetrap three-story wooden barracks and a third, standing apart, made of brick. One-story mess hall, judging by the garbage cans and multiple chimneys. Three two-story brick houses. A crooked rusty narrow-gauge railroad spur that ended in the camp, with three log-cars half-loaded and more logs waiting for the jaws of the loader boom. Metal-sided industrial garage with three tall overhead doors, probably for logging equipment.

And two steel passenger railroad cars with small, barred windows. Prison cars. Prison labor camp. Wooden barracks for the convicts, slightly better brick barracks for the guards, houses for the officers.

He focused back on the buildings. No windows on the first floor of any of them. Not even rifle-slits visible at this distance. Otherwise, they looked like frontier forts.

He moved his attention back to the cemetery. The *large* cemetery, lying outside the perimeter of the camp and flanking two sides of it, row upon row of markers. Row upon row of mounded grass-covered graves. Some with dark fresh dirt, not old enough for the grass to sprout.

Too damn many graves.

No wire fence, no wall. Probably no place for the prisoners to run *to,* out in the howling wilderness. If his vagrant and unpleasant memories of Siberia were true, the next humans might be fifty, a hundred miles away, in another prison camp just like this one. Run away and die. Most people preferred to live as a slave than die as a free man, no matter what the brave slogans shouted.

He lowered the binoculars, for a general scan. Movement caught his eye—a guard stepping out on the catwalk of the nearest tower. Albert froze, no motion to catch the *guard's* attention. Then he brought the binoculars back up, slow, slow, and caught the guard in their focus. He couldn't see much detail at this distance, even with ten-power lenses. Rifle, with curved magazine sticking out the bottom, looked like the ones the trackers had carried. Cloth cap rather than a helmet. Dark hair, brown skin, no way he could check out the eyes or cheekbones or nose, but the general impression was the same as those trackers. Not dark enough for African, but not European.

Vague memory told him that some of the Eastern Woodlands tribes had been doing a fair imitation of empire when the Europeans landed, back in the so-called Real World. So had the Inca and Aztec, down south. Looked like they'd grown up to true "civilization" in this parallel world.

He inched back into the cover of the rock. They needed to give the camp a wide berth. Even if they *could* talk to the people here, had a mutual language between them, they wouldn't dare. Didn't matter whether they met guards or prisoners, all the possible outcomes his brain offered ranged from bad to worse.

This place forced a decision. The Seal called to him now, he could sense its direction. It lay somewhere beyond the camp, in the general line of the railroad. The not-smell smell of sandalwood lay on a different course. Not a *huge* difference, but a bit south. The salamander, the *ghost* of the salamander maybe, didn't want him following that rail line. Didn't want him taking a direct route to the Seal.

He hadn't mentioned this to Mel. He didn't plan to. No need to add to the ton of doubt they carried. But, he had to assume that sense could be something Mother planted; it could be Legion, ditto; it could be some unknown Tertium Quid acting with some unknown third purpose.

It could be a guide or a trap or totally irrelevant.

Which side are you on?

He handed the binoculars to her, so she could see the camp for herself and draw her own conclusions about this land.

She poked another note under his nose. WHERE THE HELL ARE ALL THE PEOPLE?

Albert went back to searching the forest, bit by bit by detailed bit, from his nest underneath a thick old maple tree, hoping she did the same from her post on the other side of the trunk. If he was a god, why the fuck couldn't he see behind him? Everything about this place made him twitchy. So many things were . . . off . . . about the whole scene, including her question. Why so much empty forest? Where had those fireflies come from? What made some of the tracks they'd crossed? No animal he'd ever seen . . .

And they had people with guns chasing them.

They were still using scribbled notes, even though his hearing was getting better. Slowly, but better. He'd actually heard a crow or raven just a few miles back, croaking imprecations as it flew off when they disturbed its crow-business. Must have been *really* loud complaints.

She had backup pads and pencils in the pack, so they didn't have to swap back and forth to carry on a conversation. Albert shrugged to himself. *No people* meant *No people shooting at him.* That was great. He'd forgotten how much he hated having people shoot at him.

He still couldn't remember where and when he'd learned that basic truth. Where he'd learned the skill-set of a scout or hunted prey surviving in a hostile land. The damned Seal wasn't weakening fast enough for so many memories to come back. Yet.

He chewed on the second half of his bacon bar, deferred from "breakfast"—just a compressed brick of fat and dried meat but he preferred it to the beef bar because of the salt and smoke flavor. Which was strictly academic at this point, as they had now finished off her supply of both. She'd packed a week's food in the most compact, high-energy form she could find, meat bars and bar solid chocolate and walnut meats and such, all things that didn't need cooking, all vacuum packed and stable for long storage. That meant, a week for one person. Which looked an awful lot like three, maybe four days for two.

Tomorrow, they started hunting or started going hungry. Free choice. *What* they would hunt was a different question. They'd have to find some animal as deaf as they were, with the amount of noise they must be making, not able to hear the crack of a stick underfoot or the shuffle of dead leaves. Or something with defenses like a porcupine, that didn't damn well care. Not enough open space to see game before it heard them.

Can a god starve to death? Interesting theological debate. I've never tried. But then, I never thought I was a god before. Not sure I do now. He wiped his fingers on his pants, swatted a persistent mosquito, and picked up pad and pencil.

We're in Siberia.

He chose that as a generic big empty place with trees. And mosquitoes. Besides, the one place they *had* seen people, yesterday, looked a hell of a lot like a Soviet or Czarist labor camp. Not a death camp, not the Nazi thing, no gas chamber or crematorium, but none of the workers got paid and nobody but the bosses ate anything like decent food or enough of it and if you died, nobody important cared.

But this was good land. Not the Russian taiga, where you couldn't do anything with the miles and miles of trackless boggy bug-infested land *except* grow trees on it. Slowly. This was northern hardwood forest, decent soil at worst, and if these kinds of trees grew well on it, the climate wasn't too wet or too dry, too cold or too hot. The kind of land people grabbed, white people or brown people or black people, when they found it. And, if they could, killed off any prior inhabitants who objected.

Another one of the things he couldn't remember was that he couldn't remember how he knew all those things.

She took the pad and wrote, THEY HAVE AIRPLANES. THEY HAVE HELICOPTERS. THEY HAVE RAILROADS. WHY DON'T THEY USE THIS LAND?

They'd seen a flight of four helicopters headed in the general direction they were running *from*. None of the choppers strayed from their flight plan, none of them seemed to be searching. They'd seen jet aircraft overhead, contrails high in the daylight or blinking lights high at night. Flyover country. Nobody in any hint of a descent or takeoff pattern.

Or searching pattern. That baffled him. And her winds reported emptiness in the forest around them, just the deer and other game and predators you'd expect. And not very much of *them*. One of the odd facts he'd picked up in his centuries—a mature forest didn't support much wildlife. You got more deer, for example, in cut-over or burned-over land where the food grew within reach. In late spring or early summer, all the chestnuts and acorns and the like on the ground had been picked over. He'd found an un-chewed beechnut or two, cracked them, all empty hulls. The squirrels knew. They were professionals.

She'd finally admitted that her hearing was shot to hell, too. Admitting her injuries was . . . a weakness, he guessed, un-godlike behavior. Just admitting it took her a full day, and she'd looked ashamed when she scribbled it out in the early twilight. They'd been talking—well, scribbling—about standing guard in the night.

Another note from her. That logging camp. Doors looked like they were built to keep things out more than in. She paused and pulled her notepad back. He hoped she was paying more attention to the forest, to standing guard, than to her writing.

My winds don't recognize anything i don't know, but they see things i don't know. Same as back at the bunker. I told you they sensed something out there. It wasn't the guards and booby-traps.

Now she was admitting that she lacked omniscience. Next thing to go in the godly triumvirate would be omnipresence, he guessed. All this humility was probably good for her character, bitter as she seemed to take it. *He'd* never felt like he was all-knowing or all-powerful or everywhere, but he was a trivial god at best.

Not like Mother. She'd *never admit there was anything she didn't know, couldn't do.*

He scribbled Dragons? and passed it to her.

Once again, choosing a generic title for the whole spectrum of big unknown dangers. Maybe he should have gone with evil djinn haunting the wastelands, but she'd told him to lay off the cultural and Qur'an references. He didn't feel up to coming within an inch of killing her again. A quarter inch.

The note came back. Here be dragons? No. Dragons would leave trails. Tracks. Piles of dragon shit.

They hadn't crossed any trails or tracks larger than a large deer. Elk, maybe, or moose, cloven pointy hoof. Not reindeer, those had rounded hooves. These critters looked *heavy*, judging by tracks at one of the marshy areas, softer ground but not *that* soft. Also something like a bear, broad pads and toes with claws, weight similar to the moose by the depth of the print, but the track didn't look quite right to him.

He couldn't remember where he'd learned to read tracks, either.

She moved around the tree where he could see her, turned her back to the arc of forest *he* could watch, and scribbled some more. Conversation works better when you can see faces.

Look. Those trackers we killed? Winds say nobody followed them. Bodies just lay there. Food for ravens and crows.

That gave him second thoughts. He already knew she hadn't been telling him everything. Sometimes ignorance could indeed be bliss.

She was writing again. Apologize for not telling you. I'm used to living with humans. If I tell them everything, they go crazy.

As if he wouldn't go crazy. But if she was going to start apologizing for things, he'd have to start thinking of her as a person. Not just a royal pain in the ass. Upsetting to his worldview, that.

Those guard towers with the big searchlights. Biting things that don't like lights. Hunters who had quit chasing two murderers from another world. A song, maybe fifty years back, about a sheriff who didn't worry too much about a fugitive in the Everglades—if the mosquitoes didn't kill him, the snakes and gators would . . .

No windows on the ground floor, not even rifle slits. A lot of insects seemed to stay close to the ground.

He wrote: Fireflies?

She cocked her head to one side, thinking. She didn't wince while doing it. The bruise on her face had faded, and his own aches were settling down to a background murmur.

Maybe. Or something like them. Some reason why people don't dare live alone out here, can't hunt and fish. But if that's it, why haven't they attacked us?

He thought about the few game trails they'd crossed, the animals they hadn't seen, about the scarcity of game her winds reported. Not enough food? They have to hunt more territory, so we haven't run into them? Yet?

Or they didn't attack in masses until their scouts had time to gather a swarm together. Like in the tunnel. And then he remembered the cemetery, all out of proportion to the size of the camp that fed it. With fresh graves, judging by the heaps of dirt. At least they buried their dead, which implied they hadn't been eaten alive by the fireflies.

Disease?

She stared at his note. She stared at him. He wished she would go back to staring at the forest behind him.

Mosquitoes transmitted yellow fever, malaria. Bugs carried other nasties: dengue, sleeping sickness, dozens of diseases— hell, fleas transmitted plague.

Something transmitted by fireflies, maybe?

She stared at his added note. Stared at him. Then scribbled. I don't get sick. Do you?

That sort of implied that she bought it—plausible working

hypothesis. He tried to remember. He'd been injured more times than he could count, but sick? No. BUT THESE AREN'T OUR GERMS. DON'T KNOW IF THEY'RE OBLIGED TO RESPECT FOREIGN GODS.

Then: NO FIREFLIES IN OUR WORLD. He swatted another mosquito. They seemed to think his blood would work for breeding purposes, human or not.

What diseases did this crew carry? If the hypothetical Big Boss God had a master plan, why did He or She have to include so damn many parasites? The last creek they'd waded across had leeches, equally interested in minor-god blood.

Could tie into the apparent brown tint to the population. Wouldn't have taken much more to wipe out the first few waves of European colonies—both Jamestown and Plymouth tottered on the edge, and the Spanish focused down south where they could steal the silver and gold.

She was scribbling again. JUST KEEP MOVING.

He nodded. That had been the prescription in that old song, as well.

Addendum, from her note pad: WHICH WAY TO THE SEAL?

Decision time. Trust that buzzing annoying ache in his molars, the shortest route to the Seal, or trust the unknown source of the smell that wasn't a smell, the sandalwood?

I've always thought salamanders were like friendly unknown cats met on the street, walking up to me expecting a chin-rub and ear-scratch before we go our separate ways. I should trust one for tactical advice? Elementals aren't that smart. Am I following a salamander, or something else? To what end?

Which side are you on?

He pointed a bit south of "east" and the railroad line—the direction the sandalwood told him. The railroad would be the path of least resistance. The sort of thing Mother would set up.

That was east by Mel's compass, anyway, and it agreed with the observed data. Like, sunrise happened off in that general direction. Plus, it still led away from the bunker that had guarded against their entry. Putting more miles between his ass and the guns suited him just fine.

Any idea how far?

He glared at her. Shook his head. I've never done this before. It's getting weaker. I'm probably getting stronger. I didn't know how far away it was when we started. All I know is, we're closer today than we were yesterday.

He grunted his way to his feet, leaning on the cane. All this backcountry mileage, chancy footing and up and down and around hills, irritated his hip. As the other aches died down, that one grew and grew. Downhill actually seemed worse than climbing, a side effect of the shorter leg, and orthopedic shoes didn't soothe all the difference. Just keep moving, as long as the land didn't throw a wrench into their gears in the form of a wide river, a gorge or cliff they couldn't pass, a swamp like the one in that song.

Or even a damned ocean. He felt the Seal, but like he'd told her, he had no idea how far away. All he knew was, it was closer. Closer than an unknown distance still added up to an unknown distance. Half of infinity is still infinity.

If it faded away, if that crack broke all the way through and killed it, would he lose the tracking of it? He didn't have experience to judge, not even a guess. In theory, observer interacting with observed, as it grew weaker, he grew stronger. Maybe he'd even be able to find it if it broke. When it broke.

If he believed Mother.

Who, Mel reminded him on a regular basis, wasn't his real mother—who had been damned flexible in her interpretation of the truth in all the years he'd known Her, in other ways as well. Centuries.

But he was beginning to think "when" rather than "if," the longer this took. What the hell would he do with broken magic first dreamed up and then forged by Suleiman bin Daoud?

No illusions—I'm a smith, not a wizard. I never even knew this shit existed before last week.

He shouldered the pack with another grunt. Still heavy. Using up all her bombs and eating almost all her food hadn't lightened it that much. He wasn't carrying it out of misplaced chivalry. *She* was the deadly warrior goddess, swift as her mountain winds. He didn't want anything to slow her down if the shit hit the fan.

XVII

*S*o that's *what made those tracks.* Albert concentrated on looking *both* non-threatening and non-tasty at the same time. Maybe "dangerous enough to not be worth the trouble" was a better choice.

He studied the thing in the low, late afternoon light. Best name he could come up with on short notice was an armadillo bear. And short notice was what he had. They faced off across a small clearing in the forest. By the time they'd seen each other, they were maybe thirty feet apart. Bear-sized, large for a black bear or maybe smallish for a grizzly, bear-shaped with big teeth and long claws, but covered in dark brown scale or plate armor like an armadillo or pangolin. Armor on those was laminated bone or horn, wasn't it? Tough and resilient.

OKAY, SO THAT'S EVOLUTION'S ANSWER TO FIREFLIES.

How she could free up her attention to scrawl a note and wave it under his nose, escaped him. Maybe *she* could move as fast as her winds. He couldn't. That made him the obvious meal if the bear wanted one. Old joke—"I don't have to run faster than that bear, I just have to run faster than *you.*"

Albert had a conscientious objection to being a meal, even for a bear.

The "bear" gave them a glance, curious but not much, the attitude of something that was used to being the roughest, toughest bastard on the block and not needing to prove it to anyone. Then it went back to tearing a rotten log apart, probably looking for delicious squirmy beetle grubs and termites.

Yeah, a firefly would have a hard time finding anything to bite on that, if it curled up to protect nose and asshole and anything else soft. He thought they would have some problems getting either buckshot or pistol bullets through the armor, if they had to. Looked like a job for either an elephant gun or maybe a shaped-charge anti-tank rocket. Or, at a minimum, one of those automatic rifles they'd left lying on the forest floor. He could have figured out how the safety and magazine latch worked by now.

Never bring a knife to a gunfight.

They'd been looking for a place to camp for the night, some place more or less level and more or less clear of rocks and roots and without any big dead limbs overhead and not in any drainage path in case of the rain they hadn't had yet. Did *not* look like this was that place.

He felt the cool touch of a breeze on the back of his neck, wind changing around sunset, and the bear must have whuffed or chuffed or something because dust and splinters of dark rotten wood blew away from its nose. The bear jerked, all attention on the strangers now, as it rose up on its hind legs. Albert changed his mind. Big as a grizzly, seven feet, eight feet tall.

Okay, so we haven't either of us had a bath all week. No need to get so huffy about it.

Albert had been wondering how long Mel was going to be willing to share her small backpacking tent with his stinky carcass. Or for that matter, he with hers. Neither of them wanted to get downwind of themselves. But they probably smelled strange to an educated nose, as well as filthy. He doubted if minor gods wandered through here on any regular basis.

The bear was still staring myopically across the clearing. You could read its thoughts on that armor-plated ursine face: "What the hell are these strange human-shaped objects that don't smell like humans?"

The wind shifted again, bringing the reek of Big Mean Carnivore back across the clearing and with it an undertone of rotting wood and dirt. In the course of all that, Albert had unsheathed his sword-cane and added the knife in his left hand.

Showing *his* claws. He was pretty sure Brother Bear recognized them.

Yes, he still had her pistol hanging on his waist. No, his instincts didn't go for it. Rational thought followed reflexes, pointing to the armor and the fact that he'd already decided a 9mm pistol didn't measure up to the target. Always use enough gun . . .

Not that he thought he needed one. The average bear was a pacifist.

This bear dropped back to all fours, must have whuffed again judging by the spray of leaves under its nose, and bounced toward them a couple of feet before stopping. Albert had just labeled that as a bluff charge, now they could back away from each other and everyone could go off with honor satisfied, when he felt the distant boom of her shotgun by his side, sound still deadened by his hearing loss, and the bear's face exploded in blood.

Dammit, why the hell *did she do that?*

Two more booms, again as much felt as heard, and he saw chest armor dent and bounce back, shot deflected into the dead leaves and dirt splashing up. The bear charged their smell and sound even if it couldn't see through its ruined eyes and Albert jumped to meet it, more afraid of her and her shotgun at his back. His sword-cane stabbed like a bayonet through butter into the bear's chest. He sidestepped the front claws and let go of his cane's grip and the bear stopped in its tracks, head swinging around, bewildered.

Knife in his right hand now, Albert slashed the bear's neck and the scales parted as if nothing more than paper. Blood spurted. He stepped back, panting, shaking, with time now to be scared. The bear collapsed in slow motion, knee joints weakening and then giving out completely. Unbalanced bulk toppled the beast over on its side. It jerked, once, twice, and then more blood flooded from its mouth. Not pulsing now, just flowing.

Dead. After she'd blinded it, that was mercy.

Dammit.

Albert wiped his blade with dead leaves, hands shaking, jerked his sword-cane out of the corpse and wiped *it,* sheathed both blades.

Still shaking, still panting, he pulled out the pad of paper and pencil.

WHY???

He underlined it three times, squiggly lines because of the shakes. Then, on a separate page because it seemed to demand it: GODDAMMIT!!!

She stared at him. She started talking, jumped up the volume and shouted to the point where he could actually pick out syllables and words—they weren't English. Biting down on her words and rage, she pulled out her own pad.

ATTACKING YOU!!! With her own three heavy underlines that damn near tore the paper.

Then, also separate page, YOU ASSHOLE!!!

This from the woman who had gotten pissed off because the trackers had forced her to kill some dogs . . .

He scrawled. BLUFF CHARGE. Then: AHIMSA.

No underlines, this time. But her face blazed with anger and she balled up her fist, before appearing to think better of it. Maybe she remembered the last time.

Or maybe Buddha-nature conquered Kali-nature. Either way, a win. He slumped down to sitting on the dead leaves and forest duff, running his fingers through his hair. Combing some other dead leaves out of it. Sweat chilled on his back and under his arms and he shivered with it. Aftermath of combat. Unnecessary combat. The worst kind, as far as he was concerned, as if any kind was good.

Maybe she'd never lived in a land with bears in it. Never

learned their language, their bluffs and real threats. Never learned that they were gods, too.

More likely, she'd been afraid the bear would steal her blood vengeance. Not nearly as sweet, if your enemy dies by some other hand. Some other paw.

He looked up. She was still glaring at him, stance saying that she really, *really* wanted to kick his ass into next week. The way he felt, he'd almost welcome the chance to thump *her*.

She spun on the balls of her feet rather than her heel, always a warrior, always keeping balance, and stalked across the sunset-dappled clearing and halted, still stiff with anger, and reloaded the shotgun from whatever inner stash of ammo she carried. Then she scanned the forest around them, shotgun at rest against her hip, looking anywhere except at him. She did *not* ask for the pack and more shells. He wasn't going to dig them out, unasked.

Albert levered himself off the ground, leaning on the cane, and then limped across to the dead bear. Close up, he could verify the scales, dark brown verging on black, dull rather than glossy, with raised rib lines as if they'd grown reinforcing along the way. Where he'd slashed, it looked like they were a quarter-inch thick or more. And that was the throat, where a bear wanted flexibility. He laid his hand on fading warmth and blood between the ruined ears and muttered a few words that came to him, asking forgiveness in a language that he hadn't used in centuries. Didn't matter that *he* couldn't hear himself. The stars could.

Then, "Go well, Brother Bear."

Never give insult without intending it.

But he couldn't stay long enough for a proper wake and chanting the spirit along its journey. Gloom gathered in the clearing, full dark would come fast, and they didn't want to be out in it. They hadn't seen any fireflies since the gateway-cave, but assumed the beasts were nocturnal. They made camp each evening before sunset. Her miniature tent might not be much, but it seemed to be enough. So far.

A glow curved across the edge of his vision, zeroing in on the dead bear, and he jerked back. Firefly. That was damned fast, coming upwind on the scent of death.

Albert backed away. Another glow arrowed in, this time from *upwind,* that didn't make sense. And another. He spun around. One came straight at him, he was between it and the corpse, and it flew . . . *around* him.

Scavengers. Given the choice, they went for dead meat rather than live. Trapped in the cave and starved, they hadn't had a choice. Probably selective breeding for aggression, too.

I could hate the people who run this place. Easy. Really, really hate them.

The fireflies could communicate. A colony, spreading out to forage, call the others when you found something juicy? Like bees and the honey dance?

They came from every direction. Settling to feed in the darkening twilight, they made the corpse glow. More colors than yellow, here—red, orange, yellow-green, blue. They swarmed above it as well, dancing in the air. He picked out those groups of three again, the threes of three and the threes of threes of three, moving in unison. The mass of them made flames in the night air.

A king's funeral pyre, a burning dragon-ship.

He stared, frozen. Then moved one step, two steps, closer. Closer. They chewed the scales, edge in, as well as the wounds he'd made. They seemed to ignore him. He could pick out individuals and follow them. Each trio contained three different colors. They fed. They danced their patterns in the air. They settled to the ground. They came together. They separated and the glows faded.

They were mating.

New life out of death.

No clue how that worked, with three. Two males and a female? The other way around? Three different sexes, with the three different colors? Three different ages with different roles?

He backed away again and found a tree in the darkness. He sat, back against its strength to hold him up. He watched the fireflies and wept. More came, and more, and more, the later ones from further away, most likely. A bear corpse, a bear wake, would have to be a rare gift.

"Wheeled the battle-crane
"Over bodies of slain
"Of blood drank its fill
"Sated fight-gull's bill . . . "

Egil Skallagrímsson came to his tongue, unbidden. More followed from the sagas, the Eddas—praise for the fallen, the valor of warriors, the might of their kings and the wealth of their lands. He chanted the Old Norse of the skalds, since his own strength lay elsewhere. Albert sang his bear-kin off on the next voyage.

Whatever that was.

He watched all night, until the multi-colored "fire" faded into dawn and Brother Bear lay as a pile of bones. Nothing ate *him*.

Not even a mosquito. He shook himself and groaned to his feet using the tree behind him as brace and leaned on his cane, a cane again instead of a god-killer, and he needed it. Damned near everything ached, from his hair down to his toenails. He stared at three narrow rips across his right sleeve and on to the belly of his jacket. Claw marks. He hadn't seen them in the gathering darkness, hadn't felt the blow that caused them. Brother Bear had come that close to gutting him, even blind and dying.

The clearing waited around him in the dawn calm. Crows called in the distance, he had no idea how far, but his hearing seemed to still be getting better. He wondered how crows found any carrion to scavenge, in a land with fireflies. But crows ate damn near anything.

Across the clearing, *she* sat in lotus in front of another tree-trunk. She'd been crying too, he saw it in the streaks in the dirt on her face.

He limped over to her. She did not look up.

Instead, she held her notepad up to him.

PLEASE FORGIVE ME. I DIDN'T KNOW. I THOUGHT THE BEAR WAS GOING TO KILL YOU.

He stared down at her. This was going to get awkward. When you ask God to forgive you, He's supposed to do it. That's part of the bargain.

Depending on the exact theology involved, of course. Some gods aren't big on the forgiveness bit. They prefer wrath and eternal torture. Even for problems *they* caused in the first place.

He took the pad and wrote. YOU'LL HAVE TO FORGIVE YOURSELF. YOU CAN'T PUSH THAT JOB OFF ON SOMEONE ELSE.

He knew that one too well.

She read his note. She nodded. Head still down, she tucked the pad away and reached a hand up to him. He took it and pulled her up as she unfolded from her lotus and then steadied her as she staggered and worked her legs into a semblance of function. She'd been sitting like that all night? Penance?

Self-flagellation was simpler. They'd come across and dodged plenty of thorn-bushes if she felt the need.

She bent down, a reminder of how much taller she was than him, and kissed him on the forehead.

That scared him, probably scared him more than if she'd pulled a gun on him. He didn't remember what a kiss from Kali meant, but it couldn't be good.

But she wasn't Kali, not really. He *did* remember what the kiss of the mountain winds meant. Frostbite. Hypothermia. Death.

Kiss the ice goddess and die. Men who survived could be maimed for life, scarred cheeks and ragged ears, missing fingers, toes, even whole hands or feet.

She pulled away from him, dropped his hand, and turned to pick up her shotgun from where it lay next to the tree. Turned back and drew interlocking triangles in the air with her free hand. The Seal.

That way, he pointed, going by the sandalwood "smell" rather than the Seal's own buzz.

It felt closer, enough that he thought, he *hoped* to think, they'd reach it in another couple of days of trudging. That was going by the way the feel of its distance had changed as they walked, extrapolating. The weakening had a different feel than distance, not one he could explain even to himself, but he could tell. It almost came down to the pitch of a harp-string as the harper tightened its peg. The buzzing in Albert's teeth changed pitch as the Seal weakened, as the crack widened and lengthened across that ancient iron, he could *see* it in his mind.

Anyway, the distance they'd already covered was greater than the distance that remained. Whatever that meant. Simple distance didn't *mean* that much, to feet on the ground and headed across the grain of the land.

He knew he could be twenty feet from the Seal and not be able to touch it. That depended on what guards Mother had set on it. She wouldn't leave something important to chance. He knew her better than that.

The way led generally downward, but not continually so. First a slow slope through dense forest, then faster slope with scrub cherry, hawthorn bush with its wicked two-inch spikes, ravine and rocks and a tangle of briars—looked like raspberries but not fruit season—then slippery moss and a creek of algae-greased stones tipping underfoot, trying to spill him. Climb out again, skirt a tangle of fallen rotting tree-trunks that looked like windstorm blow-down or a giant's game of jackstraws, climb down to another wider creek with a wade and more leeches looking for lunch and another climb—they'd have an easier path if they headed just about any way but the one they followed, the one his sense of the Seal told him to follow.

That would be Mother at work. She knows where we had to come from, where we'll be trying to go. She hid the Seal wherever reaching it would be hardest. As soon as she knew Legion had dragged me into this, she grabbed the Seal and moved it and planned her new defenses and told me to leave it be. I can just see her bending over a map and drawing the straight lines she knew I'd have to take and cackling like an evil witch out of fable at the thought of us taking this route or that between the gate and the Seal.

And then offering that rail line as bait, an easier way, level and clear and headed in the right direction. If Mother offers an "easier way"—

Mel is right. "That bitch" would fit just fine.

Across another ridge, down into another ravine, larger still, he could probably call it a valley and not be wrong. He hated this uphill and downhill, it played hell with his hip, with his calf and thigh muscles. He could walk for miles in the city or on level ground, but rough land just took it right out of him. Mother knew that. He wondered what she had planned for further on, once she'd worn her victims down.

A swamp, maybe, worse than a river or lake because you can't take a boat. Assuming you could find a boat, steal a boat, in lands where no one lives. The ocean, maybe, hiding the Seal on an island far offshore in treacherous waters filled with sharks. Whatever.

I've never been worth a damn in boats. I need to set my anvil on solid ground.

She knows I can't swim.

Can Mel?

They topped another ridge, looked down through trees over a steeper slope still. One he didn't want to have to climb down. Sharp rocks and loose soil and slippery moss and a tangle of brush.

At the bottom, a river. Naturally.

Not a *big* river, as rivers go, no Lower Rhine or Mississippi, but a couple-hundred yards of flat water and serious current, he could see ripples from the rocks and gauge that from here. He saw buoys marking a channel, throwing their own wakes on the water. Which meant boats.

Of course they'd use boats. Rivers meant easier, safer access in a land where building roads was dangerous and difficult.

He looked down again, trying to sort out the bottom of the slope in his head. From this distance and angle, it looked like it dropped to bare gray rock and then steepened into dark water. They stood on the outside edge of a bend, where the current struck head-on and had eaten right down to bedrock.

No floodplain, no landing.

Choosing this route, choosing the sandalwood rather than the buzzing, led them to a dead end. He still could "smell" the sandalwood, on the far side of the water.

Which side are you on?

XVIII

T*HIS LOOKS LIKE THE BEST CHOICE WE HAVE*, Mel wrote.

Albert looked down at her "best choice." The slope of bare gray rock and tangled brush looked a little less steep than some of the routes they'd studied, steeper than others. None of it looked good to him. He wasn't a rock climber. And his hip hurt. And that river looked *cold*. It looked . . . sinister—dark gray-green with milky eddies and boils like something that flowed straight and gritty with rock-flour from a glacier, although some of that was reflecting the gray sky overhead. He was pretty sure they were about to get wet from above as well as below.

The major difference he could see, between this particular bit of canyon edge and the half mile upstream or down they'd scouted, was it had a couple of possible places to stand on the way down and a little pocket of grass and trees and dirt at the bottom reaching to the river's edge. The rest of the stone face fell straight into water and looked like it headed down from there to a considerable depth.

Mother had laid out her plans well, aiming the shortest distance between two points right over a river *gorge* rather than just a valley. Jumbled hard dark stone, basalt looked like, and tangled blow-down timber blocked them at either end of this section. Going around *that* would take them a mile or more back into the forest, rough going if possible at all, and wouldn't guarantee a better view at the end of it.

Of course, they could have followed the railroad. Which meant following Mother's script. He didn't find that attractive. It probably led to a choke-point of some kind, army garrison or whatever, and Major Trouble.

He shrugged. Mel was the mountain goddess. He had to assume that she knew climbing. He scribbled his foremost thought on his pad and poked it under her nose. I'VE TOLD YOU I CAN'T SWIM?

She responded with a visible snort.

They could actually talk, if they had to. If they shouted directly in each other's ears. Jotting notes still came out ahead. She flipped her notebook back to the all-purpose page, getting rather wrinkled and smudged by now.

PACK.

He shrugged out of it and set it in front of her. He hadn't poked around inside of it—that would be like searching her underwear drawer—and didn't know what other miracles she could draw from the depths. A helicopter? Or, both more compact and more true to her heritage, a magic carpet? But if it held infinite resources, they wouldn't have run out of food.

Rope. She pulled out the hank of parachute cord they'd already used, no new revelations. It wasn't long enough to reach the bottom of the gorge, but those knobs and ledges below them started to fit together in his mind. Drop down to *that* one, use it as an anchor to the next, then to the next.

Yes, she knew what she was doing. At least that far.

If the rope is as strong as she said it is. If it doesn't rub on a sharp outcrop and chafe through. If. If. If.

And if I trust her not to drop me headfirst on the rocks. She wants me dead. Blood pays for blood.

Insha'Allah.

Which he did *not* write down. She'd told him to lay off the cultural references.

She was scribbling. TIE ON. WALK DOWN. STOP ON <u>THAT</u> LEDGE AND UNTIE. She pointed. He nodded. I'LL KEEP TENSION

ON THE ROPE. DON'T FALL—THIS WILL HOLD YOUR WEIGHT BUT IT WON'T TAKE IMPACT LOADS.

That reassured him a hell of a lot.

He looped the rope around his chest this time, wanting the pull higher on his body, as she anchored herself to a tree with the other end of the line. He tucked his cane inside the loop to have both hands free. Then, backing up step by step, he edged out on the bare gray stone and worked downward. He *could* walk down, back down, using the brace of the rope to keep his feet off at an angle to his body. The slope started at maybe forty-five degrees, the limit of what he could walk on without the rope but it got steeper below.

I'll stand out like a cardinal in full ceremonial regalia in a whorehouse if a boat comes along the river right now.

That thought hurried him along, as well as the reminder from his hip that this wasn't any more fun than walking. Worse, even. It moved from a throbbing ache to a jab of fire each time he took his weight on that side. Something about the angles, maybe.

He reached the ledge. He knew there had to be a lot more rope left, but he assumed that she knew what she was doing. If she didn't, they were fucked anyway. He untied, trying not to think about her just pulling up the rope and walking away to leave him to starve and die of thirst in the middle of the rock face . . .

Well, I can always just step out and roll down to the bottom and splatter all over the rocks or fall in the river and drown. Faster, either way.

But she said she'd tried the falling on rocks thing, and it didn't work. Can gods drown?

She'd pulled the rope up, all right, but it was coming down again with the pack. Which kinda sorta implied that she was going to follow it.

I'm not sure that makes me feel any better. She's been acting funny today. As much as I can tell with somebody I've known for less than two weeks now.

As if time was any sort of reliable measure, with Legion buggering around in it.

He untied the pack and watched the line snaking back up across the rock face. She was coming down then, moving about three times as fast as he had across the rocky slope. He understood why she'd had him stop well short of the length of the rope. Less than half the length, to be more precise. Because she was using it doubled, slung around the tree at the top, so she could pull it down after. Clever woman.

Or maybe it's such a common move in climbing that she didn't even think about it. An automatic part of analyzing a slope, like me looking at a fire in the forge.

She was standing behind him on the small ledge with brush and one scrawny weather-beaten tree. Listening to her winds, and yelling "Down!" loud enough for him to hear and emphasizing it with a push that could have shoved him off the ledge if she'd half tried. He tucked and froze behind thin shrubbery as she sprawled flat behind the tree. Reaching out, she pulled the pack in behind her.

A boat nosed out from the bend upstream. More a barge than a boat in shape, river cargo rather than open water. Broad and flat black hull and orange deck with big white tarp-covered rectangular blocks stacked high and tight by the boom and mast. A winch at the bow, a red wheelhouse and black stack in the stern. Sooty diesel smoke billowed from the stack. The cargo was, most likely, lumber from the prison camps. He watched as the barge slewed sideways with the current against the engines, a skidding turn that carried it wide around the horseshoe bend but safely inside the buoys.

A *lot* of current. River must be pinched here, chewing on the rocky gorge. To have any control in the rudder and engines, the boat had to push faster. Albert knew *that* much about boats. Maintain steerageway. The pilot or captain must be having fun, adrenaline rush of speed and danger even in that flat-bottomed tub.

It vanished around the bend downstream a lot faster than he would have thought possible and left Albert staring at its wake foaming green over the rocks on either shore. How the hell were they going to cross that?

I can't swim. Mother knows I can't swim.

She set this up on purpose. The love-hate meter is swinging pretty strong over to hate.

At least everyone on board would have been concentrating on the river and rocks, with no time to spare on searching rock ledges for random passing gods. Mel pulled herself up by the twisted spruce, not the kind of bounce he'd expect of her, and listened to her winds again. And nodded.

He tied on to the rope again, walked down the stone face again, found another ledge much like the first. Pack down, Mel down, repeat, repeat. He landed on the small flat—almost a beach behind an eddy, scrubby shrubs and some stunted trees tangled with driftwood cast up. A couple of empty beer bottles in the river's discards, with labels he couldn't read even where they hadn't been worn away or soaked off. Looked like beer bottles, anyway.

Pack down. Mel down. She vanished behind a clump of scrub, wilderness toilet, and Albert spent his privacy emptying his own bladder off in the other direction of their tiny rock-bound world. That need had been growing more and more urgent the more he thought about crossing the river.

The other side of that boat's speed downstream is, it'd stay in sight forever *headed upstream. I hope her winds give us plenty of warning.*

Then he was done and she was done and she was burrowing in the pack again. And wrinkling her nose. He smelled it, too, a sour animal smell on the air, some critter that he didn't want to meet, judging by their run-in with the armadillo bear. It probably used this landing as a picnic spot while fishing in the river.

Good excuse to hurry. That, and the spattering of rain that had just started, cold hard drops. Mel pulled out plastic bags. She pulled out a lump of camouflage *something*, pulled an orange string, and it inflated into an air mattress. No, a float, about three feet by four, heavy airtight fabric with rope loops sewn along the edges and tie-down tabs with metal grommets, some kind of military gadget for exactly this kind of military problem—getting people and heavy gear across streams on a scouting mission.

She was stripping and he was gaping at her. Dirty torn coveralls, bloodstained yellow bulletproof vest, leotard, all her guns and knives and spare magazines of ammo, stowed in plastic bags until she was tying everything on the float in her underwear. Thin underwear, female bits visible through it.

She glared up at him. Scribbled. YOU WANT TO LIVE IN WET CLOTHING FOR A WEEK, YOUR PROBLEM.

Then she stowed her pad and pencil in with the rest. He started stripping, police gun-belt, knife, jacket, and on down to *his* underwear. All into plastic, sealed. He tied his cane down next to the pack. She kept her shotgun, tied to the float but on a leash, so to speak, so she could grab it and aim it and fire, but couldn't lose it. He didn't want to think about a firefight while swimming.

I can't swim.

But they both tied on to the float with the parachute cord—he might drown but she could recover his body. Large consolation, that.

And then, wading into water, cold water, *icy* water, he gasped at the bite of it. It grabbed them and she kicked up a froth driving them out of the eddy and into the current, aiming upstream and across. He tried to help, kicking and probably wasting half his effort, more, on splashing and spinning them in the current.

Just keep moving. If I'm moving, I haven't drowned yet.

Cold. A wave smacked him and spun them around and he spat water. He couldn't tell which riverbank was which. She kept them moving. He hoped *she* knew which way. Cold. His hands cramped on the rope edging of the float. Feet numb. Keep moving. The riverbanks were moving. Fast. Spinning. Around. Around. Seal *that* way, he felt it. Heard it.

He bumped against something. Hard. It hurt. He pried one hand loose from the float and tried to fend off. Slippery. He focused. Worn black wet knobby wood. Driftwood. Tree trunk or thick branch, with the bark long gone. In an eddy.

Water splashed in his face, Mel still kicking, head resting sideways on the float, still driving them, but slower. The cold bothered her, too, mountain goddess not immune to her own weapon. He grabbed at the wood with his numb right hand, hooked a slimy broken limb, and pulled himself up against it. Looked around. Small rough cove. Inside of the bend. Cobble beach. He dragged himself, dragged the float, dragged Mel along the log from handhold to handhold closer to the beach and out of the pull of the eddy and bumped against bottom as he tried to get footing with numb feet.

Across.

Mel kept kicking. Her eyes were closed. He grabbed at her, fumbled under her armpit and missed and probably touched anatomy he shouldn't and hauled her into the shallows. She was going to kill him anyway, didn't really matter *what* he touched. Easiest way to haul her out was to flip her over and grab her with an arm under her breasts.

Doesn't count as groping her if both of us are too numb to feel a thing.

He dragged her up the cobbles and they snagged at her panties and pulled them halfway down her thighs. He just pulled them back up again. Even though they didn't do much to hide anything now, soaked and plastered tight against her body. She struggled against his arm and he let go.

She rolled over on her hands and knees and vomited. Same smell as at the cove on the other side. Hadn't been an animal. Wasn't the effort and the river.

She looked up at him and shook her head. Tried to crawl away from the tiny blotch that was all she could haul out of her stomach. Collapsed.

Cold. He remembered—clothing on the float, clothing for both of them. He dragged it up on the stones, tore open plastic bags, hauled dry clothing out and put it on. How the hell could he put a leotard on a woman who wasn't moving? Didn't try. Same with the bulletproof vest—bullets weren't the problem here. He shoved legs and arms and torso into the coverall and zipped it up. Then wondered, brain finally coming back on line, where she was going to get the body heat to warm the coverall from inside.

Fire. She has to have some matches and fire-starters in the pack, just hasn't pulled them out because we weren't making fires. Smoke not a good idea for fugitives.

To hell with the same problem of smoke here. Burn that bridge when we come to it. Have to live that long, first.

Besides, this weather will hide smoke. Except the smell.

But it might be a good idea to get them and the gear out of sight from the river.

He lugged her and the pack and the float back into the scrubby trees until he couldn't see water. If he couldn't see it, it couldn't see him. Then, the pack. Pockets first. She'd had him dig into most of them, hadn't noticed matches. Tried the last one. Pulled out more things that weren't matches, didn't even remotely *resemble* matches. Then stared at a plastic package in his hand. Red letters wrapped in orange flame.

HEAT.

Chemical heat pack. He stirred up enough brain cells to read the label. Followed the directions. Did the same with a second pack. Read the directions again. They promised the stuff wouldn't get hot enough to burn you. Unzipped her coveralls, really rude thing to do to a woman who couldn't say yes or no, tucked the heat inside on both sides of her body—he could feel it starting to work on his hands—and zipped her back up.

Rain splatted on his face. If he wanted to *stay* dry, he'd better move his ass. Whatever the hell was wrong with the Goddess of the Mountain Winds, cold rain wouldn't help. His jacket was supposed to be waterproof. Water-repellent, really, that was the extent of the claim. He didn't trust that after the beating he'd been giving it, not even counting the bear-claw rips. He tore armholes and a neck hole in one of the plastic bags and pulled it over his head. Big, it hung down about to his knees. Instant poncho. Another one over Mel.

Tent. He needed a level place, a place with a minimum of rocks. He scouted. The best site lay on bare sandy gravel about three feet above the stream that flowed into their cove. No way he was going to set up that close to water in a rainstorm.

He found another, not even near level, not quite as wide as the tiny backpacking tent, tucked in between a tree-trunk and a rock face. Maybe eight feet above stream level at the moment. He tried to guess how much water a rock high overhead would dump on them.

The cliff looked like it would split runoff, not concentrate it. Any port in a storm. He set up the tent with one side pinched in a foot by the tree, damn good thing he'd had practice when his brain was working. Hauled Mel, hauled the float and used it to pad the worst of the lumps and bumps inside. Hauled the pack and the scattering of gear he'd pulled out of it.

Mel was mumbling something, he couldn't hear what and didn't think she was up to writing. Wasn't sure it would make sense, anyway.

What the hell was wrong with her?

Was this what he looked like, when he collapsed after a siege at the forge? He'd never had anyone with him, to tell the tale after. Not even Mother. Too personal, too vulnerable. Who could you trust with your life like that?

Wind shook the tree overhead, splattering him and the tent with icy rain blown loose. Heavy mist flowed down the side creek. Had she called this on them, to hide them from any eyes on the river? She was the Goddess of the Mountain Winds. Had that effort pushed her over the edge?

He sorted through the backpack. To hell with privacy, if she had anything in there like the heat packs that could save her life. If she *could* die.

Inventory.

Plastic sheet—good. Could be used as an improvised tarp to add dry space to the tent, or ground sheet under it. Another uniform coverall, pristine, probably keeping that clean in case she needed to impress the peasants. Spool of monofilament fishing line, thick and strong enough to land a sailfish. Or to serve as garrotes. Fishhooks and basic spinner lures. He set those to one side.

Aluminum pot, with lid. Second one nested inside of it, the lids would serve as plates or fry pans. Yes, clamp handle that fitted the lids, fitted the lips of the pots. Inside further, small camp stove a little larger than a can of beans. And matches. Finally he found her matches. In waterproof match safes.

All that padded with clean underwear. So he hadn't heard it rattling. No space wasted.

Like I said, searching through her underwear drawer.

The camp stove made sense out of the aluminum flask of white gasoline. He'd pulled that out before, digging for toilet paper. At the time, it had seemed like a damned dangerous way to start a campfire . . .

He packed everything up again before it got soaked. Tucked it inside the tent with Mel. Who had curled up into a ball and felt hot now, deadly feverish hot and running sweat, instead of clammy cold. She'd pulled out the heat packs and tossed them across the tent and left her coveralls unzipped after. Too hot to care.

If she was a human, he'd say she was sick. Damned sick. She didn't, he didn't, *get* sick.

He grabbed the heat packs and jammed them into his pockets. If she didn't want them, *he* did. He'd started shivering from the cold and wet.

And he was going to be sitting out in that, in the rain, in the damp wind by the river, fishing. Yeah, she might die without his help. She might die *with* it, just as easily. He wasn't a doctor.

Besides, she wants to kill me.

XIX

Albert woke with a jerk to pitch-black night and rain—the fishing line jerked out of his hands. At least he'd had the sense to tie it off on a springy cedar close to the water's edge, the closest thing he could find to a fishing rod.

He needed a minute to sort out where and when he was. He pulled his left arm free of the sheltering plastic bag and stared at the faint glow of his watch until his bleary eyes consented to focus. His even-more-bleary mind processed the numbers. He blinked. The numbers stayed the same. He'd slept for twelve hours. Which was just the *least* bit scary . . .

And nothing had eaten him. Or shot him, stabbed him, fanged him with poison, or arrested him. The river hadn't risen enough to drown him, either. He ran through a whole arm's-length list of calamities that *hadn't* happened.

Unusual. Suspicious behavior on the part of the universe.

He'd really, *really* needed that sleep. Even if he felt like his spine had molded itself to the tree trunk behind him in a permanent lumpy curve of aches and cramps.

He didn't hear anything sneaking up on him to change that uneaten status. He could hear the water rushing and gurgling against the rocks, the rain dripping on leaves and rattling off the plastic-bag poncho. He could hear . . .

He could *hear.* The sounds came deadened like he still had *some* cotton in his ears, but he could hear. And he didn't hear any boats chugging along out on the river, either. Even so, he checked for running lights or the stabbing glare of searchlights or even reflected glow off the clouds and fog. Nothing. Then he took a chance and flicked on the flashlight.

First check, the river hadn't risen. Second check, the creek *had*, by about six inches. Nothing drastic there. Quick look around, and no eyes of potential Albert-eaters gleamed back at him from the shadows amid the meteor-streaks of raindrops across the flashlight beam. Fog soaked up the light before it reached the other side of the river, even on his tightest beam. The fishing line gleamed its reflection across that dark fog . . .

The fishing line. He shook his own fog off and pinned the light on the cedar branch. It bent over, jerking with enough force on the monofilament that Albert had visions of a sturgeon or gar or a river catfish big enough to swallow a dog. Or a small blacksmith. Then he remembered the current. Enough weight of moving water, even a sunfish could put a respectable bend in a two-inch tree branch.

Still, a sunfish would be more food than he'd had all day. He stumbled across the rocks and roots and slippery wet moss and laid his hand on the line. No, that wasn't a sunfish. Wasn't a sturgeon, either, but he felt muscle and size on the other end. One tug, and the thin line started to bite into his fingers. He knew he wanted gloves.

He set the flashlight where its beam would cover the water downstream, and pulled them on. Hand over hand, jerking, line dashing out into the current and back toward the shore, he pulled and pulled. Then the pull eased, he'd dragged the fish out of the main stream and into the eddy, foot by foot with the line curling at his feet and threatening to tangle in roots and twigs. Fishing reels were a good thing, stow that line as you pulled it in. She hadn't packed one.

Is she still alive? I've seen too many humans that looked like that, chills and fevers and sweats and thrashing and mumbling incoherent nonsense, even if I knew what language they were mumbling. Most of them died.

Hand over hand, line jerking. He hadn't snagged an old boot or tree limb as it swept downstream. Whatever fought him was definitely alive *here,* no matter what had happened back at the camp.

She hadn't packed any medicines, either. Bandages and elastic wraps and other "first aid" supplies yes, but no antibiotics or anything beyond a small plastic bottle of aspirin. After all, gods don't get sick.

Besides, *if* she was sick, since gods don't get sick, he didn't have a clue whether it was bacteria, a virus, or some kind of parasite like malaria. He wasn't a doctor, but he knew that the treatment for one could kill you if you had the other.

He didn't know whether he could catch whatever she had. *If* she was sick, and not just crashing from pushing her powers too far. Two of them down and dying wouldn't help Legion even a little bit.

The fish jumped, a bright splash against the dark water, and dove again. It looked heavy-bodied, at least two feet long. Not an eel, he'd been hoping against an eel. Good to eat, most of them, but not as much meat as a fish and he disliked slime. Get someone else to clean it, he'd be glad to do the eating.

Steady, hand over hand, more line tangling at his feet, and he could see a dark shadow under the river surface. It could see him, probably, against his light. It jerked sideways and fought harder, thrashing the surface into froth. Strong. Heavy. Frantic. Then Albert saw another shadow in the water, larger, *much* larger, and he jerked the line and fish—*My* fish, *my* meal, you can't have it!—clear of the water to flop on the moss and rocks at the river's edge. The other fish vanished in a swirl.

Did we swim over that *thing's head? Six feet long if it was an inch, and a hunter. Long and lean like a barracuda.*

His fish flapped wildly, snapping at the air with impressive teeth. Everything in this world had teeth. Albert drew his own, the knife, and tried to figure out a way to use it. He finally planted a boot on the silver flashing tail, tightened up the line until he had slowed the head into a target, and just slashed. He barely felt the jerk as his blade took the head clean off as easy as lopping a dandelion. It *was* a good blade.

The body kept flipping, the teeth kept snapping, but they couldn't work together. They finally slowed and stopped. He pried his hook from the jaws, multiple rows of vicious backward-pointing needle teeth, and threw the head out into the darkness. He heard a double splash out there, smaller and larger, the head and whatever ate it.

Stay out of the water at night.

Hell. Stay out of the water, period.

He was left with the body, pounds and pounds of meat, dark green scales on top and silver on the bottom, dark stripes the length of the body, spiny fins. It reminded him that he didn't know this world. A pike, maybe? With those teeth? But heavier and deeper-bodied than any pike he'd ever seen, and the nose had curved down to meet the mouth. More like a bass.

Food. To hell with Carolus Linnaeus. It's food, and anything that's food attracts other feeders in this world. How long until we attract the fireflies?

He gutted it, skinned it rather than wasting time trying to scale it, cut two heavy filets of meat free of the bones and diced them small for quicker cooking and wrapped them in a plastic bag, tossing everything left over into the water. Double splashes again. He hoped that whatever lurked out there wasn't amphibious, like a crocodile. Then he washed down the moss and rocks where he'd worked, washed his knife, his hands, his boots—didn't want to leave any food-smell, blood-smell, behind.

He might revere bears, but didn't want to invite one into his camp.

Then he untangled and coiled the fishing line on a thin slat he'd cut from a driftwood plank. Set the hook in the wood, stowed it in a pocket—he might need it again. He fumbled and stumbled back through the wet shadowy brush and trees to their camp, such as it was. Faint green light glowed through the mottled camouflage of Mel's tent, a small camping nightlight he'd left on so she could tell where she was if she woke up lucid. It had been a coin-toss, risk either way—attract animals or humans, or have her panic in the night.

If she had the strength to panic.

"Hani? Hani?"

Okay, he could hear whatever she was babbling now. Which also proved that she was still alive. He hadn't decided yet whether that was a good thing. Risk either way.

"HANI?"

What or who was a Hani? That wasn't a word *or* a name he recognized. He dumped the fish chunks in the larger pot with some chopped-up cattail roots and wild onions and garlic he'd gathered and cleaned and already part-way cooked while he still had light. Fish stew. But before he started up the stove—complicated dance in the wind and rain and he'd better watch it for a while until the cooking settled down—he thought he'd better check on his patient.

Flashlight on, not shining full on the tent but bright and moving, he didn't want to startle her. At least three guns in that tent . . .

"Mel? Lieutenant? Goddess?" Cover all the bases. "It's Albert."

Silence.

It continued long enough, he was debating whether he dared open the zipper. He did *not* want to startle her. She was the kind of person who, if you startled her, you could end up hurt.

"Hani's dead." Her voice came across almost dead, itself. But at least rational.

He wrestled with the zippers, two of them, storm flap and then insect netting, and didn't get shot even though the flashlight threw his shadow ahead of him. Maybe she was waiting for a clear target, couldn't tell which way his shadow offset from his body.

She looked like hell, green wan light reflected off the camouflage tent not helping. Hair soaked with sweat and tangled. Eyes hollow over hollow cheeks. Hands almost skeletal plucking at the Mylar rescue blanket he'd spread over her, but not bothering to pull it up to cover her soaked underwear. She'd thrown off the coveralls again—too hot in the fever.

"Hani's dead."

Even so, it looked like she was home. She focused on him. She appeared to know who he was, where she was.

"Who was Hani?"

"A man. He made the Kali. Centuries ago."

Oh, *hell*. What did the kids say, these days? Been there, done that? "I quit having human lovers. They die. Every damn time, they die."

Mel shook her head. "He didn't die. I killed him. There was a woman . . . "

"Thou shalt have no other gods before me . . . " Albert couldn't help himself, the words just slipped out. Jealous gods. Everywhere, the jealous gods.

She managed enough strength for a glare, looked around as if searching for one of the guns. The shotgun lay right next to her . . .

"No. She was a slave. He beat and raped her. Strangled her as he raped her. I killed him. He'd just finished the statue. We'd—" She buried her face in her hands.

It's not as simple as it looks. It's never as simple as it looks. You'd think you'd learn that, after a few centuries.

Albert started to ask her why her winds hadn't warned her, and then didn't. People, even gods, get stupid when sex enters the picture. He knew *he* had.

And she kept the statue. She set it right in front of her Great Wheel, part of her meditations. Life is struggle, life is pain, life is illusion. Life is death. Endless. Life is a wheel, ever turning and ever coming up again to repeat. He flinched away from the image.

"I've caught a fish. I'll be cooking it with some wild vegetables. Should be done in half an hour or so. Do you think you'll be able to eat any?"

She looked up. "You haven't left. You know what I am, and you're still here. Why haven't you left?"

Good question. "Fish stew, in about half an hour. Think about it."

He zipped the screen and the storm flap closed, leaving her to whatever he was leaving her to.

Albert ducked back under the plastic sheet he'd rigged for some minimal shelter against the wind and rain. The pot felt dead cold, of course, more than twelve hours since he'd boiled the roots with salt from the pack and a few herbs he'd found along the creek. Not what he'd call an elegant stew, but hunger provides a reliable sauce.

The tiny gas stove didn't have a pump—preheat the tank enough to force gas into the burner, he'd puzzled that out by the scorching on the bottom, then shut the valve and ignite the puddle of gas around the burner stem. Open the valve again just before the flames around the burner guttered out. Do it right, you got a jet of vapor and then a roaring blue flame. Do it wrong, you got liquid gas and went through the steps again.

He did it right. He'd always been good at studying a machine and figuring out how it worked.

This time he could *hear* the roar, just inferred on the previous run. Setting the pot back on the burner took another delicate touch, really too big and heavy a pot for the small stove, but he got it balanced and solid enough. Cautious, he set a couple of rocks where they would block wind and keep the pot from tipping over if it shifted. He sat back, watched, and waited for the first wisps of steam. Once the lid was bouncing over a strong boil, he cut back the heat, another temperamental thing, until he had a decent simmer.

Hunger sauce, the steam smelled *good*. Good enough he was tempted to cut back on the cooking, take at least a sample early. But he wanted that fish to boil long enough to cook clear through—meat and anything living in it. He did *not* trust sashimi. He'd seen a short pale worm crawl out of a plate of sliced raw fish once, and had to assume this world had its own.

After all, those mosquitoes had wanted his blood. No reason to think intestinal or muscle worms wouldn't.

Cook 'em long enough, they're just added protein.

He nodded off again, twelve hours apparently hadn't been enough sleep, but he heard the tent zippers rasp and snapped awake and the pot hadn't boiled over or boiled dry or fallen off the stove and spilled. He checked his watch—more than twenty minutes into the half hour he'd said.

A flashlight beam climbed out of the tent and stood and headed off into the bushes toward the stream. He wondered where she would find anything to shit or piss after the last two days—nothing had gone in that needed to come out again. *If she was a human, she'd be dead.*

Back from the stream, stepping into the almost-light of the candle lantern hanging in his kitchen, her hair shone slicked down with fresh water. Face wet. She'd been washing up. She'd left the top of her coveralls unzipped a bit, from washing, and he could see that she'd put on both the leotard and the bulletproof vest. That probably meant she felt she was fit for duty. He assumed she'd stowed her arsenal as well.

I should have warned her about the fish. Either the one I caught, or the bigger one that wanted to eat it. Dip water out of the stream into a pot, don't splash your hands around like bait. Something might decide to take the invitation . . .

There's other things I don't think we want to talk about, just yet. Find a safe tangent to keep our tongues out of mischief.

"Helps the soup a lot, but any *particular* reason I've been hauling a pound and a half of kosher salt up hill and down dale for a week? That pack's heavy enough without it."

She blinked and stared at him, then nodded. Fast brain there, even just staggering out of a sickbed. "I don't like slugs. Plus, a complete circle of pure salt, thick enough to mound and overlapping all the way around, keeps some things out or in. It's a simple magic, no words or gestures or secret ingredients needed."

He looked around at the shadowed pattering rain, steady like it intended to settle in for days. "Wash away before you could get much done, right now. You think it would work on Legion?"

She cocked her head to one side, considering. Then she smiled, tight lips and narrowed eyes. "I'd like to *try*. Just as an experiment . . ."

He nodded. Just as an experiment. A chance to test his blades.

"Okay, I'll keep carrying it."

Steam billowed out into the damp air when he lifted the pot lid, steam fragrant with onion and fresh fish and the wild tarragon he'd found. He poked at chunks of meat and they fell apart under his spoon. Cooked through. The peeled cattail roots had softened. He set the pot off the heat and shut down the stove. Wind and rain and the rushing water of the creek filled the silence. That stove made a *lot* of noise for its size. He hadn't noticed, before.

He scooped stew into the deep pot lids and set them on rocks to cool. His stomach growled that it didn't care if the tongue got scalded.

A couple of pounds of fish, a couple of pounds of starchy roots, a quart or two of water—they vanished. He could have saved more meat, gathered more cattails, but they wouldn't have fit in the largest pot. He didn't want to keep food in the camp. It could attract Things.

She scraped the last dribbles out of her pot lid and then licked the aluminum. Then started to gather stuff for cleaning. "You cooked, I'll wash."

But she staggered when she stood up, and caught herself against a cedar trunk.

He took the pots and lids away from her. "No. Get back in the tent. I just hope that all stays inside of you."

She blinked and sagged back onto a rock. "Silly Mel, thought she couldn't get sick. You cook good. Think I'll marry you rather than kill you."

Her voice slurred as much as if she was drunk. Then she twisted herself onto hands and knees and half-crawled back to the tent. He listened to the rasp of the zippers, open and shut again, and shook his head.

I'm not sure that's an attractive choice. And I don't expect you'll remember it in the morning, anyway.

He shook his head again and went to scrub the pots in the stream. He kept his hands out of the water as much as possible, and used a shallow eddy of water rather than the main channel. Then, bit by meticulous bit, he packed the stove inside the pot inside the other pot, blew out the candle lantern, and listened to the rushing water and the rain in the darkness. He didn't hear anything else, which was just what he hoped to hear.

By the time he crawled into the low narrow tent, she seemed to be sound asleep. He left the dim nightlight glowing.

XX

Albert opened his left eye, just a slit, trying to figure out what had wakened him. Faint pre-dawn light shone through the tent, and the nightlight wasn't glowing. She must have turned it off sometime after he went to sleep, probably going out in the night to pee, and the thought startled him more awake. Apparently his sleeping brain trusted her enough that he didn't wake up for *that*.

Either that, or his subconscious wanted to die . . .

He didn't like the image either way.

Drips still tapped on the tent fabric. He couldn't tell if they meant continued rain or just the trees dumping their overnight load. He could hear the river and stream out there, water muttering around rocks and logs. A brief stir of wind whispered in the branches, and more drips showered down on the rain fly. Nothing suspicious *there*.

But something had changed and his "sentry" noticed it, that part of him that processed the world while the rest of him slept. It had poked him awake.

He lay there, both eyes open now, ears sorting through some early birdsong and the muttering river and the occasional touch of wind in the trees. And the quiet sigh of Mel's breathing behind his right ear.

Mel's warmth against his back.

That was it. He hadn't had someone snuggled up warm against his back while he slept for, well, centuries. Now that he noticed it, he welcomed that gift against the dank night chill. She hadn't packed any sleeping bags, no room in the backpack. She'd made do with a couple of those flimsy emergency blankets, aluminized plastic.

She probably hadn't even woken up to move, just tossed and turned and rolled in her sleep and found some warmth and wanted it. It's not as if the lumps under the tent made a comfortable bed—rocks and roots, and everything sloping down to the rear left corner, and he hadn't had time or daylight or energy to find a better site.

Any port in a storm. Literally.

He felt her draw a ragged breath and let it out with a sigh and *also* felt her arm move with it, draped across him, and that told him she was awake. She couldn't have done *that*, asleep, without him noticing. His "sentry" would have screamed out loud. She had to have moved slowly, gently, consciously, to avoid waking him.

Then his brain processed the faint sounds behind him, good thing his ears were still getting better, and the shudder of her breathing clicked with everything else. She was crying. Silently.

Probably remembering . . . Hani? That was his name, the artist? Or some other deep wound from the past. God, whichever god, knows I have enough of those. Some of which cut too close to this.

If I let her know I'm awake, I can think of at least twenty-five ways it will turn out bad. Including, if she's anything like a human female . . .

The last time he'd tried to comfort a crying woman, they'd ended up doing things that both of them regretted. Not at the time, not the next day, but later. In his case, forever, or so close as to not matter.

I quit looking for human lovers.

He lay there for the next eternity, concentrating on slow breathing. Only allowing himself the small movements people make in normal sleep. But his right arm was going numb and his bladder and gut kept nagging, growing more insistent by the minute. That fish stew wanted to be released back into the wild.

He stirred a bit more, just what a sleeping man would do if a rock was poking in his ribs. Which it was. She jerked her arm back and eased away from him, silent, as far as the tight width of the tent would allow. He could pretend to wake up now. And do something about his bladder.

Keeping as quiet as possible, as if he was trying to avoid waking *her*, he unzipped the bug screen and the weather flap and slipped out of the tent and zipped them up again. Out from under the rain fly, he could stand and stretch and wince. His back still ached from falling asleep against that tree.

Fog, dead calm now, dripping trees, smell of moss and forest and river, but it didn't seem to be raining anymore. He had enough pre-dawn light to pick his way across the roots and rocks and around wet dark tree trunks to the clump of bushes of the designated toilet. Something boomed wings overhead, sounded like a startled grouse, dumping a fresh shower of drips, and then rattled through the leaves to vanish in the silence. He got back to breathing again, and waited for his pulse to quit pounding in his ears. Maybe being deaf wasn't such a bad deal, after all.

If it was a grouse, it probably had teeth. And was carnivorous. This world *would* have carnivorous grouse. More likely, it had been a vulture of some kind, hoping those bodies in the tent would live up to their stink. But he wasn't inclined to take a bath in the stream or river. Not after what he'd seen trying to steal his dinner.

When he got back to the tent, she was up and out and had her shotgun stripped down and spread across a bit of plastic sheeting, drying the component parts. To hell with cleaning clothes and bodies and such. The weapon comes first. He remembered that.

He didn't remember from *where*, though.

She looked up at the sound of his feet, reached into a pocket, and tossed him one small package and then another. "Breakfast."

He caught them. Heavy. Unwrapping aluminum foil from the first one gave him a thick granola bar. The second offered a large flat chunk of bittersweet chocolate.

"Keep some snacks in the coveralls. That's your half. I get really bitchy on a long shift in the field. Keep the blood sugar up, at least the rest of the squad won't take a secret ballot on shooting me."

How would we tell "really bitchy" from the ordinary day? He ate "breakfast" and copied her, clearing and then field-stripping the pistol and drying it as best he could. He couldn't remember ever handling this particular model of pistol before, but the metal told him to click *this* and slide *that* and push *there* to tear it down.

He didn't find any visible rust. Yet. As far as he knew, she hadn't packed a cleaning kit for any of the weapons, or gun oil.

She fitted a couple of shotgun pieces together with a snick of metal. "Don't count on lunch, there ain't no more. I'd been saving it for when we got across the river, but . . . things happened."

Like, she'd collapsed.

Then, "How's the Seal doing? Still holding together?"

He consulted with the ache in his upper molars. "Weaker. We're a lot closer. General direction is upstream on the creek." Which also was the direction of the sandalwood smell that wasn't a smell. Whatever trick he'd been following, trap set by whoever, they had walked right into it. Had swum into it.

He thought about it for a moment, running memories back through his head. "I was kind of aiming for that feel, crossing the river. Tried to keep kicking in the right direction."

Another click and another and another, and she had a whole shotgun in her hands. She started pushing shells into the magazine, snap snap snap. First one in the chamber, of course.

"You should have gone on without me. Find that thing. Fix it. You've lost one day, two? Jeopardized the mission."

The mission outranks any soldier, any day. Or all of them

combined. One reason why he'd always hated armies. Not a one of them agreed with the high value he put on his own skin.

What armies? Where?

Some of them had had guns. He remembered guns, various kinds, various eras. Some had carried spears and swords and bows. He couldn't sort them out, put names and dates to them. What had he done for the armies before bronze and iron? Chipped blades and points out of flint? Carved really, *really* superior clubs out of blackthorn roots?

He shook his head. "Drop the Warrior Goddess Sacrifice bit. People matter to me. *You* matter. To me. If that Seal dies, we'll deal with it. Even frigging *Legion* hasn't ordered us to fix it."

She stared at him. She stared some more.

"Thank you."

That made him blink. "For what?"

"Pulling me out of the river. Feeding me. Pretending you were asleep." Pause. "You jerked, just a hint of it, when you woke up. But I needed to touch someone. Hold someone. A warm, living someone. It's been a long time."

The loneliness of the long-distance god. Been there, done that.

Then, in an "If you ever mention this moment of weakness, I'll kill you . . . " brisk tone, "Pack up and get moving. We can't waste time waiting for the tent to dry out."

Yeah. Packing a wet tent is so much fun. It weighs three times as much as dry, and when you next set it up all that weight has turned to slime and mildew stink.

Another memory, unbidden and without proper provenance or attribution. I wish that damned Seal would collate the archives and unlock the index as well.

He studied her—eyes still sunken, cheeks less so, hair combed and glossy rather than the dead rat's nest of yesterday. She seemed to be moving close to normal. Thinking close to normal. From what he knew of "normal" as that word applied to her.

"You well enough to hike? Climb? Looking across from the other side, this looked just as high, just as rocky."

That got him a shrug. Typical. "I can hike. I can climb. Slope's shallower on this side, inside of the bend without the river eating into it, and we have the creek to follow. Gentler climb."

Until we come to a hanging waterfall, that is, cut off by the glaciers. I've seen those in the fjords and mountain valleys . . .

He rolled up the rain fly and moved on to knocking down the tent, packing the pots, shaking out and rolling up the plastic sheets. That float of hers, the gas cartridge was used up, no more instant inflation, but it had a nozzle and valve to blow it up with good old-fashioned lungpower. Maybe she could talk her winds into doing the hard part. Anyway, he let the gas out and rolled it up and packed it, too. Might meet another river. Not that he liked the thought of swimming with this world's fishes.

And yes, when he hefted it, the pack weighed about five pounds more than when he'd last put it down. About five pounds of water weight, and they couldn't even drink it. His hip twinged at the thought of hiking and climbing. He buckled the waist-belt anyway and headed upstream along the creek, toward his sense of the broken Seal.

She'd been pacing like that caged leopard again, waiting, not trying to pretend that packing was a two-man job. Now, moving, out in the open, she kept stopping and listening. With the air dead calm, maybe her winds didn't want to talk to her? Then he heard it—a low thumping growl through the fog, a boat headed upstream against the heavy current. No reason to think they were searching, but . . .

Following the creek had brought them back into view of the main river. The sides of the ravine had narrowed to force them out into wading cold shallows—too steep and too tangled with brush for them to sneak along on either bank. He picked his way over slippery rocks, plunging into knee-deep icewater, using each bush and low-hanging branch as cover, glancing back into the fog. He could see the river. The river could see him. At least he'd had the sense to buy a gray jacket.

Never *had* liked standing out in a crowd.

Mel's uniform coverall, dusty blue, had gathered enough dirt and soot and lichen-smear to pass as camouflage. She crouched, froze, and turned into a rock on the stream bank. He ducked behind a tangle of . . . mountain laurel? Something with glossy leaves that loved the wet, anyway.

A ghostly lump nosed out of the fog, dark hull with white at its nose—bow-wave. A smaller lump stood up from the bow, in front of the mast and boom for loading. Lookout—should be concentrating on the river, watching for the next channel buoy, watching for any washed-out tree trunks or snags riding the current. Should *not* be worried about rocks and bushes on the side creek.

Albert concentrated on being a bush. Nothing more than a bush. Gods are hard to see. Everyone knows that.

The lump inched upstream, slow as a walking pace against the strong current. He could see the wheelhouse now, faint red through the fog. Nothing here but rocks and brush and trees . . .

Gronk, gronk, gronk, three blasts on the ship's airhorn, Albert's heart almost stopped as the blasts echoed back from the gorge's rocky walls. But the bulky shadow faded, easing further out into the current. They had to signal before rounding the curve in the river? Damn sure you wouldn't want to meet another ship in the middle of the channel, and radar wouldn't be worth shit in this gorge. Radio might not work, either.

Or—belt *and* suspenders. You don't take chances on that kind of thing.

The shadowy bow passed out of sight behind a tree. Each inch of the hull passed out of sight, taking a minute for each foot. The wheelhouse grew faint as the ship eased over to the far side of the channel, must be some rocks that forced them out into the fiercest current.

The wheelhouse vanished. Albert straightened up and dared to breathe. *Gronk, gronk, gronk,* three more blasts, fainter, echoing again, signal for the next curve. All in a day's work for the pilot and helmsman.

Had the boat signaled like that, the other day? Headed downstream? He'd thought he heard crows, deafness wearing off.

The Buddha tells us to live here now. The past and future are Maya, illusion. Be here now.

Here and now, Albert's feet were freezing. So much for the battle to keep clothes dry. He climbed over the next rock, and the next. His hip complained. A bend in the creek put the river behind them, out of view. The ravine widened a bit, and he could pick his way through shallows along the bank. He looked back. She splashed through the same holes, over the same rocks, teeth gritted and shotgun held in her right hand as she braced or grabbed branches with her left. She seemed to be moving okay. Gods heal fast.

Deep pools, mossy boulders, cold water, laurel and cedar along the banks and overhanging the eddies—this creek should hold trout. If this world had trout. He picked out and cut a maple sapling flush to the ground and smeared mud over the stump it left. He stripped and tucked the branches deep into laurel tangles, shadows where even wilting leaves could hide.

No reason to leave a clear trail behind them.

Then he cut a spear from it, about seven feet long, splitting the end for a couple of feet and barbing the insides of the split and spreading that point into a narrow fork with a thin shaving to hold the springy jaws open. A fish-sized fork. He'd seen this used, Inuit or Native Americans, couldn't remember where . . .

Shadows darted in the water, disturbed by feet in the current. They *looked* like trout, too bright for browns, maybe speckled or rainbow. Lunch. No way to fry them, no cooking oil or butter, but even poached trout were good. Should be more wild garlic and onions around, and herbs.

I used to know someone who lived to fish. Any fish, but obsessed with trout. Had dozens of ways to catch and cook and present it, pulled from cultures throughout the world. He'd love this place. Not a friend, not an enemy, someone strange. Beyond strange.

Where and when and who?

Water splashed behind him, and he turned. It hadn't been a fish jumping. She'd fallen. She struggled to pull herself up—not a hole or drop-off, she'd just slipped. She still held the shotgun out of the water, keeping it dry. Protect the weapon that protects *you.*

She was *not* moving well. She put a good face on it, but her rueful grin looked more like a grimace. How hard could she push, recovering?

He waded back to her, careful of his own footing on the slippery rocks and strong icy current, and offered her a hand to pull her up on the bank. What was worse, she took it. That told him things.

He turned and found a trail on the bank. No one used it much, no one had used it recently, he could just trace it out under the leaves of last fall. Still, someone had tended it, someone had cut saplings flush with the ground long enough ago that the sawed cuts had weathered gray to blend in with the dirt and moss. Old saw-cuts, also dark with age, had cleared branches that crossed the trail, up far above his head. Granted, he was short, but whoever had cleared this wanted room.

And the whoever liked a neat path, everything tidy, flush cuts, no scars of a careless saw or axe. Tended.

She pushed away from leaning on him and nodded thanks. She'd seen it, too. A path meant people, and people meant no talk, or whispers.

They followed the path upstream, and she nodded again as he pointed out spurs leading to open rocks here and there, to ledges, to spaces with a clear line upstream or down over pools and eddies in the stream. Something caught his eye, a red spot on a twig, and he stared at it, moving closer when it didn't stir to flee or try to bite him.

A tiny hook had snagged there, feathered, crimson silk body and dark fuzz at each end, white wings, tail. He plucked it from the twig and felt the metal. Not old. No rust. A thread of leader still clung to the eye of the hook with a tiny fancy knot. That "fly" hadn't spent the winter hanging in the shrub.

He laid it in the palm of his hand and held it out to her. Low voice, "Fishing. For fun, not to survive. You'd set fish-traps if you *needed* the food."

She nodded. "Someone lives out here."

He checked with the ache in his teeth, judging direction, then consulted the sandalwood. "We're getting closer. Need to go uphill now, that ridge." He pointed, this side of the creek. "You able to climb?"

Another telling sign, she didn't snap an answer. Then, "I think so. That's not too high. Winds say, five hundred feet or so."

He followed the trail, the path of least effort, and another trail led off it, upward. This looked like it had more use—dead leaves and twigs cleared from a gravel surface. Tree roots and rocks made steps, not sized for him, so he'd climbed for maybe fifty, sixty feet before they clicked in his head. He stopped and waited until she caught up within whisper range.

He pointed at a slab of rock angling across the path, big rock, looked totally natural, but . . . "Rain diverter. Channels runoff out of the trail, prevents erosion. Someone put a lot of work into this. Over a long time. Centuries."

She nodded, no answer. Catching her breath.

Upward, a steep climb, he kept stopping at shorter and shorter intervals, waiting for her. And cooling the fire in his abused hip. Every time he stopped, he saw rocks placed for steps, roots gnarled across the path as steps, swaths of packed river-washed round stones for drainage.

All of this was fitted for someone who took larger steps than either of them needed or wanted on this slope. With that clue, he saw worn spots on the bark of trees, stone outcrops bare of moss, places where a hand might fall. If the person carrying that hand stood four feet, five feet taller than he did.

She caught up with him, panting with the climb. No, *not* recovered. But she gritted her teeth and waved off his gesture at a seat-sized rock waiting by the side of the trail, with a scenic overlook into the fog-shrouded valley of the creek below. Trees framed Chinese watercolor serene beauty, layered greens and grays with shining laurel leaves in the foreground and pointed cedars fading to nothing in the depths. The fog seemed to be thinning as they climbed, with a hint of where, beyond all that murk, a sun might actually be offering light and warmth. He could use some of each, thank you. If he was still wet, still chilled, what about her?

He pointed at the seat again, worried.

"No. If I sit down, I won't get up. Not without a nap and some food."

He handed her the spear, now a walking-stick, not much chance of collecting trout up here. She slung the shotgun over her shoulder and took the stick. More signs and portents.

"You going to be able to keep going?"

"Winds say, not much further."

He grunted and climbed again, his slow steps paced as much to ease his own hip as to allow her to keep up. The fog thinned. Sunbeams struck down through it, shafts of steam against the shadows. Another ten feet up, another twenty, and the trail leveled in front of him, a grove of spruce and pine framing a tunnel around the view ahead.

It opened on blue sky. They'd reached the crest, and looked out over whatever came next.

A blanket of fog spread out beneath his feet when he reached the end of the tunnel. Across it, another ridge humped dark fir green against the sun, with gray stone rising above it to a double summit, rounded bald stone hills, with one face sheared off by some glacier long gone and thawed.

She'd come up behind him and stood leaning on his fish spear. He pointed out across the valley, across the fog.

"I know that hill. I've been here. Long ago."

XXI

The fog chilled him again as soon as they started down. Wet dark trees, all dense tangled spruce and fir and threatening shadows, canceled any joy and warmth they'd grabbed from their brief glimpse of sun. Crossing the ridge had been like changing worlds, from welcoming hardwoods to a barrier that wanted to keep them out. They *had* to follow the path, much as that made Albert's back itch with the sense of crosshairs. He didn't trust *any* forced move, particularly one forced by Mother. Was her offer of the "easier" railroad route a pawn sacrifice, masking her real trap? A chess game played in blood?

That brief glance of sun told him they'd gone from a south slope to a north-facing land that felt and gave little warmth. And downhill *hurt*. Albert leaned on his cane as a cane now, more important than the blade inside, avoiding as much weight as possible on the fire waking in his hip.

Schwarzwald, he thought. *Black Forest. I've been here before. Even the word in German clicks some locks open. Are we climbing down to the Rhine? Did we swim across the Neckar?*

Whatever "Rhine" or "Neckar" meant, in another world.

"Hold up a minute." She leaned on the spear, catching her breath again. A sorry picture, both of them.

"This trail. Are we walking into a trap?"

He thought about it. "Well, yes . . . we're going wherever Mother hid the Seal. That *has* to be a trap. The path seems to be going toward that damned headache." Another pause for thinking—thinking took too damn long when he was hurting and tired and hungry. "You have enough energy left to go *off* the trail? Cut straight through *that?*"

He waved his free hand at the tangled forest around them—green-black prickle-needle spruce with interlaced low dead branches weaving into a wicker wall, glacier-tumbled mossy rocks, and low-growing briars and shrubs wherever a shaft of light could poke through the thick dark canopy. He could see thirty, forty feet into it, either side sloping sharply up or down. The trail cut across the slope, with switchbacks and stairways—stairways meant for longer legs than his. Each jolt down sent shooting pain from heel to shoulder, but whoever had laid it out, took the easiest way. Any other route involved a scramble. Neither of them was up to scrambling, now or in the foreseeable future.

She was studying him. "You're awfully calm about this. Just put your head down and keep going, that's all? No matter what?"

"That's the kind of person I am. Tortoise. You find a tortoise crossing a road and want to help it, keep it from getting splattered by the next truck roaring along at highway speed uncaring, make damn sure you know which way it was heading before you do anything. If you pick it up and put it down on the wrong side of the road, it'll just start out across the pavement again. Slow and steady, but it knows where it wants to be. Just like Aesop's story. I'm not fast or flashy, but I finish my job. I'm not smart enough to quit."

"Even when going straight ahead shoves your head into a noose?"

He thought about it with his slow tired brain again. "You want a military genius, you're looking at the wrong man. I'm a smith. I know fire and iron, hammer and anvil. I make weapons. I'm no expert on using them." Then, after a pause, "You want to turn around?"

Mel shook her head. "Not flashy, no, but you're fast enough to beat *me*. Three times. Good enough with that knife to cut a bear's throat and survive. I want to see how you'll handle whatever surprise Bilqis has waiting for us."

I wish she hadn't reminded me of that bear.

The way Mother set this up, this forest I half remember, there are other things in the world that I'd rather not have to kill. She's probably counting on that.

"I don't want a fight. Neither of us is in any shape for one. Please don't shoot first."

Mother, Balkis, she's not like me or Mel. She doesn't face her enemies head on, on an open battlefield. She's no warrior goddess. She'd never set up a fight she didn't know she'd win. She'll have a trick, a trap . . .

But she may not have laid that trap with Mel in mind. Not in her first planning. Later, yes, but she'll have to improvise. Not her strength, because she has a hard time thinking that the whole world won't obey her every whim.

Know your enemy. Know yourself. Sun Tzu. But I don't want to face a hundred battles. Not even one.

But if Mother hadn't started planning with Mel in the equation . . .

He pulled the knife and sheath out of his jacket and took the fish-spear from her. Then he tore long narrow strips of bark from another scrub maple growing tall and thin in its search for light in the forest gloom. Trimmed the split spear-end back to match the knife tang. Unpinned the pommel and pulled the grip, leaving the minimal guard that his blade had asked, married blade and shaft, and lashed the joining tight with twisted bark. Tested its strength. Handed the result to her, with the blade sheathed.

"Don't just stab with it, slash. Use it like a *naginata* or halberd. Sword on a stick. You ever use one before?"

She nodded. Unslung and set her shotgun aside, leaning against a tree. Flexed the shaft a few times between her spread hands, testing its strength, then unsheathed the blade and tried the balance with a few stabs and slashes. Nodded again.

She bowed to the trail, took a guard, and stepped forward with a shaft-block followed by a parry and counter, slash-stab-parry-slash, whirl and staff-block overhead, on into what had to be a *naginata kata* from some low-stance Japanese style he'd never seen, a whirling deadly flow that ended in a stab through a fallen enemy, frozen. Then a bow to the dojo, the forest trail.

Yes, she knew how to fight a *naginata*. Some people called it the "woman's spear," a weapon for the last-hope defense of the home. Fitting. The last-hope bit, not the "weapon of the weak" part.

She leaned on the shaft, panting, knees shaking a bit. Not the stance of a warrior goddess. Maybe "weapon of the weak" fit better than he wished.

Avoid fighting. If at all possible, avoid fighting. We're not going to win that way.

She straightened up, steel back in her knees and spine, sheathed the knife, and bowed to him, the formal bow of the dojo. "I will attempt to bring honor to your blade."

"*Domo arigato!*"

"*Banzai!*"

"I could do without the resonance of suicide charges and *kamikaze* pilots, thank you." But thanking her for taking the blade moved the dangerous weight of gratitude from her shoulders onto his. Safer there.

She just grinned at him, teeth bared. Looked too much like a skull with those hollow eyes. "We're immortal, remember? Wishing 'ten thousand years' doesn't seem out of place."

As if immortality wasn't a curse. He shook his head and limped down the trail again, leaning on his cane. At least, if they were walking into a trap, the tended path made that walk *possible*.

Another switchback, another run of stone slab steps far too tall for his stride and old enough that wear hollowed their lichen-spotted treads. Tree roots crossed the trail, tended like bonsai to serve as runoff diverters. He revised his age estimate for the trail from maybe a hundred years to a thousand. They had to be headed toward one of their own kind, god or demon or djinni.

And an ally of Mother. Of Balkis. Solomon's Seal, the Star of David, grew closer with each step, bait for Mother's trap. He kept looking for pit-traps and deadfalls, trip-wires and pressure plates. Military jargon, again. Memories came by fits and starts.

Switchback and switchback, stairs and trail and stairs, and he turned a corner and the dark forest shadows opened out into grass. Which wasn't natural—trees and brush would have filled that within a decade. The grass led up to a cliff face looming over them, wet weathered smooth dark gray, probably granite or basalt.

With a cave mouth lurking black in the center. The arc of grass rather exceeded a bowshot in depth.

Another place he'd been. Who did he once know, who laired in a cave like a dragon?

A man stood in the shadow and lingering fog of the cave mouth. He'd known they were coming, had felt them on *his* trail, *his* land. He lifted an open hand, peace, and waved them forward. As they walked along the stone-grit path to the cave the man grew, and grew, and grew, the closer they got, where they could read the size of the cave mouth. Not a man. A giant. A brown giant, twelve feet, fourteen feet tall, wearing brown scale armor of an age long past.

Not armor. His skin. Like that bear. Like a dragon.

Close enough to speak, Albert could see dark eyes and pale skin in the eye sockets, pale skin on his palms. More memories woke with the weakening of the Seal.

"Fafnir?"

A smile wrinkled the smaller scales of the face. "Welcome, little Alberich. It has been long and long. Come inside and rest.

Sweet mead and a fire and roast boar and a hot bath and a soft bed wait for you. You both look to need them all."

Albert heard the click of Mother's trap, arming. He shook his head.

"Lord Fafnir, your halls are known far and wide for hospitality. But we cannot guest with you. My wyrd forbids it."

Mel stared at him, then stepped sideways while keeping her eyes to the giant and *naginata* at the ready. Close enough for a whisper.

"You shithead, you know how long it's been since I had a cold beer?" Somehow she made the whole sentence hiss, even the parts without an "s" to sound.

He matched her whisper. "Guest-law. If we take his offer, we're bound to peace until we leave his lands. And the Seal's in there."

Even as he said it, he wondered if Legion had forced his memory back to this. That whole charade in the beginning, accepting bread and salt and then setting the place on fire . . . or, the illusion of fire. Demons saw things that hadn't happened yet. They weren't bound by space and time.

Never trust a demon.

"Besides, the beer won't be cold. Cellar-cool, at most. He's old-fashioned."

"Can we kill him and *then* drink the beer? Any rule against that?"

"None that I know of. It's pretty much traditional, even."

She stared from him to Fafnir and back again. "Wait a minute . . . " and stepped away, to a point where Fafnir couldn't attack them both at once.

"Fafnir. Alberich. Didn't Siegfried kill a Fafnir? To get the ring and Tarnhelm?"

The giant shook his head. "Siegfried, Siegfried. The little boy liked to brag. He drugged my mead and stole my treasures while I slept. No honor, not like your Alberich. Siegfried made up that tale about me turning into a dragon to guard my hoard. Killing a dragon made him a bigger damned hero, after all. Even bigger than killing a giant. Look at me."

He waved a massive hand at his chest and down to his feet. "Scales, yes, but do I look like a dragon? Can a mammal turn into a reptile?"

He shrugged. "Anyway, what do I have that you want to kill me for? As if you are up to killing a *mouse*, the condition you're in."

Albert remembered he had never liked Siegfried much. Yeah, the boy lied. A lot. And then Wagner added more lies. After all, none of those people were still around to say otherwise. Never let facts get in the way of a good story.

He waved negation at Mel. "Forget the stories. Siegfried told people he forged that sword, Nothung. Lies. I made it, and a good blade it was. Siegfried was a big strong dolt, just about smart enough to build a fire and roast dinner. Only time he ever lifted a hammer, was to bash someone over the head with it. And I never stole the Rheingold, either. I did some work for those Rhine maidens, and they tried to stiff me on the fee. Just like Old One-Eye and the rest of the Æsir, trying to squirm out of a contract once the work was done."

Again I remember why I don't like gods. Slimy arrogant thieving bastards, with morals worse even than the men they claimed to rule . . . at least Loki was up-front about it, not a smarmy hypocrite.

Fafnir laughed. "They weren't maidens, either. Come on in, and I'll tell you some tales over hot meat and a cool drink."

Albert shook his head. "The wyrd. We're not after gold or silver or gems, Lord Fafnir. Nothing valuable. An old iron star, six pointed, a Star of David. It's cracked. I know it's in your cave. I can feel its iron. I'll trade you a blade as good as Siegfried's Nothung."

The giant looked tempted, eyeing Albert's cane and the knife on Mel's spear. Then *he* shook his head, eyes sad in that scale-armored face.

"Can't give you the star. It isn't mine."

Honor can be such an awkward thing.

Albert twisted his cane, freeing its blade. Mel unsheathed the knife on her *naginata*. Fafnir didn't move.

"Please stand aside. We'll be thieves, then, just like Siegfried. As I told you, I'm under wyrd."

"No. I'm honor-bound to protect my guest."

Oh, hell. And damnation, too.

Fafnir looked down on them, twice as tall and more, weighing four times both of them together, and armored in scales heavier than that bear's. Faster. A hell of a lot smarter, a trained fighter. He studied the sword cane and the *naginata*.

"Those are good blades. But I doubt if they could kill me, even if Siegfried himself held them. All of us are very hard to kill. And you, you're both worn ragged. I saw you, coming down the ridge. You needed that cane, that staff, to keep you on your feet. Go away. Leave my guest alone."

The other side of guest-law. Once you accept a guest, you defend him. Her.

Another voice joined them, from the shadow deep in the cave entry. "Don't underestimate those blades, Faffy. They killed a full-grown shield-bear a few days back. The Wind Goddess moves as fast as her winds."

Mother.

Fafnir's eyes widened, and he stepped back a pace from Albert and Mel. Now Albert could see her in the gloom. Dark face, dark sari-drape of some kind. She held a darker shadow in her hands. The Seal? He felt its whining, sharper now that he could see it and yet weaker. He smelled the sandalwood, the . . . soul . . . of the salamander that had died to crack it. But that soul, that ghost, had led him to one side, separate . . .

Mel pointed the *naginata* into those shadows. "I am a police officer in pursuit of an outlaw. That Seal is stolen property. Your *guest* is wanted for arson in the nighttime, desecration of a holy place and theft of religious artifacts, and murder of an elemental, a salamander, in the commission of a felony. Also, interworld flight to avoid prosecution. I request your assistance in arresting this fugitive!"

Albert doubted if that last charge existed in the laws or customs of any nation.

Fafnir glanced back at Balkis. "*You!* You did not tell me of these things. You stretch the bounds of custom! Once you leave my house and land, I will never welcome you again!"

He turned back. "But, she is my guest. I am sworn. I cannot dishonor my hearth."

Fafnir stood in the mouth of his cave, in light while his guest remained in shadow. In order to get at Balkis, get that Seal, they'd have to pass him. *Kill* him, an innocent, like that bear.

. . . killed a shield-bear . . .

Albert stared at that shadowy figure, Mother, Balkis. "You've been following us."

He saw movement, a shrug. "Not following, tracking. I have humans to do such things. I told them to keep well away, a day behind, for their own safety."

Mel growled, deep, a mountain wolf with fur bristling. Then, "The dogs weren't a day behind . . . "

That rage still smoldered.

"Not my fault. That was the province governor. He did not understand what was happening, who you were. None of this would have happened if you hadn't killed the first guard. He would have called the outside post, they would have disarmed the mines, you would have walked out safely. All of those defenses are designed to keep *humans* from walking the path between the worlds.

"There are easier ways from that gate to here. Swimming the river, with the things that live in it, that was foolish. There's a railroad bridge a few miles upstream . . . "

She let that hang in the air between them. As always,

nothing was *her* fault. It couldn't be. That wasn't how the world worked.

I wonder what we would have found if we tried to cross that bridge, Mother dear. The salamander warned us. All things in all, I think we were better off half-drowned.

But he didn't say that. "He went for his gun."

Another shrug. "A fool. Because of a fool, ten other men are dead. You can scarcely blame me for *that*."

As if she hadn't set up the whole scene. Nothing was *ever* her fault.

Albert felt too tired for anger. "Give us the Seal and we'll go away. Too many deaths already."

Another wolf growl from Mel, fangs in the throat and ready to tear. "Speak for yourself. Justice calls for that woman's blood."

"I bind the blade you carry!"

That just slipped out. She'll kill me for it . . .

But all Mel did was glare at him.

"Mother, the Seal for your life. *You* warned Fafnir about these blades . . . "

She stepped out into the light, dark and beautiful and graceful as always. Yes, she had the Seal in her hands.

"Your word. Your honor. If you think a grubby little blacksmith can match the mind and hand of Solomon the Great . . . "

She glared down at the Seal. "Three thousand years, this thing has been eating at me. Eating at all of us. Three thousand years of treachery, and you want to *fix* it."

He saw her grip tighten, knuckles pale on her brown hands. The Seal whimpered. She started chanting in a language he'd never heard before. Her voice rose to a scream full of hate and power. Hairs stood up on the back of his neck and on his arms.

A whine joined her chant, the Seal vibrating like a tuning-fork, growing into a shriek of tortured metal. She raised the Seal over her head and smashed it down point-first on a rock.

"Take it!"

The Seal broke. Albert grabbed at his chest, at the knife-blade pain in his heart even stronger than the blinding flash in his head. The world turned gray, and he felt his bones chill as if damp grave-mould sucked at his soul.

He fought. He kept his balance. Deep in the shadow world, he caught glimpses of Fafnir, of Mother, of Mel standing with her *naginata* between him and the others, death ready for any threat. She glowed, warrior goddess with a glowing blade.

The Seal's pain faded, the sunlight returned, he could see again. Fafnir was gone. Mother was gone. He stood outside the cave mouth, Mel at his side, the broken Seal at his feet.

The broken Seal at his feet.

One point of the six lay separate from the rest, split off at the intersections of the two interlocking triangles. The breaks leaked tears of power. He could feel them. The blood of the iron, the blood of the spell.

Dying.

Mother's trick was simply time. She set things up so whatever we did, we'd get here too late. She stalled for time for the Seal to weaken enough. Enough so she could finish killing it.

XXII

"I don't suppose that offer of a cold beer and a hot bath is still open?" Mel stared wistfully at the cave mouth.

Albert knelt and picked up the shards of the Seal. They whimpered in his hands.

"Probably not. *I'm* not going to walk up there and knock on his door. You can, if you want. But I don't think he'll chase us out of his lands, either. We have an implied verbal contract, as they say."

"I'm not sure saving the world is more important than a cold beer. Even without all the other things he offered."

He wrapped the ancient pieces of iron in dry plastic bags— everything else in the pack was wet and rust would be adding insult to injury—and stowed them. What's another pound or two on the back, anyway?

When he stood up, his hip told him what, with red-hot knife blades. Another two notches on the pain meter. Why carry that dead weight? Haul it to some place where he could provide burial in consecrated ground? It's not like he could rebuild Solomon's work . . .

But it wasn't dead. It had whimpered at him, like a hound that had been run over by a boar in the hunt, spine broken, but still licking his hand.

Memories. This business of getting memories back had its bad side. He'd had to ease that dog from life, his last kindness to a faithful friend. He didn't have the forge and hammer and anvil to do the same thing for the Seal.

"Faffy?" Mel's voice broke into his thoughts. "She called him *Faffy?* Is she screwing him?"

Albert blinked at the image. "Not impossible. Not something I want to think about."

"Then size *does* matter?"

He glared at her. "You must be feeling better."

He bent down and picked up his sword-cane, its steel sheath, and joined the two. He must have dropped them when the shock of the Seal's breaking hit him. She took that as a cue to sheathe the *naginata* blade as well, custom for the weapon. Prospect of battle over, for the moment.

She was studying him with her head cocked to one side, eyes narrowed. "Okay, little man, what was that nonsense about a wyrd?"

"Norse and Anglo-Saxon lore, a fate or personal destiny that you can't escape. Irish equivalent is a geas. Or the Arabic *qismah*. Kismet."

"I know what one is. I thought that was supposed to be some kind of curse laid on you by the gods. Or the Fates, if they aren't gods. I recall you saying Legion hadn't ordered us to fix the Seal."

"As you keep reminding me, we *are* gods."

"So you are self-cursed?"

"The best kind of curse. Find them throughout literature and myth. Tragic flaw, and all that."

Mel shrugged and shook her head over the tail-chasing idiocy. "If you insist, Mister Driven-by-Fate. Okay, what comes next? Where do we drive now?" Then, "Implied verbal contract. That's so . . . *very* comforting. You think we have at least twenty-four hours to get out of Dodge? Or don't let the sun set on our asses within his lands?"

What do we do next? Good question. I hadn't planned to find the Seal too late for me to save it. For that matter, I hadn't planned on ending up some place where I couldn't just walk home again. Or take a bus.

"I think first thing, we try to find a way home. Then you can get that cold beer and hot bath."

"Sounds like a plan. You're invited."

Huh? I'll assume she meant just the beer. Safer that way.

Albert looked around, actually *studying* this place rather than searching for threats and then concentrating on the one he'd found. Fog still shrouded the peculiar Nordic gloom of dark wet softwood forest, but the gray seemed to be lifting. They stood at the focus of a grassy clearing, shaggy with spring growth and glistening from the wet, a half-circle centered on Fafnir's cliff face and obviously not natural. Three tidy stone-dust paths led from the cave mouth. One central, that was the one they'd come in on, one off into the woods along the sharp stone rise in either direction.

No signs saying, *This way to the egress.*

After all, Fafnir knew where the trails went. If *you* didn't, you shouldn't be here.

"Got a three-sided coin to flip?"

She sniffed at the air and then switched on the blank introspective look that said she was listening to her winds. "The path west leads to another stream and then the river, seems to be fishy. No sense of an exit of any kind. East, climbs this ridge and down the other side and ends up smelling of river and overloaded cesspools and pine lumber. I'd lay odds on a sawmill camp, probably where those riverboats dock and load."

She sniffed again. "The path we came in on, there seems to be more to it than fish. My winds don't know what. But you remember, when we turned to climb that ridge, the path went on upstream."

"So we should be good Buddhists and follow the Middle Way?"

"Someday your tongue is going to get you in trouble."

Albert shrugged. "Has before, will again. I'm used to it."

He glanced back at Fafnir's cave. *Yeah, she's right. Sometimes a cold beer outweighs saving the world. It's not as if they'll thank you . . .*

Throw in a deep-dish pizza or hot greasy lamb kebabs on curried rice and I'll let the gods return.

He limped back the way they'd come. Retracing steps, somehow that made the pack weigh more. Through the field, into the wet dark forest full of the smell of spruce and rot and mushrooms, up the first set of ancient steps—now he knew who had sized the treads and risers, could fit them to Fafnir's stride. He had to pause on each step.

"Give me that damned pack, you pig-headed idiot."

"You've been sick. You need that spear to hold you up."

Mel paused and cocked her head. "You said something about me feeling better. Why, yes. I am. As soon as that Seal broke, I felt the difference. Still tired, still hungry, but I can see better, hear better. My legs are longer than yours, better suited to these steps. And I'm not the God that Limps."

So she'd noticed. He had to admit, the pack had gained a lot more weight than the couple of pounds of iron could explain. He shrugged out of it and took the shotgun in return. Hell of a lot lighter.

"What's this loaded with?"

"First round is birdshot, close range and won't go through a wall to kill innocent bystanders. Rest is police-standard buckshot. Have some rifled slugs in my vest."

So if he saw one of those grouse-things, they had a potential snack. Good to know. But he wasn't going to carry the shotgun at the ready.

Up the next set of steps, shotgun slung across his back, still fire in his hip but not as much, into the fog on the trail, switchback, trail, steps, trail. The fog grew thicker, colder, wetter. It forced him into tunnel vision. His focus narrowed to one foot in front of the other. Lean on the cane. Pause to rest. Gray. Black shadows. Trail. Gray. Black shadows.

The Seal spoke out of the shadows. He might have shrugged off its weight, but not the touch of it. It remembered fire—both the recent blazing pain of the salamander's death and the ancient heat of forging that had brought it some strange form of life. The salamander lay bound in the Seal, some trick of Mother's witchery at the synagogue, and he could smell that touch of sandalwood deep in the iron. *It* wasn't exactly dead, either.

But locking an elemental's soul inside cold iron? Sadism. Now that he had held the Seal again, he could feel that *other* terror and pain, deep within.

Circuits and spells wove through the fibrous wrought iron, the words of Suleiman bin Daoud, Solomon son of David. I the Lord thy God am a jealous God. Thou shalt have no other gods before Me. Or even behind Me. Not even Balkis the Beautiful, goddess of Sa'aba. But we won't tell her that. We'll make this subtle, so she won't notice. Sneak up on them all, slowly, with centuries of patience.

Like a sponge. Soak up the fog, soak up the power, slowly, slowly, the rivals diminish, fade, slink away into the shadows. If tribal gods forget, we can beat them defeat them eat them. One God to rule them all one God to bind them. Take their lands their goats their oxen their women. Savor their precious delicious tears and lamentations. Smell the sweet incense of their burning cities. Their gods forgotten. Never were.

Forget.

Forget.

Forget.

He'd fallen into a delirious death-march, tired, so tired. *Shut up and just keep moving. One foot in front of the other. If you're moving, you're still alive.* Stairs. Trail. Stairs. Shadows. Pause. Lean on cane. Rest.

Cold.

Wet.

Dark.

Resinous incense. Roasting meat. The sweet smell of burning cities that warm the hands of God. Warmth. The rankness of wet cloth drying by the fire without first washing. Cedar incense, more precise. Roasting . . . chicken? A white dove, pure and without blemish, was a sacrifice acceptable in God's eyes. If you couldn't afford better. Oxen were better. Priests have to eat.

Hungry. His stomach growled. Albert opened his eyes.

He lay under a dark stone overhang spreading out to light—sky, blue sky and trees in low-angle sunlight, cedars and maples and birches. Smoke. His gaze wandered down the smoke to a fire, snapping, sparking, smoking, crackling, hissing from wet wood, a wooden spit above the heat with three, four, five small chickens roasting. No—grouse or pheasants or some other plump chicken-shaped bird.

Movement caught his attention beyond the fire, cloth hanging on rope, on parachute cord—clothes drying far enough from the fire that sparks probably wouldn't burn buckshot holes. How'd she get five birds with one birdshot cartridge? She?

Mel. She stepped into view, walking carefully around stones, to turn the spit. Wearing clean coveralls from the pack. Her old coveralls on the line, ragged but somewhat cleaner than he recalled. Next to his jacket, shirt, pants, socks, underwear, also ragged and somewhat cleaner.

All of it.

Well, she'd seen him before. He'd seen her. No big thing.

But he didn't feel naked. He stirred, summoning up enough strength to lift his arm. He found green cloth, stretchy, baggy as if a couple of sizes too large—her leotard. She'd slipped that on him. He hadn't pulled it out of the pack, when dressing her after she got sick. Still dry, in the plastic bag, despite the river crossing.

He wasn't lying on rocks. The bed felt springy, but it wasn't the inflated float. Then his nose told him—cedar branch tips, under one of the reflective blankets, woodsman's bed. Smelled clean, strange smell after the week or so they'd been out.

"What?"

She glanced up from tending something on the far side of the fire—pot? Steam beyond the smoke?

"Good. I was hoping you'd come over for the party."

"What happened?"

"True gentleman that you are, you proved that I am *not* some kind of substandard goddess who gets sick while others display proper godly strength and immune systems. You caught whatever I had. Less lucky, because you were dressed when you started leaking at both ends. Hence the laundry flapping in the morning breeze. Before you ask, you've been out of it for two days and nights. The evening and the morning are of the third day, about an hour after sunrise."

He struggled up to leaning on his elbows, looking around some more. This looked like an established camp—fire ring of blackened stones, and the crotched stakes holding her spit had seen some weather. He lay in a cleared area, prepared and leveled. Some of the stones moved to each side would weigh hundreds of pounds. Whoever used this had left a cache of firewood tucked way at the back of the overhang, dry and ready.

The stone overhang stretched out twenty feet, thirty feet, and would deflect almost all weather. He guessed they were at least ten feet above the stream, he could hear it and smell it beyond the crackle of the fire. Fafnir's fishing camp?

"Hope you're not using up his firewood. Bad manners."

"No. Blow-down cedars well away from the path or the stream, dead wood, enough heartwood to start the fire and dry the rest. Cut them up with the folding saw from the pack. I'll leave more wood than we found."

He nodded and inched up further to a full sit. His head spun a bit before clearing.

"Five grouse? Good shooting."

"Didn't shoot them. They're dumb, sat frozen pretending I couldn't see them until I got close enough to whack their heads off with the *naginata*."

Grouse are dumb, and *she's fast.*

He finally spotted the backpack, leaning against some rocks and propped inside-out to dry. The tent and rain-fly lay beyond it, stretched out for the same purpose. He felt the Seal lurking over there, still whimpering, still crippled. But not rusting.

"I guess Fafnir isn't following us?"

"Winds don't give me any word of him or Bilqis." Then, after a pause, "Look, I'm sorry about hooking them up as an item. Tabloid gossip. Touchy subject, you thinking she's your mother . . . "

Albert shook his head. "I got used to her men-friends centuries ago. Plenty of practice. As I said, not impossible. I'm getting used to her not being my mother, too. That explains a lot. Like her sending us on a wild-goose chase through a minefield and plague. And why I don't look anything like my brothers and sister, who don't look much like each other."

"Brothers? The way you talked with Fafnir, I got the idea that Mime and Siegfried and some of the other legends got . . . stretched in the telling. Including five different names for the same person."

"Yeah. I'm the only smith in the so-called family. Wagner came along and screwed everything seven ways from Sunday. Mixed about twenty different legends into one, and made up crap on the spot. Now I remember why I never liked Wagner."

"You up to eating? Birds are done, just keeping warm, and I can dump this wild asparagus into the water and have it ready in a couple of minutes."

She'd been hungry as hell, just about as soon as she came out of her fever. Albert consulted with his stomach. Yeah, food sounded like a great idea.

But . . . "I don't think that's *wild* asparagus. Fafnir likes his food. Now I know why I could find wild onions and garlic so easily."

She stirred stuff in two pots, dumping green and brown handfuls into steam. "Left plenty, even for a giant. It was bolting, starting to turn woody. Doing him a favor by forcing new sprouts. These morels would have gone by, too. Don't have any butter, but we can make do with grouse drippings . . . "

No, I'm not going to ask her if she's sure about those mushrooms. She's got easier ways to kill me.

The grouse had cooled enough to barely scorch his fingers and tongue. Good. *Damned* good, seasoned with juniper or something like, and garlic, and how she kept them that juicy while fully cooked on a spit over a campfire . . .

And salty asparagus just crunchy-steamed and sautéed morels savory with grouse fat. He mumbled appreciation around mouthfuls.

She studied the pile of bones and the empty pot lids used as plates. "You know, I remember a fish stew that vanished just as fast. If I went through the same things you did, the last day or so, I'm surprised you didn't just toss me in the river and have done with it. That must have been ugly."

"Was. But *you* didn't, now. Same thing. Common decency."

"Philosophy one-oh-one, necessary prerequisite for any ethical system is reciprocity—do onto others as you would have them do onto you. Morality has to work both ways, in order to be moral. From what I've seen, damn few people or gods practice that. Common decency is about as common as common sense."

Which is to say, not common at all.

She cocked her head to one side and smiled that peculiar half-smile of hers. "Speaking of the river, if you can turn into a fish, how come you claim you can't swim?"

Oh, hell. "Which version?"

"Andvari."

"Okay, that was probably Norway. What's *now* Norway. No, I can't swim. Hell, unless I've been eating really good, I can't even float worth a damn. You've probably noticed, not much body fat. Anyway, I was after some placer gold in a mountain stream deeper than I could wade. I figured out what you'd call a snorkel these days. I guess some of the locals saw me go into the water and stay down a lot longer than any of them could hold their breath." He paused and then shrugged.

"One of the things the legends have right, gold makes me do funny things. That water was *cold*. Needed to come up and bask in the sun on a rock like an otter, after each dive."

She giggled. That seemed weird, given who she was, the image she projected. Not the kind of woman who giggled. Kali? You couldn't even *think* of Kali giggling. If you did, she'd take three days to kill you.

"I bet you came out looking like a blue prune. Dick shrunken to a stub about *that* long." She held finger and thumb about an inch apart.

Well, yeah. Rude of her to say it, though.

"So. Alberich, Andvari, Ottarr, all those names, all those totally mythical dwarves that let gold overcome common sense and decency—what do I call you, now that you remember things?"

He had to snicker, himself. "I'm just Al. Albert, if you feel more formal. Or pig-headed idiot, as needed."

"I was hoping you wouldn't remember that. Sorry. I should have seen that you were getting sick. Allah and Buddha both know, *I* didn't enjoy the experience."

She paused and spent a moment or two with a narrow bone, trying to work a bit of grouse out from between her teeth. Also not something you ever visualized Kali doing. Then, "Did I rave like that in the fever?"

Damn and double damn. "Some. Most of it was in dialects I've never heard."

"Except for the Hani part."

He nodded. Some things, you can't unsay. It wasn't like he'd *wanted* to hear that. To find out what it meant. Should have kept his damned mouth shut.

She waved it off. "'S okay. I've never been able to talk about him. Amateur psychotherapy, maybe letting it out will help." Shrug.

"Anyway, you used four or five languages I've never heard, so we're even. But several times, English and Latin, you mumbled something about circuits or paths in the iron. Steel computer chips. And silicon in the ore."

She paused, staring into the fire. Made with cedar wood, it cracked and popped and spat sparks and sooted up the pots, not prime campfire wood, but you go with what you got.

"Look, I'm no authority on either the wily ways of Suleiman bin Dauod, or working iron. But, if someone cuts a bunch of wires in a radio, it isn't gonna work. That doesn't mean I have to know how to design or even build a radio, to fix it. Just reconnect the red wire to the red wire, the blue wire to the blue, and so on. I even know that *this* stub of red wire doesn't want to connect to that other red one over *there,* because it just won't reach. Can't you do something like that with the Seal?"

She looked up from the fire. "You know, I have to admit that both of us were grubby as hell. Nor can I fault Bilqis saying that you're small. But I think you're rather more than a blacksmith." She paused.

"One thing about pig-headed gods—we don't give up easy."

XXIII

Albert wiggled and then shrugged his shoulders, trying to lose the itching and twitching along his spine. Not that anything *he* did would help. He could hear Mel behind him, quiet footsteps crunching the path's gravel and dead leaves, and the problem was *her.*

Her, and his hyperactive imagination. He kept seeing her sneaking up on those grouse and then a sudden flash of steel as she whipped the *naginata* around faster than the bird could see, faster than anyone could see, and the bird flopping from its perch, a fountain of blood where its head had been. Flailing wings scattering dead leaves. Slowing. Stopping. Blood soaking into the forest litter.

Then another, and another. Five of them, she'd crept up and lopped their heads off. If she'd wanted more, she'd have killed more. Nothing to stop her. Kali, Goddess of Death and Destruction.

Reminded him too much of a praying mantis, motionless or a slow stalk, then the spiked forelegs flashing out and grabbing a victim. Then the jaws, and death.

He knew what that blade would do. He'd forged it, after all. And he'd used it to kill the . . . shield-bear . . . Mother had called it. Slashed through those scales like tissue paper.

That blade walked behind him. In *her* hands. She'd sworn to kill him . . .

"Quit twitching, damn you. I promise I won't chop your head off like a damned grouse. Or stab you in the back, or shoot you, or any of the other dooms you're imagining with every step you take."

So it will be one I don't imagine. Thanks a hell *of a lot.*

"Look, I swear, oath on Allah's love, I won't kill you before I have a washing-machine handy. I *hate* washing blood out of my uniforms once it's had time to set."

Meaning, she's done it. Now she's mocking me, to rub it in. She said she's not a Believer, not one of the umma *or* ulema. *Not what you'd call a binding oath, under those circumstances.*

"Fuck it. I'll take point, if you won't trust me behind your back. You'll have to carry the pack, though. It'd slow me down in a fight."

Taking all in all, he decided that was a good tradeoff. Though that brought him closer to the dying whimper of the Seal. Anyway, she heaved the pack down on the stream-side path, he set the shotgun against a tree, and took up the load. Not any lighter, for all that the tent and assorted gear had had a chance to dry. That Seal couldn't weigh more than a pound, at most two, but it dragged at him like twenty pounds of lead.

Why couldn't Mother have the decency to kill it? *Decency? Mercy? Her? She'd probably hamstring an enemy at sunrise in the desert ten miles from an oasis, and hang around to gloat over the dying.*

Typical god. Life isn't painful enough, so I'll invent eternal hell. Can't escape by dying.

The path led on, not steep, praise be to Allah, following the slope of the trout stream it tracked, surfaced with stones and roots and gravel mostly, cleared high and wide enough for Fafnir with a fly rod. He glanced out through and over swamp maples, cedars, thickets of laurel, a grove of dark fir here and some tall pines on a knoll over there looking like a Japanese *sumi-e* ink painting, expressive brushstrokes.

Something waited, ahead of them. Mel's winds had sensed it. She hadn't explored further than the immediate area of the campsite, keeping watch over his sickness. Now he could feel that something, his own power waxing as the Seal's waned. Neither of them had much clue as to what they felt. That had been part of Solomon's ancient work, stealing their memories and powers and more than half their skills.

At least Mel had known she was a goddess, because her people filled in the blanks. They told her what she was.

Do I want to fix the Seal? Cripple myself again, Mel again, after Mother has set us free?

Gods invent hells.

They climbed beside a waterfall, fifty vertical feet of cascade whitewater and rainbowed mist, stepped pools and black mossy rocks and trailing wet ferns, one laurel clump perched on an outcrop in the middle to supervise the whole. Thing looked like it had been built as a Zen gardener's fish ladder to allow spawning runs upstream. How much of this had Fafnir *made,* anyway?

He'd had centuries. He liked fish. He'd helped build Valhalla for gods he *didn't* like. Gods who cheated.

This is the other side of what gods do, if they take the time. None of that six-days-and-rest nonsense. Takes me longer than that to make a decent blade from scratch. Making a good universe, one that passes detail, that takes years. Like, billions of them, what with the geological epochs thrown in for checking up on long-term consequences of this tweak here and that one there.

Constant tinkering. Not a one-shot deal.

Albert soaked up the smell of wet moss, clean water, healthy trees and soil. The roar and hiss and boom and chuckle of falling water. Fafnir must have tuned the stream for pitch and timbre. Need a plunge pool over here for the low register.

Adjust again each spring, as the ice-out and high water changed things, shifted rocks and dumped washed-out trees across the current and gouged new pools. Study the results. Keep the good and adapt the bad to make it good. Life is change.

Except for us. Can gods change?

The path crossed side-streams or the main current by stepping stones—Zen spacing, you had to alter your stride and pay attention to balance, live in each step. Be here now. Zen teahouse views—framed to snatch a glimpse of shimmering pool and overhanging laurel or cedar in mid-stride, you only caught it once, from one exact angle. A trout jumped in the middle of one such glimpse, snatching a mayfly or some such glinting morsel at the peak of the leap, then vanished into spreading silver rings of water.

I'm glad we didn't have to fight him. Kill him. Guest-law requires him to defend Mother to the death. Once he let her shelter under his roof.

Damn her, for setting such a trap.

He'd lagged behind Mel, savoring the place and time. Now he pushed harder to catch up, burning hip and all, panting and sweating with the weight of the pack and the Seal. He could feel the ancient iron dragging at him on the climb. He'd had to tuck his cane into the pack, to free his hands to hold the shotgun ready.

Dammit.

"Whatever's waiting ahead of us, it has to be a trap. That's the way Mother thinks."

She didn't pause or even glance back, keeping her attention on the trail and any dangers, searching the treetops, the rocks, every clump of shrubbery, the shadows, even the water in case of kraken.

"You say this like it was some kind of news."

Sometimes, paranoia represents an accurate world-view.

They topped another slope next to another artwork cascade, and the valley opened out in front of them. Water meadows framed by forest, grass and cattails and sedges and the stream snaking deep and dark and cold through it all, perfect for the clean back-cast of fly-fishing, here and there a beaver lodge to harvest the bordering aspens. Across it all, a rise of glacier-carved gray stone much like the cliff that held Fafnir's cave.

Another giant's home? Albert didn't care. All he cared about was the route ahead looked flat for a while. Mel had been staggering, the morning she'd recovered from her sickness. He'd turned his fish spear into the *naginata* because she needed the support, not because he thought she knew that weapon.

He felt like she had looked.

Well, half dead is better than the whole dish. On the other hand, half a fish is better than none. Metaphors are almost as slippery as eels.

He shook himself and took one step, then another. If you're still moving, you're still alive. Mel had paused and waited while he caught his breath. Now she studied him with narrowed eyes, head cocked to one side.

"Want to take a break? I'm pretty sure I could scrounge up some lunch around here."

Temptation. Get thee behind me, Satan. Except, he didn't trust her behind his back. Dilemma.

He pulled up a couple of quotes from the Qur'an and then discarded them for the sake of his hide. She'd told him to stick to Shakespeare. "'Twere well it were done quickly.' If I sit down, I won't get up for a day or two."

And then, by association and not out loud, *By the pricking of my thumbs* . . . now that they had a clear view over the water-meadow, he recognized what he felt from the bare stone outcrop ahead of them. "We're getting closer to one of those gates. Same feeling as the alley outside that old door that wasn't there."

She nodded. "I didn't want to mention it, in case I was just wishing. Glad to know you feel it too."

"I think people like us, gods or whatever, we're supposed to be able to find the gates. Maybe we even built them in the first place. One of the powers Solomon stole from us. If you believe Mother."

They plodded on. Or, she strode and scouted and radiated deadly speed while he plodded. That amount of bustling energy

could have aggravated the hell out of him, if he had the strength
to spare. Instead he just filed it as a fact, possibly important. Let
her take the hard part in the coming battle. Not being a coward,
just recognizing reality when it rose up and smacked him in the
face. Like the trail kept threatening to do.

A mile winding around the water-meadows and in and out
of aspens and birches, past the gnawed pencil-point stumps that
said the beaver lodges were still active, a mile of one foot in front
of the other and wishing he dared take a break on one of the long
stones placed here and there along the trail—rounded glacial
stones with gentle flats or depressions of the correct size and
height to receive a giant's butt for lunch or quiet contemplation
of a particular view.

Glacial stones not placed by any glacier. Fafnir had been
working on this for a *long* time.

*Damn shame I can't pause and admire his masterpiece. Those
vistas. But if I stop moving, it's gonna take dynamite to get me
started again.*

One foot in front of the other. His view narrowed to the
trail in front of him, leaving the vistas and any possible threats
to Mel. If you're still moving, you're still alive.

He moved into shadow. He looked up into a bulk of vertical
gray stone spotted with lichen and the wash of dark and light
that rain brought below the lichen, its acids painting or etching
the rock. The trail ended at a door, a weathered wooden door of
rails and stiles and inset beveled panels that looked a hell of a
lot like the one back in that alley, except this didn't have a cross
and shield at the peak of its pointed arch. And just like the alley
door, it didn't offer a knob or handle or other outside hardware.
It did have an inscription winding up and over the peak and
down.

He stared at it. He tried to make sense of the Gothic spiky
scroll-letters, not really designed for carving into stone, but not
in any Germanic language he knew, ancient or modern. Then

he shifted gears and it clicked into place. Italian. *Old* Italian. Fafnir's little joke.

Lasciate ogne speranza, voi ch'intrate. He translated, out loud, "Abandon all hope, ye who enter here."

He blinked and woke up to the fact that he had just about literally banged his nose on the door.

"No bunker. No defenses."

Mel stood leaning on the staff of the *naginata,* studying him studying the door and inscription. She nodded.

"No *outside* defenses. Your old drinking-buddy isn't worried about riff-raff coming through, and apparently figures that nobody can get at this side without his knowledge and consent."

Albert thought about that, slow as molasses in Svalbard. "Lord Fafnir's lands. The district governor or whatever Mother called him, the guy that sent those trackers, he doesn't have power here. And the bugs and the mutated malaria or whatever keep all the tourists out."

Mel ran her fingers over the wood of the door. "Illusion. No barking guards, this time. Not worried about scaring off street-people. I wonder what's *really* here, hiding behind this face . . . " A pause. "Not locked. Not even latched. Just like the other one." She looked back at him. "Might be a good idea to click the safety off that shotgun."

In one smooth flow of motion, she kicked the door wide and vanished through it. He followed. He didn't have much choice. He wondered if he should have dug out a flashlight or something before heading into a cave.

No. Inside matched the other gateway hall—sunlit courtyard surrounded by galleries. To hell with impossibility, those tons of stone overhead. Instead of a fountain, the courtyard held a . . . cactus? Eight feet tall, maybe, and fat. Not spiky—furry brownish green, the kind of tiny barbed spines that practically leapt out at you and burrowed into your flesh and left you with an inflamed rash that lasted weeks. He'd met those spines before.

And then the cactus opened its eyes. A ring of eyes—blue-green with black cat-slit pupils, he could see four of them on this side and the edges of more around each side. Lumps formed on the fur and extruded into tentacles.

Forbidden.

Not a voice, a statement hanging in the air, inside his head. The cactus, the Thing, could write in his mind. In Gothic lettering.

Tentacles with claws, he'd seen those on octopi and squid, demons from the deep, catch prey and drag it to the crushing beak. They lashed out at Mel. She wasn't there, wasn't where they sought, so they stretched toward Albert and he fired the shotgun from the hip, first round birdshot blasting the eyes, second and third buckshot cutting through the tentacles closest to him, avoiding the blur that was Mel dancing in and out with the *naginata* spinning like a propeller in a deadly baton-twirl of keen hungry steel. Chopped tentacle-bits flew away from her, green blood spurted into the air, but more and more buds formed from the body and the cut ends.

Hydra.

Cut off a head, two replaced it.

Albert clicked on an empty chamber and dropped the shotgun. Emptied two magazines from the pistol, the hollow-point bullets opening gaping holes in the central trunk of the hydra. Holes that lasted seconds only, before closing as if they'd never been. Useless.

Herakles had used a torch. Seared the hydra's wounds to prevent regeneration. No torches. Hell, they'd need a flamethrower or napalm for this one, anyway. Too damn fast.

Albert shrugged the pack off, broke the buckles holding the flap, no time for stupid buckles. Rummaged into it. Pain seared across his face as one of the tentacles whipped past and then dropped to the floor as Mel slashed it off halfway.

Salt. Heavy bag of kosher salt. He tore it open, grabbed a

handful of the coarse crystals, threw them at the closing wound of the tentacle stump.

The hydra screamed, no sound, pain in *his* head, white across *his* eyes. When Albert could see again, that stump still oozed green, no healing, no regeneration.

More salt, more wounds, he waded into the nest of snakes as Mel cut and cut and cut, now slicing at the body rather than the tentacles, fillets of cactus, of hydra, and each time she cut he flung salt and the green blood oozed. Uncut tentacles grabbed at him. She slashed them as she jerked back and forth herself—the hydra found her by touch, no eyes now, and she had to cut her own body free. Then, a whipping downward slash as she dropped to one knee, the central trunk fell in two halves and Albert dumped salt on both.

Both shuddered and screamed, a scream in his head that faded and dopplered down as if the hydra fled.

Silence.

Green blood oozed.

The rest of it didn't move.

He still had a handful of salt. He stood with it in his palm, waiting for some part of the hydra to twitch, to stir. Nothing.

Not much structure he could see on the cut halves, tubes for circulation or whatever, layers of fiber. Muscles? Growth rings? The green slime covered anything else. He couldn't even tell if it was plant or animal or some mix of both.

To hell with that. He sank to his knees and then his butt on his heels, barely able to stay upright that much. He sucked in a breath, another. Dumped the salt back into the almost-empty bag in his left hand.

Still breathing.

Mel leaned on the shaft of the *naginata*, staring down at green-spattered paving stone. Red blood dripped from her cheek where one of the whipping tentacles had caught her, caught even *her*. Again, more red on the back of her right hand. If that had broken her hold on the shaft . . .

Fire burned in both of his own cheeks, his own forehead. He felt warm blood oozing down. That must have lashed across his eye-sockets. Just a touch deeper—blinding him—he couldn't have seen to throw.

The hydra had known how to fight. Not just flailing, it had gone for targets. It had thought. It knew weak spots, like those fireflies in the tunnel.

Mel stirred and looked up. Blinked back into focus. Studied Albert, across the carnage. Took a deep breath.

She stepped across bits of hydra and pools of ichor to him, reached out, and offered him a hand up. He checked with his knees—would they hold him up if he accepted?

Provisional agreement. He stood, swaying. "Those words outside. Fafnir would have used runes, not silly Gothic lettering. He'd have quoted the Elder Edda or some such thing, not Dante. That was Mother's joke."

He looked around at the carnage staining the stone flooring. "Probably this, too. Fafnir loves a good party. He wasn't tricking us with that offer of roast boar and beer. Wouldn't be surprised if he didn't keep any guard at all on his own personal gate."

Mel waved at the slime and chunks of . . . flesh? "What the fuck *was* that thing? Never seen or heard of anything like it."

Albert shook his head. "Some kind of non-Greek hydra. Maybe it came out of the lost myths and mists of ancient Sa'aba, along with Mother. Or maybe she just invented it out of ectoplasm. Whatever. I hope it *stays* dead."

He switched his attention from the hydra, it seemed to offer no *present* danger, and looked her over. That *had* been her clean uniform. Red blood and green, chunks of hydra, rips from the clawed tentacles, what looked like powder burns, near-misses from his frenzied shooting. Well, she shouldn't jump around so much in a fight, dammit.

Or maybe she was fast enough to dodge bullets.

Judging by her expression, he didn't look any better. She

reached out and ran a finger though the pain on his left cheek. Pulled back a bloody finger, his blood, and licked it.

"There. I have drunk your blood. We're free of that."

What the hell is she up to?

"My words, you idiot. When I didn't know who or *what* you were. When I hadn't seen our fight through your eyes. Self-defense."

First time I've ever heard of an Afghan tribeswoman, tribesman, letting go of a blood feud. The feud is life and more than life. Give it up and you give up your honor.

As Snorri Sturluson tells us in the Old Norse of the Prose Edda, *"When pigs fly."*

XXIV

Adrenaline ebbed into picking up the pieces. She wiped the blade of her *naginata* but didn't sheathe it, her eyes searching the galleries and doors and clear blue sky overhead for any further threat. Now that he had time, nothing trying to kill him *Right Now,* he could look around.

Near as he could tell, this place was a twin to the one that had moved them into the firefly tunnel—one "door" in, twenty-seven wooden "doors" out from the same four floors of stucco galleries rising to a red tile roof around the courtyard, pierced marble screenwork railings, marble stairs in the same corner, four single "windows" to the front.

Only difference was the cactus/hydra instead of a fountain, in the center of the flagstone courtyard. He wondered what that fountain had really been. And why they hadn't triggered its attack. Perhaps because Mother had been there already, lurking? She'd turned it off, or it had recognized her?

He found the empty magazines for the pistol and reloaded them from the backpack. Did the same for the shotgun. Neither of the guns seemed to have suffered a scratch, for all that he'd tossed each aside on what *looked* like worn flagstone pavement.

Which made him study the flat stone between the two halves of hydra leaking green goo. A line scored the stone, mark of the blade from her final slash. He'd winced when the sparks flew, but he couldn't fault her intent. Cut that damned thing clear through—no ifs, ands, or buts. And then maybe nuke the corpse, to be sure.

He took the *naginata* from her and checked the blade. No visible damage. He ran his fingertip along the flat of the blade, feeling the soul of the steel. No way he was going to test the edge. He knew better.

The blade told him it was fine, the bindings tight and shaft undamaged. He stared at the line scored into the stone, at the blade, at her. Knelt, and ran his fingertips across the groove in the stone and felt it sharp and fresh under the slimy ichor. He shrugged.

"Illusions."

The hydra's body had shrunk from when he first saw it—both shorter and less thick, probably bulk lost from extruding those tentacles. Even so, his blade had cut about three inches beyond its own length in splitting the thing. He'd wrought better than he knew. Or Mel had stretched its cut with *mana* from her Kali avatar.

He stood and handed the *naginata* back to her. Added, "Is any part of this *real?*"

She echoed his shrug and then went back to sentry duty. "The pain. The exhaustion. The hunger. The deep aching thirst for a cold beer."

And the need for a hot bath. He wiped his fingers on his pants to get rid of the slime—God knew the pants were filthy enough already. Would it dissolve cloth? Dissolve the washing machine, assuming they ever saw one again?

He nodded at the bastard improvised weapon in her hands. "You used that well. I never intended it to stand battle."

She focused on the bare blade, a frown narrowing her eyes, questioning. "I think it used me as much as I used it. You forge strange weapons, old god. It seems alive. It knows what I want it to do."

He checked the bits of hydra again. Still not moving. The salt pulled water out of the tissue, making it shrivel, and ooze, spreading puddles of musty sewage stink like a flooded cellar after pumping out. But he damn well wasn't going to waste energy on cleaning it up.

Not their problem. For all he knew, it would either vanish or regenerate as soon as they left. Just as long as it didn't try to do *anything* while they were here.

He turned and tucked the pack cover back in place, couldn't buckle it since the buckles lay scattered in bits on the paving stones. He wondered if he could break them without the adrenaline boost of something trying to kill him—that kind of plastic was strong. Anyway, he hoisted the pack onto his shoulders and grunted at the weight.

"Well, we've paid blood for this hill. Let's see if it was worth the price. Wouldn't put it past Mother to make us fight our way into a blind alley, then fight our way out again. Her brain works like that."

Speaking of their line of retreat . . . the door waited behind them, closed. No way they'd shut it behind themselves, kicking it open and then fighting the hydra. He edged up to it, palms sweating, and eased it back with his left hand while holding the shotgun braced on his hip with his right. The open door yawned at him, offering them the gravel path, spring-green water meadow bordered by aspens, trout stream, sunshine. Fafnir's Idyll, just like they'd left it. He ducked his head out, checking either side. Worn stone cliff. Including a hundred feet or more straight up overhead, where the inside courtyard opened to blue sky.

No sense. No sense at all. He closed the door again.

While he had been doing that, she'd moved over to the nearest of the ground floor doors and checked it. Now she was leaning her forehead against the middle one, the one she'd said led back to her hills in the previous incarnation of the gates. Her slumped shoulders said this one didn't smell the same, didn't tell the same tale to her winds. She mourned the loss. Funny, he'd learned to read her body language that well.

Hair prickled on his arms. Mother had said that the doors changed. Did this place offer them any way home? Whatever "home" might be?

Over to the front wall, he looked out the window there. A view into a dark forest glade with a shadowy stream in the depths, fairly wide, black spruce and fir like they'd found on the far side of the ridge they'd crossed. *Schwarzwald.* Through probably a mile of stone.

He climbed the marble stair—as far as he could see the *exact* same stair they'd climbed back in the "real" world—and checked his "Finland" door. He didn't recognize the smells behind it. But the middle door on the far side spoke to him, smelled familiar, except it wasn't raining on the other side this time. More birch, less spruce and fir than the Black Forest. Different tang to the damp earthy dead leaves and needles. Opened it and got the same gray nothing that troubled his stomach. He tried poking his cane through the space that wasn't a space, thumped it on what felt like dirt and maybe roots, and got it back again. He ran his fingers down the shaft—dry to the touch, not particularly cold. It had picked up a bit of spruce gum and a seed scale on the tip.

Maybe it wasn't *supposed* to make sense. Magic was like that— why it was magic, rather than science or even smith-work. The works of gods are mysterious, sort of by definition. Mysterious, whimsical, and tending to bite the incautious hand.

I'm going to put some serious effort into killing Legion, if we ever see its demonic ass again. This is all its fault.

At least his hand had stopped bleeding. He touched the ache of his cheek and flaked dried blood off it. If anything, he was healing even faster than normal.

Define normal, as applied to gods.

She'd also been poking around. Probably a bad tactic, both of them checking doors at the same time, rather than one on guard while the other searched. It hadn't gotten them killed yet. But he heard her boots overhead, definitely her, another thing he'd learned in the last couple of weeks. Nobody else walked quite like that, a stalking cat with rubber-soled boots.

Then, "Al, you'd better come up here."

Voice strange, tight, but not scared. Puzzled.

He climbed to the fourth level and found her staring at a door on the far side. He followed the gallery around, passing the front "window" on the way. *That* vista looked out on a grassy valley with a small stone-built mill and millpond on the stream. People could live in the land outside that window, no plague that attacked even gods.

She wasn't staring at the door. She was staring at the doorjamb, or rather at the stucco next to the wood frame. Which had an arrow on it, three slashes of orange lumber crayon. The mark he'd left on coarse dark gray stone in the firefly cave.

The exact same mark. He remembered the curve at each starting end, just quick jabs with most of his attention on the fireflies. He could see a couple of skips where the speeding crayon had jumped a dimple in the stone. They didn't match with the rough-smooth trowel prints on the stucco.

Which were illusions, anyway.

This place spooked him. "What do your winds tell you?"

"You sniff first. You've got a good nose. Tell me."

He tested the air, just as he had with the Finland door. "Cold, damp, smells like an alley, a *dirty* alley, touch of diesel exhaust, not close or fresh, cat piss and wet cardboard and a hint of coal smoke—sulfur. City. Not a good neighborhood, all in all. Probably night, going by the heavy air, or raining. Maybe both."

She nodded. "My winds know it. They think it's the alley outside the other gate."

"How much do we trust that?"

"I left two six-packs of Sam Adams in the refrigerator."

Talk about incentives . . .

"If it's *our* city, you'd better wear the cop-stuff to go with your badge and patches." He unbuckled the pistol belt and handed it over. Kept the shotgun. He wasn't up to a knife-fight, just now, and the *naginata* had gotten used to her. It knew her hands and fighting style.

Yes, it was a person. It had a soul. The shotgun, on the other hand, didn't care who held it.

He sniffed again. Got the same answers. "What are the odds that we're actually going into *our* alley?"

"Three things. Your marks. The smell, both to my winds and your nose."

"And?"

Wry smile. "Nothing else comes close. I tried all the doors. Couple of other cities, but none of them are ours. This, or nothing."

Great.

"Any caves?" And, he had to ask it, even though he knew it could hurt, "Any connection to your hills?"

"One on the courtyard level could be the cave we came in by. Nitrate smoke added to the smell, fits in with the shit that went down there. Middle door, other side of this level, *could* be Tibet or Nepal. Both fit the logic of the other place."

First floor for moves within the same world, fourth floor for moves between this world and however you define our home. Which also means that isn't my Finland. No matter what the nose may say.

But close. Might be worth a look sometime.

"So we try this?"

She nodded. "Same drill, but I'll go first this time. Healthier. You go left, I go right, we keep our backs against the wall. Safety off, but don't shoot unless you absolutely *have* to."

Because, if this is "our" alley, shots will draw the cops. Her cops. Who we don't want to meet just now. Plus, anyone in that alley at night is likely to run at the sight of people stepping out of a solid brick wall. They can't see the door.

She pulled the door open. Blank gray, without either surface or depth. She vanished through it, *naginata* unsheathed and ready. He took a deep breath and followed.

Spinning disorientation just as before, but this time he was ready. Darkness. Cold damp air smelling of cat piss and wet cardboard and all the rest. Splash of icy raindrop on his cheek. His eyes didn't have time to adjust before a flashlight blazed to his right, where *she* should be, and splashed brightness away from them across pavement and a brick wall opposite, picking out that rust-spotted junk-shop door and then shooting up and down what looked, indeed, very like the alley he remembered. A shadow vanished around a corner, leaving an echo of scared running footsteps behind.

Colder than when they left. Spring had stepped back a couple of weeks since then. Spring did that sort of thing, didn't mean they'd reversed time.

The light vanished. Silence. Into which flowed the sounds of a city, distant traffic and a siren, switching to warble and horn-blasts as it came to an intersection. A helicopter overhead thumping its way to business elsewhere. That undefined rumble that lay beneath it all, machinery and the heartbeats of a hundred thousand people.

Rain spattered on the asphalt. Rain that felt like it was half sleet on the back of his hand. Not much of it, but 'tis enough, 'twill do.

His eyes started to adapt, and he could pick out rooflines against streetlights in fog beyond. A couple of lighted windows down to the left, where he remembered windows in daylight.

"Switching the light on again." Her voice, a couple of yards away.

He closed one eye. Light splashed between them, picking up the weeds he remembered in the wind-blown dirt, now mud, light sweeping up and across the stone door jamb and pointed arch and shield with cross he remembered.

But no door inside the stonework. Just the same formless depthless gray that offended his eyes and gut and balance. She focused the light on that. The beam vanished without reflection.

The light skipped away to flicking up and down the alley again, not landing on any threats, then into darkness. Apparently she didn't like looking at that gray, either.

Out of the darkness, a pensive voice, "I wonder how long it takes to reset."

"Huh?" *Witty discourse our specialty . . .*

"We could cross back to the same gallery and gate, just like you did the first time. Sooner or later, that option is going to vanish. This will go back to being a door that humans can't see, opening into choices."

Logic. Does logic work on this stuff?

"Any way we can check if this is *really* our world?"

"Best way I can think, is that Sam Adams in my refrigerator. And I can check the date there, too."

Yeah. Time. Everything that involved Legion, screwed with the time.

"Flick on the light again, across and about ten feet left."

She did. The beam splashed on red spray-paint graffiti on brick, looked like a Russian Orthodox cross, three crossbars with the bottom one slanted, with an Islamic crescent added to the base. Probably a gang "tag" claiming this turf, he didn't know. But he doubted if that sort of thing stayed constant across the multiple universes of magic gates.

"I remember that."

She switched off the light. "So do I."

He sagged back against the wall, feeling the solid reassuring brick. Whatever it really was.

Home. They had actually found home. That cold beer she craved, the hot bath, the bed, walls he knew around him. His forge. The center of his life.

Senses stronger now, he could *feel* his cold forge and the heavy steel of his anvil, over there beyond the streets and buildings. Now, to find the strength to reach it.

His hip burned. His legs wanted to fold under him, reminding him that he'd just crawled out of a plague-dream this morning. Getting here, knowing he was here, drained him. No fight left. His teeth started to chatter from the cold wind and exhaustion and the rain pecking at his hair. He slung the shotgun and pulled his cane out of the loop that held it to the pack. Used its strength and both hands to heave himself away from the wall and upright again.

"You okay to move?" Her voice in the darkness.

Sounded like she had learned to read his sounds and body language, as much as he had learned hers. Funny thing, that. They'd started this as shadows in the dark, fighting. Enemies.

Shadows again now, but not . . . enemies. He wasn't sure what they were. Some kind of weird combat team.

"Yeah, I guess. We'd better get going while I still can."

"My place is closer."

She switched on the flashlight, keeping the beam low to pick out their footing through the rain-spotted puddles, and led. He shuffled along behind, thump thump *click,* feet and cane, while her boots made no noise.

Asphalt pavement and brick for the side alley, concrete sidewalk—his focus narrowed to five feet in front. Where his feet were going. Vague shadows scuttled away, human and other, none of them interested in hanging around people who came in twos and carried obvious weapons. He didn't know if they could see her badge or not, but they damn sure could see light glinting off the guns.

He didn't *think* he was dropping back into the fever dream, but it had . . . similarities. Especially, the "if you're still moving, you're still alive" part. Cold. Wet. Tunnel vision. So damn tired, his hip had quit hurting. He knew it was still out there, still screaming at him, but those nerves had lost touch with Central Command.

One foot in front of the other. He heard the snick of her sheathing the blade. They must have reached some point where bare steel could draw attention, but looking up, looking around, took someone with the will and strength for it. Someone not him. He shoved his free hand into a pocket, trying to warm icy fingers.

Stop. Stand in the cold and wet. Shiver. Hear the hiss and roar of traffic. Start again when she started. Stop when she stopped. She probably should be carrying the shotgun—went with the uniform. How many bloodstained limping dwarves walk through the city carrying a shotgun and a backpack? One foot in front of the other.

Stop. Cold gust of wind. Shiver. Click of locks. Apartment foyer, wind went away, hooray. Grumbling, more clicks and clacks, day's mail falling on the floor, fumbling to pick up, should be more than one day's mail. Maybe her "people" knew to collect it if she didn't.

Stairway lock click clack clunk. Stairway, dammit. Now he had to lift each time for the one foot in front of the other. Tap of his cane, grab the railing, grunt. Up. Up. Up. Stop.

Door without outside locks. Hers. Into that sparse room, lights, Wheel of Life, meditation pad, gleaming gold statue of Kali. Stand shivering. Teeth chattering. Dripping half-sleet on the floor.

"Fucking exhaustion and hypothermia. You! Into the shower! Now!"

He stood. Not enough brainpower to walk. To hell with chewing gum at the same time. Shotgun pulled from his shoulder, backpack pulled from his shoulder, coat off, someone's strong impatient hands. Shirt off, boots off, pants off, underwear off, sense of flying, hot water. Blessed heat. Scrubbing.

Slippery soapy body scrubbing his. Sting of soap and hot water in half-healed wounds.

"I'd *planned* this to be a little sexier, dammit." Somewhere behind his left ear. No beer breath, so it couldn't be Mel. She'd be in the kitchen with a cold Sam Adams. Not washing him. Not washing his ass.

Towel. Bleary focus, more stings where the towel caught at scabs. Dark-skinned naked body pulling him. Dark wet hair. Strong hands, strong arms. Bedroom. Bed. Blankets. Darkness.

Warm damp body pressed against his back.

Darkness.

Wake to darkness, still or again. Wrong. Windows in the wrong places, wrong number, streetlights outside the windows in the wrong places, throwing the wrong shadows. He lay there, blinking, sorting. Even the bed was wrong. It was too big. It had someone else in it.

"You're awake." Mel's voice. Things clicked into place.

"Come over here and make yourself useful."

Eventually they fell back to sleep.

Warmer.

XXV

Albert woke alone. He could feel it. He lay there, eyes closed, for a couple of minutes until he figured out why that mattered, why that was a change. "Alone" had been his default state for centuries . . .

Mel.

He opened his eyes and looked around. Shades pulled now, they hadn't been when he woke in the night, but daylight outside. Gloomy daylight, with the patter of rain on the glass, so he couldn't tell the time by sun angles and besides, he didn't know which way her windows faced. She didn't seem to have a clock in her bedroom. The air felt somehow afternoon-ish. At a guess.

He studied the room, her bedroom, it should be damn near the most intimate of her spaces. He never had *seen* it, not really. He'd ended up in her bed by teleportation.

One long low dresser stood opposite the foot of the bed, dark golden fancy-grain wood, maybe walnut and damn sure not cheap veneer, with mirror. No pharmacopoeia on top, no cosmetics, just a hairbrush and comb and a hand mirror for checking the back of her head. All laid out precisely parallel and neatly spaced.

And a pistol, looked like a Colt .45 automatic from where he lay, also precisely squared with the dresser top. That sort of fit her personality. He assumed it was loaded. With a round in the chamber.

Closets ran along the wall across from the windows, all closed, all austere six-panel off-white paint like her kitchen and her meditation room. Wooden chair on either side of the bed instead of tables, the one on his side—well, the side where he was lying, he couldn't really claim it as *his*—looked like the ones he remembered from her kitchen. The other didn't. So she didn't keep two chairs in her bedroom. Which also fit what he knew of her.

Clothes folded on that chair, his. Cleaned. How long *had* he been sleeping, anyway? His bladder suggested, quite a while. He sat up. Where did she keep her bathroom?

One of the "closet" doors stood ajar about six inches, a signpost out of character with her obsessive tidiness. Tiled wall visible next to the doorjamb. QED, bathroom.

Bathroom large, off-white tile and fixtures, large soaking tub that *could* have taken two friendly people, separate shower. Again, nothing left sitting out on the sink top or toilet tank, no toothpaste stains or hair in the sink.

Tidy. Compulsive tidy. He tended more toward casual. Or, to be more truthful, a slob. That could be a problem. He dared to poke into the mirrored cabinet, just in case she kept a razor, conscious of a week or two worth of stubble. She hadn't complained, but . . .

No razor. Everything inside the cabinet just as neat.

Back in the bedroom, dressing, the pants and shirt smelled twice-washed but still carried the memory of stains. Like she said, blood "sets" if you give it half a chance. Apparently, the same went for hydra goo. He found rips mended with the tight precise handstitching of someone who had learned to sew long before the invention of sewing machines. That added some further hours to the answer for the "How long have I slept?" question.

He finally noticed what woke him up, an indication of how groggy he still was. Food. More specifically, the smell of gourmet cooking—lamb, onion, something the Western world generically called "curry"—turmeric, coriander, cumin, touches of cinnamon, ginger, cardamom. He wasn't ignorant enough to think that what he smelled came out of a jar labeled "Curry Powder." She'd have her own range of blended spices for each specific dish, if she was any kind of cook. With variations that depended on the season and the weather and what she thought his aura needed.

His nose told him that she *was* a serious cook. It told him to follow that smell. His stomach agreed. Vehemently.

Delicious smells wafted his way through one of the "closet" doors. No, not a closet but a corridor leading to the middle room, the meditation room, dark now but with enough light spilling in from the kitchen to guide his feet. He wondered what, *who,* he'd find there, which Detective Lieutenant Melissa el Hajj, Goddess of the Mountain Winds.

Mel. Definitely Mel, of all her multiple personalities. She was wearing a narrow *shalwar kameez* in thin blue silk, pants and top clingy enough that he could tell she wore nothing under them. He remembered the shape and touch of her hard stringy body in the night.

And remembered other things. They'd been . . . excessive. Product of a couple of centuries of celibacy, at least on his part, and she'd responded with a ferocity that told him she'd also been a long time between lovers. He expected bruises. Worth it.

He hoped he'd lived up to her standards. She hadn't mentioned Hani in any of the random noise, anyway.

She turned, not that he'd made any sound, probably sensing a change in the air. "Just to clear this out of the way right from the start—half dead, you're a better lover than he was on his best day. Or night. You have much more stamina, and he couldn't let go of some cultural baggage. Inhibitions. Whole different league. You should turn pro."

He blinked at her mind-reading, and then thought of something lost in the fury and haze. "Should we have been using birth control?"

She laughed, a touch of bawdy cackle in her tone. "I'm a few thousand years old. All that time, I've never gotten pregnant, and that's not for lack of chances. Contrary to what some guys on the force might think, I don't have 'that time of the month.' Don't worry about getting stuck for child support."

Then her eyes narrowed. "Of course, I don't think I've ever screwed another god before. Who knows? Maybe we're just not fertile with humans." Another wicked grin. "We've got two families of babysitters downstairs. They'd fight over the chance to help raise a Mel-baby."

How many arms did that statue have, anyway? Durga instead of Kali? Also a warrior goddess, but Maa Durga, mother goddess . . . more protector than destroyer. But Durga was a mother, and she just said she's never been pregnant . . .

Quit trying to fit her into the Hindu pantheon. She's Mel. Not a Hindu in the first place.

Just, Mel. With aspects of other goddesses as needed.

Too much theology on an empty stomach. She dished out the, the "lamb curry" for lack of a precise name, orange lumps of rich sauce and meat over rice. He fetched the chair from her bedroom—if he was going to spend much time here she'd need another chair or two—and settled down to serious eating. While he was moving furniture, she'd popped a couple of beers, Sam Adams, and poured them with a proper head. Yes, those *would* go with the aroma rising from his plate.

The . . . curry . . . woke tears in his eyes. Not that it was hot, not as hot food goes, just enough bite to focus his mind on the flavors, but an exquisite blend of foods and herbs and spices cooked just long enough for each—lamb seared by itself, same with the onions, not stewed in the sauce, so they remained distinct, rice just gummy enough to hold the sauce, some non-ethnic touches like tomatoes that couldn't have been in her original cuisine.

Non-ethnic original cuisine bullshit! Curry isn't native to her hills. Lamb isn't. Even the rice. One last time, quit trying to classify her. It ain't gonna work. She's at least as old as I am, and has lived in as many different cultures. Just savor the food. The moment. The things that go bump in the night.

If she got bored with him in bed, maybe she'd at least invite him over for dinner now and then . . .

He swallowed another lump of bliss and sighed. "How'd you get the timing on this just right? I stagger out of bed, and everything comes together to perfection after a couple of hours of work? Won't be nearly as good if it sits for even fifteen minutes."

"I'd hoped smelling food would wake you up. This time, it worked. I've finished off three meals by myself, your loss. Second day, now."

"You must have gone out shopping. That was fresh meat, fresh tomatoes, all the rest. Not frozen or canned. I could taste the difference."

She laughed again, less wicked this time. "You'll be meeting the Goddess Mel Support Society soon enough. Bismillah and Lakshmi, downstairs. They heard we were back and, morning after, brought in enough fresh groceries for a small army. Feeding holy beggars, or something. They acquire merit thereby."

"Muslim and Hindu names . . . "

"And a tribe of refugee devil-worshipers from so far back in the hills we're probably half Chinese. Yes. People tend to be more ecumenical, when you bring your own goddess incarnate with you."

Actually, she's *probably what made them ecumenical. Her worshipers didn't have much choice.*

"They heard us. We made that much noise?"

The ribald laugh again. "Trust me, they approve. They're relieved, even. They worry about their goddess. In their world, people and gods should come in sets. Not necessarily in *pairs,* mind you, they can get creative. But celibacy isn't natural. My people are rather . . . earthy, is the polite term. They didn't ask where I was, but they were glad I brought back a souvenir."

"How long have we been gone?"

"Nearly three weeks."

Ouch. "Any problems with your job? With the police force, I mean?"

She shook her head. "I'm on medical leave, remember?" She lifted her left hand. "Broken wrist? Not fit for duty? And I think the chief marks any day he doesn't have to deal with me as a good day. I know the rest of the squad does."

They're probably too scared of her to raise questions, anyway.

She looked around at the wreckage. They'd managed to demolish two heaped steaming plates of curry on rice each with just enough leftovers to prove her guest didn't want more—laws of hospitality observed—and two beers each. Part of the goddess thing, she'd cooked exactly the right amount.

"I cooked, you wash up. Now you owe me a good meal, fair exchange. I figure the grouse and the fish stew come out even."

Albert took a good deep sniff of the remaining curry before she scraped it into glass bowls for the refrigerator. "What makes you think I can equal this?"

Raised eyebrows. "I've cooked in your kitchen. I saw what you had, raw materials and tools. You wouldn't have all that, care properly for all that, put that much wear on pots and pans and cutting boards and stove, and not be able to use it to good purpose. Besides, you couldn't have appreciated this," hefting one of the bowls, "without some talent of your own. I've met damn few people I'd cook this for. Too much like work."

She cocked her head to one side, remembering. "Comes down to it, I knew from your cutting boards. Five of them. Different boards for different foods. I sniffed them. I may have been pissed off at you and Legion just then, but I wasn't going to insult good food by cutting sausage on a fruit board. Five boards—bread only, cheese and fruit on opposite sides, onions and garlic, herbs and vegetables, and meat. Don't mix tastes unless you intend it."

An afterthought: "Oh, and the plastic cutting mat for fish. But you hadn't cooked fish lately. Probably couldn't get it fresh enough to suit you. Or fresh enough is too expensive."

I knew she'd used the right board. Just felt damn glad for the good luck.

As for wear, well, damn few people put enough mileage on a cast-iron skillet to wear the maker's mark off. She's got me there.

With a wicked grin she walked over to the corner and opened a cabinet revealing a stereo system, *expensive* stereo, he knew the brand and lusted after it. Speakers must be built into the walls or ceiling—he couldn't spot them. She punched a button, and Wagner filled the room. The Nibelheim scene from *Das Rheingold*, those tuned anvils, she must have cued up the track and kept it lurking while she waited for him to wake up.

"You're just playing that to annoy me. Wagner really screwed up the story."

Her grin widened. "Me, annoy someone? On *purpose?* Never. Or, hardly ever . . . Anyway, I sort of hope you haven't forsworn earthly love for all eternity."

Well. "First thing, that doesn't say a word about hot raw animal sex. So, last night or whenever, that's not covered."

She glared at him, the corners of her mouth struggling with a grin.

"Second, Wagner made that up. Yeah, if one of the Lorelei jumped into bed with me, I'd jump out the other side twice as fast. You've never met them. Vicious bitches, wrecking ships and then stealing from drowned sailors. That's how they got the Rheingold in the first place. I *did* swear off human lovers, for reasons we both know."

Sobered, she stared at him for a moment. "Available evidence says, I won't grow old and die on you. Because of that, I'm not asking or giving any vows. Just, come by every now and then. I'm okay with a little on the side." Pause. "Or on my back, on top, standing up, down on hands and knees . . . "

That ribald grin again, and another pause. "You're fun, both in and out of bed. A little *strange,* but who am I to talk?"

She waved at the stereo. "Anyway, the leitmotif is because your Seal wants you up and working. It bit me yesterday. Taking it out of the pack when I was cleaning and fixing."

She held up her right hand, flexing it, a red line across her palm. He couldn't tell if that had been a cut or a burn, now that it was healing.

She could have used the "Anvil Chorus" instead. But no, it had to be Wagner. Because she is who she is. Get used to it.

She headed through the door, tossing words back over her shoulder. "I need to change out of this harem gear and you need to wash up. Break's over, back on your head."

How would she know that I know that old joke?

Because of the old part.

And because he found her dish detergent in the logical place, and the scrub pad and the drainer and the dishtowels. They had a lot in common. He only had to try twice to find where she stowed her empty beer bottles before returning them.

And she wasn't *that* annoying. She'd set up a play list on her stereo, and as soon as the short snippet of Wagner finished, it went on to Irish fiddle and then North African flute with drums. Moroccan? All of it good, if eclectic. He found the speakers, flat acoustic panels set into the ceiling and with some smooth surface that looked pretty much like plaster until you followed the sound to its source.

I wonder what else she has hidden around here. More to everything than meets the eye.

Like in my place.

Then she was back, dressed in uniform coveralls and cop aura again with the gun-belt and radio and all. Arson Squad Lieutenant, from tip of cap to spit-polished boots.

She blinked at his stare. "Don't know *what* you're going to do about that Seal, but I want to look official if you blow up the forge or take out power for half the city. It could give us a head start on our getaway. We're fucking around with Powers Beyond Those of Mortal Men—just being gods doesn't mean we can't screw the proverbial pooch."

Putting on the uniform even changes her idiom.

"Where's the Seal?"

Mel led him into the middle room, flipped on a recessed ceiling light, and opened a deep closet. She reached inside, not even looking. She knew where she left things, and they'd damned well better still be there . . .

First, the *naginata*, then the pack. He stared at her weapon. *Her* weapon now, no doubt about it. She'd killed some time with it, double meaning, trimming the rough cuts he'd made in the forest and smoothing a bevel on edges of the remaining bark, replacing his bark-strip lashing with cord. Looked like silk or maybe nylon, tan but glossier than hemp, and more of it for long wrapped handgrips on the shaft. It wasn't *kumihimo*, more like the tight twine "serving" a mariner would wrap on a ship's wheel for grip.

It fit the rustic flavor of the weapon and turned it into intentional design. Not makeshift any more. He touched it, running fingers over the sheath. His blade felt comfortable there. It had found a new home.

She looked a question at him, had she pushed too far? Taken a gift where none was intended? He nodded acceptance.

There's the difference between her and Mother. Mother wouldn't have asked. Would never have thought of asking. Anything she wanted, was already hers.

And then, the Seal. She pulled it out of the pack, wrapped in plastic again, and he saw she was wearing gloves. Even gods are pain-averse.

He felt the whine. She stepped back, waving a gesture that said she wasn't gonna touch *that* thing again. *All yours, Maestro . . .*

He unwrapped the pieces. They looked like they had when he picked them up in front of Fafnir's cave. Two pieces of old gray wrought iron, five points of the Star of David and a separate full triangle, ragged edges at two angles where Mother broke it off.

He floated his right palm over each piece, trying to make sense of what he felt. Stared off into space. Vibrations, strings of molecules twisting into spaghetti, like one of those microchip computer circuits . . .

She didn't ask, but he could see the question hanging in the air above her head, like a cartoon.

"It isn't dying. It isn't working, either. The smaller piece feels like the larger, sort of like when you break a bar magnet, it doesn't stop being a magnet. Instead, you get *two* bar magnets. Just, smaller."

But it wasn't doing what Solomon had intended. Mother's plan had worked that far. But she hadn't killed her enemy.

The Seal knew him. He touched it and it didn't bite. He picked up the pieces, one in each hand, and tried to add their weight and temperature and molecular vibration to their story. He tried fitting the broken pieces together.

They repelled each other. Magnet analogy, again, as if each jagged jigsaw piece was trying to fit "north" to "north" against the will of physics. He studied the broken faces, making sure he was matching the correct ends with each other.

He was, no question. They hadn't broken clean. One ragged corner of the triangle had a dent that matched a outcrop on the main body. The curve followed those internal lines he sensed.

But the piece didn't want to go back there. He set the main body flat on the floor and tried to drop the triangle into place. It flipped over.

Out of curiosity, not really thinking it would help him find a solution, but . . . she'd dumped his keys and wallet back in his pants pocket after washing. He'd felt the weight. He pulled out his keys. Most were brass, but some of the old locks took old keys, skeleton keys, cast steel keys. He dangled one next to the main piece of the Seal, and then the detached triangle.

No attraction—not magnetic.

He looked up at Mel again. Again, unspoken questions hovered around her head.

"I don't know what I'm doing, no. Not a clue. But I'm glad Solomon didn't use magnetism as part of his working. Forge heat will destroy a magnet. Lets the lines of force escape, the molecules turn out of alignment. Or something."

And I don't need any further complications.

XXVI

Albert squinted at the flat gray sky. *Not* raining. No thunder and lightning providing theatrical backlights for the mad scientist's ruined castle silhouetted on the ridge overhead. No typhoons or tornados, either. Not even snowing or sleeting or hailing or dropping a plague of frogs on him. He distrusted that. How can you have a proper apocalypse without storms?

Still, the sky offered at least a *threat* of storm. Of proper drama. Gusty winds, puddles dotting normal dirty stinky city streets, enough lingering damp chill that he needed his jacket. His nose had forgotten diesel soot and dogshit and overflowing dumpsters and just too damn many jostling-elbows people in the last few weeks. Forests smelled better.

But apparently the Powers That Be weren't throwing a fit about them walking to his forge. That probably meant there was no way in hell he'd be able to fix the Seal. Jehovah's apocalypse didn't need to rush to beat the deadline. It could keep its own schedule.

Mel was doing her cop thing, striding along in her starched-uniform official aura that flowed out fifty yards and owned the street, making half of the scattered pedestrians look like they had something to hide. The ones that hadn't seen her first that is, and vanished before he ever noticed them.

He glanced over at her. "Look, I don't know whether I can fix this thing or not. But it's not just a technical question. Beyond that, should I even try? Actions have consequences.

'Let a hundred flowers bloom. Let a hundred gods contend.'
Why should I cut off my own arm to make Solomon's Yahweh
supreme?"

"You're misquoting Chairman Mao. Besides, he just used that
as a trick to smoke out troublemakers so he could spot them,
nab them, and send them to camps for reeducation. Cultural
Revolution. Dude, I was *there*. It wasn't fun."

He grimaced. "You know, sometimes we sound like we're
singing a 'bragging song'—built the Garden of Eden and the
pyramids, told Wellington how to win at Waterloo, all that
stuff. Been everywhere, man. Done everything, man. Some of
my blades fought in the Battle of Hastings, on both sides . . . "

She glanced over at him and then went back to scanning the
sidewalks and streets and the roof parapets overhead. Restless
eyes. "You made Excalibur?"

"No. Some other guy. My blades aren't magic and they
aren't fancy. They just do a damned good job of cutting things,
and don't break unless you really, *really* try. Besides, it was the
scabbard that made Caliburn special."

"How much of *that* story is true?"

Albert thought for a minute as they walked. He'd known
people, who knew people, who . . . "About the usual one percent,
I'd guess. Arthur lived. He tried. And failed and died. No, I
don't know whether Merlin was a demon or a god like us or just
a clever man. About five minutes after Arthur died, the lies and
mixed-in bits of other stories started piling up . . . "

Then, "You dodged my question."

She smiled. "Yes."

Another couple of minutes, walking in silence, and she
stopped and turned to him. "Look, I got along okay with what
we had. I could take care of my people. That's all I really need.
From what I've seen, you could still work miracles with iron.
In iron. As for memories, well, I'd managed to forget Hani.
And a bunch of other things I'd rather not talk about. Some

of them worse. My take on all this boils down to: This world doesn't need more gods. Hell, I don't think it needs the ones it *has*. If I held Shiva's trident, I'd be tempted to melt Rome and Jerusalem and Mecca down to radioactive glaze, three birds with one stone . . . "

Okay, back to Kali for a reference point.

"So yeah, if you figure out a way, go for it. Fix the damned thing. And modify the spells to include Bilqis while you're at it. We wouldn't be in this shit if Suleiman bin Dauod hadn't tried to slip one past her."

Then that quick grin of hers that verged on a leer. "Or slip one *to* her, as the case may be."

Back to Durga.

They walked on. He felt his forge looming in front of him, his power, *his* altar, like golden warmth spreading from his *hara* to all his other *chakras*. Just to mix theologies and languages all to hell.

That's the problem with long life. It melts together. Interferes with "Be here now."

And then, as she points out, there are the memories you'd rather forget.

Remembrance of things past. "Now that we have our memories back, what's your real name? The original? I mean, Legion called you Noshaq or some such thing."

"It called you Simon Lahti. If you start believing demons, God knows where you'll end up. No, my name is Mel. Always has been. Damned if I remember what language it started out in, or what it means or who first called me that. That's *way* too far back. But 'Melissa' and 'Melanie' and the other names, I just take those to fit the changing world. Noshaq is the tallest mountain near where we lived for some centuries. My people sometimes call me 'Goddess *of* Noshaq.' I'm betting you lived in Lahti for a long, long time. I'm sure people called you 'The Smith of Lahti.'"

True, that. "What about the 'el Hajj' part? You ever make the pilgrimage, or is that just sticking plumes on the donkey?"

"So I'm an ass, now?" She wiggled her hips at him. Didn't really fit her cop persona. "No, I made the pilgrimage. Long ago. Wanted to see what all the fuss was about. Stoned the devil and walked seven times widdershins around the Kaaba and kissed the Black Stone and all the rest. Talked to a few mullahs and sheiks who didn't tack ancient tribalism onto the good parts of the Prophet's advice. Came away knowing nothing that I hadn't known before. Served me right."

That brought them to the turn into his alley, the back alley of his apartment. He half expected to find Mother waiting, holding a flaming sword to bar him from returning to Eden. She'd been in front of them and waiting at every step of this personal Hajj. Everyone hates a know-it-all.

But the alley stood empty except for the pizza joint's Dumpster and some other trash, and a mangy-furred yellow dog that took one look at them and slunk away into the shadows and vanished into a slot between brick walls too narrow for most people to follow. Judging by the trash spilling out of the dumpster, it must be Thursday—regular pickups were Friday and Monday mornings, early, and stores had been open on their walk, so it wasn't Sunday.

He hadn't asked Mel what day it was . . .

He hadn't asked how much spoiled food she'd had to toss when they got back either. Gone three weeks, he expected his own kitchen now harbored an advanced ecosystem in the breadbox and the refrigerator. Maybe the penicillin mold would fight back the salmonella. Or maybe the hobs and brownies and house-elves had feasted behind his back. He *had* invited them past the door of his house and then went away.

His cellar door stood closed, just as he'd left it that dawn long weeks back. There too, he'd half expected Mother to have interfered. But she'd never liked entering his forge. Temple of another god, perhaps, and it felt chill and unwelcoming to her?

And then there was the iron. She'd never liked iron. Came after her time, probably.

Anyway, he locked the door behind them, barred it, and stood sniffing for a minute before he switched on the lights. Nothing out of the ordinary, no smell of anyone passing the door since he'd locked it—cool dry dust and darkness, old brick and wood and stone, the memory of charcoal fires and hot iron and bitter sparks. Normal. He led Mel down the stairs to the second door and locked and barred that behind them too. After all, Mel was on the inside. Nobody else could get past those locks just by talking to them.

Except Mother wouldn't need to use those doors to get inside. She knew the hidden ways. He switched on every light he had and poked into dark corners, looking and sniffing, just in case. No Mother.

At last, he took the pieces of the Seal out of his pockets— separate pockets because they didn't seem to like each other now—laid them on his largest anvil, and stared at them. What did they want him to do? Forge them, that was obvious. They asked for heat and hammer and anvil. And magic of some kind, the touch of a forge god. Which wasn't the same as the touch of a wizard-king . . .

How could he fix it?

What did it want to be?

Would forge-heat and hammer make the two pieces one again? Flow metal together in alliance, bring those strings of spell-iron into a working circuit? Did *Mother* do something in the breaking that caused the matched edges to repel?

His mind turned back to how Mother didn't like iron and steel all that much. Maybe it tied into the myths that the Old Ones, the fairy people, feared cold iron. Used copper and bronze and flint in their weapons, rather than steel. The stories said humans had driven them from the world with iron. Solomon had used iron for his Seal, to drain power from competing gods. That meant something—normal people didn't use iron to decorate their god's temple. Iron was too utilitarian. It wasn't rich and rare and pretty.

He stared at the pieces of the Seal. "I don't know what I'm doing here. I'm just going to start doing it. The iron wants heat. Maybe once it's hot, it will tell me the next thing and the next."

He looked up. Mel just nodded, no words. This wasn't her department.

So. Charcoal. A wide bed this time, not long like he'd made for his cane. Deep around the tuyere, and he checked to make sure he had plenty of charcoal in reserve. The iron was asking for a *lot* of heat. Something beyond normal—beyond forging, beyond welding, into the range of casting or the transformation that was smelting from the native ore. The magic thing again. Or maybe it was the salamander's soul, looking for escape and rebirth on some kind of elemental's Great Wheel. He kindled the fire with shavings and wood splits, and checked tools and quench tubs and room to work while the coal took fire.

All was as he'd left it, where he could find things without thinking. Of course. But he kept expecting to find some sabotage, some further trap Mother had set in advance in case she hadn't blocked him before this point. A bomb camouflaged as a lump of charcoal, a flaw hidden in hammer or anvil that would shatter like glass under impact. Plots within plots within plots. She'd *intended* him to get his hands on the Seal, but too late to save it . . .

But she hadn't killed the Seal. He held that thought.

Fire in the heart of his forge, spreading, awakening it to life. He pumped the bellows. Sparks branched like fireworks. Blue flame. Yellow glow, edging toward white. He knew the fire. The fire knew him. They talked.

He laid the broken star in the heart of his fire. Tried to add the triangle. It wouldn't go. He turned it. Still the part would *not* join the heat of the main body. They wanted to be forged apart. Once broken, they became new things. He set the triangle aside.

More air and fuel and heat. The iron stayed dark in the glowing heart of his fire. More heat. More air. More charcoal. Still dark. He turned the iron, half expecting letters to glow on the surface, like that ring in the story, Solomon's magic made visible by heat. Ancient Hebrew it would be, he didn't know that language, wouldn't be able to read it. Bellows. Charcoal. Air. Fire.

Hand on his shoulder, Mel, shaking him out of communion with his fire, his forge, his iron. No words, she waved him away from the bellows. Goddess of the Mountain Winds. She didn't touch the bellows, just stared at the fire. It blazed white.

Dull red now in the iron. He sank his mind back into it. Lines, threads, circuits, the grain of wrought metal. Incomplete. Broken.

Not to be mended.

But, maybe *changed.*

More wind. More charcoal. More heat.

Red heat. Orange. A tinge of yellow. He grabbed tongs out of the air and pulled his iron from the fire, laid it on his anvil, raised up his hammer. What did the iron want to be? How would the threads weave back together in a working whole?

A gentle tap, then harder as the metal spoke to him. Collapse the form, collapse the remaining points of the Seal, fold them, make a forging blank that could become anything. Anything at all. Feel the grain of the iron under his hammer, through the tongs, against his anvil. Fold. Fold. Fold. Back to the fire.

The charcoal glowed beyond purple now, near ultraviolet, heat never seen. Forge god and wind goddess. More fuel. Carbon. Iron. Steel.

Heat that wasn't heat flowed over him, spreading, thinning, escaping, leaving a hint of sandalwood and joy behind. He'd, *they'd,* freed the salamander from its iron prison, undone that part of Mother's cruelty. Now the iron could speak to him, listen to him. It wanted revenge. He caught a sense of direction from it. That structure waited, still a grain within the metal, Solomon's touch that made this iron strange.

Hammer. Anvil. Tongs. Turn. Fold. Weld the grain back on itself. Heat. Hammer. Anvil. Stretch the form, stretch the grain. Back to the fire.

Shape. Long. Narrow. Taper. Bevel.

Blade.

Tang.

Point.

Change anvil. Change hammer. No grinding. No polishing. Nothing to touch the grain. Nothing to break the grain. No metal lost. Too precious. Polished anvil, small hammer, small fuller, polished faces.

Point. Edge. The blade knew his mind. The steel flowed under his hammer. He flowed with it. Soul bound in blade. Balance. Hand, particular hand. Arm, particular arm. He knew that hand, that arm, the span of them, the strength of them, lover's caresses in the dark. He felt them on his body, on his manhood, on his heart.

Shaped the blade. Heated the blade. Quenched the blade. Drew the temper, hard and keen and tough and eager.

Cross-guard. Triangle, into the fire. It felt the need, drew the heat, formed under thoughts and taps that wouldn't kill a fly. Cut, hot chisel. Two pieces. Larger shaped, split center. Laid across tang of finished blade, attraction, no repulsion. Driven home against taper, no sharp shoulder to concentrate stress. Chill of blade. Shrinking metal. Blade and guard, one again.

Grip. No waiting. A thing of days, his habit. Not this time. The blade's need drove him. Hardwood, oak, straight-grained. Carved to fit that hand again, that hand that held his heart. Heart hollowed to meet the tang, bound with silver chain, jewelry chain, little coarser than a horsehair braid. Sandpaper rough, sweat or blood would soak in and leave firm grip. Tap chain round and round with peen to set it in the wood, meet the ridges and hollows of that hand he knew.

Pommel. Second piece. Heat. Shape. Punch. Drive home to pinch chain end, hold, smolder, tap to thicken against wedge of tang, never come loose. Quench.

Sword.

Sword to kill a god.

Any god.

Albert fell out of his work. Out of his trance. Out of the timeless space.

He held a short sword or long knife in his hands, gleaming. No, glowing with the forge's heat bound within the steel. Straight, neither narrow nor wide, double-edged. Ripples on the steel, from hammer, fine scallops on the edge from hammer. Watered-silk grain of the folded steel, pattern of breaking waves without an acid etch. Edge without file or grinding wheel, polish without rouge.

Masterpiece of a god.

Not made for his hand.

Made for hers.

He scrounged around in the darkness cast by the dying fire and found a rag. He dropped it on the blade's edge, just gravity. The rag split before it touched the blade's edge, and fluttered down. He found a length of steel bar stock and dropped that on the blade's edge. The bar split and clanged to the stone floor.

That eased sound back into his ears, the snaps and clicks of his forge cooling. He broke his focus from the blade. Firebrick had melted at the edge of the forge, flowed, freezing now. Charcoal gone. Even the ash gone. Heavy anvil scorched. Wooden beams overhead, scorched. Air scorched.

The skin on his face and arms ached with a dry tightness like sunburn. Muscles shook and twitched. He set the blade across his small anvil. Let his knees fold. Sat on low wood, the edge of his stock bin.

Mel.

He found her in the shadows, face soot-smeared so that it blended with those shadows, her stare moving like a metronome between him and the blade. He waved for her to take it. She stepped forward and reached as slow as if she thought it would bite. Venomous bite. As if that blade would ever bite *her.*

She took the grip. Lifted the blade.

"Oh. My. God."

The point twitched to one side and then the other, up, down, her testing the balance. "It reaches up my arm and into my head. If I *think,* it moves. How the hell do you make a blade like this?"

Albert groped for words. "I don't know. I've never forged a blade for a lover before."

She looked around and then focused on the scorched ceiling beams. "That fire . . . we should have burned your building down around us."

He thought back. "That's just leakage. I focused the heat. *We* focused the heat. That's how the sword knew you before you ever touched it."

He glanced at his charcoal bin. Empty. Not just empty, clean. No charcoal dust, no crumbles. He didn't remember feeding the fire. Not past a certain point in the forging.

"I guess I need to buy more fuel."

She was eyeing the sword again. "This blade could cut the moon out of the dome of heaven."

"It will cut anything you want it to. I've never forged like that before. Never forged *iron* like that before. Solomon did something to it. Now *I've* done something to it. Added . . . I don't know *what* to it."

She still focused on the thing in her hand as if it was a snake that could turn and bite.

"How do you sheathe a blade that can cut diamond with a thought?"

He took a deep breath. His ribs ached. His shoulders ached. "That, that I can answer. I mold copper sheet around it to line the sheath. As long as I'm the one who forms the copper to the steel, they know each other. The blade won't cut its friend. Brass or bronze throat to the sleeve, has to have copper in it. Then, wood or leather or whatever you want, the outer sheath. Hangings depend on how you want to carry it."

"That's why the *naginata* sheath is heavier than it looks?"

She'd noticed. Of *course* she'd noticed. "Yes."

Then, from the shadows across the cellar, "Such a clever boy. Sholomo ben David would have been impressed. Now give me that abomination before you hurt someone!"

Mother. How long had *she* been there, watching, just in front of the false wall that hid one of the secret ways?

XXVII

"No." Mel shifted her blade so that it pointed just a bit away from Mother, not actually threatening but not *not* threatening. Her stance growled a quiet, "Go ahead. Try and take it. Make my day . . . "

"Give that . . . that *thing* to me!"

Albert couldn't remember ever hearing tense fear in Mother's voice before. She'd always been so sure of herself and her command of all around her. The universe *would* obey her. It didn't have a choice.

He sagged back against one of the dirty square brick pillars that supported the floor beams overhead. *Oh, god. Gods. Mother. I've just forged the greatest blade of my life. That means I'm on the edge of falling over dead where I stand. I think Mel would have to carry me upstairs and pour soup down my throat. Not even strength to eat. And Mother turns up, looking for a fight.*

She turned her attention to him. "Make her give it to me. You've proven how great a smith you are. How great a wizard you are. Greater than Solomon. Now we have to destroy it. Before it destroys us."

Mother stepped out of the shadows. The light didn't flatter her. Cobwebs and dust from the old airshaft sullied her perfect hair. Sweat beaded on her forehead and stained her silk drape, another sexy thing in green that clung like a second skin to the bits it didn't reveal. Not suitable for a forge—she'd brushed up against something that left a black smear on one hip. Looked like grease or dust from a chunk of scrap iron . . .

Mel fit into his world a hell of a lot better. Soot-smeared coveralls and sweaty tousled hair and ragged fingernails sort of goddess. Mother had never liked getting her hands dirty. That was for others.

He looked around for his cane, forgotten in the heat of forging. "I can't give you the sword. Like with Fafnir and the Seal, it isn't mine to give."

"Nonsense. You made it. It's yours. Now give it to your mother."

As if *she* could unmake that which he had made . . .

But, "You're not my mother. We're not even part of the same family. Gods of different tribes."

Memories. Two-edged blade, giving us back our memories.

There. I've said it. Out loud. Not anything like hearing Mel say it. Cutting the apron strings.

She winced like he'd slapped her. Rage blazed dark across her brown cheeks. She said something, three syllables, four, five, but his ears and brain wouldn't process them. Wouldn't even make *sounds* out of them, much less meaning.

His cane. Over there, that long shadow leaning against another of the brick pillars spaced through the cellar gloom. He wanted a weapon, with Mother in a rage. He *needed* a weapon. That blade had stabbed through a shield-bear's heart . . .

He couldn't move. He couldn't even move his eyes.

Mel glanced from him to Mother and back again and back to Mother. "That won't work on me. How long ago did you tamper with his brain? Centuries? A thousand years ago? Did you booby-trap his 'brothers' and 'sisters,' too?"

She moved the sword's tip. It waited, directly between them now. He wondered if that was Mel's thought, or the sword's.

Mother wasn't taking care of us, she was controlling us. Part of her plan. Control every god and goddess she could track down. She only kept me *close to break the Seal, if she couldn't do it herself. So many lies, for so many years. Centuries.*

Mother shook her head. "Give that thing to me. You don't know what it is. All those thousands of years, sucking life and memory and power. Now he's fixed it. Worse. He's made it into a weapon, not just a drain. That thing can kill *you!*"

Mel had circled away, stepping sideways to where brick pillars and the fieldstone foundation guarded her flanks, her back, choosing her battleground, and he could see her face now. Bitter smile. "You say that like it's a bad thing."

She asked for a blade to kill a god . . .

Mother jumped on that. "If you want to die, give me the blade."

Mel's sword dipped an inch, as if she considered the offer. Then the point came up again. "No, I don't think so. I'm not bored with Al yet. Did *you* teach him?"

Ohhhh, me*ow* . . .

Mother's face flushed darker. Goad your enemy—rage makes bad decisions. Always trade insults before battle. Mel *was* a warrior goddess, *was* Kali, plus all those other aspects and avatars.

Mother snarled. Then, "Give it to me. Or I'll destroy you."

Now Mel's smile turned mocking. "What part of 'no' don't you understand? I've been around for a long, long time, O mighty Bilqis of Sa'aba. You wouldn't say that if you were sure. You'd just *do* it."

Achilles and Hector, two champions out in front of their armies. Trading insults. Hectoring.

But jaw jaw is better than war war. Churchill knew. He'd *seen* war. Not like some other leaders.

Then something moved at the edge of his sight, fuzzy, and he couldn't turn to focus over there. His anvil? The big anvil? Two-hundredweight of steel, plus the elm-wood block it sat on, floating through the air? It accelerated into clear sight, aimed at Mel.

Yes, his big anvil. Flying. Mother's witchery.

Mel flicked her gaze at it, didn't flinch, didn't step aside. A flash of glowing steel, and the anvil split and flew past her shoulders in two pieces, clanging to the floor. The basement shook around them.

Mel shook her head. "You know, I never believed that part of the story. That Siegfried cut the anvil in half with his re-forged sword. Not possible. But, I'd never held that sword's brother before . . . "

She stepped forward. Mother stepped back, fear replacing the doubt on her face. Albert had never seen *that* before, either.

Dust swirled, as tongs and hammers and swages and chisels flew in a hornet-swarm around Mel's head. Her winds blew them away to clatter and thud and ring off other metal. Flame blossomed in the dust and then died, lacking fuel, blown out. Mel stepped again. Mother retreated again.

The floor shook, not impact but cracks opening in the concrete, nipping at Mel's feet. Bricks shattered and dropped from the pillars. Screams overhead, heard through the wood flooring, an earthquake.

Oh, God. The pizza shop. Don't know what time it is, what day it is, but I can smell their ovens, the sauce, the cheese. They're open. People up there, working, eating, picking up take-out. What did they ever do, to get caught up in a war of goddesses?

Albert couldn't breathe. Dust settled. Mother stole the air, to kill Mel's winds?

His ears popped, air returning. Idiot Broadway tune ran in his head, "Anything you can do, I can do better."

Albert slipped down the pillar, brick by jerky brick, his knees giving out on him. Tired. So damned tired. Price of that forging. Mother's magic didn't hold him up, just kept him from commanding his own muscles. His tailbone thumped on the concrete floor with a stab of pain. Something in his balance and the pull of gravity turned his head enough that he could still see Mel, see Mother, as they angled away from him.

Blue lightning flashed between the goddesses. It touched

neither. He couldn't tell who had thrown it. Thunder followed, as if the bolts had flamed half a mile away rather than less than twenty feet. The floor shook again, rocks falling from the foundation wall. Something larger thudded down in the shadows to one side, he tried to map what. Nothing of his, nothing of the forge. It had the ring of dry hard wood, splintering.

Must be a floor beam. The whole building was caving in around them. Dust, fine dark brown mummy-dust of old floors and beams and horse-hair plaster walls and brick and mortar, centuries of dust showering everywhere. Dust billowed between him and Mel and Mother, and when he could see again, they were close together.

Shrouded in fire, as if that dust had exploded in frozen time. Fire leaping from the blade he'd forged for Mel, purple into ultraviolet, it hurt his eyes but he still couldn't turn away.

Mel raised the blade and thrust without effort. The point caught Mother square between her breasts. Sprouted from her back. Fire blooming, Mother's fading shape blasting out in the same purple light that threatened to burn his eyes to blindness. The floor bulged above them, exploding upward. Gray daylight peeked through cracks as the building tore apart.

The people. May God have mercy on the people. We'll survive. We're gods. But they're doomed. Take a miracle to save them. How much of the city will die with Mother? Sodom? Gomorrah?

We're gods.

WE are gods.

WE make miracles. As well as the wrath of God that melts cities into radioactive glaze.

The shattered wood froze in mid-air. Albert could move again. Could speak. Mother's spell had died with her. He remembered the fire in his apartment, the stench of his own charred flesh, the demon moving through frozen time with a curl of smoke caught in its golden nostril.

"Legion! I command you!"

The air hung silent. Mel turned. She also moved outside of time. Nothing else could. Until . . .

Golden air condensed into the shape of a human.

"Who dares to command us?"

Ah, this is the point where I get my head ripped off. Never used it that much, anyway.

"We are gods. We outrank you."

That was why Legion couldn't stop Mother, couldn't punish her. Why it had to trick *them* into acting. Gods outrank demons. Are more powerful, if they know who they are. And Mother had still remembered who she was.

Legion glared at him. Albert didn't know how a blank face of glowing ectoplasm—it hadn't bothered with eyes, with mouth, with nostrils this time—could glare. But Legion did it.

"Prove that you have such power over us!"

Albert lay there, half dead and propped up on the collapsing brick with tons of shattered building poised to fall on him, staring up at an angry demon, and almost laughed. He looked beyond the sexless golden form.

"Mel?"

She lifted the sword. Legion grew a second "face" on the back of its head and saw, however it was that it could see without eyes.

The demon cringed. "We obey."

About damned time . . .

If damnation is possible.

"Demon, I command you. Repair the damage. Heal the humans. Wipe this from their memories, as if these minutes were cut out of time."

Albert sagged back against his brick pillar. Surreal bits of golden light chased splinters of wood and steel and brick. Legion really *was* legion. The main shape stood between him and Mel, no visible change. But, those bits unbound by space and time, each was also the full demon. The building reformed overhead.

Smoke vanished. Char vanished. Dust sucked back into the cracks between floorboards. Video reversed, except he and Mel and Legion kept moving forward. Thought couldn't follow it.

Dizzy. Tired. Hungry. Tired. Thirsty. Tired.

Mostly, tired.

Words pulled him back from his fog. "We cannot repair what the blade has cut. All else is as you command."

What the blade has cut. That's okay, we don't want Mother back. Dead goddesses tell no tales.

He tried to focus. The anvil still lay on the concrete floor in two halves, the cut faces shiny. Some other tools also lay in separate pieces. Got in the way. Collateral damage.

Cut face of the anvil looked . . . strange. He found enough energy to crawl across, rough concrete grabbing at the knees of his pants, tearing, but that was the pair he'd already ruined. No big deal. He still had Legion's pile of gold. Could buy another pair.

Unless that gold was a demon joke.

Steel. Just below the working face of the anvil, the steel body . . . pockmarked. Honeycombed. Crystalline. He'd ruined it, forging Mel's sword. Too much heat.

And. The finished sword had weighed more than the Seal. His hands remembered. He'd drawn metal out of the anvil into the blade. Part of the alloy. Part of the soul.

Part of the magic.

The blade had forged itself. He wondered what *he* had given to it. Would he ever lift a hammer again?

Would he ever lift a hand again?

Focus through gray swirls, golden demon. "Take us upstairs. My kitchen."

He *felt* the wood passing through his flesh and bones, him through the wood, through the ovens of the pizza kitchen, up through each floor in turn. He was lying on cold vinyl flooring over wood, against plaster. In between the seconds of time.

Stale air. Moldy bread. A sour hint of rotting oranges. *Don't even think about what's mutating inside the refrigerator.*

"Make the food fresh."

Air cleared. He could get used to this, having a demon at his beck and call. Perquisites of godhood.

Power tends to corrupt. Absolute power tends to corrupt absolutely.

"Give Mel back her gun. Exactly as it was when you took it."

He forced his eyes to focus. The Colt materialized, a vague floating transparent shape that turned solid, blued steel and checked rubber grip. Mel plucked it out of the air with her left hand, sword still in the right, and hefted it, sighted it, glanced at the engraving and the serial number, flipped the safety on and off and on again. She nodded. All present and correct, to the gram.

"You want Legion to lick your boots?"

Horror flashed across her face. "God, no. Take the polish right off, probably ruin the leather." She paused and grinned. "Nice thought, though."

"You insult us. You treat us like common djinn. We are not servants!"

Albert shook his head, a serious effort the way he felt right now, and forced his eyes to focus on the demon. "I treat you the way you treated us. 'Do unto others as you would have them do unto you.' You knew what you were doing. You knew we were gods. 'As ye sow, so also shall ye reap.' I should tell you to go fuck yourself and die."

He didn't have the strength to wonder if demons *could* die. Or, for that matter, fuck themselves. Sure, that ectoplasm could take any necessary form, but the physics wasn't the same as the metaphysics.

Too tired for theology. Fall asleep right here.

Work left unfinished. Sword. Deadly. Cut the moon from the vault of heaven. "Make a sheath for that blade. A sheath suited to Mel. Safe. Will only give the blade to us. Mel. Me. No one else may draw it. Not even gods."

Copper sheet formed from the air and wrapped itself around the blade—the demon knew Albert's mind. Wood, pale wood, close-grained, and then leather, dark leather, black like Mel's cop belt and boots. But not official, not uniform issue—gold at the sheath's throat, a handgrip wide, he could feel the weight of it hanging in mid-air, ounces of pure gold, engraved, with silver inlay, a scene of high snow-capped mountains and clouds. And an emerald for a green sun over the mountains. Big as his thumb.

Sheath.

Much more than simple. Much more than his command. Was Legion . . . grateful? Rewarding them? Did such concepts even exist, in this world between moments?

Hungry. Tired. Too tired.

Food. Image, on his palate. "Onion soup. Double-reduced chicken stock, yellow Spanish onions sautéed in butter, sourdough bread toast, fresh grated Parmesan. You know how I like it, damn you. Enough for a second meal, leftovers, for both of us."

His big stockpot materialized on the back burner, which had turned itself on to simmer heat. Warm chicken/onion savor filled the air, overlaying the sharp tang of Parmesan cheese, *good* Parmesan, steaming on top of hot sourdough toast, from bowls on the counter. Albert sorted through the aromas.

Yes, Legion knows the right recipe. Probably read it straight off my brain, like a laser reading a CD.

"Now. Be gone. Don't come near either of us ever again unless we summon you."

The demon vanished, far faster than it had come.

"Good riddance to bad rubbish."

He couldn't tell if he had said that, or Detective Lieutenant Goddess Melissa el Hajj. Not that it mattered.

He crawled over to his kitchen table on hands and knees and pulled himself up on one of the chairs. Sat. A bowl of soup appeared in front of him, steaming, golden transparent butter dotting the surface. Beautiful. Fragrant.

Mel was talking, somewhere off in the fog. "I think I've changed my mind on that long-term commitment thing. If this is your version of onion soup, I'll hire you for live-in cook any day you're willing."

He was still staring at the soup, holding his head up with his hands, elbows on the table. His spoon sat there, an immeasurable weight.

Mel pulled a chair up beside him. A spoon, full of soup, nudged his lips. He opened them. Soup. Good.

More soup. Sometimes the spoon came to him, sometimes to Mel. Still good. Same spoon. No problem. They'd shared other fluids. A second bowl. Empty.

She reached out and lifted his chin. Stared into his eyes. "If I scoop out another bowl, you'll collapse face-first in it and drown."

Something wiped his lips. He moved, rose, without effort. She was bigger than him, and strong, those whipcord warrior-goddess muscles. Carried him to the bedroom. Stripped off his clothes.

Grunted. "Can I throw these out? Not even worth washing up for rags . . . "

He opened his eyes. Pants, torn. Shirt, torn. Not just torn. Buckshot holes in both, with singed edges, sparks from the forge. No leather apron . . .

The whole right arm of the shirt burned off, from armpit to cuff. He checked his own right arm. No burn. Not even the hair singed. Had the salamander done that?

Bloodstains on shirt and pants. He wondered whose.

He nodded. Yes, she could throw those out. Although the service they'd given, should be a burial with full military honors.

Rifle salute and all. Where had that scene come from? Smoke from the salute, black powder, century or more ago. It hurt, but he couldn't remember why.

Memories still jumbled.

Maybe, he'd fixed the Seal, it would take memories away again. Good riddance to bad rubbish. Mother wouldn't admit to bad memories. She'd never done anything she regretted. That would have required her to care about what her actions did to others. Her brain didn't work that way.

"Ah, sleep, that knits up the ravell'd sleeve of care." Mel had asked him to switch to Shakespeare . . .

Singed sleeve, in this case.

"Go ahead and sleep. I'm on guard."

She had the sword, and her pistol back. She could summon Legion. She was Mel.

Nothing could touch them.

XXVIII

Albert woke in darkness, streetlights in the right places glowing through shades on windows in the right places and in the right number. He didn't keep a clock in *his* bedroom, either. After all, he didn't have to get to work at a certain time.

Mel was awake. He could tell by her breathing. Then she moved enough, just a little shift of hips and shoulders, to say that she knew that he knew, that he would be welcome over on her side of the bed.

He reached across the bed and met her hand reaching for him. No words necessary.

This time, they made love. The last time, it had been some kind of mutual consensual rape, not even as genteel and refined as fucking. She hadn't asked before she did things. Neither had he. Must have burned off enough of that pent-up need.

And now they didn't have to worry about waking up the downstairs neighbors . . .

Afterward, snuggled, he noticed something. "Where'd you get the pillow?"

He hadn't had two on his bed for centuries. It felt like a silk pillowcase . . .

"Other bedroom."

Oh, shit. "That's Mother's. She'll . . . "

"No, she won't. It's mine now, by right of conquest. All her lands and cattle and slaves belong to me."

She wriggled a bit more in his arms, nestling her butt warm and muscular against his groin, and went to sleep.

So did he.

Light again. God only knew what day it was. And Mel wasn't still lying next to him to say.

He sniffed the air. Something baking. Yeast bread—raisins, cinnamon, almonds, saffron. She'd been up for a while, if she'd had time for yeast bread. His nose told him *he* had time for a shower before the bread would be out of the oven and cool enough to slice.

She'd been there first. The towel rack held a second set of towels, still a little damp, that used to be Mother's. Right of conquest again. She'd used his toothbrush. No problem. Any germs to share, they'd already shared them.

Silly question, that, but they'd both found out the hard way that some germs *could* bite them.

She'd gotten up and showered and been clattering around in the kitchen, without waking him. Either he had been really, *really* tired, or his subconscious really, *really* trusted her. Or both.

Anyway, he shaved—Mel hadn't said yea or nay on a beard, but he wasn't going to grow face-fuzz again until that librarian died or at least retired. No need to look even *more* like those memories . . . and he cleaned up the beard hairs and shaving cream and the rest, much neater than usual. Mel liked things tidy.

Dressing, he saw no sign of his old clothes—she'd followed up on her threat. Her coveralls and leotard and Kevlar vest and underwear lay in a neat stack in one corner, still dirty, waiting for him to tell her where the washing machine lived. He lifted his eyebrows at that—nude cooking could be hazardous to delicate parts of the anatomy. Especially since the aroma of frying bacon now mixed with the baking bread . . .

And not any kind of bacon he kept in the apartment. Maple sugar cured, maple wood smoked, he could smell the cost. He knew the shop and the smokehouse—excellent pork but he rarely scratched that itch. Other things he liked as much or more, that cost a lot less. Speaking of cost, he remembered that he hadn't replaced the saffron, last time he'd used it up. Too damned expensive, for the amount he used it.

She'd been out shopping. Which upped the "nude" question by an order of magnitude.

Maybe she'd stepped outside of time to do it. Or, like Mother, she made the world conform to her own ideas of what was proper.

She'd left a neat array of weapons sitting on his dresser. Two Colt pistols, large and small, the third would be within her reach in the kitchen. That would be the one she'd carried on their quest, not the one he made Legion give back. She wouldn't trust *that* one until she'd tested it on the range.

Next to the pistols, spare magazines. A wicked little serrated-edge knife with a flip blade. Machine forged stainless, but honest steel like her KaBar. Probably *not* for gutting alleged perpetrators in back alleys—for cutting seatbelts for rescue or escape, cutting tangled ropes and wires, that sort of thing. He hadn't known she carried it.

And . . . the sword.

He stared at it while buttoning up his shirt. That sheath. He didn't trust it, didn't trust Legion. He floated his right palm above the sword hilt, above that gold decorating the sheath, above the black leather. He felt more to all of them than met the eye. He *knew* what the sword hilt was telling him. The rest . . .

It didn't feel like a threat. Or even an invasion, not some kind of magical bug planted by Legion that would let the demon spy on them and control them from afar. He touched the gold. He touched the emerald. He'd wakened with a slight headache, no real bother, just the forge hangover. So familiar, he'd barely noticed it.

The headache vanished. The ache in his hip vanished, also an old acquaintance, background noise that told him he was still alive and moving when he woke up in the morning.

O . . . kay.

Trust, but verify.

He drew the blade. It slid out of the sheath's throat as if it had been greased, but he could feel both the blade and the sheath agree on that. He was authorized. Step two okay.

The blade . . . it had a pale blue tinge on both edges, less than an eighth of an inch wide. He hadn't done that. He touched one fingertip to the flat of the blade, not going anywhere near either edge. The steel told him it was fine, that the blue *was* metal, not some kind of poison or magic on the surface.

Killing Mother had changed the steel. It had become even harder, tougher, sharper. Sure of its own way. Anything that got in that way would die. It had taken on some of her character.

He winced at the thought. But those weren't bad attributes in a sword. Just, not so good in people.

Last, he checked Legion's gold coins—still hidden where he'd left them. Weight the same. Mother hadn't taken them, which meant she hadn't found them. And Legion hadn't played a demon's joke.

Mel was slicing the bread, fresh yeasty-sweet steam with a touch of saffron and sliced almonds rising with it, when he stopped in the kitchen doorway. Back to him, bent over the cutting board, she didn't look up. She wasn't nude. He recognized some of Mother's less . . . aggressive . . . attire, loose gray velvet drawstring pants and a light blue silk top. With this type of clothing, it didn't matter that the two women had rather different shapes. The outfit didn't bare any controversial bits and was more or less opaque. While leaving the male eye—or female, if so inclined—with no doubt that those bits were there, in proper and enticing shape. No visible evidence of underwear.

Which made sense. Mother was shaped like an ancient

fertility goddess. Her bra or panties—if she owned any—would have fallen right off Mel.

"You are a most peculiar man. Easier to wake you up for good food than for good sex."

He thought about that. "Everything considered, all angles, food costs less in the long run."

She straightened up and turned around. Lifted her right eyebrow. "If I'm available at all, I'm a cheap lay. No diamonds necessary."

Albert grimaced. "That's not the kind of cost I meant."

"No. It isn't."

She turned back to the stove and shuffled some scrambled eggs. He saw flecks of red and green in the fluffy light yellow, and his nose identified them as three different peppers. One of which promised to bite back. Also, an artisan cheddar he couldn't quite place. Should go well with the saffron bread. Whatever name and ethnicity it went by. And bacon.

Which was done. Precisely, according to his nose. Perfect timing again.

She dished food out and added a block of farmhouse butter from the refrigerator, another luxury he didn't indulge. Orange juice. The bread, the bread, the bread, a low braided loaf baked on a sheet rather than in a bread pan, exquisite. Thick slices. Hot. Moist. Savory. The butter verged on gilding a lily. Except, it completed filling his senses. Texture as much as flavor.

"Need to get you to talk to my kitchen knives." Mumbled around a mouthful of eggs. "They won't slice bread this warm." She swallowed, a concession to good manners, before going on. "Which reminds me. I felt you drawing the sword. Touching that . . . emerald. I'm not used to having a psychic shadow. What the hell have we gotten ourselves into?"

He shook his head and got up to slice the second loaf. Somehow, the first had vanished. "Whole bunch of things about this that I don't understand. That sword is what it is. We forged it together. Some kind of wedding ring, or maybe a suicide pact. And we won't know what Legion was up to with that sheath, for maybe a century or two. All I know is, it's complicated. I *think* it was thanking us. Maybe."

She'd joined him at the counter, switching on his coffee maker. New smells blossomed, fresh-ground Sumatran beans and cardamom. Sensory overload. More stuff she'd bought when she was out. Maybe second or third trip.

"How long?" He didn't need to specify what he meant.

"Two days since I woke up. Hate to disappoint you, but I polished off all the leftover onion soup and sourdough. You missed out on braised garlic lamb shanks with new potatoes. Yummy."

"I thought you said that good food would wake me up faster than good sex?"

She punched him in the ribs, hard enough to hurt. Those muscles again. "Teasing. Sex was last night. Won the race."

She leaned over, still taller than him, and nipped his ear. "Good."

But they went back to eating.

"Two days. You could have found the washing machine by now. Wouldn't have to rummage through Mother's closet and wear *her* idea of fashion."

She took a sip of coffee. "Item the first: silly man, I *like* dressing up slinky-sexy like a damned expensive whore. I just haven't had an excuse for it, last couple of centuries." Pause for another sip. "Item the second: this is *your* apartment, and the former home of Bilqis of Sa'aba. I'm *not* poking around any more than necessary. I'm not just being polite—I remember those stairs. Very tricky. Bilqis had left a surprise or two in her room. Including one in that pillow."

Mother. He'd learned, long ago, to stay out of her things. Which reminded him . . .

"Why didn't she catch us earlier, before I finished the sword? Why wait until I *finished* it?"

Mel cocked her head to one side and squinted at him. Shook her head. "No, you wouldn't know. You're always on the inside."

More coffee. Which was good. Albert savored another sip of his.

"That first night, way back when, I damn near had to sell my ass to Shaitan himself in order to follow you into your forge. Not just opening those locks. The doors didn't lead anywhere. Like your power had moved the whole forge and cellar sideways into another world or a place outside of time. Turning the Seal into a sword, that stepped up to another level entirely. I don't think Bilqis *could* enter the forge while you were working. Couldn't enter the heart of another god's power. Once you were done, the sword complete, the fire cold in the forge, then the walls opened again. Inside and outside of the doors lined up. Whatever."

I always did feel that I worked off in another world somewhere. That's why days vanished.

She took another sip of coffee and savored it. "That reminds me. Where do I go to buy an anvil? Haven't seen them in stock at the local hardware, and I owe you a new one."

What?

She read his face. "I ruined your anvil. Don't you remember? Sliced it in half."

Uhhh . . . "Self defense. Mother threw it at you."

"Could have dodged, could have had my winds throw it right back at her. I had time. But the sword felt *good,* best weapon I've ever held, and I wanted to show off, biggest baddest warrior goddess in ten galaxies."

And she cut the anvil clear through, even splitting the elm block. And elm wood doesn't split worth a damn. Then she stabbed Mother . . .

Dead.

The word froze him.

They'd killed Mother. The two of them. He made the blade. She held it. Mother was dead.

He saw the point entering her chest. Poking out of her back. No blood. The exploding blaze of purple light, instead. The frozen time. Legion rebuilding the world around them, squeezing that light back into a point and vanishing it. Somewhere. Somewhere in demon-space.

Dead. He'd held that word squeezed away in his own demon-space. Now it exploded.

He was shaking. She was holding him, warm chest and arms cradling his head. Mel. Kali. Death-goddess. He felt his tears damp and hot in the cloth. Mother's cloth, shirt from her closet. Slinky-sexy, damned expensive whore. Untouchable goddess.

Balkis. Bilqis of Sa'aba. Mother. Eternal. Dead.

She wasn't my mother. She didn't even belong to my tribe. She controlled me, tampered with my brain. She was a monster—nothing mattered to her but her own whims. She wanted to bring gods incarnate back into the world of humans. Turn humans back into slaves. Slaves to the gods.

If she had gotten her hands on that sword, she would have killed Mel with it. Killed me.

"She was a monster. But she was *my* monster. I loved her," he whispered that into the damp cloth between Mel's breasts.

He felt Mel's lips touch the crown of his head. Heard her whisper.

"I know. Hani was *my* monster. You heard. He still haunts my dreams. I loved him."

He felt her arms around him. Her hands on his back. The hands that killed . . .

The hands that caressed and demanded. He remembered how he had formed the sword's grip, fitting to the ridges and hollows of her hand on him in the darkness. Her hunger in the darkness, both times. Even back in the tent, no sex, just needing someone to hold. What it said of the hollow space in *her* life.

Mother. Men or women, she took humans and discarded them. Not even worth the slight trouble of killing. They worshipped her for a brief time, each, and she left them. Any hollow spaces were strictly *their* problem.

She could have had immortal lovers, gods or goddesses. She knew them, alone of all the victims of Suleiman bin Dauod's magic.

She didn't want them.

I wonder what Mel stabbed through, to kill her. It wasn't a heart. Mother didn't have one.

But she was my *monster.*

He wrapped his arms around Mel, just above her butt, that butt he knew the exact roundness and muscular hard warmth of in the darkness, so comfortable nested against the hollow of his groin. He wept into the hollow between her breasts.

Ruining the silk, most likely.

Some time later, he loosened his grip around her waist. The same instant, she relaxed her hold on his shoulders.

"I'll wash up, just this once. Don't get any ideas about making it a habit. And now you owe me another meal." She turned to the counter, the sink, the stove, leaving him some privacy to grab a napkin and wipe his eyes and nose. Eating and then grieving, they'd used up enough time that the bacon grease had congealed in his frying pan. She turned on the gas to melt it, and pulled the jar out of his refrigerator where he saved leftover grease for cooking.

"I can stay here for a few more days. But, I have some people I need to guard." She glanced at him, emphasis. "A couple of people I need to hide. And a job. Which sometimes helps with the first two. Things to do that you probably don't want to know about."

Probably related to "illegal aliens" and "racial profiling" and some people considered "terrorist suspects" because they have brown skins and funny names and worship in the wrong god-house . . .

She nodded, seeing him work through that. "And I haven't seen a phone anywhere around here. So I have to get back to my apartment soon—shouldn't have been away as long as I was."

Pause. Clanking dishes in the sink. "And I know *you* can't live with *me*. Your forge."

Yes. My forge. My altar. My temple. Why I keep coming back here. I didn't know that, before. Nothing really to do with Mother.

She might have thought *it was. But, no.*

Mel was still talking to the wall, the sort of hesitant things easier said without eye contact. "I'm not breaking up with you, horrible phrase. But I don't think our worlds and days fit together all that well. Even if *we* do. You're welcome in my world any time you want to visit. And I hope I'm welcome here."

She paused, and he saw some laughter come into her stance at the sink. No sound, but he knew the way she stood, the way her hips and shoulders set . . .

"Just whistle. You know how to whistle, don't you, Al? You just put your lips together and . . . blow."

"Bacall, to Bogart. *To Have and Have Not.*"

Did *she* see *him* as Bogart? The world twisted, just a bit. That she could fit him into Bogart's role, him the little gimpy gnome with ears too big for his head . . .

He'd seen that movie, new, on the silver screen. Likely she had, too. And he wouldn't have to cook up a lie about how he knew the reference, renting tapes or DVDs of oldies to play on a TV set he didn't own . . .

He stood up. He whistled.

She turned off the heat under the bacon grease and, mountain wind-goddess fast, flowed up against him and squeezed him hard enough he felt bones creak.

THE END

About the Author

James A. Burton is also known as James A. Hetley. This revelation makes it easier to explain why Jim Burton's website is www.sfwa.org/members/hetley and his blog is to be found at jhetley.livejournal.com.

He lives in the Maine setting of his Hetley-authored contemporary fantasy novels *The Summer Country*, *The Winter Oak*, *Dragon's Eye*, and *Dragon's Teeth*. His residence is an 1850s house suitable for a horror movie, with an electrical system installed while Thomas A. Edison still walked the earth, peeling lead-based paint, questionable plumbing, a furnace dating back to Teddy Roosevelt's presidency, a roof perpetually in need of shingling, and windows that rattle in the winter gales. He's an architect. Not just any architect, but he specializes in renovation and adaptive reuse of old buildings. Go figure.

Other diverse connections to his writing include black belt rank in Kempo karate, three years in the U.S. Army during the Vietnam War, a ham radio license, and such jobs as an electronics instructor, auto mechanic, trash collector, and operating engineer in a refrigeration plant. He continues a life-long fascination with antique crafts and the hand-tool skills of working wood and metal.